As the Prince spoke to the other nobles gathered at his table, I knelt and poured the drink, stealing a glance at the Khelid's face. Smooth, pale white skin, absolutely unlike the ruddy, weathered Derzhi or the reddish-gold color of my own race. A pleasant, narrow face. Ageless. Smiling. Then his eyes met my own.

Eyes that terrified me beyond anything I had seen as a slave, beyond nightmares, beyond the most fearful encounters of my youth, for never had I faced such eyes defenseless. I stopped pouring and bowed my head, breaking off the contact instantly. Brandy was of no use to him. Nothing could ever warm those eyes or what was behind them.

However crippled I was, however lost, however removed from the person I once had been and the life I had once lived, I could still recognize one when I saw it.

He was a demon. . . .

TRANSFORMATION

CAROL BERG

A ROC BOOK

ROC
Published by New American Library, a division of
Penguin Group (USA) Inc., 375 Hudson Street,
New York, New York 10014, USA
Penguin Group (Canada), 90 Eglinton Avenue East, Suite 700, Toronto,
Ontario M4P 2Y3, Canada (a division of Pearson Penguin Canada Inc.)
Penguin Books Ltd., 80 Strand, London WC2R 0RL, England
Penguin Ireland, 25 St. Stephen's Green, Dublin 2,
Ireland (a division of Penguin Books Ltd.)
Penguin Group (Australia), 250 Camberwell Road, Camberwell, Victoria 3124,
Australia (a division of Pearson Australia Group Pty. Ltd.)
Penguin Books India Pvt. Ltd., 11 Community Centre, Panchsheel Park,
New Delhi - 110 017, India
Penguin Group (NZ), 67 Apollo Drive, Rosedale, North Shore 0632,
New Zealand (a division of Pearson New Zealand Ltd.)
Penguin Books (South Africa) (Pty.) Ltd., 24 Sturdee Avenue,
Rosebank, Johannesburg 2196, South Africa

Penguin Books Ltd., Registered Offices:
80 Strand, London WC2R 0RL, England

First published by Roc, an imprint of New American Library,
a division of Penguin Group (USA) Inc.

First Printing, August 2000
20 19 18 17 16 15

Copyright © Carol Berg, 2000
All rights reserved

ROC REGISTERED TRADEMARK—MARCA REGISTRADA

Printed in the United States of America

Chapter 1

Ezzarian prophets say that the gods fight their battles within the souls of men and that if the deities mislike the battle-ground, they reshape it according to their will. I believe it. I have seen such a battle and such a reshaping as could only come about with the gods' devising. It was not my own soul involved—thank Verdonne and Valdis and any other god who might eavesdrop on this telling—but I did not remain unchanged.

Crown Prince Aleksander, Palatine of Azhakstan and Suzain, Priest of Athos, Overlord of Basran, Thryce, and Manganar, heir to the Lion Throne of the Derzhi Empire, was perhaps the rudest, most callow, ungenerous, and arrogant youth ever to ride the deserts of Azhakstan. From the instant of our first meeting I judged him so, though it could be said that I was prejudiced. When one is standing naked on a slave-auction block in a wind cold enough to freeze a demon's backside, one is unlikely to have a fair impression of anyone.

Prince Aleksander had inherited the intelligence and strength of a royal family that had ruled a constantly expanding empire for five hundred years and had been clever enough not to diminish itself through inbreeding or internal mayhem. Older Derzhi nobles and their wives despised his lack of respect even while shoving marriageable daughters into his path. The younger nobility, themselves no paragons of virtue, named him a fine fellow on the basis of the lavish entertainments he permitted them to share, though that opinion often changed when they ran afoul of the Prince's whims and irritability. Derzhi military commanders judged him fit, as his heritage demanded, though rumor had it that they drew lots among themselves, the loser forced to serve the rash and stubborn Prince as military aide. The common folk were, of course, not allowed an opinion on the issue. Nor were slaves.

"You say this one can read and write?" said the Prince to the Suzaini slave merchant after examining my teeth and prodding the muscles in my arms and thighs. "I thought only Ezzarian women learned to read, and that just for deciphering potions and spells. Didn't know the men were permitted it." Then, while poking at my private parts with his riding crop, he leaned over to his companions and expressed the usual humorous opinions on the question of gelding Ezzarian slaves. "Completely unnecessary. Nature's already seen to it when they're born a man in Ezzaria."

"Aye, my lord, he can both read and write," said the fawning Suzaini, his bead-woven beard rattling as he babbled. "This one has many refinements as would suit him for your service. Quite civilized and well behaved for a barbarian. Can keep accounts or serve at table or do hard labor as you prefer."

"But he's been through the rites? None of their sorcery nonsense hanging about in his head?"

"None. He's been in service since the conquest. Went through the rites his first day, I'd say. The Guild always makes sure of Ezzarians. Got nothing left of witchery inside him."

No indeed. None of that. I was still breathing. There was still blood inside me. That was about all that was left.

More rude poking and prodding. "It would be decent to have a house slave who had some semblance of intelligence—even barbarian intelligence."

The merchant glared at me in warning, but a slave learns quickly to pick and choose the points of honor for which he is willing to suffer. As the years of servitude pass, those become fewer and fewer. I had been a slave for sixteen years, almost half my life. No mere words could raise my hackles.

"But what's this?" I tried not to jump when the riding crop touched the lacerations on my back. "I thought you told me he was well behaved. Why the stripes if he's so virtuous? And why is his owner getting rid of him?"

"I've papers, Your Highness, where the Baron Harkhesian swears this one is as fine and obedient a slave as can be found, with all the accomplishments I've said. He's only getting rid of him to settle his financial affairs and says the marks were a mistake and should not tell against the slave. I don't understand it, but you can see the lord's seal on his papers."

Of course the slave merchant would not understand. The old warrior baron I had served for the past two years was dying and had decided he would sell me rather than allow me to become the property of his only daughter—a woman who took singular pleasure in abusing those she could not command to love her. Deciding whom to love was one of my remaining points of honor. No doubt it would crumble along with all the rest, given enough time.

"If he doesn't suit, perhaps one of these others . . ." The slave merchant's small eyes darted nervously about the barren, walled enclosure and the ten restless spectators. As long as the Prince was interested in me, no one else would dare bid, and the weather was so nasty, there was no assurance anyone would stay around to buy the other four wretches huddled together in the corner.

"Twenty zenars. Have him delivered to my slave master."

The slave merchant was horrified. "But, Your Highness, he's worth at least sixty!"

The Prince gave the man such a look of strained patience as would make a sensible person check his back for daggers. "I'm reducing it fifty because he's damaged. With scars on his back I'll have to keep him better clothed. But I'm giving you ten extra because he can read and write. Is it not fair?"

The slave merchant recognized his defeat—and his danger—and prostrated himself. "Of course, Your Highness. Fair and wise as always. Twenty zenars." I had a feeling the merchant was going to have an unpleasant surprise ready for

whatever well-meaning friend had notified the Prince that a
literate slave was up at auction.

The Prince was in company with two other young men.
Those two were dressed like gaudy birds, in bright-colored
silks and satins with gold linked belts, and carried daggers
and swords so ornately wrought and crusted with jewels that
the things would be absolutely useless. From the soft look of
the pair and the way their eyes were set so close together, I
wondered if they could figure out what to do with weapons.
The Prince himself, lean and long-limbed, wore a sleeveless
shirt of white silk, dun-colored doeskin breeches, tall boots,
and a white fur cloak that could only be the pelt of the silver
Makhara bear, the finest and rarest fur in the world. His red
hair was caught in a single braid on the right side of his
head—the Derzhi warrior's braid—and he wore few adorn-
ments: arm rings of beaten gold and a single gold earring set
with a diamond that was likely worth more than all his fop-
pish companions' baubles put together.

The Prince slapped the arm of one of his finely dressed
companions. "Pay the man, Vanye. And why don't you bring
the creature along? Except for the scars, he's a league more
handsome than you. He'll look well in my chambers, don't
you think?"

The pockmarked young lordling in blue satin and cock
feathers dropped his receding jaw in horrified astonishment.
Well he might. With a single phrase, his prince had banished
Lord Vanye from Derzhi society forever. It was not the humiliating public comment on his physical shortcomings that
had done it, but the fact he was named a slave handler: a job
ranking just above those who tend dead bodies before
they're burned and just below those who skin animals. As
the Prince turned his back and strolled out of the gate, the
chinless man pulled out his purse and threw the coins at the
feet of the slave merchant, looking as if he had just eaten a
green dakhfruit. It was astounding how proficiently Aleksander could destroy a friend, insult a reputable merchant,
and cheat an influential baron in a short five minutes.

In the way of slaves, I looked no further to the future than the next hour. Rather than spending an entire day chained to the wall of the slave market in the dismal weather, I had the prospect of clothes and shelter almost immediately. Not a dreadful result. Far from my worst day on the auction block.

But as was to happen frequently in the ensuing months, I was to reap the consequences of Prince Aleksander's carelessness. The furious slave merchant said he had no time to replace the choke-collar, arm chains, and hobbles that were designed to make delicate female slave buyers feel secure, and he refused to supply so much as a loincloth to cover me. My journey across the crowded, cosmopolitan city, naked in the freezing rain, hobbling frantically behind Lord Vanye's horse to keep from being dragged, ranked with the more ridiculous events of my long captivity.

As for the chinless lord . . . well, having one's body in the control of a man who sees himself grossly ill-used is not the way to improve on a miserable situation. And when the man thinks himself clever, but is not, matters can get much worse. Instead of delivering me straight to the Prince's slave master, Lord Vanye took me to the palace forge and ordered the smith to mark me with the royal seal . . . on the face.

What breath I had left was sucked away in horror. On the day of their capture, all slaves were branded with a crossed circle, but it was always on the shoulder, as I had been, or on the thigh. Never on the face.

"Is he a runaway, then?" asked the smith. "Prince Aleksander don't brand none but runaways in that fashion. Don't like the ugliness, even in those for the mines."

"No, I'm only—" I tried to protest, but Vanye shut off my cry with an iron bar he'd been fondling since we'd entered the smithy.

"See the lash marks on his back, and how we've had to chain him up like a wild dog? Of course he's a runaway."

"He's an Ezzarian. Durgan says—"

"Are you afraid of groveling filth like this? The only magic that's going to happen here is when I turn you into a tongueless gelding for disobedience. Now, do it."

Vanye's blow to my head had left me groggy, but I soon

wished that he had hit me harder. Claiming long experience with the Prince's whims, the uncertain blacksmith used only his smallest iron to sear the seal of the Derzhi royal house on my left cheekbone. The larger iron would have exposed bone and teeth, creating enough damage that sepsis would eat away what was left of healthy tissue. But, at the moment, gratitude was not in my mind.

And so I was delivered to the Emperor's Summer Palace in the middle of winter, deposited on the straw-covered floor of the slave house, shivering, nauseated, and half out of my head.

The burly slave master, a bearded, flat-faced Manganar who called himself Durgan, looked down at me in puzzlement. "What's this? I got word of a new house slave for the Prince's service, not a runaway fit for nothing but the mines."

I was certainly in no condition to explain Vanye's pitiful attempt at revenge, his clever plan to ruin the Prince's bargain.

"This is the only new one bought today. Lord Vanye said—" The smith's lad who had dragged me across the courtyard almost swallowed his tongue when Durgan grabbed his throat.

"Demonfire! Vanye! Smith burned the Prince's new slave on the word of a dolt not clever enough to open his pants to piss?" The slave master looked like he wanted to put his head through a brick wall. "Tell your master Smith he don't ever, ever in this world mark a slave but the word comes from the Prince's own mouth or from me. I was told to get this one cleaned and sent up to serve supper. Just look at him!"

I could not have been a happy sight. My stomach emptied itself again at this mere hint of food.

"At least master was careful with the branding," stammered the boy, backing toward the door. "Not too damaged, is he?"

"I wouldn't set great hopes for living much past fourteen if I were you. Be off with you. I've work to do."

Half an hour later I was climbing the back stairs of Aleksander's palace carrying a monstrously heavy tray filled with a platter of peeled fruit, cinnamon-dusted pastries, a round of stinking Azhaki cheese, and an urn of scalding nazrheel; their tea that smelled like burning hay. Every few steps I had to stop and let my muddled head clear, my churning stomach settle, and the throbbing firestorm in my cheek subside.

I was dressed in a plain white sleeveless tunic that reached from shoulders to knees, a concession to the Prince's distaste for seeing open wounds or excessive scars. The Derzhi usually kept their male house slaves in fenzai—short, loose pantaloons—and no shirt. It was some remnant of their desert heritage, singularly inappropriate and unpleasant for those of us held captive in the mountainous northern regions of the Empire. The tunic was not much warmer, but felt slightly more modest at least.

Strangely enough, the slave master's biggest dilemma had been my hair. I had no beard—Ezzarians just don't produce them like most races. But, unlike the usual custom in Derzhi slave houses, the Baron's daughter had commanded my hair be left long. Durgan wanted it off, but was afraid that would leave the burn marks on my face too prominent and expose the swollen, bloody lump where Vanye had laid the iron bar. So instead, he had me tie it loosely to one side in the Derzhi style—not braided, of course; only blooded warriors wore it braided—hoping it would cover Vanye's folly. He also put salve on the burn, a gesture I did not mistake for kindness. The slave master was praying to see the next sunrise.

"Ah, supper!" said the Prince as I walked through the gold-leaf doors and into a sumptuous sitting room. I bowed—awkward with the tray—and congratulated myself when I managed to straighten up again without passing out. There were seven or eight people in the room. Three men and two women were seated on cushions around a low table playing ulyat, a Derzhi gambling game that involved painted stones and wooden pegs and not a few blood feuds. I studiously did not look at anyone as I set the tray on another low table surrounded by blue and red silk cushions. The slave master had been very specific about keeping my eyes down. I wasn't sure if it was a household rule or just a way to keep my swollen, seeping cheek out of view.

"Look, all of you. I've got myself a new slave. An Ezzarian who can read."

"Impossible . . ." There were titterings and a repetition of the standard remarks.

"Quite accomplished, I hear. Perhaps even some royal Ezzarian blood in him."

"A barbarian sorcerer! I've never seen one of them. Will you lend him out?" asked a low-voiced woman with more on her mind than food.

"Ah, Tarina, why do you ask it? What pleasure would you find in such a scrawny fellow, all dark hair and dark eyes?"

"Though nowhere near your own stature, my lord, he looks quite fit. If his face is pleasing, I could be tempted . . . when your eye wanders, as it seems to do constantly. Will Lydia allow such dallying when you are married?"

"Now you've done it. I will certainly not lend him to anyone who reminds me of the sharp-tongued she-wolf. Come take your pleasure with my food, for you will surely not get my slave."

I very much disliked being the center of such sparring. As I had discovered again so recently with the Baron's daughter, it was more dangerous than serving a warrior on the front lines of the Empire. I bowed and mumbled. "If that's all . . ."

"Speak up," said the Prince. "How can you read if you can't speak clearly? And no, that is certainly not all. We must let Tarina see what she's missing." Before I could be properly afraid, a hand reached under my chin and jerked it up. By the time my eyes could focus after the nauseatingly sudden movement of my head, they were looking straight into the hot amber gaze of Prince Aleksander. "Get Durgan!"

Someone scurried past us, hearing the unrefusable menace in the Prince's voice. I was held immobile by the iron hand under my chin. He had me stretched up on my toes, and I was sorely afraid I might be sick again from the position and the mingled scents of heavy perfumes, cinnamon, and the rank tea and half-rotted goat's cheese the Derzhi so prized.

Durgan's account of the afternoon's events was somewhat muffled by the carpet under his mouth. Complete prostration was perhaps a bit overdramatic in such a private setting, but the slave master was fighting for his life. When the tale was done, the Prince released his grip and shoved me aside. I knelt down and crossed my hands on my breast as would be expected, encouraging my stomach to return to its proper venue.

Ezzarian Seers teach that in nature's pause before disaster strikes, a discerning listener will hear the clicking of the victim's bones. On this occasion a stone could have heard them. When the Prince gave the order summoning Lord Vanye, the bone rattling was as noisy as an earthquake.

I was sent outside the palace gates to await the young lord. The night was freezing, and I had no cloak or shoes. But neither the gate guard's bonfire nor the blazing torches on the wall could have warmed the chill inside me. Perhaps the Prince thought it would unsettle his chinless friend to see me, though as I led the gray-faced young man through the gates, I doubted my presence had anything to do with his terror. He knew he was done for.

The Prince met us in the front courtyard of the palace. He wore his white fur cloak and gave his hand to Lord Vanye as the trembling man dismounted. "You see I sent this slave outside to greet you . . . freely, with no concern that he might run away. You've done me quite a service, Vanye." The young lordling gaped stupidly at the Prince, who laughed, took the young man's arm, and strolled toward the kitchen courtyards and workshops. "Come, I want to thank you for it."

Though he laughed uncertainly—more of a squeak than a laugh—Lord Vanye could not have been easy. In addition to two torchbearers and two attendants, there were four liveried soldiers following him and the cheerfully chattering Prince. The soldiers shoved me after them. I wrapped my arms about myself, silently cursing winter and royalty and my life.

Dread and surety gnawed at my gut as we stepped inside the smithy, the heat of the thundering flames searing my cheek anew until the very air quivered with the burning outlines of the falcon and the lion that I would wear to my grave. The smith stood ready.

Vanye tried to pull away as they strapped him to the post, but he was not half strong enough. Then he began to beg, his pockmarked face a pasty gray. "Aleksander . . . Your Highness. You must understand. My father . . . the disgrace . . . handling slaves . . ." When the smith pulled the largest of his glowing irons from the fire, the gibbering turned to a low wailing.

I would not watch it. I had been very close to howling two short hours earlier, and the smith had been careful with me. I closed my eyes . . . so I was not at all prepared when the burly smith crammed a heavy iron handle into my hand.

"Do it," commanded the Prince, who smiled and folded his arms, waiting. "Vanye is not content to be a slave handler. He thinks he can fall no lower. Prove to him how wrong he is."

"My lord, please." I could scarcely speak for my revulsion. Everything I still held sacred, everything I prayed was still tucked away inside me . . .

The hot amber gaze shifted to me. I wanted to look away, knowing that no good could come from anything I might do or say. But there are deeds that are impossible, no matter what the consequence of leaving them undone.

"I'll hear no womanish Ezzarian scruples. I'm giving you the chance for revenge. Surely a slave craves revenge."

I held my tongue, but did not look away. I could not let him mistake my intent. While staring straight into his blazing fury, I raised the vile implement to toss it back into the fire. But before I could loose it, the Prince roared, curled his powerful hand about my own, and forced the red-hot iron onto Vanye's face.

I heard Vanye's screams and smelled his burning flesh long into that night, long after I was locked in a cell beneath the slave house in the frigid darkness. I pulled the filthy straw over my nakedness and fought to retrieve some semblance of the peace and acceptance I had striven to build over sixteen years. But all I could think was how much I detested Prince Aleksander. I could not judge Lord Vanye or whether he was truly worthy or unworthy of Aleksander's scorn, but how could I not despise a prince who would mutilate one man and trample the pitiful scraps of another to remedy his own foolish mistake?

Chapter 2

It was three or four days before Prince Aleksander had need of someone who could read. Not just anyone. Someone that he trusted. Palace scribes were notorious for spying and intrigues, being privy to private information as they were. Of course, it wasn't so much that he trusted me, as that he could remove my tongue should I repeat a word I read. I understood that. Misplaced trust is an extremely painful lesson.

I was asleep when Durgan dropped the wooden ladder through the ceiling and yelled at me to come out of my barren little hole. Through years of such intermittent punishments, I had learned to make the best of the silent hours. I had taught myself to sleep through almost anything: sweltering heat, bitter cold, chains, ropes, unending damp, pain, filth, and vermin. Hunger was a little harder, but only rarely had I been starved—slaves were too expensive to ruin frivolously—and, in general, I had managed to give my masters little reason to go beyond the normal beatings and degradations that seemed to make them happy. On this particular occasion I feared I had gone too far and might not get out of it, but even so, I had managed to sleep away most of the time.

"There's a cistern just outside, and your tunic on the hook," said Durgan as I climbed squinting and shivering into the cold daylight. "You're to make yourself presentable. There's a knife beside the cistern. Take off the hair. And don't think I won't check to be sure the knife is still there when you go."

I sighed and did as he told me. The knife was very dull, and my head throbbed at every jerk. It seems ridiculous, but being forced to cut off my hair had come to be more irritating than any of the other petty annoyances of servitude. It was so pointless.

"You're to go straight to the Prince's chambers." Durgan gave me no word as to what was wanted. Whether I was to serve dinner or be murdered, it wasn't his business to know . . . or to tell me even if he did. I ran across the bustling, slushy courtyard to the kitchens, cleaned the mud off my bare feet in the footbath by the outer door, then hurried up the stairs, regretting the savory smells and billowing warmth I left behind as I passed by the spits and baking ovens. Perhaps I'd get to linger a moment on the way back. Surely the Prince wouldn't have bothered to have me cleaned up if he was going to kill me.

I tapped on the gold-leaf door and swore at myself for violating my long-held rule by thinking beyond the moment.

"Come."

A quick glance about before dropping to my knees and averting my eyes told me that only the Prince and one other man were present. The other man was much older, with a weathered face, long, wiry gray hair only partially tamed into his braid, and upper arms that looked as if he juggled boulders for pleasure.

Aleksander was reclined on a blue brocade couch. "Who are . . . ? Ah." It wasn't a deadly sort of ah, but neither was it an "I'm going to forget that you defied me" sort of *ah*. With my luck he would have a long memory. "Come here and read this."

Derzhi nobles did not learn to read or write, or if they did, they certainly wouldn't let anyone know about it. The Derzhi were a warrior race, and though they prized the literacy of their scholars and merchants, it was much in the way they prized their dogs who did tricks, or their birds who could carry messages unerringly, or their illusionists who could make rabbits turn into flowers or sultry maidens disappear. It was not something they would want to do themselves.

I touched my head to the carpet, rose, and knelt again beside the couch where the Prince lay, waving a rolled paper at me. My voice was hoarse to begin with, as I'd scarcely used it since being sent to the slave merchant almost a week before, but after a paragraph I got the words to come out clearly.

Zander,

It sorrows me greatly that I'm not able to come for your dakrah. I'm bogged down in getting the Khelid legate installed here in Parnifour. His list of requirements for his residence is unbelievable. It must back to the hills. It must accommodate at least three hundred. It must have a superior view of the city. It must have two wells that are not connected. It must have enough garden space with its own spring that their delicacies can be grown there. And so on endlessly.

Why your father chose to send his most junior dennissar to see to such a matter is beyond me . . . though I am still interminably grateful for the appointment and honored to be entrusted with such an important duty. I feared the Khelid legate might be offended at my assignment, thinking it less than his due, but he is everlastingly charming and accommodating—as long as I meet all his demands. I may have to turn Baron Feshikar out of his castle if I can't find anything better. Dispossessing a landed baron of the Fontezhi Heged is an ordeal I would as soon avoid. But I carry the Emperor's warrant, so anything that must be done will be done.

So as you can see it is impossible that I be there, though I know it will be a celebration worth a man's life to miss. My throat aches already, thinking of the bottles that have been laid down these twenty-three years for the day of your anointing, and everything else aches for the women that you will leave aside for the rest of us to enjoy! You must save me a bottle and a wench, and enough fire for a race from Zhagad to Drafa next spring. My Zeor is faster than ever and with a superior rider— myself—will have no difficulty against your pitiful Musa and his feeble master. I'll set you a thousand-zenar wager right now. That will give you reason not to forget me while I languish here in the backwaters of the realm.

Your desolate cousin,
Kiril

"Damn!" said the Prince, sitting up abruptly. "It won't be a proper feast without Kiril. It's only a two-week journey on a good horse. You'd think he could manage to be here for at least two or three days out of the twelve." The Prince snatched the letter from my hand and stared at it as if to send his displeasure back to its writer. "Maybe I should have him recalled. Kiril is a warrior, not some diplomatic lackey. Father can send someone else to do this servant work." He pushed his boot into the older man's back. "How could you let Father do this to Kiril? I thought he was your favorite nephew. Would you send a son into such dismal exile? Perhaps that's why the gods never gave you any."

"Did I not predict this?" said the older man, more worry in his voice than an unavailable cousin seemed to warrant. "As the Khelid weasel their way into your father's favor, they start making more and more demands. I'm told they insist that only their own magicians can practice in Karn'Hegeth, and that a Khelid must officiate at every marriage and funeral and dakrah. It's only been three months since your father gave them the city, and already they shape its working as if they were its conquerors."

I knelt unmoving, my eyes fixed on the intricate red and green designs of the thick carpet, trying not to give the appearance of interest. The Baron was the only one of my masters who had permitted me to hear anything of the world beyond uninformed slave-house gossip. It had been a small pleasure in a life with few of them, and I had regretted losing it more than almost anything when he put me up for sale.

"You worry too much, Dmitri," said the Prince. "You've been on the borders too long, and you're still upset with Father for giving away the city you took from the Basranni. Learn to enjoy yourself again. Even in this ice pocket to which my father consigns us, there are distractions aplenty. You've not been hunting with me in six years, and still owe me a new bow from the last time."

"You worry too little, Zander. You are Ivan's only son, the future Emperor of a thousand cities. It's time you worked at it. These Khelid . . ."

". . . could not defeat so much as a single Derzhi legion with their finest troops. They ran away, Dmitri, and hid for twenty years. They were so afraid of us, they came back groveling for peace. Who cares what they do with Karn'Hegeth? Who cares what they do with their magicians? Might as well worry about their jugglers or acrobats. Actually . . ." The Prince poked at the other man who sat cross-legged on the floor beside him. ". . . I've decided to hire a few of their magicians for my dakrah feast. I've heard they're astoundingly good."

"You must do no such thing. The anointing of the Derzhi Crown Prince on the day of his majority is not a spectacle for foreigners. No outsider should even be in the city on that day. And if their magicians are a part of their religion as they claim, then why would they hire them out for entertainments? I'd like to send all of them packing with their books and crystals shoved up their asses."

My shriveled Ezzarian soul could not hear such frivolous talk of true power without a twinge of anxiety. "Magic" was the common term for the illusions, sleight of hand, and smatterings of spell-weaving used for entertainment and mystification. Sorcery was altogether different. True power could alter the workings of nature and could be used for purposes most men and women could not imagine. I had heard enough of the Khelid to believe they knew something of sorcery. The Derzhi played with things they did not understand. There were mysteries . . . dangers . . . in the world . . . I closed my eyes and slammed shut the doors of knowledge and memory, the doors locked and barred on the day the Derzhi had stolen my freedom and the Rites of Balthar had stripped me of true power.

Lord Dmitri must have sensed my uneasiness, for he

seemed to notice me for the first time. He reached for my
arm and twisted it almost to breaking behind my back.

"You understand the penalties for sly, sneaking slaves
who so much as think about the private conversations of
their masters?"

"Yes, my lord," I squeezed out. I had seen such penalties
early on in my captivity and had needed nothing further to
persuade me to keep my counsel. I could forget as easily as
I could sleep.

"Get out," said the Prince, his cheerful manner clouded.
"Tell Durgan to put you back where you were."

I touched my head to the floor again and returned to the
slave house, informing Durgan that I was to go back underground. The Derzhi enjoyed seeing slaves carry the messages for our punishments. They would have had us lash
ourselves if they thought it possible we would do it to their
satisfaction.

In the dark, cold days before Aleksander called for me
again, between my long hours of sleeping and the three minutes a day I was fully occupied by a cup of gruel, a hard
lump of bread, or a chunk of rancid meat wild dogs would
disdain, I did some thinking about the Khelid. My previous
master, the Baron, was the most traditional of Derzhi, and
mistrusted any foreigner that had not been conquered by
force of arms. Even Ezzarians were more palatable to him
than the Khelid. We had held out for all of three days once
the Derzhi set their minds on the soft green rain swept hills
beyond their southern borders. The Baron thought us weak
and stupid to let ourselves be ruled by a woman, and muddled in the head with our sorcery, but at least we had put up
our best effort before we were dutifully subdued.

"These Khelid, though," he had said, confiding in his
slave because no one else would listen to him, "never really
fought us before they ran away. I never believed they were
engaged in a real battle. They did not ride, you see. No
horses. But look at them now, prancing around on these stal-
lions they've brought with them—beasts that Basranni

would worship as gods. You cannot convince me the Khelid do not fight on horseback." He was not a particularly intelligent man, the Baron, but he knew horses and he knew war.

When I asked him what the Khelid had been doing if they were not fighting, he said they had been "testing" the Derzhi. "They would probe here and there, then disappear," he said. "Show up in another place, get whipped, and run away. One day they just never came back. They learned where we were and how strong we were. Do you know we never captured any of them alive? Only dead. Always dead."

"But why is this so different?" I asked. "They learned you were stronger . . . as did we all. They just endured the loss of their independence with less death and destruction."

The Baron had no answer for that. He had no vocabulary for concepts beyond war.

I wondered if Lord Dmitri knew the Baron. It seemed he shared something of the same sense about the pale-haired strangers from a land so far away few Derzhi had ever seen it. It had been three years since the Khelid had reappeared, offering their tongueless king to the Derzhi in chains and vowing subjugation to the Derzhi Empire in return for peace, friendship, and mutual respect. Their king had been executed straightaway, and his head dispatched to Khelidar with a military governor and a small garrison. Messenger birds arrived regularly with reports from the governor detailing the good relationship with the Khelid in their remote and harsh land. It was a very different relationship than with other newly conquered peoples. The doomed king—or whoever he truly was—had been the only one to wear chains.

"Wake up and get out here! You sleep like the chastou at noonday."

I had almost given up on ever seeing daylight again. Seven days had passed since I'd read the Prince's letter. I assumed I had not pleased him, for in the last three of the seven, no cup had been lowered with my daily scrap of food. I couldn't muster enough spit to wet a dust mote, and hadn't even been able to eat the last hunk of dry bread they'd given

me. Death by thirst was very ugly. Better to be killed outright.

In the great paradox of the desert, I was so dry I no longer
desired to drink. But even in my muddled state I knew I was
not one of the sturdy desert beasts, and I'd better do what
was needed. I knelt to Durgan once I was out of the hole,
and I held out my hands. "Please, master, may I drink?" The
words ran together, stumbling over my tongue.

Durgan growled and called for someone named Filip. A
scrawny albino boy, a Fryth, scurried into the long block-
shaped room, where it appeared that at least a hundred men
must sleep on the straw-covered stone floor. "When did you
last give water to the one in the hole?" demanded the slave
master.

The pale-eyed boy shrugged. "You just said feed him.
Didn't say nothing else."

Durgan laid the back of his hand into the boy's head so
hard it flipped the child end over end. The boy bounced up
and shrugged his skinny shoulders, then strolled casually out
of the door. "Drink as you need." Durgan threw a tunic at me
and a tin cup, and pointed me at the cistern at the end of the
room, all the while mumbling, " Cursed Fryth. Don't have a
brain to share out amongst the lot of them."

There had been a time when I believed that drinking and
washing from the same basin was impure, a sign of inner
disorder that prevented one from discovering universal
truths, and put one at risk of corruption. Youth can be so
laughably serious. On that day the only difficulty was leaving any of the brown, brackish stuff to wash with. When I
was dressed, Durgan informed me that I was to go to the
Prince yet again. "Best behave yourself. He's had me asking
around for another reading slave. He don't trust you."

Well, I certainly shared that feeling. If I had thought the
only penalty was to be sent away, I might have considered
misbehaving, but I knew better. I didn't want to attract any
further unpleasant attention from the future Emperor of the
Derzhi. Survival was still of interest to me, though it was not
the passion it had been when I was eighteen and still learn-

ing what manacles and whips were all about. "Thank you,
Durgan. And thank you for the water. I'll do nothing to draw
his wrath upon you." I gave him a bow of true respect. He
had not been required to let me drink my fill before answering the Prince's summons.

"Off with you, then," he said.

This time the Prince was alone in a modestly propor-
tioned map room attached to his chambers. The walls were
covered with maps of the Empire. A rectangular table and
most of the floor were littered with map rolls, and ebony
pointing sticks, and gold and silver markers used to indicate
troop positions and supplies. Massive candelabra hung low
over the table, casting bright light upon the strategist's tools.
Prince Aleksander was standing beside one of the maps trac-
ing his finger idly over a part of it and sipping a glass of
wine. Unlike his larger chambers, this one had no perfumes
sprayed about to cover the stink of gathered bodies. Though
the Prince seemed reasonably clean, his race—a race with
origins in the desert—was, in general, not keen on bathing.
The only scents in the map room were candle smoke and
wine.

In the first months after my capture, I spent an inordinate
time wallowing in the pain of looking backward. But another man, one who had been in bondage for forty years, had
taught me the self-discipline required to stave off that particular madness. "Look at your hand," he said. "Trace the
bones and examine the skin and the calluses, the fingernails,
and the iron band about your wrist. Now re-create the hand
in your mind with the joints knotted, the skin hanging loose
and dry like paper, the nails brown and thick, the flesh spot-
ted with age like mine. The same iron band about the wrist.
Tell yourself . . . command yourself . . . that only when
there is no difference between your hand and the image . . .
only then will you be allowed to remember what has been. It
will not be forever, so it is not an impossible command to
obey. And when the time comes, you'll not remember so
clearly why you weep, and no one will take you to task for
it." I had followed his lesson faithfully and became quite

good at it. But there were moments when the exercise failed, and I would glimpse a piercingly clear image from my true life.

Such was the moment when I knelt just inside the door of Prince Aleksander's map room and inhaled the homely scents of hot beeswax and strong red wine. There flashed before my eyes a vision of a comfortable room, lined with books, hung and carpeted with the rich, deep autumn colors of my mother's weavings. My sword and my cloak lay on the floor, dropped after a long day of training. A beeswax candle burned softly on the dark pine desk, and a man's strong and vital hand pressed a glass of wine into my grasp. . . .

"I said come here! Are you deaf or just insolent?"

When I lifted my eyes, the Prince was glaring at me from across the room. I was up quickly, trying to regain my composure, trying to suppress a hunger that had nothing to do with food.

The Prince motioned me to a stool. Paper and pen, ink and sand were set out on the table in front of me.

"I want to see a sample of your writing."

I picked up the pen, dipped it, and waited.

"Well, get on with it."

I steeled myself for his displeasure. "Is there anything particular you would like me to write, my lord?"

"Damn it all, I told you I wanted a sample of your writing. Did I say I cared what it was?"

I deemed it prudent to answer with deeds, and that the deed had best be well considered, so I wrote, "May all honor and glory come to Prince Aleksander, Crown Prince of the Derzhi." I turned the paper so he could see it over my shoulder, dipped the pen again, and asked, "Would you like to see more, my lord?"

"You wrote my name," he said, accusing.

"Yes, Your Highness."

"What did you put with it?"

I read him the sentence. He was quiet for a moment, and I kept my eyes pinned to the paper.

"Not very original."

I glanced up in surprise at the wry humor behind the un-smiling words. Perhaps it was because I was off balance from the vision . . . unguarded . . . still weak in the head from hunger, or drunk with water after three days with-out . . . but I grinned at him and said, "But safe."

He stiffened, and it appeared for one instant that I might regret my moment's madness, but then he slapped me on the back—spattering ink all over my composition—and laughed heartily. "Indeed. Hard to find fault with it—even for me." He drained his glass of wine and shoved another sheet of paper in front of me. "Your hand seems good enough. So now write what I tell you."

He walked around the table as he dictated. The faster he walked, the faster he talked, which did nothing to aid my dizziness. I tried to think of something to make him stop, but he was accustomed to scribes, of course, and knew when his thoughts raced too far ahead of my hand. He would pause his words to give me time to catch up, but would not slow his walking.

> Cousin,
> I am dreadfully annoyed with you for taking your du-ties so seriously. Give the cursed Khelid legate a hovel and be done with him. These are my subjects, for the gods' sake, not my masters. If you are not here for my dakrah, I'll have your balls in my tea the day after.
> I despise these damned Khelid and wish they would crawl back to their rocks and pits, wherever they are. Fa-ther is so preoccupied with this Khelid Lord Kastavan and his clever ideas that he has sent me here to Capharna to hold his winter Dar Heged. The weather is uniformly dreadful, my duties tedious, and of course, Father has sent Dmitri to be my schoolmaster. Was there ever any-one so preoccupied with plots and conspiracies as our unerringly grim uncle? I know I am truly bored when I start listening to his warnings and taking them to heart. The only reason I allow him in my chambers is that there

is so little other amusement. The company in Capharna in the middle of winter is dismal—all imbeciles or ass-lickers. Who else would give up the glories of Zhagad's finest season for this? Between the mistrust Dmitri hammers into me and the hatred they have earned through this despicable winter's banishment, I'll confide to you that I plan to behead or exile all of the fiendish Khelid the moment I am crowned.

The wager is doubled to two thousand. Musa will not allow your plow horse to beat him.

Your equally desolate cousin,
Zander

I read the letter back to the Prince, made the few minor corrections he wished, then, in all innocence, asked if he wished to sign it himself before I melted the wax for his seal.

"You insolent pig!" He raised the back of his hand in a painfully familiar gesture, and I dropped instantly to my knees, pressing my forehead to the floor. In my first years of bondage, I could not assume the submissive posture without my stomach gnawing on itself and my hands trembling in anger. But over time I learned that such a position made it much more difficult for an angry man to lay his fist to your head. Somehow it seemed to take a little more thought or preparation before they began using their feet.

"My apologies for my stupidity, my lord! I beg you command me." My tongue rattled off the necessary words. Not too many. No excuses. Prattling or excuses always made them angrier.

He was silent for a long while, and I dared not look up.

"Melt the wax."

I got to my feet and stepped back to the stool, but as the blood rushed out of my aching head, another wave of dizziness made me stagger slightly against the table.

"What's wrong with you?"

"Nothing, my lord." He didn't really want to hear it.

"Would you prefer the white wax or the green or some other?"

"Red. For Kiril, always red."

I bowed my head and got about the business of sealing the letter. When he had pressed his signet ring into the soft red wax, he rang a bell, and one of his gentleman attendants appeared before the ringing had ceased. There were at least two of the gold-clad young men outside the door at all times in addition to the four heavily armed bodyguards.

The Prince dispatched the letter on its way to Parnifour, then turned back to me. I was uneasy, sitting idle on the stool under his unwavering eye.

"Get out. Tell Durgan you're to have ten lashes for insolence. You think too much, and you don't say what you're thinking."

I performed my obeisance and said nothing . . . certainly not what I was thinking.

Chapter 3

It was another seven days until I was brought out of my cell again. The day was brilliantly sunny, a rarity in Capharna's high valley, which seemed to capture every fog, mist, and cloud that hung in the northern mountains of Azhakstan. Perhaps it was this ever-present cloud of mystery that convinced the Derzhi, who had their origins in the dune seas of central Azhakstan where the sky was a constant flat steel blue, that Capharna was a holy city, sacred to their gods.

The doors of the slave house had been thrown open to the sun. It was still cold enough to show your breath, but anything was better than the stale, fetid air of my burrow under the floor. I stretched and inhaled and felt half-human. My other half was itching, stinking, and squinting to keep out the painful glare of sunlight on snow. But I wasn't greedy.

"What's the matter with you? I've never seen anyone smile after nigh on three weeks down there." Durgan held the white tunic close to his brawny chest, as if planning to withhold it until I had confessed my secret sin.

"I've slept enough for ten men, I've not had a lash in seven days, and yesterday's meat was only half gristle and not quite off. I've had worse weeks."

The slave master stared at me as if I were mad. "You're an odd one, Ezzarian."

I could have said the same for Durgan, who had not only made sure the Fryth boy sent my water down every day, but had sent two cups instead of just the one. And the portions of food in my one meal a day had been noticeably larger than before. But it's never wise to point out a kindness in your master, lest you find out it was all a mistake.

I pointed to the tunic. "Is that for me?"

"Oh, aye. As before. In his chambers. Be quick about it."

I bowed, took myself to the cistern, and, once the slave master had inspected me and given his approval, started for the palace. As I left the slave house, Durgan called after me, "Watch your tongue, slave. Better than last time."

I was not averse to watching my tongue. I just wished I knew how to go about it with Aleksander.

On this occasion the bodyguards outside the Prince's door searched me before I was allowed to knock. As they prodded and poked self-importantly, I heard the disconcerting sounds of glass breaking and cursing from behind the door. At the snappish, "Come," my fading lash marks stung in warning.

The Prince was throwing things: pillows, statuary, wineglasses and bottles, and the occasional knife. Evidently this had been going on for quite a while, for the priceless Induit carpet was stained with wine and littered with fragments of glass, porcelain, feathers, clothing, and cushions. I worried that I might slice my forehead on the shards, and it was difficult to convince myself to rise up again after my obeisance. So I stayed down. I didn't want his attention. And, in truth, he seemed to have forgotten me already.

"Intolerable! I'll see them all dead. Better, I'll see them all in chains. I'll send them to the Veshtari Overlord to spread dung in his fields. The Veshtar know how to use slaves."

"Aleksander, control yourself." It was the Lord Dmitri, brother to the Emperor. "Your rash behavior has caused this mess."

"You blame me as Father does. It's my fault that this city is filled with inbred imbeciles who can't find their mouths with a spoon, but who dare spy on their Emperor's son. And I am to accept it? You're the one who keeps warning me of these Khelid, and now I'm taken to task for speaking my mind in private correspondence. By Druya's horns, Dmitri, he'll have me married to one of them, if this doesn't stop."

My equanimity, already unsettled by Durgan's warning, lay in ruins.

"I'm as concerned about the Khelid as ever, Aleksander. But if you're to be Emperor, you must think before you act. You mutilated the son of the oldest family in northern Azhakstan. You taunted and shamed him—and therefore his kin to the sixteenth degree—setting them at odds with your father and yourself. And to compound your stupidity, you make fatuous threats against your father's new favorites and trust the letter to one of your attendants who happens to be Vanye's brother-in-law! How can one intelligent man be so thickheaded?"

"Get out, Dmitri. Until my father revokes my birth, I am your prince. You will watch your despicable tongue or I'll have it out of your mouth."

"Zander—"

"Out!"

I glimpsed two well-worn boots, elegantly crafted of the finest leather, standing beside my head.

"Here is your slave, Aleksander. Consider carefully what words you have him commit to paper. I love you well, but I will not stand between you and Ivan. Never think it."

An oil lamp crashed into the door as it closed behind Dmitri. I knew it was from the combination of shattered glass, rattling brass, and peach-scented oil that splattered over my back. It took all the control I could muster to stay still. It was daytime. The lamp was not lit.

"Insolent, damnable wretch!" I hoped that was aimed at Dmitri. I kept my head to the carpet. I would have preferred to keep it there all day rather than allow the Prince to glimpse the barely healed mark on my face—the abstractions of a rampant lion that threatened to devour my left eye and the falcon that still throbbed on my cheekbone. From the conversation I had just heard, I was much too involved in this unpleasantness—exactly the last place a slave should ever be.

Droplets of oil dribbled slowly down the backs of my legs. How could something so complexly wonderful and mysterious as the human intelligence devise a world so utterly, absolutely absurd?

"Come, take up your pen, Ezzarian." Anger transformed to cold bitterness. Very dangerous.

"In the map room, Your Highness?" I asked, speaking clearly, not in some annoying craven whisper. I kept my face averted.

"No. Right here." He pointed to a small desk beside the window where he stood. It was a simple piece, made of dark cherry wood, planed and shaped into smooth, elegant lines, far less exotic and elaborate than the other tables and chests in his chambers. Out of place, yet far more pleasing to my eye. The drawer slid open quietly at my touch. Inside it a small, sharp knife lay beside the stack of creamy white paper. While I unstoppered the ink and used the little knife to sharpen the three pens that lay on the desktop, the Prince absentmindedly ran his hand over the satiny, tight-grained finish of the desk, muttering. "Damn you, Dmitri. Damn you."

"All is ready, my lord."

I waited a good five minutes while Aleksander stared out of the window, folding his arms in front of his chest, his jaw rigid, in the very posture of controlled rage. When he began to release his words, they were like the first few pellets of sleet spit from lowering clouds, so hard and biting that they would send villagers scurrying to gather in their children and their stock to protect them from the coming fury of the storm.

> Sire,
> I accept your righteous rebuke for my decision to reduce Lord Vanye's rank. It was a thoughtless act, contrary to the best interests of the Derzhi Empire and reflecting dishonor upon myself as your son and heir, and therefore upon you, my father and my liege. Such result was never, and could never be, my remotest intent. To

bring the least blight, the most minute taint of unseemly dispute to your glorious reign or your honored person is so vile a thought I can scarcely voice it, as if by saying the words, my tongue must blacken and fall out with the poisonous taste. Upon the life that you have given me and the honor that you have nurtured in me, such a lapse will not happen again.

But for any act beyond this, I accept no chastisement. Vanye purposefully and contrivedly sought to destroy the property of his prince and liege. This is nothing but treason. To treat such a crime with lenience is to invite further affronts or open rebellion. The penalty for treason must be death or enslavement. So I was taught by you, honored sire. Vanye brought this shame upon his family, not I.

As for the other matter, it seems but a confirmation of the earlier results. If Vanye's family are loyal subjects wronged by the Emperor's justice as they claim, then why is Lord Sierge found spying on his Emperor's son? This is yet another act of treason to augment and compound the first. A price must be and will be paid for it.

My words to my cousin were private, and I will offer no apology for them.

I have received your Khelid messenger graciously and heard from his mouth my Emperor's rebuke. Your choice of a non-Derzhi voice for this most painful missive is, of course, not a matter on which I would dare express misgivings. But I most determinedly resist the long-term companionship with this Khelid lord that you have suggested. The Khelid people may be worthy allies and have a culture deserving our scrutiny, but when it comes to the governing of the Derzhi Empire, I wish for your tutelage only, sire. Not that of foreigners who treat for peace with their sovereign in chains.

With all respect and deepest humility,
Aleksander, Prince of Azhakstan

A masterpiece. I was absolutely in awe of Aleksander's craftsmanship and came near blurting out my compliments. To pull in the reminder of the Khelid king in chains . . . to couch his own stupidity in such noble sentiments . . . I wanted to stand and applaud him. Perhaps the man had more intelligence than it seemed at first. Perhaps he had learned a lesson from the whole nasty mess.

I shook the sand off the letter and prepared wax for the seal. Aleksander pressed so hard he almost squeezed all of the stuff from under his ring.

While I cleaned up the desk, including glass fragments and feathers and the oil that had dripped from my hair and my arm, Aleksander spoke to a servant outside his door. In only a moment his uncle Dmitri entered and genuflected quite formally, expressing his surprise at being recalled so soon.

"I have a mission for you, Uncle."

"And what is that?"

"I wish you to bear my answer to my father."

"You jest!"

"Not at all. I can't seem to trust my messengers not to pry into my correspondence, but you would not dare deliver a letter with a broken seal to your Emperor, brother or no. You are the only one I can trust, therefore, you must go." The Prince stuck the letter in his uncle's thick fingers.

The Derzhi warrior was furious. "You young fool—"

"Do not defy me, Uncle. This is not the day for it. I want you on your way within the hour."

Dmitri dipped his knee again. "My lord." Then he stomped out of the room. I would not have been one of his slaves at that moment for an extra year's rations.

The Prince did not stop my cleaning, even when I moved from the desk to the couch, where I had seen him recline. He was tapping his foot and staring out of the window again.

The man who arrived next was so bulbous his gold breeches and vest could scarcely contain his bulk. One could get nauseous from watching the undulating waves of gold satin. His scant hair was swept across the pink ball of his head into a braid of a most unnatural color of red, and it had been a goodly while since the fellow had seen the desert from the back of a warhorse. Amazingly enough he could sweep a bow as gracefully as a slender boy. "Your Highness, all blessings of Athos and his brethren upon you this glorious day. How may I lend my poor talents to the service of my most gracious lord?" His speech was bulbous as well.

"We are having special guests this evening. I wish every first-degree noble of the House of Mezzrah to receive a personal summons from my Lord High Chamberlain. From his very lips."

The florid face was a bit disconcerted. "From my—"

"From your lips, Fendular, from your lips. I believe there are some nineteen of these gentlemen. You are to greet them with my heartfelt good wishes, my promise of leniency in all our dealings, my most sincere respect, my desire to treat with them, to hear their grievances, and heed their wisdom . . . whatever particular flatteries you think appropriate. You are wise in these matters as I am not."

Another bow. "Your Highness is too generous with—"

"You will tell them that I wish to receive them as soon as possible and introduce them to the Emperor's Khelid emissary, Korelyi. In fact, they will be in my reception rooms no later than four hours from the next striking of the clock."

"Four—"

"Your life is forfeit, Fendular, if even one of these lords is not present. And I will not have them brought by force. They must come willing, despite any . . . misgiving . . . they may have about my favor. Do you understand me?"

"Indeed, my lord." The man had lost a good deal of his robust coloring, and had, indeed, sagged into his clothes a bit like a slip of gold leaf set too close to the forge.

"What anxiety is this, Fendular? You understand these northern nobles as no one else in the Emperor's service understands them. You know the right words to bring them."

A straightening of the overburdened spine. "It shall be done as you command, Highness. I am honored by your confidence."

"Good. And because these lords may be apprehensive—some scurrilous rumors that they are out of my favor—you will arrange for suitable gifts of greeting to await them upon their arrival. Fine gifts. Once I have received our guests, we will surprise them by having them dine at my own table with my Khelid guest. You will give the necessary orders?"

"Of course, Highness." Fewer words as the tasks of the next hours grew impossibly complex.

"Be off with you, Fendular, with all haste."

"Your Highness." Another bow, not quite so sweeping, and the Chamberlain backed toward the door.

"Oh . . . one more thing," said the Prince.

"Yes, my lord?"

"You need not invite Sierge, Lord Vanye's brother-in-law. I am issuing his invitation myself."

Fendular withdrew with his orders and was quickly replaced by a tall, thin Derzhi warrior dressed smartly in the Emperor's green livery. His face was shaped like a shovel, narrow at the top, spreading into a flat wide jaw. The Prince acknowledged his crisp bow.

"You value your appointment as the palace guard captain and the trust I bear you, do you not, Mikael?"

"My life is yours, as you know, Your Highness, since the day you were fifteen and saved—."

"You have told me many times that you will neither question nor falter in your duty, no matter what I ask of you. For the honor of your Emperor and your Prince. This is still true?"

"I would sooner fall upon my sword than fail you, my lord."

"Following my instructions to the letter will suffice. You are to take a troop of well-armed guardsmen, and exactly four hours from the next striking of the clock, you are to arrest my attendant Sierge of the House of Mezzrah at his home. The charge is treason. He is to be taken directly to the public square of Capharna and hanged. Without discussion, without announcement, without forewarning to his family.

Absolutely without delay of any kind. Do you understand me?"

"Aye, my lord." To his credit, the guard captain's voice did not falter as his sudden pallor might warrant. "I would assume that no word is to be spoken of this, even in the palace itself, until the deed is done."

"You are perceptive as always, Mikael. At the same moment that you are arresting Sierge, two of your finest officers will be extending my gracious invitation to our Khelid guest, Korelyi, to witness an event of great import. He will be escorted to the square, where I will await him. I wish him to be at my side to witness this execution before I entertain him at dinner."

"As you wish, my lord, it shall be done. May I suggest doubling the watch this night? The House of Mezzrah has a large standing force and owns at least five assassins."

"No. No doubling of the guard. We are not afraid of an honorable family of such long and distinguished service to the Emperor. You will make this clear to those at Sierge's house and to the guard and to all who may inquire or be concerned. I have judged that only the two men, Vanye and Sierge, have been involved in treason. No one else in the family. Even their wives and children will reap no ill harvest from their deeds."

"Yes, Your Highness. Four hours from this."

"Go with the gods' protection, Mikael."

"You are Athos' priest, my lord, and his wisdom guides your hand."

As the man bowed and left the room, I sincerely wished that I believed enough in a god—whether the Derzhi sun deity or some other—to think he or she was taking an interest in Aleksander's plotting. The Prince was either an inordinately brilliant strategist or the maddest fool ever to wear a coronet. I suspected the latter. I suspected he was starting a war over an ugly face and a twenty-zenar slave.

Once the guard captain was gone, I hastily resumed my cleaning, suspended by the extraordinary events I had witnessed.

"What is your name, slave?"

I had hoped he would not care to know it. I should have known better than to hope. It was the ultimate expression of subjugation—to be forced to give up the most personal, the most private self to one who had no claim, no right of friendship or kinship or guesting, to one who had no idea of the power of names or the dangerous entry they gave to the soul. "Seyonne, my lord." No violation of body or mind was so bitter, save the rites they used to strip us Ezzarians of our power.

"You are a lucky man, Seyonne."

I paused with my hands full of broken porcelain and feathers, trying to keep the foot I had just punctured with a shard of glass from dripping blood on the carpet. I kept my eyes averted and tried not to break into hysterical laughter.

"When I discovered that the contents of my letter had found their way to Khelid ears . . . and thus to my father's ears, I presumed it was you had done it. The death I planned for you was an artwork."

I swallowed my rising gorge.

"But Durgan and his men convinced me that you had been locked up securely since the day you scribed my words, and therefore, of all the inhabitants of this city, only you were proven innocent. Ironic, is it not?"

"As you say, Your Highness." It had been half a lifetime since I had considered myself at all lucky.

"I've heard that you Ezzarians claim you can see the future. Is it true?"

"If we could see the future, my lord, how could we not have prevented our own destruction?"

"You asked a question. You did not answer mine." So he was not a total fool.

"No man can see the future, Your Highness."

"Pity."

Aleksander dispatched me to fetch wine, and other house slaves to clean up the mess, and his body slaves to bathe and dress him. Once I located what he required and poured him a fresh glass of wine, he sent me back to the slave house. I was to clean myself and report to the kitchens, where I was to learn the customs for serving at the Prince's table . . . to begin that very night.

Chapter 4

The Summer Palace of the Derzhi Emperors had dominated the misty valley of the Ghojan River for some four hundred years. Built on the site of an ancient fortress that had guarded the mountain passes from barbarians to the north, it had been expanded by one after another of Aleksander's forefathers. The farther north the boundaries of the Empire stretched, the less fortified and more luxurious the palace became. By the time I was taken there, the sprawling palace walls encompassed some ninety hectares of buildings and courtyards, workshops and barracks and armories, butteries and gardens and stables. The city of Capharna itself was scarcely larger.

The newer rooms of the main keep had large windows and high ceilings, elaborate columns and arches and elegant carvings, a splendor of decoration that seemed misplaced in the harsh mountain setting. For six glorious weeks a year, the sweetest airs of the Empire wafted through the graceful archways, and the gardens exploded in an ocean of flowers. But on almost every other day the bitter winds rattled the huge windows and gusted through the desolate courtyards. In the long winters thick rugs and tapestries were hung over every opening, making the short daylight hours nonexistent for those who didn't venture out of doors. Unending wagon loads of wood had to be carted from the thick mountain forests to keep the hearths blazing. Even so, the heat all drifted upward to hang in the ceiling vaults, and the residents . . . and certainly the lightly clad slaves . . . were forever cold.

This palace would be the entirety of my universe until the

Prince decided to dispose of me. Only rarely were Derzhi house slaves permitted beyond their master's walls. We were always chained at night and closely supervised during the day. As universes went for slaves, though, the Summer Palace would be quite fine—with a variety of interesting people and events to observe.

Zeroun, the slave commanded to instruct me in the customs of the Prince's table, was sure that some dreadful mistake had been made. "An Ezzarian, a branded runaway, serving the Prince and his table guests? Impossible. His Highness would never reward such deviance with his favor, and would never tolerate a scarred face in his sight. You don't even wear fenzai . . ." He pulled at my tunic and peered at my back. "As I suspected . . . a disobedient barbarian. Impossible. Scandalous impertinence."

Three times he sought confirmation of the orders, until he was at risk of stripes himself. His problem, of course, was that he was a Basranni, which meant that he considered himself far above the level of an ordinary slave. The Basranni were a horse-worshiping desert clan, who'd had the misfortune to slay a Derzhi prince when they were trying to assassinate their own tyrant some fifty years previous. Though related by culture, blood, and intermarriage, and allied in war for three hundred years, the Derzhi had leveled every Basranni town and village and killed or enslaved every Basranni man, woman, and child. Still, Basranni slaves believed they were part owner of every Derzhi household, and were more concerned with upholding Derzhi tradition than were the Derzhi themselves.

"Derzhi table customs are quite refined and quite specific. What concept could you have of the graceful presentation of delicacies? How could you know of hand-washing rites or how to pour—"

"Zeroun, I have served in four noble Derzhi houses, most recently that of an excessively traditional baron of the most traditional of the noble houses, the House of Gorusch. I know how to lay the meat on top of the loaf. I know how to kneel just behind the cushions, yet serve without touching the guest. I know how to pour the nazrheel on top of the lemon, rather than drop the lemon in the tea. I know never, ever, to offer meat, cheese, or eggs if the guest's knife is laid crosswise. Just tell me how the Prince's table differs. If I do something wrong, we will both suffer the consequences."

That seemed to stifle his objections, though he took special care not to touch me and to point out to every other slave that passed by us that I was the lowest of the low and could not be trusted. I supposed that would make no difference if I was to be kept forever in the slave-house dungeon rather than join the other men who slept chained to the walls above my head every night. Trust among slaves was a fragile thing; once lost it was hard to recover, and one could find oneself a pariah among pariahs. I didn't blame them. Trust had been bled from me long years in the past. But Zeroun was a good teacher. By the time the female slaves had laid the richly patterned cloths and gold plates on the low tables, set out the carafes of wine, and spread the freshly aired cushions alongside, he had crammed my head with every nuance of the Prince's preferences.

I had no thoughts to spare for Aleksander's scheming. When the hour struck, the hour the Prince had set for his plot to unfold, I was trying not to drop a tray of twenty-one small basins of warmed, scented water between the kitchen and the Prince's table. There were three tables set up in one of the small dining rooms. The Prince's table, set for twenty-one, was elevated above the other two tables on a low dais. It looked like sixty or seventy people would be at the lower tables to witness whatever the Prince had in mind. A cold draft made the candle flames waver, and a servant stoked the great hearth in the corner of the room behind the dais. Whoever sat at the Prince's far left would bake; whoever sat at his far right would freeze.

About fifteen minutes past the striking of the hour, finely dressed, bejeweled Derzhi men and women began crowding into the dining room, jockeying for places at the lower tables. The Baron did not entertain, nor did the master before that, a less than prosperous merchant who could not afford to do so, so it had been on the order of five years since I had been in the midst of so many hostile people at once. It made me uneasy, but I distracted myself by listening for any snippet of conversation that might reveal what had transpired with the House of Mezzrah. Surely there were rumors of the execution or the summoning of the Mezzrahn lords. But I heard nothing beyond curiosity as to who would sit at the high table, what lady did the Prince fancy this month, and when was he ever going to get down to the business of the Dar Heged, the winter joining of northern Derzhi families, the business that had brought Aleksander to Capharna in the first place.

I wondered if Aleksander planned to kill the eighteen nobles. Surely he was not that big a fool, though his own father had done something similar on more than one occasion. Hostages were another favorite Derzhi tactic, but it seemed too obvious. The nobles would not be naive enough to lay down their arms when entering the palace, and if Aleksander threatened them, they would fight. Unless . . . I glanced at the elegantly laid head table with its twenty-one seats. The Derzhi had very strict guesting customs, drawn from their origins in the desert. When water was life to all, deprivation of water was seen as a crime unworthy of a true warrior. The bitterest enemies could share a well peaceably on one day, even while planning to slaughter each other on the battlefield the next. Guesting . . .

The great double doors behind the dais were thrown open and a line of fur-clad men—all wearing the orange-striped silk head scarf of the House of Mezzrah—began to file in and take places at the head table. They were glowering suspiciously, but seemed to relax at the sight of the table, the other chattering guests, and the feasting dishes being carried in by a parade of female slaves. They didn't know. These powerful, ruthless warriors had no idea that their kinsman's body hung lifeless and freezing in the public square of Capharna, executed less than an hour past by the smiling, red-haired Prince who graciously followed them through the doors, honoring each man with his special attentions. If they drank only water, they would not betray themselves, but the moment they ate

Aleksander's meat or drank his wine, they would become his guest-friends, all past disputes, all grievances settled and forgotten . . . whether they knew of them or not. They could not take revenge for the hanging without betraying a thousand years of Derzhi tradition, because they would have shared Aleksander's table after the murder was done.

Breathless with astonishment at the Prince's brazen stroke—and the enormity of the risk he had taken—I took my place at the back of the table and helped arrange cushions and swords and boots and cloaks until the guests were as comfortable as they could be in Prince Aleksander's house. The sourest of all of them was Lord Barach, Vanye's father, his gray braid hanging well below his bare shoulder, who sat in the place farthest from the Prince. From the look of him, he was there only at his House elders' command.

It was time to put aside my distracting speculations lest I be noticed. Derzhi nobles had been known to cut off a slave's fingers or scald his hands in boiling tea if food was dropped or spilled or improperly served. Carefully I filled the crystal wine goblets and doled out the hot flat loaves of herbed bread, then offered the platters of succulent roast lamb and savory brown-crusted pork. There were fruits to be sliced or peeled, pickled eggs, sugared dates, and tiny salted fish to be laid out for those who wanted them. Nazrheel, the bitter tea, to be poured. More wine. Zeroun's lessons and those of other forgotten teachers repeated themselves continually in my head—the sum of a slave's scholarship.

Always kneel just behind. Never allow your body to touch the guest. Always offer to the Prince first. If he points at it or nods his head—the gesture can be so slight as to be almost undetectable—give the taster, the shivering slave who sits in the shadows behind him, a portion first, then arrange the remainder on the Prince's plate. Do not breathe while serving the Prince, lest your breath offend him at dinner. Never let the guests run out of meat, lest the Prince appear ungenerous. Never let them run out of nazrheel, as this is seen as a bad omen. The gray-haired lord has his knife across his plate. He is in the middle of the ephrail, the purification fast.

*No meat, cheese, or eggs—nothing from a beast can cross
his lips. No wine or spirits. Only fruit and tea. When the
Prince is finished, nothing more must be served to any guest.
The hand washing must be done before. . . .*

When would they hear of it? When would they know
how they had been tricked? What would they do? When
would they understand why one cushion, the seat at the far-
left end of the table, remained vacant? Sixty witnesses to
their guesting, too many to kill to remedy their mistake.
Even Lord Barach had eaten and drunk.

"Is there no mead or brandy to be had in Prince Aleksander's household?" asked the slender man in dark purple
who sat just to the Prince's left. "I prefer a sweeter drink to
ward off the night's chill."

"Of course, my lord," I said quietly, then quickly fetched
Suzain brandy from the sideboard. It was the sweetest and
fieriest available. I knelt behind him and poured a few drops
into his goblet. "If it does not please, I can bring mead."

He lifted the glass. "Ah. Well chosen." As I filled his goblet
with the dark amber liquid, he drew his fur-lined cloak about
his shoulders. "One would not mistake the Summer Palace of
the Derzhi for the Winter Palace. The names are most assuredly switched." The mild voice bore a trace of an accent.

I glanced at his face very quickly. He must be the Khelid.
How could I have failed to notice how different he was?
White-blond hair cut short and straight about his face.
Smooth, pale, white skin, absolutely unlike the ruddy,
weathered Derzhi or the reddish-gold color of my own race.
A pleasant, narrow face. Ageless. Smiling. As I indulged my
idle curiosity, his eyes met my own . . . eyes of ice-blue,
eyes as clear as the morning sky in the highest mountains . . . eyes that terrified me beyond anything I had seen
in sixteen years, beyond nightmares, beyond the most fearful encounters of my youth, for never before had I faced
such eyes defenseless. There was no difficulty with keeping
my breath from offending. I could not breathe. I bowed my
head, breaking off the contact instantly. The brandy was use-

less. Nothing could ever warm those eyes or what was behind them.

The rote of my lessons kept churning senselessly in my
head.

*Always lay the meat across the bread. Never look the
guests in the eye. Slaves have been killed for looking into a
guest's eyes . . .*

. . . and they were not such eyes as the ones I had just
glimpsed. Did he know I had recognized him? Did he know
it was possible, that there were those of us in the world who
had been trained to see what he carried within him? However crippled I was, however lost, however removed from
the person I had once been and the life I had once lived, I
could still recognize a demon.

I set the bottle of brandy within his reach and began to
withdraw my hand, but he caught my wrist in short cold fingers with smooth, tight skin and perfectly manicured nails.
Surely there were many reasons why a slave's hands would
tremble.

"You're the one," he said, soft enough that neither the
Prince on his right, nor the Derzhi lord on his left could have
heard him. He pulled me closer by twisting my wrist with
fingers of steel until my face was just beside his own. I kept
my eyes fixed on the table. Then, with his other hand, he
traced the lion and the falcon on my cheek, the touch of his
cold fingers setting a blaze on my skin that was far more terrible than the smith's glowing iron. "You're the cause of all
this. The catalyst . . ." I felt him try to peel back my skin
with his razor eyes. ". . . the damaged property. This Aleksander is clever beyond all our imaginings. To bring you
here within sight of them . . . Charming. Dangerous." He
was not talking to me, but to himself. Well and good. He
could not recognize me; they didn't know our names. I
wanted nothing . . . nothing . . . to do with him.

Perhaps I should have looked about the room and tried to
read the souls to find one who might be worth saving. Perhaps I could have mustered the skill for deeper looking even
after so long. If I had cared for a single man or woman in that

assembly, I would have stood up and cried out a warning and welcomed whatever punishment would come. But time had taught me that care for any being carried consequences too painful to be borne—consequences far beyond lashes or starvation—and even in the presence of uttermost terror, I could not face them. Desperately I wanted to be back in my hole in the ground, naked in the dark. Hidden. Asleep. Alone.

"Seyonne!"

The Khelid released my hand, even as I cursed the Prince for speaking my true name in the demon's hearing.

I moved quickly around the Khelid and knelt beside Aleksander, bowing my head as low as I could without putting it in his lap or his plate. "Your Highness."

"I wish you to wash the hands of my table guests."

"My lord . . ." I almost choked on the words that tried to tumble out of my mouth. What in the name of the gods was he doing? The washing at the close of a meal was usually the job of younger slaves . . . attractive women or youths made available for a night for those guests who took a fancy to them. I had not been required to do it since I passed twenty-five and had enough scars to make me less than pleasing.

"And you will use this for the drying cloth." Into my hands he placed an orange-striped silk scarf. Sierge's.

I was beyond all speech. I bowed my head and said the prayer of the dying . . . even though I no longer believed in prayer.

The room was noisy with conversation and the clattering of dishes and bottles. I'd hardly noticed it until I walked numbly to the end of the table to take up the jug of hot water with rose petals floating in it. Magicians were drawing rings of fire in the air and producing bouquets of flowers from out of them, as I poured water into the small porcelain bowl beside the first Mezzrahn Lord. Though I could not look up at him, I felt his eyes on me as I held out the bowl. He would be curious. One male slave, clearly past the bloom of youth, to do the washing. Two greasy thick-fingered hands dipped into the bowl, sloshed about a little, then stopped abruptly. He had noticed the scar on my face. He could not avoid it as

I knelt in front of him. His hands began to quiver as he withdrew them from the hot water. I emptied the bowl into a slops jar and pulled out the scarf. A wrenching moan of dismay rumbled from his chest, and I had scarcely touched his outstretched hands with the scarf when he clenched his fists. I steeled myself for a blow, but he did not do it. Could not. For once I blessed Derzhi tradition. I moved to the next man.

Four of them grabbed the scarf, and I had to remain kneeling in front of them with my hand open, waiting until they released it to me again. Three of them came near breaking my fingers. Three of them grabbed my ear and twisted my head to look closer at the mark on my face. The last seven refused to have their hands washed at all. Though considered somewhat barbaric, it was not a full breach of etiquette. None of them killed me. None of them broke the guesting laws. They knew they were guilty. They had forsaken their caution for whatever blandishments the stout Fendular had whispered in their ears. Perhaps they had convinced themselves that Vanye was indeed ugly and stupid and not worth offending the Emperor's heir or his Khelid emissary. They could blame no one but themselves.

I left the Khelid and the Prince until last. That was the custom. I could scarcely bring myself to touch the Khelid's small fingers again, but at least I didn't have to look at him. After I cleansed the Prince's hands, Aleksander lifted my chin and smiled at me wickedly as if I had been his accomplice instead of his tool.

"Well done, Seyonne. Are we Derzhi not a polite people?"

"Yes, my lord," I whispered.

"You are dismissed. None of my guests have asked for you."

I touched my head to the floor and withdrew. I could not get out of the palace fast enough, and I barely made it into the cold night air before heaving up the scant contents of my stomach.

Chapter 5

I could not sleep that night. I tried everything I knew, but never had the cold seemed so bitter or the darkness so filled with dread. Whether open or closed, my eyes could see nothing but the Khelid's ice-blue eyes, and my haven of darkness became a well of madness. I huddled in the corner; I paced the five steps from wall to wall until I was dizzy and could not stand upright . . . anything to keep myself from thinking, from remembering, from seeing. I peered at the ceiling until I found the thread of gold that marked the square of the trapdoor, and I hung onto that thread as a drowning child hangs onto his father's hand. I translated the muffled steps and voices above my head into human beings who had souls, who had eyes that were not demon's eyes. And when all grew quiet and the thread of gold winked out, I moaned and buried my face in my arms.

Not a week this time, Durgan. Not five days or three. If you have a soul, slave master, don't leave me here too long or you'll find a raving lunatic when you open the door again.

One might have thought the demon had taken up its residence in me, feeding on anger I could no longer recognize in myself, because I had forbidden it for so long. I told myself it could not know me. It was not a demon's nature to associate a bodily form with those it had encountered at other times in other places. Yet such reasoned arguments held no sway when I crouched naked in the dark and tried so desperately to lose myself in sleep.

Well, we can always bear more than we believe possible.

By the second day from the execution feast, I was sleeping again, though not peacefully. I received three rounds of food and water, and thus I believe three days passed before Durgan dropped his ladder to me again. Though I had regained my composure, I was up the ladder almost before it touched the floor.

The sturdy slave master examined me curiously as I knelt shivering in the clean straw of the deserted slave house. It was early morning.

"These last days have not been so easy as before, have they? I heard you cry out."

"It's no matter, Master Durgan." A slave barracks was one of the noisiest places in the world to sleep. Most slaves had plenty of fuel with which to feed nightmares; I happened to have more than most. But one could not afford to let slip any hint of madness. Mad slaves were dangerous; they disappeared very quickly, and one didn't ask where.

"Make yourself ready. You're to be in the First Audience Hall today. I'm told a table sits beside the Prince's chair. You're to be seated at the table, prepared for writing work, by the first hour of third watch. You can get paper and ink and whatever else you need from the Third Steward. Any questions?"

I asked where the Third Steward was to be found, then asked what I might be expected to be writing in the large drafty First Audience Hall.

"It's the Dar Heged begins this day. There'll be letters and messages and judgments and proclamations."

"Is it usual for a slave . . . ?"

Durgan cocked his head to one side and ran his gaze over me. "No. Not usual at all. I've heard"—he flicked his eyes to the left side of my face—"that maybe His Highness thinks to have a little reminder of recent events on view when his lords come." Durgan caught himself up and flushed. He'd been thinking out loud rather than answering me. I had just happened to voice the question that was already in his head. "Get on with you and mind your tongue."

"Always," I said, and bowed to him before taking myself

to the cistern. On that gray morning I had to crack ice to get to the water for washing. Others had been there before me, for the surface of the cistern was a miniature mountain range of ice shards: broken, pushed aside, and frozen to each other again, as if some ghostly hand had done it. The dull shaving knife lay in a scattering of frozen hair of every color and texture. I had yet to see those who shared the slave house with me. The men who glided through the palace passageways and kitchens in their fenzai and shorn hair might have been players in a traveling company for all I knew. Only three people in the palace were real. Durgan, for he fed me and spoke to me. Aleksander, who controlled my life. And the Khelid . . . the demon. I shuddered at the memory and put him out of my mind. There was nothing to be done about the demon.

Durgan was sitting on the floor at the far end of the slave house in front of a small brazier, sharpening a long, old-fashioned sword. On my way out the door he glanced up. "I've been told you have a name."

I halted, but said nothing, prepared for another taste of bitter truth.

"Ezzarians don't like their names used." He resumed his sharpening, moving the blade rhythmically across the gray stone. It was a statement, not a question, yet it was left open at the end. He was not finished with what he wanted to say. It was very curious.

"You know something of Ezzarians," I said in the same manner, though I was certain that whatever he knew, it did not approach the truth. Privacy . . . secrecy . . . was our lifeblood.

"My family is from the south. Karesh."

Karesh was a small town in the rolling southern grasslands of Manganar, perhaps four days' journey from the Ezzarian border. We had traded in Karesh when I was a boy, and it had seemed a crowded metropolis to a child from a land of small, scattered woodland settlements. "Karesh has the finest ale in the Empire," I said. "And our miller would buy no other wheat."

"Aye." The thick fingers pressed the shining blade to the stone. The conversation was finished. Much more had been said than words could convey.

I started out the door again, then paused, closed my eyes, and spoke quietly over my shoulder. "Master Durgan, do not cross paths with the Khelid."

From the corner of my eye I saw his head jerk up, and I felt his eyes on my back as I ran across the busy courtyard to the kitchen door, thinking I was the greatest fool ever to draw breath. One kind word changed nothing. Durgan carried a lash.

The winter Dar Heged was held for twenty-three days in the first month of the year. Every Derzhi House in the northern Empire would send representatives to present the Emperor with their tax revenues, to hear what levies of men and horses and food would be needed for spring campaigns, to resolve disputes with other families, and conduct whatever business needed the attention of their sovereign lord. The streets of Capharna were teeming with warrior nobles and their retinues, grim-faced soldiers guarding the tax-levy wagons, excited families reunited with distant kinsmen or children who had married out of their House, street vendors and shopkeepers and innkeepers raking in revenues from the influx of visitors, fights breaking out between parties to land or property disputes. Dar Heged was a time for marriages and betrothals, treaties and alliances, trades, bargains, and negotiations of all kinds.

I did not observe any of the activity in the streets, only the business brought before the Prince. He sat in the lesser of two huge gilded chairs at one end of the smoky Hall, flanked by ten counselors representing the ten oldest Derzhi families. The counselors were only for show. The Emperor, or in this case his son, had the final and only say in any matter. The line of taxpayers and petitioners stretched across the cavernous room, and the walls were crowded with observers: families, servants, and whomever else had managed to get themselves past the door wardens.

My table was just to the Prince's right, close enough and angled such that I could see and hear both the Prince and the petitioners who faced him. Just beyond me was another table arranged with scales and balances and an array of gleaming brass weights. It was manned by the Emperor's chief redyikka, the magistrate of weights and measures. Every village large enough to have a marketplace had a redyikka to keep traders honest with their measures and to ensure proper coinage and fair dealing.

The daily session lasted from early morning until well after the usual dinner hour. My hand cramped from so much writing, and my fingernails turned black from all the ink. Every judgment had to be recorded in a large, leather-bound ledger, and many of them involved additional letters or writs to be sent to other parties not present at the Dar Heged.

The presence of a foreigner and a slave was an affront to the Derzhi, and as they passed behind me or waited for me to finish a paper they needed, they made sure I knew it: some whispered curses and some extremely rude and unlikely suggestions for physical abuse. I wondered if Durgan was right that I was on view for a purpose. I could always tell from the quick intake of breath when one petitioner told another of my role in Lord Vanye's fall and Lord Sierge's execution. When the Prince scowled at the disturbance, the Derzhi stopped for a bit, but would start up again once Aleksander was distracted.

Despite all that, I enjoyed the days well enough. The giant hearth fires were well stoked, there was a variety of people to watch, and though most of the disputes and petitions were mundane, occasionally there were matters of interest or consequence to observe. Best of all, when I returned to the slave house on the first night, Durgan had received orders that I was not to be returned to the underground cell. Though Zeroun had soured my reputation thoroughly among the slaves and no one of them dared speak to me, it did my soul good to feel the breathing of other human beings in the room as I slept. It made it easier to put away fears that I could do nothing about. Easier to strengthen my barricades against dreams that came creeping back from where I had banished them.

Aleksander, on the other hand, detested the whole business. From the first moment of the first day he snapped at every comer, even if they were presenting a chest of riches to be transported back to the treasury at Zhagad. "What crime did I commit to be trapped in this hateful chair?" he fretted on the third morning, just before the doors were opened to the line of opulently attired Derzhi. He tugged and jerked at the heavy red robe attached to his shoulders. "If Father is to have the privileges of being Emperor, then he must take the duties with it. Why do I care that the House of Gorusch has usurped three grainfields from the House of Rhyzka? What interest have I in some Hamraschi girl's marriage portion? She's an ugly wench, and I'd not have her in my bed for triple the dowry. I'd like to tell them to burn the cursed fields and throw the maiden into the fire."

The stewards cringed at the Prince's ranting and groveled appropriately when it was time to open the doors and let the people come. Though he was rude and uncivil, the Prince seemed to maintain somewhat better judgment in public than he did in private. He knew when to use his authority and when to keep himself out of it and induce the warring parties to settle things between themselves. In major disputes he would yield to the suitor who paid the most taxes or brought the most men and horses to his father's armies or had the most beautiful daughter in tow. Not an arguable position, unless you were the one who happened to be wronged or had some insane notion of justice. The Emperor would probably feel that his interests had been properly looked after.

I tried my best to pretend that nothing had changed since the execution feast, but as the days passed, I found my eyes skimming the crowds for the demon Khelid and watching in uneasy curiosity as he insinuated himself into palace life. It was not so strange for a rai-kirah to come hunting in Capharna. A Derzhi palace would offer succulent opportunities for a demon, and even if one of them yet lived, no Ez-

zarian Searcher would dare venture into a Derzhi stronghold. It was surely no more than odd coincidence that a
demon happened to come to a place where one who knew
what it was—perhaps the last living person who could recognize it—existed powerless to do anything about it. But I
could see no overt signs of demon possession in the Khelid.
No extraordinary cruelty. No wild madness. Only smooth
charm and polite interest in the proceedings. Why? Fifty
times I dismissed such musings, but they lingered in my
mind like the taste of rancid meat.

Late on the afternoon of the fourth day, the proceedings
were disrupted by an unusual excursion into the city.

The Fontezhi Heged was possibly the most powerful
Derzhi family in the Empire save the Emperor's own Denischkar family. The Fontezhi holdings included a sizable portion of northern Azhakstan, plus millions of hectares in the
conquered territories of Senigar and Thryce. Unlike most of
the hegeds who owned large palaces in Capharna, but whose
land holdings were elsewhere, the Fontezhi claimed about
two-thirds of the land on which Capharna stood. Merchants
and householders of the city worked diligently to keep rents
flowing into the Fontezhi coffers.

The Jurran Heged, on the other hand, was a minor house,
not one of the Ten who sat on the Emperor's Council, nor
even one of the Twenty who held the bulk of lands and the
traditional Derzhi titles. The Jurrans were closer to being a
merchant house than a warrior clan. They needed no sympathy, however. They had a stranglehold on the spice trade and
were very rich. But as all their holdings were in gold and
spices rather than land and horses, they were dismissed as
unimportant.

On that afternoon, when Aleksander was quite obviously
bored to insensibility with a succession of minor disputes
and tedious speeches, Baron Celdric, the head of the Jurran
Heged, came before him with a protest over the Fontezhi decision to burn a crumbling district of Capharna that lay
southwest of the river. It was the poorest district of the city,

populated by maimed and diseased veterans, elderly people
who had no kin to care for them, widows without resources,
and all manner of thieves, dead-handlers, lepers, and mad-
men. The Jurrani spice warehouses were situated right in the
heart of the district.

Aleksander yawned through Baron Celdric's presentation, then sent for a representative of the Fontezhi Heged to
answer it. The outcome was foreordained. The Jurrans could
never prevail against so powerful a heged . . . except that the
Fontezhi made a serious mistake. They sent their most junior dennissar, someone's cousin's nephew's son, to appear
before the Prince.

"And where is Lord Pytor?" the Prince snapped at the
quaking, bewildered eighteen-year-old whose appearance
had sent him into a froth. "Does the lord of the Fontezhi believe he is too important to appear at his Prince's summons?
Perhaps he expected me to wait upon him."

"N . . . no . . . Your Highness. Lord Pytor is out riding
this afternoon." The downy-cheeked young man did not
know when to keep his counsel.

"And have the Fontezhi no messengers, no aides, no
horses available to contact him? And perhaps every first-,
second-, and third-degree noble of your house is similarly
occupied? I cannot believe that such a quailing fish as yourself could have attained even fourth-degree status.

"Of course not, Your Highness . . . I mean, it was just
thought . . . as it was only the Jurrans and it was not the
Emp—" The youth almost swallowed his tongue. "The district is nothing, Your Highness. A filthy, plague-ridden
haven for thieves and beggars. Lord Pytor wishes to make it
beautiful . . . worthy of the Derzhi summer capital."

"And how does he plan to make it beautiful by burning
it?"

Recouping a bit of his confidence, the junior dennissar
puffed out his chest and tugged at his purple satin vest. "He
plans to build a shrine to Athos—your own patron, Your
Highness."

"But that would take only a small part of such a tract.

What else has he planned? Tell me truly, now, or I'll have it from you less pleasantly."

Less sure now. "Only a residence . . . for his son . . . a small palace . . . that's all."

"Well"—Aleksander jumped up from his chair—"as this is so unimportant a matter as to send a puling child before the Emperor's representative, I had best go look at this disputed land myself. Perhaps I may have some use for it."

The Fontezhi youth gaped and turned pale. It was not a wise thing to lose your heged lord's lands by virtue of your incompetence.

Lord Celdric bowed deeply. "My lord Prince, the Jurran Heged will, of course, accept whatever judgment you see fit. We are honored by your hearing." His expression was properly solemn and respectful. But I was sitting to the side of him, and I could see his gleeful grin of satisfaction as he bowed.

So it was that I had to pack up my writing case and ledger book and hasten barefoot through the city streets after Aleksander. He set off walking, sending his hastily saddled mount back to the stables. It was unheard of for royalty to walk the streets rather than ride, and I wondered if the Prince wanted to shock the staid palace staff. Or perhaps it was just to stretch his legs and wake himself up after four days of boredom.

It was not a quiet journey. Ten hastily mustered torch-bearers lit the way through the afternoon gloom, the smoke settling heavily about us in the cold, still air. Fifty guards, an equal number of attendants, cloak-bearers, boot wipers, and every manner of dennissar were still scurrying about, deciding on positions and precedence long after the party passed through the palace gates and into the town.

Townspeople gathered quickly along the road, gaping at the fabled young prince most of them had never seen. At first it was well-cloaked ladies and children who watched, merchants, shopkeepers, drovers, and clerks who deserted their posts for the chance to catch a glimpse of royalty. They cheered and waved at the flesh-and-blood manifestation of the Empire's glory. Aleksander did not acknowledge them. They would not expect it. Out of perverse habit they would most likely lose respect for him if he looked pleasant or waved in return. Rather he strode vigorously through the afternoon, talking only with Sovari, the captain of his personal guard.

After we crossed the arched Ghojan bridge, the lanes grew narrower and muddier and the onlookers not so well turned out. They were thin and ragged, quiet and fearful. Hollow-eyed children hid behind their bony mothers, and crippled old men gaped toothless. In an attempt to mask the growing stench, one of Aleksander's attendants began swinging a censer that emitted a cloying smoke, but Aleksander shoved the man aside and made him douse the burning herbs in a mud puddle. "That makes the stink worse. Do you think I am some woman who has never smelled the back end of a horse?"

But I don't think Aleksander had ever seen the dregs of his cities—and certainly not from his own feet where he could look at them eye-to-eye. His gaze did not remain fixed and ahead as before, but darted from one pitiful sight to another. He wrinkled his nose in disgust at three scabrous beggars who were wallowing in the river of mud and excrement, fighting over a whimpering mangy dog. He drew away from a gaunt-cheeked, rheumy-eyed old woman who was kneeling in the mud with her hands outstretched, wailing in mindless misery. He peered curiously into alleys where groups of rag-wrapped men, women, and children huddled listlessly around pitiful fires, too weak and cold to pay him any mind.

Two whores pushed aside ragged customers and gaped brazenly at the Prince. One of them, a buxom young girl with long curly hair grinned and wagged a finger at him. Aleksander laughed, and the girl blew him a kiss, lifted her skirt, and went back to her business.

As the Prince's procession rounded a corner, a woman with a squalling infant bound to her back was shoved out of a dark, rag-draped doorway, two grimy children clinging to her skirts. "There's no work here and no bread," bawled a harsh voice from behind the door. "Die somewhere else." The woman tripped over a torchbearer and fell right at Aleksander's feet.

The young Fontezhi dennissar, thinking, no doubt, to redeem himself in his prince's eyes, screamed at the woman to give way and kicked at her viciously, sending her sprawling in the filth of the street. One of his bodyguards grabbed the two terrified children by the necks and flung them to the side into a crusted heap of dirty snow. The two little ones burst out wailing and tried to run back to their mother, but I was standing nearby and grabbed hold of them to keep them out of harm's way. In horror I watched as Aleksander drew his sword. I believed he was going to slay the stunned woman for daring to touch his feet. But instead he laid the tip of the blade at the Fontezhi youth's throat and fixed his eyes on the youth's disbelieving face, while extending his other hand to the fallen woman. She stared at him blankly, mud dripping from her lank hair, her starvation-dulled eyes asking only from which direction the blow would come.

"Here, here, woman," said Aleksander, shaking his hand at the woman, though still not looking at her. "Take it and get up or these cretins will trample you."

She reached out a hand as if putting it into the mouth of a wolf, but the Prince pulled her up and shoved her away. Then he sheathed his sword and with cold ferocity backhanded the Fontezhi guard who had throttled the children. Astonished, I urged the two little ones toward their mother, and the three of them fled down an alleyway. I wondered how many days they had left to live. Unless the weather eased up a little, I guessed it was not many.

The Prince said nothing more of the incident, but he did seem to take notice of me as I stood shivering in my sleeveless tunic, waiting for the expedition to proceed. He stared at me so long I wondered if I had angered him by interfering even in so small a way. After a quick glance about, he started to speak, but thought better of it and motioned me to stay close behind him. When we reached the Jurran warehouse, he commanded one of Lord Celdric's attendants to find me a cloak and some sandals lest I be too cold to write properly. I was confounded.

The Prince took only a few moments to inspect the warehouse before rendering his judgment. The district could not be burned. It might encourage all the unsavory residents of the place to converge on the rest of the city, he said. The Fontezhi dennissar was speechless and kept fingering the tiny scratch on his neck left by Aleksander's sword. No doubt the Fontezhi lords had assumed that the residents would burn along with the other filth.

But Aleksander was not done. "The Jurrans will pay for the land on which their warehouses sit," he said. "Not rent, but in full for proper ownership. Before the end of the Dar Heged, Lord Celdric will bring me a notice of the settlement. Make a note of it, Seyonne. And for the next twenty years the Jurrans will contract solely with Fontezhi caravans to transport their spices within the boundaries of Azhakstan."

Masterful. The Fontezhi would lose land for their insult of the Prince. The Jurrans would lose gold for their insult to a more powerful house. The two hegeds would be forced to work together, and would likely both profit handsomely from the contract, leaving good feelings all around. It was well-done. But it was Aleksander's treatment of the woman I found intriguing. It seemed wholly out of character.

We were soon back to normal. On that evening as I sat at the Prince's writing desk copying dispatches for the military commanders on the northern borders, Aleksander came in from the bedchamber and poured himself a glass of wine, then summoned one of his aides. He pointed at the curtained door to the bedroom and jerked his head.

"What shall we do with her, Your Highness?"

"Throw her back in the cesspit where you found her. She stinks and is more crude than a Veshtar. Sovari was right."

The aide disappeared through the curtain and did not return.

"What are you looking at, slave?" said Aleksander. "Was she a friend of yours?"

I suspected it was the whore from the streets, though I never saw her.

Chapter 6

On the fifth morning of the Dar Heged the Prince began act-
ing strangely. He could not sit still. He tapped constantly on
the arms of his chair. He shifted and settled in the red velvet
as if he could not get comfortable. He fiddled with his knife,
twisted his braid, and played with a jewel on a chain about
his neck, then threw the cushions from his chair aside before
commanding a servant to bring them back again. He called
for wine, but did not drink it; rather he threw the goblet on
the floor when he got irritated at a petitioner. An elderly ma-
triarch of a powerful family accusing her son of falsifying
the lineage of a prize horse—a crime more serious than murder in the Derzhi Empire—almost fell out of her chair when
Aleksander jumped up in the middle of her droning argument and yelled at her. "Be quick about it, woman. There are
a thousand others waiting to stand before me." He circled
his chair and drummed his fists on the back of it, trying to
induce the woman to talk faster. She got flustered, and I
thought he was going to have her hanged when she started
panting and holding her breast and had to be carried away. A
steward stepped up to the Prince and whispered quietly in
his ear, only to have Aleksander yell at him. "I'm perfectly
fine. Just get the next person up here before I have you
flogged."

On the next day things were worse. The Prince could not
sit for more than a minute at a time, so he paced back and
forth across the dais as people spoke to him, their heads following his movements. It made them stumble in their words,
which made him angrier. As the hours passed, he fought to

control this restlessness, folding his arms tight about his chest or clenching his wine cup until his knuckles were white. But even then his foot would drum or his head would toss. The stewards and the chamberlains were wide-eyed and fearful. He had two of them flogged for daring to suggest he might want to rest, and he was threatening to do the same for the next person who asked if they could do something for him. It was on that day, the second of this strange behavior, that I noticed the Khelid emissary among the courtiers and attendants behind the Prince's chair. The fair, slender man in the purple cloak stood watching, saying nothing to anyone, smiling to himself on occasion, though I could never understand what kinds of things he found amusing. I put it out of my mind quickly. What did slaves care about demons or their amusements?

The seventh day of Dar Heged, the third of Aleksander's odd behavior, began with a very complex case where the head of a family had died, leaving only one unmarried female child to inherit extensive lands and properties. Aleksander sat in his chair holding on to its arms so tightly, I would not have been surprised to see the ancient wood crumble in his grasp. I was close enough to see dark gray circles under the amber eyes that darted here and there, never focusing on anything. The Chamberlain had warned him that the parties to the disputed inheritance, two male members of the House who each claimed the young woman in marriage, were powerful barons of equal degree, who guarded the most dangerous frontiers of the Empire. The Emperor would not wish to antagonize either of them.

After half an hour of tedious explanation by the representative of one of the warriors, Aleksander began to tremble. His hands, his legs, his body quivered as if the bitter winter outside had snuffed out the hearth fires and settled upon him alone. "Continue," said the Prince tightly when the speaker paused to stare at him. Quiet murmuring rippled through the audience hall. "I said, continue."

The man went on, then yielded to the other party in the disagreement. I did not see how Aleksander could possibly be taking in the details of family connections, old debts, warriors' promises, marriage pledges—the very minutiae of Derzhi clan lore. He looked like a volcano ready to spew fire. Onlookers were shaking their heads, frowning, wondering. And there among them, leaning casually against a doorway was Korelyi, the Khelid emissary . . . smiling.

I quickly dropped my eyes to my ledger. Never, ever could I allow the Khelid to see me watching him, to see that I knew. I had no power. I would be helpless. There were things in the world that made enslavement to the Derzhi seem benign by comparison, and I could not allow myself to so much as think of them. Demons were attracted by fear. But in the instant of time that it took me to pull my eyes from the smiling Khelid, he made a slight movement of his fingers and my heart skipped a beat. I whipped my head back up to look at Aleksander. He was shaking his head from side to side as if to clear it. What was happening?

"I beg you, do not deny my saying, Your Highness," said the bewildered advocate. "I have not even bespoke the agreement with the young lady in the matter as to Baron Juzai's suit."

"No, no. I'm not denying . . . Proceed, Cerdan. I understand the import of this matter, and I will give you full hearing as I promised." The Prince could scarcely pronounce the words through his gritted teeth.

For another half hour Aleksander battled his strange malady, setting his jaw in iron. As I wrote down the particulars of the case, I would glance up from time to time and let my eyes wander to the slender man by the door. There . . . another flick of his fingers. The Prince tightened his grip on the chair and forced himself still. The man in purple was not smiling anymore.

When both sides had presented all their evidence, Aleksander closed his eyes briefly, then said, "I must give this case full consideration. Such noble servants of the Empire will receive all due respect. I shall retire to my chambers and issue my judgment tomorrow morning." With such self-mastery as I had never witnessed, Aleksander stood, acknowledged the two lords' genuflection and the obeisance of the crowd, and hurried out of the Hall.

The people broke into frenzy the moment he was gone.

"What ails him?"

"Must be a sickness . . . I've not seen its like before."

"I've heard he's not slept in three days."

"Ah, it's that he has no patience for ruling. He has not his father's strength."

"Arrogant twit. He'll never have wit enough to rule. Did you hear . . . ?"

"We'll pray he has fine sons and dies young."

The comment in which I was most interested was made without words. As I stood up, stoppering my ink, gathering up papers, closing the ledger to give into the safekeeping of the Chamberlain, I cast my eyes about once more. The scowling Khelid brutally shoved three servants aside and disappeared through the door.

It didn't work as you expected, did it? I thought, as I packed the pens and sharpening knife into the wooden writing case. *He was stronger than you believed. Stubborn.*

I ran my ink-stained fingers idly over the maroon leather binding of the ledger. Not sleeping. Of course that was it. It would be easy to find the cause of Prince Aleksander's malady. A gift, perhaps, a miniature bronze horse or porcelain egg . . . or something left behind under a cushion, perhaps a ring or a kerchief. No, not a kerchief. Cloth was too weak. It could be a brass box, suitable for a jewel, or a shining pebble dropped in one of the garden pots in Aleksander's chambers. All you had to know was what to look for, what to see, what to listen for when you took yourself into silence. . . .

I shook my head as if to dismiss a dream and snuffed the lamp that had illuminated my writing. The First Audience Hall was almost deserted. Sweepers came through with mops to clear away the puddles and dirt left by the hundreds of muddy boots.

What was I thinking? I had no power. No weapon. I cared nothing . . . far less than nothing for Prince Aleksander. He and his people had stolen my life, had destroyed everything of meaning to me, had maimed and mutilated my body and mind, and ruined . . . *oh gods, don't let it come. Not now.* I stared at my trembling hand that held the ledger book. I forced myself to trace its lines, the long, bony fingers stained with ink, the roughness and cracks of constant cold, the steel wrist band that would be with me until death, and then, in my mind, I transformed my hand into the aged, dried husk it would become. The reality and the illusion were not yet the same. Not yet. I banished the unwanted memory quite effectively, but I could not dismiss my belief in what I had to do.

It was not for Aleksander or any Derzhi that I picked up the maroon book and set off for the Prince's chambers. It was not for any larger purpose. My larger purposes had been stripped away with my power. It was for myself. So I would not see the sly smile in company with the ice-blue eyes. So I could sleep again in peace.

"I've brought the recording book. The Prince needs my notes to aid in his deliberation," I said to the door guard who had searched me and my writing case thoroughly and didn't quite know what to do with me.

"But he hasn't sent for you."

"Well, he may have. It's all so strange, how he can't sleep, and we've been having all these cases in the Dar Heged, and it's very confusing. I think he commanded me to bring it. Perhaps it would be best if you ask him, you being a Derzhi warrior and all. He'll not have you hanged just for asking like he would a slave. Maybe a lash or two, nothing more. But if he wanted me to come and you didn't let me in . . ." I shrugged my shoulders. "Yes, you should be the one to ask him."

The guard blanched and glanced over his shoulder as if the whip might be bearing down on him already. "Certainly not, slave. If you can't hear things right, then you'll have to take your own consequences."

"He's been here before when the Prince needs writing

work done," said one of the gentleman attendants. "And if he dies for his stupidity, who cares?"

Indeed.

They tapped on the door, opened it, and shoved me inside. It was very dark. Heavy draperies had been drawn across the windows and only a single candle gleamed on the table by the door. Aleksander was sprawled on the couch, one arm thrown over his face, and I screamed silently at myself for an idiot. He was asleep. I'd risked my neck for nothing.

"Who is it?"

Quickly I knelt, bent my head, and took a deep breath. "Seyonne, Your Highness."

He pulled his arm away, and his eyes were like dark holes in the dim room. "Have you a particular wish to die this day, Ezzarian? I did not send for you."

"No, my lord. I've come to give you back your sleep."

He sat up abruptly. "Has the whole world gone mad and not just me? I'll have you flayed and hung out for the wolves for this impertinence."

I had no doubt he would, though I hoped exhaustion might slow him down a bit. I talked very rapidly. "Before you do so, my lord, I will tell you one fact, and if I'm wrong, you may do with me as you will. Of course you can do with me as you will anyway, but . . ." I stopped and cursed myself for a babbling fool, then began again.

"In some hour just before you were struck with this malady of sleeplessness, you had a visitor in these chambers. My guess is that this visitor brought you a gift—something of brass or bronze or porcelain. He put it directly in your hand. Very shortly thereafter, he found the need to light a candle or pull a burning twig from your fire. You may or may not have noticed him draw a pattern in the air with the fire. It may have just looked like he was using his hands to express himself and had forgotten he held it. Shall I tell you who was this visitor, my lord? And shall I tell you the word he spoke when he touched the fire?"

The Prince sat motionless. "I have many visitors and receive many gifts. If there's meaning to this blathering, you'd best get to it while you have a tongue that works."

I sagged in relief. If I had guessed wrong, I would be on my way to the flogging post at best.

"If I can discover this gift . . . this artifact . . . my lord, will you listen to what else I can tell you about it?"

"I do not bargain with slaves."

"It's not a bargain. Of course not. I only beg hearing and believe that my act will lend weight to my words."

"Show me."

I bowed, then stood up and picked up the candle. After a moment's preparation—a clearing of the mind and a shifting of focus that would allow me to see and hear with deeper senses—I began to walk around the large, quiet room. I shone the candle on every surface, on every bit of glass or metal, examining every bottle, every decoration, the painted dishes with remnants of an early breakfast, bells, rings, the box of ulyat stones and pegs, scattered jewelry, the Prince's sword belt thrown on the floor, the clasp on his fur robe dropped beside it, the riding crop and gloves tossed on a table. My ordinary senses became aware of someone speaking to me, but I was not listening for voices, so I didn't hear what he was saying.

The skills I used were not sorcery. My power was long dead, methodically and deliberately destroyed in the first days of my captivity. But I had been trained from age five to see and hear, taste and smell with acuity well beyond the usual, to detect the irregularities in the weaving of the world caused by enchantment. One could not live every moment with such sensitivity; the barrage of sensation would be exhausting, akin to living inside of a pounding drum or drowning in an artist's paint pot. And so I had also learned to shift back and forth between ordinary senses and extraordinary, only calling on those heightened skills when needed.

There . . . what was that? I stepped to the small writing desk by the window, and quiet, gut-twisting music sounded faintly in my head. Closer. I held the candle high and the soft light gleamed on the polished finish of the desk. Where was

it? The music was louder, wrenching, teeth-on-edge dissonance, where the next note you expected to hear fell sour
upon the ear and the soul. *Quickly . . . before it deafens you.
Demon music eats the mind away.*

I pulled open the drawer and found it, a heavy brass seal
with an ivory handle that would imprint the same Derzhi
lion and falcon as Aleksander's ring when pressed into hot
wax. A larger seal than his ring, designed to be used for official documents of the Empire. A mark of his coming majority when he would become his father's voice and not just
his father's son. The waves of enchantment pulsing from the
handsome thing made my skin itch and my spine cold. I
shifted my focus again, picked up the heavy piece, and
turned to Aleksander, who stood not five paces behind me,
staring at the thing in my hand.

"Here, my lord. This is what the Khelid gave you."

"What witchery is this, Ezzarian?" said the Prince softly.
I could not see his face in the dark. "Were you not put
through the Rites as I was told? Or is this some more ordinary treachery?"

Stupid to think he would accept my word. "I have been
through the Rites of Balthar, my lord. I have no power of
any kind, nor any way to use it. But there are skills . . . practiced skills no different than fencing or riding or dancing . . .
that the Rites cannot take away. That's what I used to find
this thing."

"What has this gift to do with this sickness of mine?
Choose your words carefully, slave. I am not the fool you
take me for."

Careful! I almost laughed. I had abandoned sixteen years
of caution the moment I stepped into his rooms. Stupid fool.
To stick one finger in a boiling pot and, because I did not immerse my whole hand, believe I would remain unburned.
Every lesson of my life demanded I remain mute.

"I've seen this kind of affliction before. I recognized the
signs of it these three days. Such enchantments are carried
on artifacts that have been triggered with fire. This is where

you sleep. It had to be here. Throw it in the fire for an hour and the enchantment will be broken."

"And why would you tell me this? Don't say it's because you love me well. Think you to get an extra ration tonight? Or perhaps a silken pillow or a pliant female for your slave-house bed? Do you think because I've missed a few hours' sleep that I'll believe the first lunatic story that a cowardly, sniveling slave tells me?"

Before I could attempt an answer, the back of his hand sent me stumbling backward. My shoulder struck the corner of the writing desk, and I ended up in a heap at its feet. The ivory and brass seal flew out of my hand and clattered onto the tile floor beyond the carpet.

"I don't believe in sorcery, slave." His boot caught me in the side, before I could roll up to protect my more vulnerable parts. "You think you're very clever . . . yes, I've seen it. You watch me and judge me, and here is the result of it. I told you that you think too much, but you didn't heed my warning." His boots were very heavy, and his feet were very quick and very strong. " 'Tell the story to the fool of a Derzhi,' you thought. 'Tell him it's the Khelid, for he doesn't trust them. He'll sleep soon enough, and he'll believe it was his slave who saved him. He'll thank me.' Is that how it goes?"

He kept at me with both words and boots. I began to lose track of the words in a fog of dizziness and pain. I couldn't blame him, of course. What reason would he have to believe a slave would try to help him? Yet even as the darkness came rolling over me, I was satisfied. At least I would see no demon's eyes that night.

Chapter 7

It was a dreadful mistake to move my head. Something hard and pointed was poking into my eye, and I thought that if I moved my head, it would stop. But though the hard pointed thing—which was the steel band about my wrist and the chain attached to it—was no longer poking in my eye, the movement woke me up enough to realize that every bone, muscle, and bit of flesh I owned hurt. Even my hair felt bruised.

I did not have to open my eyes to know where I was. Not that it would have been all that revealing to open my eyes; there wasn't going to be any light in Durgan's hole. Besides, it was going to hurt. It would be marvelous if I could just drift back to sleep or insensibility, or wherever I had been since Prince Aleksander had reminded me of how stupid one could be when one tried to care about issues like good and evil. Issues far beyond the control of a slave.

Of course, once I was awake enough to think of all these things, I realized how parched I was and how cold. Not hungry—or at least I couldn't tell whether the dull ache in my belly was hunger or a royal boot print. Thus began a long deliberation on whether it was worth the misery of moving to find out if Durgan had left me a cup of water when he dumped me back in my cell. Thirst won. Thirst is very powerful.

Someone must have been listening for sounds of life. I emitted several inadvertent groans as I groped about the little cell and found no tin cup, and not long afterward, the trapdoor flew open. From out of the blinding light descended the very cup on its usual hook and rope. I clutched it tightly and eased myself to sitting by the wall. "Thank you," I said, the words coming out somewhere between a croak and a moan. I let the immediate discomfort subside before I began to drink. Better to enjoy it as much as possible. *One sip at a time. Make it last. Savor it.*

I collapsed back into oblivion about the time I finished the water. A blessed result.

I don't know how long it was before the trapdoor opened again. I believe I was somewhat out of my head. The square of light wouldn't stay still.

"Ezzarian, come up," said the harsh whisper from the light. "Move your feet, slave."

I peered carefully into the darkness beyond my aching belly, but saw only dancing spots of light. "Can't find my feet."

"Hush, fool, and get up here."

The words made no sense, so I rolled over and closed my eyes. Before I could sleep again, two large rough hands were pulling me off the dirt and straw and shoving me up the ladder. The straw at the top of the ladder was much cleaner than that at the bottom, so I crawled out of the door and burrowed straight into it, trying to get warm.

"Come on, boy," whispered the man who followed me out of the cell. "You've had a rough go, but you've got to get your head clear. Here—" He threw something at me. A thin blanket that stank of horse . . . the finest thing I'd felt in forever. "Wrap up and get over there by the fire. We've got to get you cleaned up. He wants you in five minutes."

His urgency could not penetrate my daze, and he had to half carry, half drag me down the aisle between the rows of sleeping men. He dropped me beside his little brazier, then poured a dram of brandy down my throat. I gasped and heaved and coughed. It had been sixteen years since I had tasted anything stronger than sour ale, and I wasn't sure that I was going to get a breath ever again.

"Is that better?"

"Don't know," I said, my voice scorched away. It was very good brandy.

"Here, get warm and eat this. I'll get some water to clean you up." He crammed a piece of soft bread in one of my hands and a lump of cheese in the other, then hurried away. The first bite of the bread gave me a hint of how long it had been since I'd eaten. Both bread and cheese were gone before Durgan was back. He had a knife in his hand.

I scrambled backward, clumsy, toppling a barrel just behind me, ending up in a quivering heap, my gut hurting so ferociously, I wasn't sure I would be able to move again.

Durgan squinted at me, then at the knife in his hand. "Awake now are you? Come back here. I said we're going to clean you up."

"Clean . . ." Slowly I crept back toward the fire. "The food. Thank—"

"Don't say it. I do only as I'm told." He thrust the old, dull knife into my hand and set a bucket of water on the fire. "You take care of the hair. I'll see what I can do about the blood. You're a mess. The Prince won't like it." To my great regret he yanked the blanket off my shoulders.

It must have looked very strange. One very large man, fully dressed, and one skinny man, quite undressed, huddled next to the tiny fire, whispering so as not to wake up a hundred snoring slaves. I hacked off a week's growth of hair, trying not to cut myself while Durgan ham-handedly dabbed at the broken, bruised skin on my forehead, shoulders, legs, and back. Every mezzit of my skin was mottled black, blue, and sickly green. I was happy I didn't have to worry about shaving. When we were both done, and I sat shivering, Durgan pointed to his steaming bucket. Not quite believing my good luck, I scooped the delightfully warm water and doused my head, which did wonders for my spirits until my head was clear enough to remember how I'd come to be in such sorry state.

"Enough," said the slave master, throwing me a white tunic. "You're to go to the Prince's chambers . . . discreetly."

"Can you tell me—?"

"I don't know anything. Just to send you up. You'll be met."

I set off through the dark, quiet courtyard, wading ankle deep in snow and trying to settle myself. *Don't think. Don't wonder. Just go. Just do. What comes, comes, and you will survive it or not.* It was much more difficult to follow my own command when every creaking step was a reminder of my last venture into the Prince's presence. I still saw two of everything, and had so many throbbing bruises that the darkness pulsed red in the same rhythm as my heartbeat. How could I have been such a fool?

Discreetly, Durgan had said. That was difficult in a palace that housed a thousand people, most of whom were there solely to wait upon the very same man I was supposed to meet. It must have been the depths of first watch, or just after the change to second, somewhere about the fourth hour past midnight. It was probably the only quiet hour in the palace. The great stoves in the kitchens stood like tombs in the darkness. The fires would not be relit for another hour. The passageways and staircases were deserted, only a few small lamps left burning to chase away the deepest midnight. Evening revels were being slept off in drunken stupor or languorous exhaustion. Lovers had stolen back to their beds, and slaves were lost in their own particular nightmares. Only the guards outside the Prince's doors stood awake and alert, though three gold-clad attendants were slumped over on their velvet benches, given up on any more midnight whims of their prince. I hung back behind a pillar at the top of the stair, wondering how I was to get past the guards discreetly, when a hand fell on my shoulder. I almost leaped out of my skin.

"I was set to watch for you," said a gold-clad Derzhi, removing his hand quickly and doing everything but wiping it on his breeches in disgust. "I'm to take you to a private entrance."

The young Derzhi—he was no more than fifteen and unblooded in battle, for his hair was still unbraided—led me along a maze of quiet passages and into a small storage room filled with candles of every shape and size. A single taper burned on a bare table. A door on the far wall of the candle room led us, not to an inner storage room as one might expect, but to a windowless sitting room with several comfortable chairs, a couch, a lamp, and an armed guard who did not look like he was guarding candles. He stood stiffly, looking straight ahead as if he was used to people passing through without really looking at them. I was not at all surprised to emerge in Prince Aleksander's sleeping chamber.

Someone was nestled among the furs and pillows on the gigantic bed, but it was not Aleksander unless his hair had changed color from red to pale gold and his legs had become decidedly more slender and smooth. Perhaps the Prince had found amusement to ease his malady.

The attendant motioned me through the curtained doorway that opened into the more familiar part of Aleksander's apartments. Only a few candles lit the room, and a small, bright fire in the marble hearth. The Prince wore a loose robe of blue silk trimmed in gold, open at the front, and he was lounging on a couch and talking with a man who wore the gold-crested pendant of a royal messenger. Just inside the curtained door I knelt and put my head to the carpet, a matter of extraordinary difficulty. My back was one solid bruise, at least two ribs were cracked, and I had to hold onto my belly to dissuade it from ripping apart. I hoped it wasn't going to hurt as much to get up as it had to get down and bend over.

"You'll be ready to leave before dawn?"

"I've already informed the stable to have a fresh mount ready," said the messenger.

"Wait outside in the passage. Shove my lazy wretches off their bench and sleep if you can."

"I will await your call, Highness."

"And tell those outside that I do not wish to be disturbed again."

I heard the door open and close. From the corner of my

eye I saw bare feet walk past me, through the shimmering curtain into the bedchamber. Surely he had seen me. His head had moved when I walked in. The blood was pounding furiously in my battered head, and I began counting the threads in the carpet, willing myself not to pass out.

Be easy. Ignore it. What comes, comes.

I heard murmuring voices from the bedchamber behind me, a quiet laugh, a door closing. Soft steps, and the feet stopped beside me. I did not move. I would not flinch or shrink away. At least he had no boots on.

Of all the things I might have expected, if I had allowed myself the indulgence of speculation, it never would have occurred to me that a strong hand would reach under my arm and slowly, gently, help me to my feet. He let go as soon as I was standing upright, only slightly bent over from the ache in my gut. I kept my eyes on the carpet, even while wishing I could twist them in their sockets to catch a glimpse of his face.

"Have you serious injury?" Cool. Even. No hints as to reasons or intentions. Yet he was asking. It was very odd.

"No, my lord. I don't think so." Ribs would heal, and I assumed the hot knife embedded somewhere at the base of my spine would stop twisting some day. If I could just be still for a while. . . .

He motioned me to a pile of cushions on the floor beside the hearth. "No, no. Sit. For the gods' sake, sit," he said as I creaked back down on my knees beside the cushions, wobbling dizzily and wrapping my arms tight about my ribs. He sat on a similar pile of pillows opposite me, leaning back and propping his long arms on his knees. I was not easy enough to lean back, but I basked in the heat from his fire while I waited for him to speak.

"Why did you do it?"

His quiet question answered my own. He had destroyed the enchantment. Good enough. Now I just needed to get out of his sight without any more damage. Yet the question was unexpected. It sounded as if he really wanted to know the truth. I shifted on my pillows, and my gut screamed a harsh reminder of truth.

I fixed my eyes on the tiles of the hearth. "My life is to serve you, my lord."

My words hung in the air, of no more substance than smoke from the hearth. He did not deign to comment, but sat quiet. Unmoving. Waiting. The fire snapped and a chunk of wood dropped into the ashes, shooting a stream of sparks upward.

I tried again. "I know of enchantments. Your other servants do not. Life is . . . better . . . when my lord is well." It was a bold statement for a slave, implying imperfection on the part of the master. But the moment was extraordinary, and it seemed he expected something beyond common phrases.

"And what reward do you expect? Is there no favor you would ask me for this service?"

"Nothing, my lord." A spark jumped onto the white tiles, flared bright orange, and went out, leaving a black speck on the polished tile.

"Yet you would do it again, if there was something else like, wouldn't you?"

"Yes." I scolded myself after saying it. It was too quick a response, as if I were interested. Better to stay dull. "My life is to serve you."

I felt him lean forward. The sheer intensity of his posture forced me to glance up at him. His eyes, burning with curiosity, were fixed on my face. "Let's start again. Why did you do it?" There was no menace in his quiet questioning. He was waiting for truth. He was listening as if he expected to hear it amidst the obsequious mouthings of a slave.

Would he recognize truth if I gave it to him? I paused for a moment, not moving, lest my bruises demand their say in the exchange. "What do you know of rai-kirah?" I said at last.

And because the moment was so far out of the ordinary, he did not rant about mindless superstitions, laugh at my barbarian parentage, or damn me for my insolence in avoiding his real question with a question of my own. "Demons? I've heard stories . . . warriors' tales told around battle-eve campfires. 'The rai-kirah gather on the night before a battle, ready to eat the souls of the dying.' Soldiers say they hear the sighing of the demons' lust and see them peering out of the eyes of other men, as the creatures seek out the ones who are most afraid. Rai-kirah are legends born of war and cowardice."

I expected nothing else from a Derzhi. But he wanted truth, and so in a fey recklessness likely caused by blows to my head—or perhaps by my desire to sit unmoving before his fire for just a bit longer before being thrown back into my cold cell—I decided I would give it. "My answer to your question will make no sense unless you suspend that belief for a moment, my lord. I warned you of the enchantment that was stealing your sleep because it was demon-wrought, and if I can say any word or do any deed that will hinder the purposes of a demon, then my life has meaning. For a slave that is an end worth any risk."

"Even to invading the chamber of a mad Derzhi prince voluntarily?"

I glanced up at his face again and recognized the flash of wry self-knowledge I had observed in him as I wrote letters in his map room. And so I answered a simple truth. "Even that."

I expected that to be the end of it. He would either have me beaten for insolence, or dismiss me as a mad barbarian who claimed that soldiers' legends were real. But instead, he reached for a bottle on a low table and poured himself a glass of wine, then leaned back on his cushions as if it were not three hours past midnight. "So you're saying that the rai-kirah are more than legend? Next thing you'll be telling me that I have a guardian spirit who rides at my side to protect me from dishonor."

Now I had begun, I couldn't figure out how to retreat. "I know nothing of guardian spirits. But demons are quite real."

"Go on."

"They come from the frozen lands of the farthest north, seeking a warm haven . . . a vessel . . . a human who will satisfy their hunger. Often they just devour the vessel and move on, but their power and intelligence grow when they find a welcoming host, one who'll feed them more of what they desire. They are as real as you are, my lord."

"But I can be seen and touched. I don't believe in anything I can't see."

This needed no answer. It would have been a logical place to end the strange conversation. Yet it came to me that there could be value in telling a little more. If the Khelid was set on tormenting a Derzhi prince, there was little I could do about it. I was no longer capable of facing a demon. But if I could make Aleksander wary, then perhaps his mistrust and his innate strength would tire the demon or its host and make them go elsewhere . . . away from me. I could not afford to be taken by a rai-kirah. I knew too much . . . a great deal too much . . . that they must never learn. And so I continued.

"They are as real as the sunlight, which you cannot hold in your hand, yet changes the very aspect of the land, making it lush and fertile or a desolate wasteland. They are as real as truth and honor, which you cannot see yet alter the very essence of a man. They are like moths, drawn, not to light, but to power and fear and unholy death."

He listened carefully as I spoke, but shook his head after. "So some invisible demon has sent me an enchanted seal by the hand of a Khelid emissary? I think your head is more injured than you believe."

I could feel the distance between us, bridged so unexpectedly by the touch of his hand and his probing questions, grow vast once again, and his thoughts settle into the usual Derzhi views of "Ezzarian superstition." We called it melydda—greater power; true sorcery as opposed to the illusion and trickery practiced by Derzhi magicians. But it was not only skepticism I felt from the Prince. He was disappointed. He had wanted more from me than fanciful tales he could not believe. The event had frightened him, though I was sure that particular word had never come to his mind, and he

needed some kind of reassurance. I sighed. As long as I had
come so far, I might as well tell him the meat of it.

"No, my lord. The Khelid carries the demon."

He burst out laughing. "Now you've done it. I have no
love for this Korelyi. He is sly and ambitious and oversteps
his welcome, which is not a long step, since I had no wish
for him to come. But he is no supernatural soul-eater. Tell
me a better story."

Enough was enough. I would not dredge up the past for
the Prince of the Derzhi. I would not tell him how I knew
what I knew, or how I could recognize a demon, or anything
else he might consider a "better story." I would not trust him
with any more of myself than he already owned.

"I cannot prove this to you, my lord, nor can I guess why
the Khelid sought to afflict you with the enchantment. The
demon has no purpose of its own save to satisfy its lust. It is
the vessel that gives direction to its evil. I can only tell you
what I see and what I know to be true." I fixed my eyes to
the hearth tiles again.

The Prince had been idly kneading a small cushion.
Abruptly he threw it back into the pile of them. "You take a
long time to come up with your answers. How am I to believe anything you say? Perhaps it's you. That's the easiest
explanation. What if you weren't properly cleansed in the
Rites of Balthar? Perhaps we should do them again to be
sure."

"I am at your mercy, Your Highness. As always." I wasn't
going to waste words answering those charges. I didn't
think he truly believed what he was saying or this nighttime visit would have started off quite differently. I hoped
I didn't need to tell him that if I was put through the Rites
a second time, I would have no mind with which to serve
him.

"Have you nothing more to say on the matter?"

Sense, strategy, self-protection . . . I refused to say too
much, yet dared not say too little. "Only this, my lord. He
will try again. A demon does not like being challenged, and
you have done so. First, because you fought his enchant-

ment with some success. I watched him grow frustrated with you at the Dar Heged. Second, because you destroyed the enchantment. He won't know why or how . . . unless you tell him, which would be imprudent . . . most imprudent. And he will certainly try to find out."

"You have a bold tongue for a slave, Seyonne."

"Only in the matter of demons, my lord."

"Well. Enough for tonight. I will find out who's behind this, be it warrior, slave, or demon."

I eased to my feet, taking his words for dismissal.

"Hold up for a moment. There's another matter." The Prince waved his hand at the couch where he had been sitting when I arrived. "Get that and read it. The messenger awaits my reply."

I broke the white wax seal of the letter and knelt close to the fire so I could see. This time I remained kneeling. We were back in a more usual context, and I did not want to try his forbearance.

Aleksander,

News of your little escapade reached Zhagad a few hours after I did. Now it is clear why you had to get me out of the way so quickly. You have acted the fool.

Ivan was ready to disown you when he heard your insolent letter, and I would have stood at his right hand as he did so were it a jackal he anointed in your place. But now, as it has turned out well, he laughs at your solution, and he is too distracted with Lord Kastavan's proposal for a new capital city to worry about what you've done with our northern bulwarks. By Derzhi tradition, the House of Mezzrah is as staunch an ally as it ever was. Yet if I were not bound by my brother's hand, I would already be back in Capharna, giving you such a thrashing as I've not done since you were a child. A soldier fights with his heart more than his arm. It is a lesson you must learn or you will forfeit the greatest heritage any prince was ever given. The arms of Mezzrah will fight for you, but their hearts never will.

I return to Capharna ten days hence. Until then I urge you to use every caution and pay sober attention to your proper business. The Dar Heged may seem trivial—yes, I can hear your childish complaining even at this distance—but it is the foundation of your power. Do not fritter it away as you have done with the Mezzrahn alliance. I believe a time is coming soon when you will need all the strength that is yours to command. There are ill deeds afoot in the Empire. We have a great deal to discuss.

Dmitri

The Prince leaped to his feet after the first sentence of Dmitri's letter, and when I was done, he snatched it away and crushed it in his fist.

"By the gods was there ever a man so everlastingly pompous as Dmitri? I'll send him to the frontiers again. Ten days. Damn all, I can't bear the thought of his preaching." The Prince flung himself on the blue couch and kicked at least ten cushions onto the floor. "I can see him sitting at my shoulder at the Dar Heged, disapproving of every decision. Not deigning to speak in front of the supplicants, but saving it all to dump on my head after, as if I could read his mind to choose as he would. And for this I was dragged from my bed?"

"Is there to be a return message, my lord?" I wanted to remind him I was there, lest he be even less cautious in his words.

"There was going to be. But not now. I daren't trust my words to messengers. Not when they have to do with poisoning the Emperor's brother." He threw the wadded letter at the fire, where it flared up with a hiss. "No, on second thought, I will send him a reply."

"One moment, Your Highness." I lit the candle on the cherry wood writing desk, and set out paper, ink, and one of the pens I had left sharp. "Now, my lord."

Aleksander paced furiously as he dictated.

Dmitri,
On the day you return to Capharna, I will release you

from all laws of fealty and invite you to make whatever attempt you desire to thrash me. It may not be so easy as when I was twelve, but we shall see. Until then I shall delight in the thought of matching fists with you. But for the moment, as you are still bound and your loyalty restrains you from disobedience, I will again prevail upon your duty to me.

I wish for you to proceed to Avenkhar to arrange safe transport to Capharna for Lydia and her party. I am not such a fool as to ask you to escort her yourself. But as much as I would like to dissuade my father from forcing her on me, I will not have my future wife displeased by less than perfect arrangements nor endangered by less than secure ones. The vixen would never let me hear the end of it, and I'll not have her carping at me for twelve days. The bandit season will be upon us by the time she comes, and since the passes between Avenkhar and Capharna are the worst, she must come another way.

Unfortunate that these arrangements may require your absence some weeks past the end of the Dar Heged, but I shall try to muddle along without your wisdom. If Father is considering replacing the Pearl of Azhakstan with a new capital city, I would say he is in much more need of mentoring than I.

The Prince's voice drifted away after the last sentence. I waited a moment, but he seemed to be done with it.

"How do you wish it signed, my lord?"

He considered for a moment. "Zander."

I shook my head to myself and wondered if the hard-headed old Derzhi, infuriated by the insulting letter, would notice the affectionate name at the end of it. Considering Dmitri's scathing words to the Prince, I judged Aleksander's fondness for the old man must be considerable for him to offer even so small a concession in the reply. After Aleksander sealed the letter, he held onto it and said he would see it off. I could go. I bowed, then looked stupidly from the door to the bedchamber curtain, uncertain which way to make my exit.

"The way you came in. And you're to be at the Dar Heged tomorrow as before."

"Yes, my lord." I started through the curtain, leaving Aleksander sprawled on his cushions, staring into the fire. "Sleep well, my lord."

He looked up, surprised . . . as I was. "I will."

Chapter 8

The portal stood open. Beyond it boiling clouds, riven by purple lightnings, obscured a landscape of twisted rock and ice. The ground shifted uneasily even as I watched. Chaos. This one would not be easy. But then none of them were. The path held steady, unmoving, solid . . . ready for my foot. It was only the stepping on it that was so difficult. To leave everything behind: life and breath, love and joy. To be utterly alone in the domain of evil.

"Never," came the whisper in the deepest corner of my mind. "Never alone." It was a comfort, but I knew better.

My weapons were ready: the silver dagger, the oval mirror of silver and glass, my hands, my eyes, my soul. They were all that I could take with me through the portal. A hundred times I had done it, but each time was more difficult . . . knowing what was to come.

The comforting whisper came once more. "I will hold until you return. Never doubt." I could not answer, for I was prepared and speech would break the weaving. Then the voice fell silent, and I had to go or not go. There could be no more delay.

Thunder rumbled, and a whirlwind caught my hair and whipped my cloak about me as I stepped through and began my transformation. I felt the eyes of evil widen with surprise at this invasion.

"Who dares come here?" bellowed a voice that shriveled the heart and infused the mind with despair. How would it manifest itself this time? A four-headed snake? A dragon? A warrior twice my height with sharpened spikes for fingers?

Would it make me give chase or would it spring up from the bowels of the earth beside my feet? Every one was different.

"I am the Warden, sent by the Aife, the Scourge of Demons, to challenge you for this vessel. Hyssad! Begone! It is not yours."

I only needed to delay a little longer, and the transformation would be complete. Already my feet left no mark on the path, and I could sense the subtle textures of the wind.

"Insolent slave, you know not your place. I own you. Everything you are and everything you will ever be is mine to do with as I please."

"I am a free man."

"All those you call friends wear my chains—or the chains of death, my ally. You are the last. And your Aife . . . have you not guessed? The Aife is also mine."

"Impossible," I said, but beneath my feet the path began to crumble, and when I turned my head in the howling wind, I saw the portal fading.

"No!" I screamed. "Love, don't leave me!" I ran toward the dwindling portal as the rai-kirah's laughter tore at my flesh like icy fingers. Darkness crept from every direction across the heaving landscape. My breath rasped; my side felt pierced with knives, but the portal was always farther and almost too faint to see. "Not here . . . don't leave me. . . ."

I woke, sweating and panicky, my heart racing, my body crying out its emptiness, my soul weeping in denial. I knew where I was. The darkness, the cold, the stink of too many bodies too little washed, the prickling straw under me and over me. There was no mistaking one place for the other. But this, too, was a land of evil, and I could not shake the horror of my dream until the gray light of morning showed me the faces of slaves and not of demons.

When I arrived at the Audience Hall that morning, I reviewed the judgment ledger to get some hint as to how the days had gone while I was imprisoned—and how many of them there had been. The Prince had not gone back to the

Hall after he had beaten me into oblivion, but he had come back the next day and delivered his judgment on the inheritance dispute. He had made the young woman his father's ward and divided the management of her estates between the two barons. It would be up to the Emperor to decide how much of the property would be the girl's marriage portion and who would be her husband. It was well-done. I didn't think the Lord Dmitri would have any quarrel with his nephew's decision. I wondered if the girl, by any chance, had pale gold hair and long legs. I would have wagered it so.

No more judgments had been issued that day, nor on the next. Quite a number of ink blots and corrections marred the notes. Clearly things had not gone well. On the other hand, the third day, the one that had run into the dark hours when I was pulled from my cell to meet the Prince, seemed to have proceeded very much like the first days of the Dar Heged, with the Prince quite efficiently in command of his business.

The encounter with the demon, even at arm's length, had left me uneasy, waking echoes of dead voices and dead fears. As the Hall filled with the usual mix of petitioners and servants, I found my gaze flicking away from my ledger, watching for purple robes and cold blue eyes. I had warned the Prince that the demon would try again. Did I believe it? I pressed my eyes to the page. *What comes, comes.*

The Dar Heged proceeded uneventfully for the next three days. Durgan was allowing me to sleep above ground again, although he had received no orders one way or another. Since my duties were what they had been before the unfortunate incident with the Prince, he assumed that my prisoner status was also back to normal. The slave master had no occasion to speak to me about anything. He unlocked my hands from the ring on the wall in the morning, locked them again at night, and he made sure that those of us who worked in the palace were fed and not filthy.

I permitted no more dreams and worked ruthlessly to convince myself that all was as before. The demon would get bored and leave Capharna. I would sleep and work and exist in my own odd peace until I died.

But peace was nowhere to be found. On the fourth day after my return to the First Audience Hall, the Prince did not arrive at the appointed hour. The stewards and the Lord High Chamberlain fussed about with carpets and footstools. The supplicants and taxpayers, already disgruntled from having to extend their stay in Capharna because of the Prince's strange illness, grumbled as they stood in line ready to proceed. The torches were lit, the trumpeters ready for the fanfare to announce the Prince. Caged birds and monkeys, brought as royal gifts, chattered and screeched. Still Aleksander did not come.

It was unlike the Prince to be late. Much as he detested ceremony and grumbled at its burdens, he had never failed to adhere to the exactitude of its requirements. Odd. Unsettling.

After two hours of waiting, the nobles got testy with the Chamberlain.

"Tell us, Fendular, where is our Prince?"

"The snows are getting so deep, we'll not make it home this season if we don't leave soon!"

"Never has the Dar Heged been in such shambles."

"Has his illness returned?"

"Is it true that he has destroyed his apartments?"

I told myself it was nothing—a woman most likely, one he could not bear to turn out of his bed. Or something to do with his horse. There was never a Derzhi who would fail to put his horse above every other concern. Nevertheless my eyes kept searching the crowd. The Khelid was not there.

"My Lord Chamberlain, should I go inquire as to the delay?" The words tumbled from my tongue before I could bid it be still.

"We've sent five messengers already." Fendular was so distracted, he forgot to insult me. "Stay in your place."

I started sharpening pens as if they were spearpoints to be carried into battle.

Happily for Fendular and the palace supply of writing

implements, the Prince arrived soon after, and carried on the day's business without further incident—though without explanation of the delay. His Highness was not at all in a good mood, however, which meant that very few petitioners left the palace happier than when they came.

A few days earlier I had been remanded to the service of the fat Chamberlain Fendular for evening work. I toiled until midnight every night, writing endless copies of the Dar Heged judgments and tax rolls. It was tedious work and cold, for the tiny window in the small dusty anteroom where I labored had been broken out in some previous century, and the Chamberlain would not waste fuel on a slave. Every few minutes I had to hold my ink pot or my fingers over my single candle flame to keep them from freezing. After a long day in the First Audience Hall, both fingers and eyes refused to behave themselves, so I was continually forced to correct my work or begin again until the numbers and names were dancing in the air in the weak candlelight. Even so, I deemed myself fortunate. I had worked at every task a slave could be given, save the short, deadly tenure in the mines. I had served seven masters, three of whom were brutal and one of whom was mad. Chilly, solitary tedium was very close to bliss. So many slaves had so vile an existence; I could complain about nothing.

At the end of the day of the Prince's late arrival, Fendular again sent me to the cold anteroom with my writing case. As the hours passed with page after page of tax rolls, I dredged up a fond remembrance of Durgan's wool blanket and his brazier, and an even fonder image of the glorious heat of the Prince's fire. Such an odd night that had been. To exchange speech with the heir to the Lion Throne of the Derzhi. For a brief moment, I had been a man again and not a slave. Not even the Baron had ever asked me a real question as if I could form a thought in my head.

"You're done here for tonight," said one of the Prince's aides from the doorway, startling me out of my thoughts so thoroughly that I almost upset my ink pot. My heart was pounding like a smith's hammer. "His Highness requires his writing slave. You are to enter discreetly, as before." It was the same youth who had shown me the private entrance before.

"Shall I put these things away before leaving, Master Aldicar?"

"Certainly not. What kind of ignorant fool are you? His Highness awaits. I am required to clean up your droppings so that you may answer your summons." The boy was most unhappy at his orders. His naturally sour disposition was likely not helped by the fact that I was more than a head taller than he. If he didn't grow a bit more and get his braid soon, he would be relegated to life as an underling, working for someone like Fendular. I would be wise to stay clear of him.

I bowed and blotted my fingers on a scrap of paper, then raced through the Chamberlain's luxurious workrooms and across a mournful courtyard of frozen fountains and leafless trees toward the Prince's wing of the Summer Palace. I was halfway through the journey when I realized what was hurrying my steps. I was excited.

I stopped at the colonnade that would lead me into the living quarters of the palace, letting the bitter air on my scarred body and the ice under my bare feet force me to remember who I was and what I was and where I was. Nothing had changed. Nothing. After so long I could not allow myself to destroy the peace I had made with fate. Excitement meant hope. And there was no place for hope in my existence.

Assuming that "discreetly" meant that I was to enter through the private door, I found my way to the candle room, wondering if I was going to have to explain to the guard what I was doing at the door to the Prince's bedchamber. But young Aldicar must have let the guard know to expect me, for the soldier jerked his head to the inner door the moment I appeared. I glimpsed an unclothed woman huddled on the floor beside the bed, weeping quietly, just before an iron hand gripped my arm and dragged me through the softly lit bedchamber to the outer apartment.

"Where is it?" Aleksander bellowed, shoving me into the middle of his outer chamber. He was wearing only a white silk loincloth. His long red hair was loose and flying wildly around his head. "Find the damned thing."

I dropped to my knees. "As you command, Your Highness, but please tell me what am I to find?"

"The foul, enchanted . . . whatever. How am I to know?"

I could have asked him the same question, but I didn't think it wise.

"Find it or I'll have your eyes for breakfast, sorcerer. I'll not be the laughingstock of the Twenty Hegeds."

I searched in all my experiences for the appropriate words for masters who were on the verge of violence, yet had not explained what they were upset about. Nothing I knew seemed to fit the case. Resigned to trouble, I tried again. "To know what to look for, I must know what kind of enchantment has been wrought, my lord. Or if you've been given something that is suspect, I—"

I was raised to my toes by a hand about my throat. "If one word . . . one hint . . . one breath of this gets out, you will die such deaths as no slave has ever suffered."

"No word," I squeezed out past his steel grip. "I swear it."

He shoved me away and turned his back. "I cannot . . . since the other . . . since I could sleep. . . . The first night I had to sleep. Didn't try. The next we were interrupted by the messenger and I sent her away. I thought it was just taking longer than usual because I was distracted. But two nights more . . . I had to pretend I found the lady unsatisfactory . . . and so tonight I sent for Chione, a slave who always pleases me. I thought, to be sure . . ."

All became instantly clear. I knew better than to relax or yield to the laughter that came unbidden. The danger was very real. To the Derzhi, failure at such matters was unthinkable, no less a defeat than one on the battlefield.

"Has the Khelid brought you more gifts, my lord?" It was

highly unlikely to be an artifact, as before. It was, in fact, highly unlikely to be an enchantment. The matter in question was notoriously unpredictable, and thus rarely an effective target for spellmaking. But that was an answer Aleksander wasn't going to like.

"No. Korelyi's gone off to Parnifour to visit his kinsman. And you've not convinced me he's the one doing it anyway. Look for it, as you did before."

"Of course." And so I did. As I expected, I found nothing save the wretched slave girl, quivering in terror that she had displeased the Prince.

I had to tell him something. There were so many reasons such a thing could happen, even to a quite virile, apparently healthy young man, but if I wanted to retain all my own body parts, I needed a good answer. "There is no enchanted artifact here in your apartments, but this kind of thing is often passed by food. Have you eaten anything unusual of late?"

"Nothing. But I'll burn the kitchens. I'll kill them all—"

I raised my hands and shook my head vigorously. "That won't be necessary. There is only one way that I know to take care of it. You must refrain from taking in any more of the poison. Perhaps . . . the ephrail. Derzhi warriors cleanse themselves by the ephrail once a year, do they not, my lord?"

"What of it?"

"Perhaps it is time for you to do so. It would purge any poison from your body—as it is designed to do." And it would keep women out of his bed for a week and allow him to catch up on his sleep. It seemed my best chance at hitting the mark of whatever ailed him.

"Ephrail," he said thoughtfully. "It has been quite a while. And it would rid me of this?"

"I cannot say what enchantment is tormenting you this time, but if someone has tainted your food, then there is no surer way to make them give it up. Such a spell cannot affect you if you separate yourself from the source."

"I'll consider it." He cocked his head to one side. "Before

he left the city, the Khelid emissary Korelyi offered me a sleeping potion. He had heard that I was not sleeping well. I refused it and said I was sleeping like a bear in winter. He spent that entire evening's conversation talking of it, trying to find out what remedy I had used. Said he once trained as a physician himself and still collected remedies when he traveled to new places. At the end of it all, he asked who was my adviser on such matters. I thought that a curious question . . . especially as you had predicted it."

"And what did you tell him?" I could not fail to ask, as the sudden pounding in my chest required easing.

"I said I had taken no one's advice since I left the nursery."

Some nine days later, at the ceremony marking the end of the Dar Heged, I watched as a slightly leaner, clear-eyed Prince Aleksander raised a tall young woman with pale gold hair from her obeisance and allowed his hand to wander from her elbow to her breast. From his look and her unblushing smile, I had no further anxiety about my remedy, only the usual discomfort I got after satisfying the unseemly wishes of a Derzhi. But Aleksander would have what he desired, so I had to take meager satisfaction that at least no slave girl would suffer because he could not do as he pleased.

Though the Khelid was away, echoes of demon music lingered in my ears like the odor of distant death on a summer wind.

Chapter 9

Involvement in such matters as Aleksander's bedchamber difficulties does nothing to help a celibate Ezzarian suppress unwilling and uncomfortable fantasies. Though I maintained sufficient self-discipline in the daytime, and I still managed to keep more serious dreams at bay when sleeping, unwanted visions did creep into my nights. It was in the midst of such a dream that Durgan roused me late one night just after the end of the Dar Heged. "Ezzarian, up with you."

"Does the Prince do no business during the daytime?" I snapped, before my tongue was awake enough to keep better counsel. Guilt battled with a ferocious desire to follow my interrupted dreamland liaison to its consummation.

"It is not the Prince who summons you, but myself."

I sat up—always somewhat awkward when one's wrists are attached to a wall with short lengths of chain—and forced my uneasy urges aside so I could pay attention. "What is it, Master Durgan?"

"We have ten new slaves brought in from tax levies, and one of them is headed for trouble. I thought perhaps it would make things easier for all if you were to have a word with him."

I was fully awake by this time, ready to spit at the burly man crouching beside me. There were slaves who spied on other slaves, who reported infractions or intemperate speech. There were slaves who lashed or branded others, or wielded the power of food and drink, thinking to raise their own pitiful status above the rest of us. Had I not considered us all half-mad from bondage, I would have throttled any of them cheerfully. I knew the limits of my existence, and I stayed within them. But if Durgan had mistaken my compliance for a willingness to be his surrogate, to buy his favor by becoming his ally, then I needed to set him straight. "Ah, no, Master Durgan. I'm not one you can trust to do such bidding. I'd not be good at it."

"Faugh! It's not what you're thinking. This one will be dead within a day if you can't make him come to his senses. Come on." He unlocked my wrists and led me to the trapdoor of the underground cell. He shoved a small lantern into my hand, then unlocked the door and dropped his ladder down. His voice fell to a whisper. "If you think it worthy to save a life, even a life in bondage, then go down. Knock twice when you're ready to come out."

My curiosity was certainly roused. If Durgan wanted to confine me in his dungeon, it was hardly necessary to trick me into it. He could throw me down there any time. But his creeping about in the night seemed to say that he didn't want his assistants or other slaves to know of these dealings. So I descended the ladder and held up the lantern.

He was no more than sixteen, huddled in the corner, shivering with cold and exhaustion. His skin was bronze, his shorn hair black, as were his wide-set, slightly angled eyes, grown huge with terror and pain and anger. His unscarred back was marked with a few streaks of blood, and the crossed circle burned into his shoulder was still swollen and angry.

"Tienoch havedd," I said softly. Greetings of my heart. It was a very personal greeting. Inappropriate for a stranger. But the boy could be no stranger. He could be no one but myself, sixteen years in the past. He was Ezzarian.

All the work I had done to forget my own first days of horror was unraveled in a moment's glance. A Luthen mirror, reflecting evil back upon itself, could be no more destructive than was the sight of that young man to my inner defenses. In an instant I lived again the degradation of being paraded unclothed before strangers, the humiliation as they touched and probed and joked of things they had no right,

the torment of the Rites of Balthar, the pain as they destroyed faith, hope, ideals, honor. And well I remembered
my determination that I would die rather than exist in such a
way.

"Would that I could ease your pain," I said. Such futile,
useless words. "Would that I could give back what has been
taken from you or, at the least, share all I've learned that
might help you take another breath."

An untouched cup of water and a fist-sized chunk of
bread lay beside him. He had probably neither eaten nor
drunk for some days.

I sat down in the straw facing him. "You need to drink.
It's no use waiting for water you believe is clean. You won't
get it."

"Gaened da," he whispered, his anger and disgust made
childish by his chattering teeth.

"I know I am unclean. I have been from the first day I
was taken. As have you."

He shook his head in denial.

"It's not your fault. Never think it. I know what our people say about those of us taken captive, but there is nothing . . . nothing . . . you could have done to deserve what's
happened to you."

"M . . . must have done."

"You don't believe me now, but you'll come to see it, if
you give yourself the time."

I wanted to pour all of it into him, to make him see, but I
knew that was not yet possible. All I could do was get him
past the moment.

I closed my eyes and pressed a clenched fist to my breast.
"Lys na Seyonne," I said, giving him an Ezzarian's ultimate
gift of trust and kinship. "I beg you listen to what I say. You
have only one choice left to you. Live or die. There is no
going back, no bargaining with fate. I wish I could tell you
otherwise. Live or die. It comes down to that. And what does
Verdonne teach us of such a choice?"

I waited for him to say it. It would not take long. The passion for life is so strong in a youth of sixteen . . . even when faced with horror and ruin.

"Live." He closed his eyes and tears ran freely down his bruised face.

I was cheating. He still believed in gods that might have an interest in what he did. Perhaps by the time he learned the truth, living—even living in bondage—would become a habit he was unwilling to break. I gave him some time, then I placed the cup of water in his hand.

"Only a sip now," I said, easing the cup away before he drained it all at once. "It will carry you through a whole day if you let it. Do you have any injuries save the lashing and the burns?" The branding was bad enough, but the smiths were never careful when closing the steel rings about ankles and wrists.

He shook his head. "They said I would be kept down here until I died. Why did they send you?" Suspicion croaked out with his question.

He was already learning what he would need. I laughed a bit. "Durgan's let me come because you are valuable alive and worthless dead, and it makes his employers most unhappy to have valuable slaves turn into worthless ones. If you refuse food and drink, they'll force it down you. If you run, they'll beat you or brand you on the face—much worse than this on mine—and they'll cut off one of your feet. A crippled slave can still work. They won't kill you, no matter how you provoke them. They'll only do that when they've damaged you beyond use . . . and that's a very long way. Durgan, unlike many slave masters, doesn't like all that mess." I was frightening him worse than ever, but it was necessary. "Durgan also understands something of Ezzarians, but you mustn't presume on it."

I longed to ask where he had come from. The few Ezzarian slaves I had encountered in my early years of captivity had been taken as I was, on the day of Ezzaria's fall. The assault had come so quickly on that last day. We who had fighting skills had tried very hard to give the last survivors time to escape, but at the moment I had drawn my last free

breath, every man, woman, and child within my view was
dead. Where were the living? Who were they? Names
danced on my tongue, demanding to be spoken. He could be
the child of my friends. Memories flooded into my mind,
crying to be shared with one who might understand. Questions about what exactly had happened after the first Derzhi
lash had fallen on my shoulders . . . an unfocused hunger for
understanding, dressed in a strange, quivering anxiety that
set my teeth on edge . . . crept to the edge of my tongue. But
I could not indulge my desires. I had to teach the boy truths
for his new existence.

"Be easy about one thing. The Derzhi won't ask you
about the others, because they don't really care all that
much. We're not worth the trouble to hunt down. It was an
accident you were taken. You did something stupid and got
yourself noticed by a Derzhi magician. Am I right?"

The boy nodded hesitantly.

"The magicians are the only ones who care about us anymore."

"Why?"

"Afraid we'll put them out of a job. They can do very little but make illusions. They happen upon things by chance,
but they've lost any memory of melydda. They know we
have power to do real sorcery, but they don't understand it
and can't figure out how to get it themselves. They can't
seem to grasp that we don't care about entertaining Derzhi
nobles with it."

"I was just trying to find my way back to . . . Just trying
to get home." He almost bit a hole in his lip.

"You're right not to trust me. Don't trust anyone. There is
even a rai-kirah housed among the people here—in a Khelid
emissary—"

"Rai-kirah?" His eyes grew huge. Panicked. Trapped. He
hadn't even thought of such a possibility. But then, neither
had I.

"It can't know you. Just be exceptionally cautious. You
no longer have any defenses. All in all, it's safer to keep to

yourself, but if I can help you, I will. Ask me whatever you wish."

He didn't want to talk to me. He kept looking away as if he could not bear the sight of one he would have shunned as unspeakably corrupt only a few days before. Yet then his eyes would flick back to me, to the mark on my face, to the scars on my shoulders and arms, to my fading bruises. "How long have you been . . . like this?" He could not bring himself even to say the word.

"I've been a slave for sixteen years. Since the fall of Ezzaria when I was eighteen." His whole lifetime. It must have sounded like eternity.

"What were you before? Did you have melydda?"

I could hear what he was really asking. If he had been blessed with true power, but I had not, then he might do better. He might escape my fate.

"This is the only thing I will answer about the past," I said, "because I've left it behind . . . as you must also do." I looked him directly in the eye so he would know I was telling the truth. "I was a Warden."

I hadn't thought he could get any paler. I put the bread in his hand and encouraged him to eat. He did so, then did as he needed to do . . . spoke of the present.

"They try to make me speak my name, to wear their immodest clothes, and kneel to worship them as if they were gods. They say I'm to serve at table. I would have to touch their foul meat and rotted foods, and use their unclean water to bathe their hands."

Of course they would want him to serve at table. He was a handsome youth . . . unscarred . . . naive . . . innocent. My heart boiled with hatred, and I hoped the rai-kirah was not hunting at that moment or it would find a proper vessel in me. "There are a few more things I should tell you about Derzhi table service. . . ."

It was half an hour more—a bleak half hour—until Durgan opened the trap and bade me come out. I took the boy's trembling hand and said, "You will survive it. Your purity is inside your soul. Untouchable. The gods will see the light in you." I wished I could believe it.

As I let go and started up the ladder, the boy closed his eyes, clenched his fist to his breast, and said, *"Lys na Llyr."*

"Tienoch havedd, Llyr. Nepharo wydd," I said. Sleep in peace.

I struggled with what to do about Llyr. Instinct demanded I stay away. Loneliness was safety, just as I had told him. And the boy had to learn his own lessons—the quicker, the better. Yet the prospect of gaining his trust and having my questions answered was so tempting as to be physically painful. Fate, in the form of Aleksander, removed my choice.

On the very next day I was moved into the palace so it would be easier for the Prince and his staff to make use of me. Preparations were under way for Aleksander's dakrah, so there were a thousand writing tasks to be performed: invitations to the local nobility, proclamations of all sorts, unending correspondence with merchants and suppliers, friends and guests.

It was a week until I saw Llyr again. The Prince summoned me, one evening at dinner; to read some poem that had been written about the coming festival and left at his place by an infatuated woman. Aleksander did not dismiss me when I finished reciting the maudlin verse, so I sat in the shadows behind him, and I watched the Ezzarian boy begin to wash the hands of the guests. His eyes were dark hollows; his skin almost transparent, stretched over his bones. My heart sank. He was not eating. He was still fighting the battle of how to avoid those things we had been taught were impure, while not killing himself—the ultimate corruption, according to Ezzarian law. It was so hard to reverse the teachings of a lifetime. And there was no answer to the dilemma unless he learned new truths to live by. Llyr could scarcely bring himself to touch the hands of the brawny Derzhi warrior. And when the man reached out and fondled his short hair, leering in unseemly anticipation, I felt Llyr's despair as if it were my own. Which, of course, it had been . . . and was.

Two nights later, as I was sitting in Fendular's cold ante-room, writing a list of extra linens needed for the two thousand guests who were expected some six short weeks ahead, a young female slave appeared at the door. "Master Durgan commands you come to the slave house."

It was an absolute breach of protocol for me to leave my assigned task to obey a lesser-ranking official, but I did not hesitate. I knew what I would find.

The fool of a boy had not known how to do it quickly or painlessly. He had put the dull shaving knife in his belly. Durgan had laid him in the darkest corner of the slave house, and thrown a blanket over him to quiet his shivering.

"Ah, child, what have you done?" I said.

He did not answer, but turned his head away from me. It was not my corruption that he could not face. Quite the opposite. *"Gaenad zi,"* he said. "Go away." He was ashamed.

I gathered him in my arms and held him to me, feeling his warm blood soak my tunic. "I am not afraid of corruption, Llyr," I said. "I'm just sorry. I wish . . ." Well, what did it matter? Softly I sang the chant for the dying, hoping it would give him some comfort.

"Were you truly a Warden?" he whispered once I was done with the ancient prayer.

"Yes."

"Will you look . . . inside . . . and tell me what you see?"

"There's no need—"

"Tell me please. I'm so afraid."

"If you wish." I gazed deep into his dark, pain-filled eyes, but I used no Warden's skill to read his soul and make my answer. "There is no evil in you, Llyr. No corruption. You are Verdonne's child and Valdis' brother, and you will live forever in the forests of light."

He relaxed and closed his eyes, and I thought he was gone. But he smiled sleepily and said, "Galadon told me he once knew someone who was a Warden at seventeen. He said I would never have such melydda as that one in a thousand years of trying."

"Galadon . . ." I came near forgetting everything in the magic of the name.

"It was you, wasn't it?"

"He never spoke such flattery in my hearing. He always said I was 'incompetent, ignorant . . .'"

"'. . . imperceptive, and ill-suited for your gifts.'"

I smiled at the echo of lost joy. "Galadon lives . . ."

"There's . . ." He choked on blood that came bubbling from his mouth, and his thin body wrenched in spasm. I held him close.

"It's all right," I said. "Be easy."

". . . five hundred . . ."

"Hush, boy."

". . . hiding, hiding, hiding. Cold and clean . . . ah . . . shhhh. Don't tell where. Gyrbeast leads the way . . ." He was drifting away and his words fell into a faint singsong like a childhood rhyme. ". . . find the way . . . find the way home . . . follow the gyrbeast . . . lead you home. . . ."

He sighed, and said nothing more.

"Nepharo wydd, Llyr," I said. Sleep in peace.

If Llyr was in peace, I was not. Durgan tried to speak to me as I rinsed the blood from my tunic and put the wet garment back on, but I would not stay to hear him. "I must return to my work," I said. "Do not call on me for such a matter again, slave master. I'd not wish the Prince or the Chamberlain to find me absent from my duties to wait upon a barbarian slave."

It was a bitter time. I would have preferred to sleep freezing in the slave house and be set to shoveling out the middens with my bare hands, than to be drawn deeper into Derzhi life. But as the weeks passed I became too busy to dwell on it much. I was ruthless with myself, forbidding any thought, no matter how fleeting, that could have an association with the past. I dreamed no dreams, permitted no visions, spoke to no one outside my assigned work. And I completely banished from my mind the astounding news that five hundred Ezzarians were hidden somewhere in the world and that among them was one who had been my mentor from my fifth birthday, the day I was found to have melydda. My encounter with Llyr had done nothing but confirm that I had been right to stay apart, right to forget, right to pretend that there was no other life beyond the moment in which I existed.

Chapter 10

It was only three weeks until the start of the twelve days' celebration that would mark Aleksander's majority. He would be twenty-three, the age at which Derzhi men became the equal of their fathers. They received their portion of the father's estates and lands according to mother, birth order, and number of siblings, and they could marry without their father's permission. They could argue against their fathers in legal disputes and fight against them in battles without danger of being hanged for disrespect. They could speak with the same authority as their father, though as to being respected for their opinions, they had to earn that in the way of all Derzhi men—in battle.

Being the Emperor's son, Aleksander's case was slightly different. He would hold title to his own property—in his case, enough land, horses, and treasure to establish several thriving kingdoms—but he could not choose whom to marry. That was too important a decision to be left to a young man's whim. And Aleksander would certainly not be the Emperor's equal, though his voice would speak with imperial authority. If he spoke against his father's wishes, only his father would chastise him. No one else would be permitted to do so. And no man or woman could refuse Aleksander's command, thinking to go behind his back and make peace with Ivan as they might have done in the past. Ivan would have their heads for it. The Prince's word would be the law of the Empire.

Every noble, every servant, and every slave in the Prince's household—and most of them in Capharna—were immersed in the endless preparations for the dakrah. A great deal of work had been done the previous fall, when delicacies and precious materials were brought in from the farthest reaches of the Empire before winter snows closed the high mountain passes. Wagon loads of silks and damasks, cases of gold-rimmed porcelain, and casks of rare wines were stockpiled lest a lingering winter prevent their arrival. Jewels from Zhagad's finest gem cutters were shipped in, and perfumed candles by the thousands, and such quantities of gold that the wagons left deep ruts in the roads.

Stewards agonized over planning twelve days of feasting for two thousand guests, and appropriate largess for the population of Capharna and surrounding villages, lest they starve when everything was appropriated for palace use. Herds of goats, sheep, pigs, and cattle, and flocks of every kind of fowl had been imported, along with enough fodder to fatten them over the winter months.

Tailors and seamstresses had been working on robes and gowns for a year or more. Aleksander was fitted for a robe studded with pearls enough to ransom all of Ezzaria, and I saw the designs for a diamond neck piece that would crush a smaller man with its weight.

Yet even with all the year's preparation, the palace was in frenzy. The Emperor's rooms must be painted and refitted, the guest quarters freshened, and accommodations found for those guests who could not fit even in so expansive a hostel as the Derzhi Summer Palace.

Gifts arrived from everywhere: jewels, statuary, boxes of ivory and jade, finely wrought knives, swords, and bows, jeweled headpieces and mail shirts, horses, fighting cocks, perfumes, exotic birds. Though still protesting that he had no belief in sorcery, the Prince had me examine every one of them for enchantments. Since my "cure" of his bedroom malady, he seemed to have confidence in my advising. I found nothing, but as no further disturbances occurred, he seemed to think I was doing a good job.

Much as I wished it, I could not forget about the demon.

The Khelid had left Capharna for a visit to Parnifour, but he was due to return for the dakrah feast. Though I told myself not to worry about it—a mountain could fall on him or an earthquake open the earth to swallow him—my bones told me otherwise. We had not seen the last of him.

As if there weren't enough complications to the whole matter of the dakrah, Aleksander decided that he needed a new sword to carry on the anointing day. Though the gift swords were elaborately decorated and enormously expensive, none of them was the excellent weapon the Prince fancied proper for an Emperor-to-be of a warrior race.

"Demyon of Avenkhar forged my last blade," he said to some friends one morning in his chambers. "He's the finest swordsmith in the Empire."

"Why not have Demyon make you another?" asked Nevari, slurping loudly at a glass of wine. Lord Nevari was the squint-eyed dandy who had been with Aleksander and Vanye at the slave auction. He always looked as if he had just sniffed a dead body.

Aleksander was watching me unpack a crate of amethyst-encrusted gold goblets, but nothing grabbed his attention like idiotic suggestions. "Are you an entire imbecile, Nevari? There are only three weeks until the ceremony, and it would take Demyon most of that time to make a decent sword. He swears that no other forge will work a blade as does his own. He could hardly come here to fit it to my hand and go back to finish it, nor could I go there and try it, and still get back here in time."

"Couldn't you send the order by messenger bird? I ordered this sword from Zhagad, and was quite pleased with the result. I saw no need to be there while they were making it." He pulled out a thick bronze weapon with a hilt so ornately wrought, so encrusted with jewels, and so immensely heavy it would have made a far better bludgeon.

Aleksander rolled his eyes at the other three young men in the room and thumped a finger on Nevari's slightly flat head. "Your sword is a whore's bauble, Nevari. How did you

ever earn your warrior's braid? Did your father hire mercenaries to set up a battle for you? Ahh! I see, I've guessed it!"

"Certainly not!" spluttered the young man clad in pink
satin, his face the very color of his tunic. His companions
covered their mouths to hide their smirking.

"Learn from me, if your head can comprehend it. No true
warrior could carry a blade not made to fit his hand and balanced to suit his style and pleasure. Not all of us are satisfied
with swords so heavy they drag the ground."

The dim young man held his ridiculous weapon high
where the candlelight caught it, and wrinkled his brow seriously at the sparkling toy. "But it looks well, don't you
think, Aleksander? How can you bear such plain work as
you carry? Yours might be the sword of a drudge soldier. An
Emperor's sword should be even finer than mine."

But Aleksander wasn't listening to Nevari. He was staring down at his scabbard, discarded on a round, marble-
topped table. Suddenly he whirled about. "Seyonne!"

I set down my work and bowed. "My lord?"

"Has there been any word from my uncle?"

"No, my lord. Not since the last from Zhagad." That was
the three-line message in which the old man had submitted
to Aleksander's scheme to keep him away from Capharna
for the Dar Heged.

> Your Highness,
> Your word is my command. The Lady Lydia will be
> provided for. I will see you in Capharna, when my duty is
> done in Avenkhar.
> Dmitri

Aleksander had taken no pleasure from that note, and no
triumph. "We'll mend," he had said to himself after hearing
it. "We'll mend."

"Dmitri has surely gone to Avenkhar by now. He knows
every strength and weakness of my hand, and exactly what
design suits me best. Who better to judge Demyon's work
than the finest swordsman ever to carry a blade? It will only

delay his return a bit longer. If he comes by the Jybbar Pass, he'll be here well before the ceremonies begin."

I was immediately set to writing at the cherry wood desk.

> Dmitri,
> As you are yet annoyed with me, I might as well get your blood boiling one more time. It will keep you warm as you come over the Jybbar to Capharna. I've decided on a new sword for the dakrah. You will command Demyon to drop everything he's doing to make a sword fit for his Crown Prince—a warrior's blade, not some ceremonial toy. The finished blade should be two mezzits longer than the last one he made for me, as you and I discussed last summer, but I expect the balance and the edge to be just as perfect. As for the hilt, Demyon knows my taste. I require only that it bear the graven device of the Derzhi lion and the falcon of our House. I trust you to judge it fit, Uncle, and to bring it in all haste from Avenkhar for the opening of the dakrah. Send me word that you will see to this commission.
> Zander

The Prince had me post the letter via messenger bird to Avenkhar, then he fussed and fidgeted for four days until a message came in reply.

> Your Highness,
> Your sword will be satisfactory. The Lady Lydia is on her way. Three weeks and I will be in Capharna.
> Dmitri.

Aleksander shook his head at the message. "I suppose I must be ready for your thrashing, likai," he said. Then, with an unaccustomed wistfulness, he added, "Why is your head so hard?"

Likai. That explained a great deal about Aleksander and Dmitri. A likai was a Derzhi warrior's tutor, the master of his apprenticeship in the art of war. Though it was unusual for a likai to be a relative, I should have guessed it. Ivan would not have allowed his son's training to be handled by just anyone. What was more unusual was that they had apparently come out of it without being mortal enemies. A good likai was a hard taskmaster—and I surmised that Dmitri was good at it. Inevitably these thoughts of mentors and students led me back to Llyr, and I returned to my work cursing all Derzhi.

The only preparation for the dakrah Aleksander found amusing was hiring entertainers. Five householders were given the duty of designing entertainments for every day and night of the celebration, and there was a constant flow of musicians and dancers, jugglers and magicians streaming into Capharna, vying for the lucrative contracts. The householders would screen the applicants, then send any who seemed likely to the Prince for final judgment. The Prince was, of course, not at all shy about expressing his preferences.

"You sound like screeching geese."

"Your mewling makes me vomit."

"You are an offense to Athos. Isn't there some god of music to throttle this woman?"

One after another the unsatisfactory aspirants slunk away. The Prince told a Basranni lore master that she could not show her face in Capharna or Zhagad for ten years. He kicked a dark-skinned Hollenni singer in the backside, just as the man reached an emotional crescendo. The singer's eyes popped open and the poor man almost swallowed his tongue.

"Seyonne, write a proclamation that Hollenni are not permitted to sing Derzhi love songs. Their slobbering sentiment degrades our traditions."

I wanted to tell him that perhaps the emotion had something to do with the fact that Hollenni couples were pledged at birth and never had an opportunity to challenge their tribal matchmaker's choice. When Hollenni sang of unrequited love and the sorrows of impossible joining, they knew what they were talking about. But I refrained.

At the end of the long day of unsatisfactory auditions, a lute player twanged an off-key string in the middle of an otherwise decent performance. Aleksander leaped from his chair, grabbed the instrument, and smashed it over the unlucky musician's head. The devastated man fled from the palace music room weeping.

"Well, what are you looking at?" The Prince caught me before I could drop my eyes.

"I'm looking at nothing, my lord."

"You see? Again, you're not saying what's truly in your mind. This past fortnight it's been worse than ever. What are you brooding about?"

"I think of nothing but doing your will, Your Highness."

"There. Clearly a lie. Tell me the truth or I'll have you flogged. It's been too long since you've had a lash, so you'd best make me believe you. You're useful, but not indispensable."

I was sitting on a high stool at a clerk's desk, staring down at my bony, ink-stained fingers that had once held a Luthen mirror, and such a great weariness overcame me that I could not retreat behind my usual barricades of words.

"I was thinking that the lute player's family is going to starve, because his instrument, which is his livelihood, is now destroyed."

"Ah, he probably has a bag of gold sewn into his cloak. Or does your Ezzarian magic tell you other?"

"No, my lord. It is only my eyes tell me. He is Thrid and therefore he has traveled a month to get here and must travel a month to get home, yet he has holes in the soles of his shoes. The five tattoos on his left arm tell me he has five children, yet he wears no ivory. A Thrid who has sold his last ivory talisman has no legacy for his children. Therefore he has nothing and his family will starve, for what merchant or farmer will have mercy on a Thrid, who are hated and despised by every race?" I let far too much bitterness leak out with my words.

"What's the matter with you today, Seyonne? What care have you for a Thrid? He has no slave rings. Thrid soldiers were in the vanguard when we took Ezzaria."

I believed I had controlled my anger about Llyr's death. But after the endless day watching Aleksander's boorish behavior, I could not check my tongue when he goaded me.

"He is a living, breathing being, my lord. He has hands and voice to do you honor, and a soul to worship his gods and bring good into the world. You have destroyed him because you are bored."

"How dare you speak to me thus?"

It was one of the most difficult battles I had ever fought to abandon my stool, force myself to my knees, and will my tongue to obey. "I do only as you command, my lord." I was shaking in rage. Never had I been so close to losing control of myself, and from the corner of one eye, I saw Aleksander's fist clench and jerk, ready to lay me flat. I prayed for him to do it before I made matters worse. But all he said was, "Get out. And bring a civil tongue tomorrow or you'll have no hands with which to write."

All that evening as I worked at Fendular's drudgery, I damned myself for a fool. *Stupid. Stupid to let him goad you into words from your heart. If you once let a trickle past the dam, how long will it be until you loose the flood?*

I hoped the Prince would forget the incident. He was quick in his humors. Quick to anger. Quick to strike. Quick to forget. I thought of him as a dangerous child, and had come to believe it was the source of his deepest difficulties with people. He could not understand long-standing or deep-held grievances, and found any reminder of them irritating or insulting. He truly believed that the Mezzrahn lords would love him again and send their sons to be his noble attendants and warrior companions. Indeed those who had suffered from his violent and thoughtless tempers or his childish, humiliating insults put on the face required before the man who would one day control their destiny. But I saw their expressions when Aleksander was not looking, and I did not believe they forgot.

Unfortunately, Aleksander did not forget my rash words. On the next morning I sat again at my high writing stool in the vast cavern of the gilded music room. The giant open hearth in the middle of the room was producing very little heat, and the Prince slouched in his cushioned chair beside it, staring at me sourly while he listened to more aspiring entertainers. For an hour nothing would please him. But as the day progressed, three performers were fortunate. The first played the mellanghar, the low-droning pipes of the Derzhi, in such fashion that he could have had the giant stone lions of Zhagad fawning at his feet. A lissome, sloe-eyed Manganar dancer merited not only a contract, but also an escort into the living quarters of the palace, where I had no doubt she would be made other unrefusable offers on the Prince's behalf. Also approved was a storyteller who made the well-lit, chilly room seem dark and hot with a tale of a warrior venturing Druya the bull god's cave.

But about midday a skinny Thrid juggler, performing a daring trick, missed a catch and came near bashing Aleksander in the head with a large wooden ball. It was not a good week for Thrid. The lanky, hollow-cheeked young man prostrated himself in abject terror. When the roaring Prince picked up the man's bag of implements and aimed it at the hearth fire, I quickly averted my face. Aleksander must have changed his mind then, for the heavy bag nearly knocked me off my stool.

"Hie, Thrid," said Aleksander, poking at the man with his foot. "Up with you and show me the soles of your boots."

The poor, gaping fellow could scarcely stand for his knees knocking together so wildly.

"Hmm. No holes. And show me your left arm. One child. And three of your ivory baubles about your neck. What say, Seyonne? May I thrash him without your disapproval?"

"You may do as you please as always and forever, Your Highness. Your will is sacred to all who live in the sunlight of the Derzhi Empire." I stared at the blank paper on my writing desk as I recited the required words.

"Begone, Thrid, and learn your trade before you appear before your prince. Lucky for you someone else offends me more than you."

I've seen few men move faster than did the Thrid juggler. He didn't even take his bag.

I held my hands close to my chest as if I could protect them from Aleksander's wrath. It gave me great satisfaction that they were not trembling when he pulled one away from me and examined it.

"Flogging would not change your thoughts, would it, Ezzarian? Nor even if I made good my threat and cut this hand from your body? And do not dare give me your, 'You may do as you please, my lord.'"

"Such a punishment would not make me other than I am," I said, "unless I went mad from it, which is a likely result. But then, of course, I could be of no use to you."

"Can I believe a woman-ruled barbarian has no fear of my knife?" He pulled the aforementioned weapon and drew its tip across my wrist, leaving a thin thread of blood welling from the taut skin.

What made me decide to tell him the truth? Perhaps I had given up. Perhaps Llyr had left me in such despair I could no longer reason. Perhaps I had not the boy's courage to put a knife in my belly, and so I would force Aleksander to do it for me.

I looked directly into his face. "I am indeed afraid, Your Highness. Every moment of my existence carries such a burden of terror you could not imagine it. I fear I have no soul. I fear there are no gods. I fear there is no meaning to the pain I have known. I fear I have lost the capacity to love another human being or ever to see goodness in one. Among such fears as these, my lord, there is little room for you."

There was no one near us. The room was quite large and the householders were cowering by the doors awaiting a signal that they should send in another candidate.

"I can make you fear me," said Aleksander, with the

quiet, deadly calm I had only seen once before—as he planned Lord Sierge's execution.

"No, my Lord. You cannot."

I felt the searing heat of his wrath as plainly as if the sun had fallen from the sky onto my head. And because I thought the end had come, and I wished to look upon the soul of my executioner, I shifted my senses and searched deep in the amber eyes . . . and found something I had never expected to find.

A glint of silver, shimmering in the silence . . . a frosty moment of heart-stopping clarity . . . a thousand possible outcomes and one . . . Oh, gods have mercy, so brilliant was the light, my inner sight grew dim, blinded by its glory.

Impossible! Not a Derzhi! Not one who had likely slain hundreds of men and women incapable of doing him harm, hundreds more who had committed no offense but standing between him and the object of his desires. Not the representative of everything I detested about the world. How could the gods play so vile a joke? I had lost my skill. It had been too long. My extra senses were not fed with melydda, nor had I ever been a Seer. It was as if I had discovered that somewhere in the bowels of a rotting, maggot-infested corpse lay a pearl of perfection that would ransom the world.

I groaned aloud in desperate denial. I jammed the heels of my hands into my eyes, but the blaze of light was still burned into my vision, like the afterimage when you glance into the sun.

"What in the name of Athos is wrong with you?"

His irritation scarcely penetrated the peripheries of my other senses. The senses that could show me the traces of demons. The same senses that could show me the feadnach, the mark that revealed a soul of destiny, a soul of possibility, raw material that could be cut and shaped by time and fate into something of magnificence . . . a soul that must be preserved at the cost of my life. My slave's chains were as nothing to this new-forged tether that bound me to Aleksander, for in the moment I discovered the luminous possibilities hidden in his depths, I exposed the irrefusable burden hidden in my own. My Warden's oath. For so long I had believed it buried in the ruin that was my soul, just another scrap in the rubble of honor and dignity, love and friendship and purpose. But that moment of my seeing was like the sweep of a giant's hand, removing the debris to reveal that the foundation still held. My oath was the core of my being, the single principle I would not compromise, the point of honor I could never yield. It committed me to do everything in my power to frustrate the purposes of demons, and it demanded that I do everything in my power to protect and nurture those who carried the feadnach—to protect and nurture Aleksander, Prince of the Derzhi.

Chapter 11

"What's wrong with you? You look as if I've already killed you. Is it some enchantment?"

"Enchantment . . . yes . . . makes me talk wildly . . . nightmares . . ." I wanted to scream. To weep. To strangle someone. Curse my infernal pride. Why had I been so bent on taking his full measure? Only one trained to read souls as I had been could see the feadnach—perhaps one in a thousand even among my own people. I waved my hands before my face as if to clear away a tangle of cobwebs. "My lord, forgive anything untoward I may have said in these past days. I was seeking enchantments . . . to protect you . . . and this is a very complex working . . . and only now . . . only now have I come to my senses."

"Curse your lying tongue!" He grabbed my shoulders and shook me until my bones rattled, as if truth would fall out of my mouth and bounce onto the floor at his feet.

Perhaps he was not going to kill me, but I was saved from finding out by a shout from across the room.

"Your Highness! News! Ill news!" Mikael, the gaunt palace guard captain, was running toward us, his footsteps ringing on the sand-red tiles. A disheveled man followed him, more slowly, but with true urgency in his weary steps. "Your Highness, a thousand pardons for the interruption," said the tall soldier, flicking a curious glance my way. "But we knew you would wish to hear Hugert's tale immediately." He gestured toward the messenger.

The grizzled man, whose padded layers of wool and leather were stained and worn, genuflected heavily and began a harrowing tale of a town ravaged and set afire by a party of bandits. What citizens survived were left freezing and without food in the dreadful weather.

I stepped away from Aleksander and began to pack my writing materials into their case. My hands, so steady in my mad confrontation with the Prince, were shaking so fiercely I could scarcely stopper the ink. I could not fathom what I was to do. How could I protect one who would likely kill me once he had a moment to do it? How could I nurture one who owned me, who considered me of no more value than a chair or a footstool? It was absurd. No oath could compel the impossible. I wrenched my mind from my madness and commanded it to stay on my task and nothing else.

Just go. Just do. What comes, comes. You will survive it or not.

But my well-worn chant did not work. It was no longer just about me. The instant of my seeing had crumbled my isolation as quickly and effectively as the Derzhi had overrun Ezzaria.

"Prince Aleksander, I demand an explanation!"

My head snapped up to see the Khelid, dressed all in white, sweeping across the red tiles toward the Prince. Chamberlain Fendular glided after him like a gilded boat upon a smooth river, an unending patter of self-abasement and apology dribbling from his puffy face. The kneeling messenger halted his tale when Aleksander glanced up in irritation.

"I have just returned from Parnifour," said the Khelid imperiously, "and my party was stopped at the palace gates and threatened with a search as if we were common criminals! Only the timely intervention of Chamberlain Fendular prevented this intolerable insult. I was assured by the Emperor that I was to be received here with all the respect he has shown—"

"No insult was intended, Korelyi," said the Prince curtly. "We've reports of bandit raids a short distance from Capharna, and the watch was properly alert. Now I must attend to the matter. Please allow the Chamberlain to make you comfortable and reassure you as to our continued welcome and high regard." The Prince turned away from the pale-skinned Khelid.

"Of course I would not intrude on state business, Your Highness," said the Khelid, bowing politely, his anger evaporated like dew at mid-morning. His voice was again pleasant and smooth, just as I had heard it at the dinner party. "Only grant me one moment to present you with the gifts sent by my counterpart in Parnifour. His duties prevent his attending the coming celebration, but he has sent three of the finest Khelid magicians to entertain you, and he asked me to see that you received this from my hand at the instant of my return. Perhaps it may be of use in this crisis."

On one extended hand the Khelid held out a slender case of finely polished wood. With the other hand he opened the lid to reveal a magnificent bronze dagger, simply and elegantly shaped, a smoothly curved hilt inlaid with silver but otherwise unadorned, exactly to Aleksander's taste. Its edge glinted in the firelight. As the Khelid expected, the Prince's face lit up in pleasure.

Remember, I whispered silently. *Think, fool.* Even without shifting I could hear the demon music from the knife. This Khelid was very serious about his dislike of Aleksander.

The Prince took the weapon from the case, hefted it, and twirled it surely in his fingers. "Fine," he said. "Quite fine. My compliments to your countryman for his excellent taste."

As the Prince drew his own knife from the sheath at his belt and tossed it onto his chair, the Khelid stepped closer . . . closer to the chair where he set the wooden box . . . then closer to the hearth, wrapping his cloak tightly about his shoulders. "A bitter night in your summer kingdom, Prince Aleksander," he said with easy amusement, and rubbed his hands together near the flames. "I think I'll snatch a bit of your warmth to carry back to my apartments and leave you to your business." He reached for a thumb-sized stick and lit its end.

Look at him, I thought. *Watch him and remember what I told you. You believed me.*

But the new knife was already sheathed, and Aleksander had returned his attention to the messenger. The Khelid bowed and turned to leave, pretending to warm his hand over his burning stick as he started moving the red tip in a circular pattern.

There was no time to consider consequences. I no longer had choices. I nudged the stopper loose in the ink jar, set the jar on the desk, then bumped the handle of the writing case that lay beside it. The glass jar fell, shattering on the red tiles and splattering ink on the Khelid's white robes.

"Kasmagh!" screamed the Khelid in fury, for as he whirled to see what was happening, the tiny flame singed his fingers and went out. No one else likely noticed the instant of heart-stopping darkness when he spoke the curse—and I was grateful that his fire had gone out before he said it. I would have been unable to counter it and so would likely have burst into flames myself. It was a very nasty word. As it was, I dropped to the floor, making sure to prostrate myself in the ink to demonstrate my humiliation.

"Forgive me, Your Highness, for being the fool as I am. Please allow me to summon a physician. The great lord has burned his fingers on his branch. My clumsiness is inexcusable, my lord, especially after your warnings to be exceptionally careful around our guests."

Hear me, Aleksander, I added in silence. *You are not stupid, so hear me. If you are what the gods have told me, then you must be able to listen with more than your temper.*

"Filthy cretin of a slave," said Fendular after screaming for a chamberlain to fetch the physician. "You will need a physician for yourself when you reap your just punishment for this deed."

"Are you much injured, Lord Korelyi?" Aleksander's voice was as cool as the tiles that pressed on my feverish face. "I'll have Giezek, my own physician, see to you."

"Easily soothed," said the Khelid, his voice smooth again, but no longer pleasant. "I carry our familiar remedies for healing. I'm surprised you Derzhi permit such incompetent servants so near your royal persons. In Khelidar this one would have never lived so long as to insult a royal guest in such fashion."

"Fendular, see to our guest's comfort. If he should so desire it, bring him to the slave house in exactly one hour to witness this slave's punishment."

"As you command, my lord," said Fendular, oozing triumph and making sure to step on my hand as he passed.

"And tell Giezek that I wish to have his personal report on Lord Korelyi's injury within half an hour."

"Of course, Your Highness."

I did not hear the footsteps approaching or see the soft leather boots until they stood right next to my head. The owner crouched down and lifted my face with the flat of a knife blade under my chin.

"The warning should have been heeded, slave. One must always carry warnings in the front of one's mind. The consequences of failure to do so are unfortunate."

The Prince stood up again and called, "Mikael, have this creature taken to Durgan. Tell the slave master fifty lashes one hour from now."

Fifty . . . gods. For one moment I had thought he understood my warning. But as the guards dragged me away, I was left in complete confusion, for the new bronze knife lay abandoned in the pool of ink.

Sometime in the long, cold hour after I was stripped and bound to the flogging post to await my punishment, a modestly outfitted Suzaini gentleman came into the slave house. He had a word with Durgan, who sat grimly beside his brazier at the far end of the deserted room. Durgan nodded and the stranger came over to me. From a brown leather pouch hanging from his belt, the slight, gray Suzaini pulled a blue vial, then opened it and held it to my lips. "Drink this. You'll be glad you did."

"Who are you?" I said, pulling my head back as far as my restraints allowed. The stuff smelled dreadful. "And what is this? I try to avoid mysterious potions from people I don't know."

He pursed his thin lips in irritation. "I was told to give it to you, but not to force you if you didn't wish it. I was told nothing about answering questions from a slave." He yanked open his pouch to return the vial.

"Wait!" I said. "I'll take it." Faced with fifty lashes, I had to scrape up a bit of faith.

It tasted as bad as it smelled—something like a mouthful of sheep entrails that had been boiled with pepper pods. But even as I felt a pleasant numbness roll out from my stomach and begin to deaden my extremities, I managed a soggy grin. "Giezek, the physician. Am I right?"

He snorted and walked away.

It was a party of twenty or thirty bandits who had raided the mountain town of Erum, only six leagues from Capharna. In most years, early spring was the best of times for bandits. When the narrow defiles through the wilder mountains began to open up, travelers and caravans started moving through them again. The caravans could move faster in the summer and a few outriders sent into the hills could protect the way. But in the spring, while snow still lay deep, wagons and horses moved slowly and bogged down easily, and those who were familiar with the snow-buried terrain could have their way with them, earning a year's livelihood in the matter of a few weeks. The caravans bringing supplies or guests for the dakrah were heavily guarded, however, so that spring the raiders were forced to seek their profits elsewhere, a town that was lightly defended due to its proximity to Capharna.

Aleksander, chafing at the inactivity of the Dar Heged and the endless consultations and fittings for the dakrah, decided that he himself would lead the troop of warriors dispatched to hunt down these latest offenders. He left orders that while he was gone, all his correspondence was to come through me, and I was to determine whether it made sense to risk a messenger to forward it on to him. It was an astonishing responsibility for a slave, and Fendular came near exploding at the news. His formidable jowls quivered in indignation.

"Your Highness, pardon my forward speech, but I have many excellent scribes and assistants available for your service. It is unseemly for a barbarian slave, one punished just yesterday for incompetence and gross insults to our honored guests—"

"You will not tell me what is unseemly, Fendular. I choose my servants as I please. Were I to make this slave my Lord High Chamberlain, who would dare dispute it save my father?"

"But, Your Highness—"

"This slave was chastised severely in your sight and in the sight of his victim. Now I require him to serve me and repay my trouble in allowing him to live."

Fortunately Fendular was not bright enough to question how I was able to walk or kneel after fifty lashes, or he might have guessed that the good Giezek had kept me well supplied with his blue vials throughout the previous night and morning. The physician had also given Durgan a salve that quickened healing, and though I was not comfortable, neither was I crippled, as I might have been otherwise. Mercifully I had felt little of the lashing itself, and I suspected that Durgan had been told to modify his strokes to make more show than true damage.

Fendular bowed stiffly and left the room, glaring at me as if I had eaten his children. I did not look forward to the next time I would be required to submit to his direction.

The guard captain, Sovari, was strapping Aleksander's sword belt about the Prince's waist. I wondered what had become of the Khelid knife. I had spoken no private word with the Prince since the incident. There were always two dozen people around him, and to summon me from the bare attic room I now shared with twenty other house slaves was difficult to do discreetly with a slave handler always posted at the door. The Prince must have noticed my glance, for he drew his knife and turned it in the lamplight. "I suppose I'll have to make do with my old knife. Unfortunate that the blade the Khelid brought was unbalanced. I had the smith melt it down. Perhaps he can do better."

After some seven or eight days, Aleksander returned from his successful foray, leaving the heads of twenty-three bandits hung on the charred walls of Erum. The Prince was ebullient. "Athos' balls, it felt fine to be on horseback again with a sword in my hand," he said to a party of young priests three days before the dakrah was to begin. "The magistrate of Erum said I should execute only the leaders of the bandit troop, that the others were only hungry, desperate men. But I've been idle too long and could not stomach mercy. The villains picked an unfortunate time to be hungry."

While my own stomach turned in disgust, the five shaven-headed servants of the sun god nodded in sympathy. They had come to plan a footrace to the top of Mount Nerod for one day of the dakrah. It was a sacred custom in Capharna. I wondered if the sun god would shine on top of the cloud-shrouded mountain on the day of the race, for surely he never did any other day. Perhaps that's why he didn't notice the despicable habits of those who governed his Empire.

"Surely your swift and forceful retaliation will make the passes safer for the dakrah guests," said one of the priests. "Many of the new arrivals tell of the boldness of the raiders."

"At least three parties have reported attacks in the western passes," chimed in another priest. "Two of them lost guards to the villains."

The mention of dakrah guests dimmed Aleksander's sunny mood. "Seyonne, has there been any word from Dmitri?"

I shook my head.

The Prince scanned my face. His eyes narrowed, then he shoved me from the stool and told me to get out of his apartments. "They asked for it," he shouted after me. "They should not have burned my town. And it is not your business." I had said not a word.

In the last days before the ceremonies were to begin, Aleksander went back to his auditioning, this time for magicians. He spent an entire day watching one Derzhi magician after another demonstrate elaborate creations of colored clouds, fountains of light, flowers, sultry maidens, monkeys, and birds. "Druya's horns," he shouted, after a trio of women magicians made yet another flock of birds appear from behind a mirror. "Is there not a decent magical entertainment left in Azhakstan? Could you devise nothing at all unique for your prince's dakrah? My Ezzarian writing slave could come up with something more exciting."

I wanted to stuff Aleksander's mouth with my writing paper. Ezzarians needed no more animosity from the Derzhi Magician's Guild. It was the Guild who had called Ivan's attention to the fertile hills off his southern borders, and convinced him that the secretive Ezzarian sorcerers were dangerous. And it was the Magician's Guild who had paid or tortured or coerced an elderly Ezzarian scholar named Balthar into devising the way to strip an Ezzarian sorcerer of melydda.

"Perhaps if we showed you more, Your Highness," said one of the magicians, a tall, anvil-chinned woman with protruding cheekbones. "This is only the beginning."

"Perhaps we should ask the Ezzarian what he would suggest," hissed another woman. It was the women of the Guild who were the most brutal in administering Balthar's Rites. Perhaps they were jealous of the status of Ezzarian women, equal in all things to men save in the matter of governing, where we had deemed it best they hold sway. Only in Ezzaria, of all the lands conquered by the Derzhi, had a woman held a throne.

"Seyonne, a proclamation." The Prince yanked me out of my wandering thoughts. I dipped my pen and nodded, having an uneasy conviction that whatever Aleksander was going to have me write, it was going to be a mistake.

"No Derzhi magician will perform at my dakrah or at a dakrah in any noble House for twenty-three years. Perhaps by the time I have a son coming to his majority, they will have thought of something new."

"Your Highness! Surely you can't mean this." The three women were aghast.

I hesitated before committing ink to paper. "My lord, I want to make sure I get the wording correct," I said. "I dare not insult you or the honorable Magician's Guild by misinterpreting your saying."

Perhaps if the women had been quiet, Aleksander might have reconsidered, but they would not leave it.

"Your Highness, this is unthinkable."

"What will the Houses think to have no magic for their most sacred celebrations?"

"You must recant this proclamation."

"You insult our Guild."

"We will carry our protest to the Emperor. He has ever shown respect for our profession. He'll not hear of our being forbidden to pursue our craft at the most significant events of the noble Houses."

"Silence, all of you," said Aleksander, leaping from his chair and sweeping their paraphernalia from a long table, "or I'll forbid you to practice your craft on any occasion whatsoever. Return to your towers and vaults and learn your business. And protest to the Emperor at the peril of your necks. He favors Khelid magicians at present. Perhaps we'll not have need for you at all in the future."

The three withdrew with such hatred boiling on their faces that I wondered if I should attempt to warn Aleksander. Could he have no idea what he had done? Even those with so little true power could be dangerous.

All further consideration of the matter was erased by the announcement of the arrival of Lady Lydia and her party from Avenkhar. The servants quickly cleared the room of the grumbling magicians when the Prince said he would be damned if he would move to the formal reception rooms to receive the woman his father had chosen as his bride.

"I'll not move a step to see her. Curse it all, why could the witch not have fallen prey to bandits?" growled Aleksander to the Chamberlain's back. "I won't marry the she-wolf. I'll hang myself first." He straightened his shirt of fawn-colored silk and flopped down in his chair by the hearth, while servants bustled about bringing chairs and footstools to set close to the fire and setting a pot of steaming wine on a table.

I continued writing out his proclamation, adding all the formalities that were required to make it law. If I was quick I might make my obeisance and escape before the lady entered, lest I be unable to get permission to leave and thus miss my evening rations.

From Aleksander's horror of the woman, I expected a horse-faced, pockmarked Derzhi harridan twice his age, someone from a rich and powerful family that no one else would have. Every female under the age of forty seemed to fawn over the Prince—whether he scorned her or bedded her. I supposed they believed that there was always a possibility that the strong-willed heir would convince his father to allow him to marry whomever he fancied, and the chance to be Empress of the Derzhi was too tempting to risk.

But my first glimpse of the Lady Lydia of the House of Marag told me she didn't care whether or not she was the Empress. She would do it if required, and do it well, but she would take not one step out of her way to make it more likely. In that and in every important way, she completely confounded my expectations.

She was no older than Aleksander, and as tall as I, taller if one counted the scarcely tamed red curls piled atop her head. Though slender and well formed, with long, elegant bones, she was neither fragile nor delicate. She was not exquisitely beautiful. Her short, straight nose, her prim lips, and somewhat narrow, angular face might even have been called plain. But her long, graceful neck could have driven a sculptor to madness, and her green eyes, stark beneath pale brows and lashes, caught wicked fire when she raised up from her deep curtsy and laid them on Aleksander. I found her breathtaking.

"Welcome, my lady," said the Prince, pointedly remaining seated at her entry, much as if he was staking out a position on a battlefield. "I trust your journey was uneventful."

He motioned her to a chair, and she slipped out of her dark fur-lined cloak and into the soft cushions in one fluid motion. Without fuss, disruption, or command, one rosy-cheeked serving woman had a footstool under the lady's feet, another held her cloak, gloves, and fur muff, and another was pressing a cup of hot wine into her slender hands. The three servants were not slaves.

"Is 'uneventful' the best you can wish me, Your Highness? I should think you could at least hope for satisfactory, or perhaps even pleasant, as we've known each other so long." Her voice was as low and melodious as the stringed viols the Kuvai played.

"Of course. Those, too." The Prince recovered well from the first assault. "We've had bandits six leagues west and heard reports of attacks on our traveling guests, so uneventful is perhaps a greater hope than it seems."

The lady nodded seriously. "I've heard likewise, but I was assured that you had shed enough blood to make us all safe again. Is it not true?"

"I did what was necessary." The Prince was picking at the threads of the brocaded chair, not quite squirming under her steady gaze.

"Of course." She smiled serenely. "Uneventful well describes my journey. The Lord Dmitri took great care to ensure it would be safely so. I've never been better guarded. Perhaps Derzhi women have guardian spirits as Derzhi warriors do? Is it heresy to say so? Being both priest and warrior you must surely know the answer."

Aleksander ignored the jab and abandoned his defensive position when his uncle's name was mentioned. He straightened and moved to the edge of his chair. "Did my uncle accompany you, then?"

"Alas, no. He said he had another commission that would delay his journey."

The morose Prince settled back in his chair, tapping a half-closed fist on the chair arm. "But he was well when you last saw him?"

"Very well. I was honored by his attentions—and yours to send him. We rode out hawking only a few days before I left. He was most gallant and charming, though I'll tell you in confidence, I don't know that he believes making ladies' travel arrangements is quite up to slitting throats and ripping bellies. I'm surprised you would use him so. You will have to explain it to me."

I found myself trying to smother a smile, and even a murderous glare from Aleksander could not subdue my moment's enjoyment. No wonder he railed at her. Even with no more evidence than this, I knew he had never gotten her to his bed. He had not found any way to conquer her, and it was driving him wild.

"My uncle is happy to serve the Empire in whatever way he is asked."

The Lady Lydia did not deign to counter such a paltry feint. Instead she followed Aleksander's glance and discovered me.

"Who is this pleasant fellow, my lord? Have you got someone to write for you? I remember your dissatisfaction with the scribes in Capharna. You always used it as an excuse not to correspond with me. Shall I find that you have acquired the means, but not the taste for it?" Her attention did what Aleksander's could not. My skin grew hot, and I dropped my eyes.

"The slave is just leaving," said Aleksander. "He can finish his work later."

I slipped off my stool, genuflected to the Prince, and rose to leave.

"Hold one moment," said the lady, jumping up from her chair. I paused and crossed my hands on my breast to await her pleasure. "No. Please turn around again."

I turned my back to her, wishing I could do almost anything else. Fifty lashes, no matter how they are dealt, leave an untidy mess. I don't know that I had ever felt so embarrassed about my circumstances. At least I wore a tunic so she could not see it all.

"You are an exacting taskmaster, my lord. Did he blot a paper or stumble over a word?" Her playful edge had grown hard.

"My slave is not your concern, my Lady." The Prince was very polite, but had regained his self-assurance for the moment. "You may go, Seyonne." I had come to believe that Aleksander, in some indefinable way, had some sense of the difference between his true authority and his fretful temper. It would explain why, though disgraced and mutilated, Vanye was living as a free man, while his brother-in-law Sierge was dead. I believed it was why I yet lived and why he had not let me suffer beyond necessity from his mistake with the demon's knife. I had no other explanation for it. "Come, my lady," he said. "I see Rakhan telling us that dinner is served, and I've friends enlisted to play ulyat tonight. Perhaps you'll win a wyr-falcon to replace the one you lost to Kiril last year. Do you still maintain the fantasy that women can compete at games of strategy?"

The lady flushed to a color that matched her hair, but her voice held nothing of defeat. "Perhaps this year our game will not be interrupted by state business just when I'm starting to win."

I bowed and retired, for once wishing I could remain behind so I could witness the next skirmish between the Prince and the lady. It could be a most interesting war.

Chapter 12

At midday on the first day of the fourth month of the year, the month of Athos, Ivan zha Denischkar, Emperor of the Derzhi, arrived at Capharna. Trumpet fanfares, parades of traditional Derzhi dancers and drummers, and showers of colored ribbons greeted the tall, powerfully built monarch as he entered the gates and progressed through the city. Eight Derzhi warriors held a red canopy over his head to keep off the heavy, wet snow. From the moment he dismounted his white warhorse at the palace gates, he trod on soft white carpet sprinkled with alyphia petals, the walkway unrolled in front of his feet and rolled up quickly behind him lest some unworthy foot touch his path. Accompanying Ivan was the Empress Jenya, Aleksander's handsome, cold-eyed mother, and Kastavan, the Lord High Ambassador of Khelidar.

Prince Aleksander met the Emperor under the towering portico of the Summer Palace, making complete obeisance to his sovereign father. Ivan raised him up and embraced him to the cheers of the onlookers. The two then proceeded to the Great Hall, where Ivan formally proclaimed the opening of the twelve days' celebration that would culminate in the anointing of his son as Emperor-in-waiting. Then, with two thousand close friends and allies, Ivan and Aleksander reclined at table and spent the rest of the afternoon and evening getting deliriously drunk.

I saw none of this. I had been up since well before dawn, carrying hot water to the guest rooms and carrying away slops jars, climbing up ladders to scrub soot from lamp glass and replace burned-down candles, hauling baskets of clean linen from the washhouse to the far-flung linen rooms, carrying in back-breaking loads of firewood, carrying out endless buckets of hot ashes, and washing away thousands of muddy boot prints from the tile floors. Every slave and servant in the palace, and many of the women, girls, and boys from Capharna, had been pressed into service. None of us were going to get much sleep in the next twelve days. My only participation in the opening night's feasting came well after midnight, when I was on my hands and knees wiping up pools of vomit from the floor of the Great Hall. I was too tired even to be disgusted.

Because I was attached to the Prince's household, I was not required to work in the slaughterhouses or the cesspits or any other outside labor, and my work, even my late night scribing for Fendular, had always been at Aleksander's discretion. But because the Prince was too busy to need my services and the staff was so pressed, I had been put at the disposal of the Lord High Chamberlain for the duration of the dakrah. As I suspected he might, Fendular saw to it that I had no such leisurely tasks as reading or writing, and certainly no business that would put me anywhere near the Prince or the festivities.

On the fourth night of the dakrah, in the midnight hours after the guests had reeled their way to bed, I was told to haul out the remains of the night's feasting from the Great Hall. I was staggering toward the door, bearing four large, heavy buckets on a pole across my shoulders, when I lost my footing on the wet tiles and fell. It was bad enough that I splattered the foul mess over one end of the hall and would have to cut short my few hours sleeping to clean it up, but I had the misfortune to splash the filth on Boresh, one of Fendular's assistants.

"Incompetent beast!" he shrilled, smashing his boot into my face. He wasn't as fast or as strong as Aleksander, but he made his point. I groveled and apologized, then spent two hours cleaning up the nasty mess, scarcely able to see for the swelling in my face. On most nights I would haul a jar of water to the attic and clean myself before sleeping, knowing

I would rest better for it. But on that night I fell onto my straw pallet filthy and exhausted, promising myself that I would jump right up when the guard yelled at us in the morning and be first in line at our single washing bowl.

There was no jumping up the next morning. I was fortunate that one of the other slaves saw me sleeping through the morning call and gave me a shove on his way out. I had time only to hurry outside to relieve myself, then report to Boresh the under-chamberlain to begin it all over again. Of course it was on that particular morning that Aleksander sent for me.

I was standing on the top rung of a somewhat rickety ladder in the Great Hall, reaching high to pry the candle wax out of a brass sconce. My right eye was swollen shut, making it impossible to judge distances properly, so the job was taking me far too long. I had already earned a lash for dawdling, but that was a small matter. It was far more important that I not overbalance the ladder. I had no wish to end up an untidy smear on the distant, blurry floor.

"Is the slave named Seyonne in here?" called the under-chamberlain.

It always left me uncomfortable to hear my name echoing about so publicly. "Up here."

"You are to report to His Highness in the gift room."

I climbed down and caught Boresh before he left. "Have I leave to clean myself first?" I asked, when his face puckered in disgust at the sight and smell of me.

"You are commanded to the Prince immediately. What do you care if he sees you as you truly are? I've heard you barbarians paint yourselves with muck."

It was not that I had any sensibility left. I had been in far worse shape, and Aleksander was welcome to see what he had made of me. It was the prospect of unpleasantness that I despised. The Prince would be offended at my appearance and yell at me about disrespect and barbarian filth, and he would demand to know what insolence I had displayed to deserve the beating. And to prepare for it, I had to walk through the crowded halls and galleries of the residential wing and feel everyone shrink away in disgust. To be noticed by so many felt like having a thousand spiders crawling over me.

The gift room was a large reception hall that had been converted to a repository for the statuary and silver, plate, jewelry, pottery, rugs, perfumes, and artworks people thought would buy their future Emperor's favor. Fifty long tables had been arranged to display the smaller gifts, and the larger offerings were set about the perimeter of the room. The room was guarded by heavily armed Derzhi warriors, and I spent twenty minutes waiting before they received word from inside that I was indeed supposed to be there. To my distress, Aleksander was not alone. With him were three finely dressed young Derzhi warriors, a dusky Suzaini woman in red satin . . . and the Lady Lydia.

I knelt as close to the door as possible and put my head to the tiles, wishing fruitlessly that the Prince needed nothing that would take me closer to him.

"Ah, Seyonne, come here." No luck at all on this day.

I stood up and stepped closer, keeping my eyes to the floor. "My lord," I said.

"Aldicar told me that these gifts have not . . ." There was an ominous pause. "Look at me, Seyonne."

I did as he told me, resigned to a hand about my throat as on the first time I had come to him with a damaged face. Instead, I saw a furrowed brow and heard a soft question. "What have they done to you?"

I spoke softly also, returning my gaze to the floor. From across the room I heard his guests laughing at a most explicit Veshtari fertility fetish. "It's nothing, my lord. I'm sorry I had no time to clean—"

"Answer my question, Seyonne."

"I was clumsy in my duties. I deserved—"

"And what duties are those?"

"Whatever is needed to serve you, my lord."

"You have spoken frankly with me in the past, and I require the same of you now. I just found out that many of these gifts have not been catalogued because Fendular has no scribes to spare, yet you have been given 'other duties'?"

"I am given the same duties as the other household slaves, Your Highness. Nothing else." Whatever it was he was offering with his quiet anger, I wanted no part of it.

His boot of golden leather was tapping on the floor like a flicker's beak. "Can you even see properly?"

"No, my lord." No use in lying about it. He was going to find it out if he wanted me to read or write anything. "A day or two will mend it."

"And lashes, too. Have you eaten today?" What was his point?

"No, my Lord."

"I'll have their heads for this."

"Your Highness, please don't." I could not believe the words from my mouth. "It is no matter."

"Aleksander, isn't it time to be off?" called one of the young men from across the room. "The dancing begins at midday."

"Yes, yes, I'm coming." The boot stopped tapping. "Tomorrow I want the rest of these gifts examined and catalogued. I've been feeling . . . odd . . . these last two days."

"As you command, my lord." I bowed, and because I had no certainty that I would see him before his birthday, I added something else. "May your gods shower you with glory and wisdom on the occasion of your dakrah." The wish I gave him was a strange melding. The prayer for glory was Derzhi, of course; the prayer for wisdom, Ezzarian.

"You may go, Seyonne."

On my way to the door I saw the Lady Lydia standing only a few paces away, beside a suit of ruby-studded gold armor where Aleksander could not have seen her. Our gaze met square on before I could pretend I hadn't noticed. Her great green eyes were full of unabashed curiosity.

I spent the rest of that day and night in the same laborious fashion as the previous ones, but on the next morning, Boresh gritted his teeth in annoyance and dispatched me to the gift room.

It was a pleasant interlude to sit in the quiet room. Except for the regular rounds by the guards and an occasional visit by Boresh to check on my progress and complain of my laziness, I was left alone with my ledger and my writing case. The windows were covered by heavy draperies to keep out the cold, so the place was lit by candlelight gleaming on burnished metal. I found myself getting drowsy as the afternoon passed, until voices outside the door startled me alert. Women's voices.

"Wait at the door, Nyrah. I want to see the Kuvai bow again. My archery master says they are the finest in the world, and I thought to have one made if I can string it. And I'll permit no knavish eyes to witness when I try doing so." It was the Lady Lydia. There was no place to retreat. I glimpsed flowing green on the other side of the room beyond the laden tables. Perhaps she wouldn't see me on my stool in the shadowy corner. I fixed my eyes on the ledger and convinced myself I was working.

"I thought I might find you here."

Even half expecting it, I jumped when the voice came from behind me. I slipped from my stool and genuflected. "My lady. May I serve you in some way?"

"Only to sit down again and tell me what you are." Her green riding skirt, rust-colored tunic, and long leather boots suited her far better than her flowing court dress. The red curls had been released to billow about her narrow face. On her shoulder she carried a well-used bow, and she held the long Kuvai gift bow in her hand.

I returned to my stool and fiddled with my pen and ink. "I am the Prince's writing slave, my lady. Nothing else."

"A great deal more than that, I think. I cannot quite believe what I saw and heard yesterday. It's why I had to come." She sat herself on a gilt chair that was crafted in the design of a snake—a gift from a Manganar village chieftain—set her elbow on the gift table, and propped her chin on her hand, calmly watching me fidget. "Who are you who can request Aleksander of Azhakstan to control his temper and have him do it? His own mother and father, who overlook his every fault, have found such a thing impossible. His uncle, who adores him, despairs of the possibility. No one else in the world would even bother to attempt it. Yet a soft-speaking slave tames him like a horse master calms a colt. It's something I would like to understand."

"I can't explain anything, my lady. I should not speak of—"

"Of course you should not speak of him. You might accidentally mention that he is a despicable, vengeful, bloodthirsty child. But there is no one to hear you say it but me, and you cannot be unaware of the Emperor's intentions with regard to me. Consider that I may be your mistress someday."

Even for one of the strong-willed Derzhi, she displayed extraordinary determination. It was very hard to refuse her. But I did. "That consideration can do nothing but assure that I adhere strictly to my place, my lady. I would do nothing to merit my mistress's concern. She would not allow me to speak of my master without his permission."

The candlelight grew brighter with her smile. "He said you spoke with frankness. I hear some hint of it . . . and sense and wit that are extraordinary for one in . . . your circumstances. So, well enough. Say nothing of Aleksander. Instead, say something of Seyonne. You are Ezzarian?"

"Yes, my lady."

"A sorcerer. Perhaps that explains everything. I've heard it said that Ezzarian sorcerers can cure madness. Is that what you've done?"

"I've been through the Rites of Balthar, my lady. It is impossible for me to do anything of sorcery."

"How long have you served the Prince?"

"Only these last three months."

"Three months to breach a bulwark of stubborn self-indulgence built over twenty-three years. I am more impressed than ever."

"My lady, my last wish is to displease you, but I should get back to—"

"No, Seyonne, you will not put me off so easily. My serving woman will warn me if anyone comes." She retrieved the Kuvai bow that she had laid on the gift table. "So what do you do besides scribe's work?"

"Only what I am commanded to do: reading, writing, household work. It would not be of interest to a lady."

"Hmm." She ran her fingers over the polished sweep of the bow and frowned. "How long have you been in bondage?"

"Sixteen years."

"So long? Well, if you will not speak of the present, tell me of yourself seventeen years ago. What has made you into a person Aleksander holds in a regard he shows no one else?"

"Please, my lady, I cannot. There's nothing to tell."

"I insist. I know nothing of Ezzarians, save the rumors of sorcery and that they were intelligent enough to allow a woman to rule them. Enlighten me."

I could not allow it. Not even for one with so engaging a manner. "Please understand, madam. I did not exist seventeen years ago. I did not exist three years ago, nor even one hour ago. A slave can exist in no moment but the present one. I beg your gracious pardon, but there is nothing more to tell. I am a slave who reads and writes, and who is honored to serve the future Emperor of the Derzhi."

"I see." I regretted the chill in her voice just as I ached when the sun would set after a rare sunny day in Capharna. "So only one more question, then. Who was your master before Aleksander?"

I would rather not have told her, but she could find it out very easily, and I didn't want to offend her further. "The late Baron Harkhesian, my lady."

"Has the Baron died today? I'd not heard it. I saw him just last evening."

I was somewhat flustered. The Baron's physician had been sure he would not survive the change of the year. "No. I mean . . . he was very ill when I was sent away. I assumed . . ."

"He is noticeably feeble, but not dead yet. He was lifting

his tankard well into the night with every other warrior. I
don't think he missed a toast or a song."

I couldn't help but grin at the thought. "I'm glad to hear
it. He always said that Suzaini brandy and strong ale would
preserve him beyond his physician's prediction."

"You see . . . even now you give lie to your own words,
Seyonne. We will continue this conversation another time.
For now I suppose I must let you get back to your work."

She rose from her chair, and I bowed to her. "Please excuse my frankness, my lady. I have no intent to offend."

"Your frankness serves you well, Seyonne. I'm not in the
least offended."

It was a long time before I could summon up enough concentration to get back to my work. I spent a great deal of it
wondering how so perceptive a man as Aleksander could
fail to recognize a prize more magnificent than any lying in
his treasury.

Chapter 13

On the same evening as my talk with Lady Lydia, after I had eaten a bowl of greasy stew with the other slaves and was being given instructions as to the evening's duties, I was summoned to the Prince's apartments. He was wearing white satin breeches and white silk hose, but no shirt. His body slaves were hovering about him, offering a filmy white shirt embroidered in gold, black boots, three jeweled rings in a velvet box, pearl windings for his braid, and a fur-lined cape, but he was pacing restlessly and came near pouncing on me when I entered.

"Skip the bowing and write a message. I want it dispatched instantly by messenger bird to the Chief Magistrate of Avenkhar. I'm tired of waiting and no one can give me any information. And Korelyi keeps asking me when my uncle will come, as if I hadn't thought of it. The damnable Khelid is like a scorpion in my boot."

His eyes spurred me on as I set out the materials and sharpened a pen.

Rozhin,
I require immediate news of Dmitri zha Denischkar, brother to the Emperor. He is five days overdue in Capharna. He was to complete business with Demyon, the swordsmith, and proceed straight here. If you value your position and your balls, you will have a report to me no later than midnight on the seventh day of this month.
Aleksander, Prince of Azhakstan

"Curse all stubborn Derzhi. Where is the man?" said the Prince as I rolled the scrap of paper in its leather covering. "Punishing me, no doubt. Decided he can't thrash me anymore, so he'll get his revenge another way. I swore I'd not ask after him, but almost half the dakrah is past. He should be here."

"The message will be off within the hour, my lord," I said.

I wanted to ask him more about Korelyi's goading. What interest could the demon Khelid have in Lord Dmitri . . . or was it only to spur this fever in the irritable Prince? But before I could get close enough to ask discreetly, one of the slaves finally caught his arm and helped him on with the shirt. As the rest descended on him like flies to a corpse, he called after me. "You're to stay at the aviary to wait for the reply. Otherwise they'll try to send it through Fendular, who won't dare interrupt anything important, but you'll come straightaway, no matter what I'm doing: even if I'm at table with my father or in bed with a woman. Do you understand me?"

"Of course, my lord. The Chamberlain . . ."

"The Chamberlain will be told. Now, off with you."

Though it was impossible that the messenger bird could return from Avenkhar before two days, I obeyed the Prince's command and spent every hour, awake and asleep, in the shed where Leuka the bird keeper nurtured his valuable little flock. Messenger birds were used only for the most urgent messages. They were expensive to train, and only Derzhi nobles were allowed to own them. Commoners were hanged if caught with one. People got nervous if crows flocked to their fields with any regularity, afraid the magistrates would accuse them of training the birds to bear messages.

After several hours of maddening idleness—I hated being so far from Aleksander now Korelyi had returned—I offered to help Leuka with his unending chores of feeding and watering the birds and cleaning their cages. He, in turn, regaled me with the names and personalities and exploits of every one of the fifty birds under his care. "Nybba is a Zha-gad bird. Can find her way there in five days. Made the trip some forty-six times. Been kissed by the Emperor himself. Of course my favorite nestlings, the ones I trained myself to come home here, they're scattered all about the Empire. Not one of 'em ever strayed. I'm forever wondering which one will show up next. They always come first to the chimney. I hear 'em gabbling . . ." I learned a great deal more about messenger birds and their role in Derzhi exploits than I had ever wished to know.

Sure enough, two days later, about the time the sun was setting somewhere behind a miserably cold rainstorm that looked to have settled in permanently, a gabbling at the chimney announced the arrival of Arello, a fat, sleek gray messenger. Leuka kissed the bird and crooned softly to it while he unfastened the leather from about the bird's leg and exposed the bit of oiled paper.

"I'm off," I said. "It was a fine two days."

"Any time," said Leuka. "The birds like you. You've a gentle hand."

I hurried through the courtyards, where the ankle-deep mounds of crusted snow had been replaced by ankle-deep puddles, skimmed with ice.

"Where will I find the Prince?" I asked Boresh, who was marshaling the armies of slaves and servants for the evening duties. "I have the message he's been waiting for."

"Give it to me," he said. "I'll see he gets it. You've three days' work to make up."

"Master Boresh, the Prince left orders that I'm to bring him the message from Avenkhar with my own hand, no matter where he is or with whom or at what time. Dare we disobey his command?"

Of course the under-chamberlain dared not disobey, not now that twenty others had heard me recount my orders. Grudgingly, he revealed that the Prince was attending the evening's entertainment in the ballroom. It took five more confrontations with Fendular's underlings before I was climbing the winding stair toward the curtained-off loge where the royal family and their selected guests could look down on the ballroom.

As I entered the long gallery that girdled the ballroom walls, I caught only a glimpse of the festivities below. Chairs of gilt and velvet had been set up on half the shining wood expanse of the ballroom floor. They were filled with a glittering crowd of guests. Colored lights flared from the vast open space in front of them, but I had no time to stop and observe. The music was odd, dissonant harp melodies that set my teeth on edge and seemed to accompany changes in the lights. Periodically I would hear applause or murmurs of awe and appreciation from the crowd.

The closer I got to Aleksander, the more uneasy I became. I could not explain the creeping shudders or the cold fingers up my spine. Maybe it was the grating music that so unsettled me. It seemed to crawl up the steps behind me and tangle itself in my legs and my arms and my vision while I waited in the dim light for the guard to whisper my name to the Prince.

I told myself that it was only the prospect of being so near the Emperor that gave me the megrims. A flick of the imperial finger could have a man burned alive or make him rich enough to buy an entire heged. Ivan's word could destroy a kingdom, could wipe out twenty thousand lives of grace and beauty, could rape a sweet land . . .

. . . *a land of thick green grass . . . of rolling meadows and open forests of oak and ash and pine, laced with clear, cool streams, a land of balmy breezes and tender, starlit nights. . . . The starlight on the circle of white marble columns was bright enough to give light to the forest glade. Why was it always night when the call would come? Nights were for walking moonlit paths to meet friends gathered around sparkling fires. To engage in long talks about the universe that made no sense in the day. To put your arm around warm shoulders and follow the music that wafted its way through the trees like wood smoke . . . inviting . . . welcoming. But that night I walked the path away from friends*

*and fire toward the circle of white, where Ysanne would
send me out to do battle. . . .*

Verdonne, what was I doing? Desperately I cast my eyes
downward and memorized the lines of my trembling hand.
Not yet. Not yet. I pushed the vision away . . . walled it up
again . . . and waited for the guard to return.

"He's coming out. I hope you've got something as he
wants to hear."

Well, he wanted to hear it, but he wasn't going to like it.

Aleksander stepped through the heavy velvet curtain. His
high-necked black tunic was trimmed in silver; silver bands
set with amethyst bound his full sleeves and his neck. Black
did not sit well on him, but left him looking pale and ill in
the lamplight. He grabbed my arm before I could kneel.
"What news, Seyonne?"

I read him the message from the rolled scrap of paper.

Your Highness,
The Lord Dmitri and five companions rode eastward
on the Jybbar Pass road ten days ago. The weather has
been moderate. I have dispatched a search party along
the route, and the House of Marag has sent its finest
scouts to aid us. I will send news as soon as I have any.

All glory and honor be yours in this time of celebration, and may this message find you rejoicing in the company of the Marshal Dmitri.
Your humble servant,
Rozhin, Chief Magistrate of Avenkhar

"Damnation!" Aleksander slammed his fist into the
gallery wall. "Ten days. He should have been here in four."

The crowd in the ballroom let out a great sigh as the remaining lamps flicked out and were replaced by whirling
green and purple and blue. The sickly light made Aleksander's complexion look dead and his eyes sink into dark
pits. "Hang all this foolery. Tell Sovari to pack my gear and
have ten of my men ready to move in one hour."

"As you command, my lord."

"Your Highness, what keeps you? The entertainment is reaching its climax." The man who stepped through the velvet curtain was in a rich purple gown, sewn with gold thread. Though his purple cape was lined with gold and fastened by a massive gold clasp, he was not the Emperor. His flaxen hair was not braided, the shoulders were too slim for a Derzhi warrior, and the soft, accented voice was not the speech of the man who ruled most of the known world. His pale face was indistinct in the strange light, but I could see that he was a Khelid.

I bowed and remained in a submissive posture, wondering who he was. I did not know how to recognize Khelid rank.

"I've received word that my uncle is missing in the Jybbar Pass. I'm off to find him."

"But, Your Highness, the ceremonies . . . the Emperor . . . your guests . . ." Surprise. Kindly concern.

"They mean nothing if my uncle is endangered, Lord Kastavan."

Kastavan. The highest-ranking Khelid in Azhakstan. He who was persuading the Emperor to abandon Zhagad, the birthplace of the Derzhi. The man who had traded his mutilated king for Derzhi favor. I stole a closer glance at him, but his back was to me.

The music grew louder and more grotesque. The colors reflected on the walls and faces around me blended in nauseating profusion. Sweat dripped down between my shoulder blades. It made no sense.

"Of course, I understand," said Kastavan, laying a sympathetic hand on Aleksander's shoulders. "Most distressing. So send your slave to make ready while you watch the conclusion of our display. Only a few minutes more. Korelyi and Kenedar will wither in humiliation if you are not there to witness their triumph—it is unlike any magical event in the history of your fair Azhakstan. Designed especially for you."

Magical display . . . Korelyi. The nerve-scraping music.

The nauseating light. The memories that would scarcely keep buried. Demons.

"Be off, Seyonne, and do as I've said. Tell Sovari I'll be at the stables in an hour." I could scarcely hear the Prince, for the thunder of warning in my head. Now that I let it loose, I thought it might crumble my bones. Was it only the one demon I had seen or were there more of them? Surely the creeping horror that chilled my soul was not just from Korelyi.

"As you command, my lord," I said automatically.

The Prince and the Khelid moved toward the velvet curtain. My skin shriveled with what I had to do. I moved as if to go, then I stepped deliberately on the flowing purple cloak, holding it long enough to jerk the heavy gold clasp hard against the Khelid's throat. He staggered briefly and choked, then whirled about furiously as I stumbled off the purple silk and dropped to my knees. "A thousand pardons, my lord!" I cried and glanced upward. Just before Kastavan's hand crashed into my head, I glimpsed what I dreaded: a pair of cold blue eyes that spoke of soulless lust, lust that had found an evil nest very much to its liking. But the magnitude of what I saw took me beyond fear. This was beyond anything I had ever known, beyond anything any Ezzarian, living or dead, had ever seen. I had glimpsed a being from our most ancient writings, so fearful that we could not believe in it lest we refuse to venture our work in terror of encountering such a one. Korelyi was a small player. Kastavan . . . Kastavan was the Master.

I crawled away, trying to shake the darkness from my head, mumbling apologies, not daring to think lest the demon somehow read it.

"The slave will be punished for this," said Aleksander.

"No need," said the Khelid smoothly. "I'll not let a captive brute spoil your celebration. The slave can repay me by doing his duty. Come, Your Highness, and view the climax of the evening."

It seemed to be my good fortune—if good fortune could be said to apply in any encounter with demons—that Kasta-

van was preoccupied with Aleksander and whatever was
going on in the ballroom. But his very interest in the Prince
spoke of monumental deviltry, and I didn't know what to do
about it.

"You are more lenient than I," said Aleksander coldly,
then opened the curtain for his guest. "Please go in." As the
Khelid and the servant disappeared through the opening, the
Prince looked down at me in irritation. "Are you absolutely
mad?" he whispered.

"Don't go in, my lord," I said, huddling over my knees as
would be expected from a slave in imminent danger of the
Prince's wrath. At a gesture from Aleksander, the guards had
moved back to their station beside the stairs. "Find a reason.
Stay away from him."

"There is not reason enough. I cannot leave without informing my father. I'll be inside no more than five minutes.
Do as I told you and be ready to explain yourself when I return from the Jybbar." He shoved me toward the stairs with
his foot, then disappeared inside the curtain. The kick wasn't
hard, just enough to knock me off balance. I did the rest,
sprawling on the gallery floor and creeping away.

The guards shoved me down the stairs, but I didn't go all
the way down. I needed to be about the Prince's errand, yet
I had to understand what the Khelid were doing. I had seen
the Lord of Demons . . . the Gai Kyallet, the Changing
Face . . . one who could assume a hundred different aspects
when forced to take form, who was accounted impossible to
slay in a demon battle, because of its power and guile. Our
oldest writings claimed that the Gai Kyallet could draw the
demons together and set them to a common purpose, could
command them all with a single thought as a queen bee
ruled her hive. I could not imagine such danger.

I stood by the railing and looked out on the ballroom. The
end of the ballroom had disappeared, and in the open space
beyond the crowd was a world of marvels. Between the
sturdy granite columns existed a magical woodland with
youths and maidens chasing each other and laughing merrily
as they caught and kissed and ran away again. Fantastical

birds and beasts cavorted with them: a deer with a boar's head, a bird with an eagle's wings and the claws of a lion, a horse with a man's head. All through their games they danced to the squawking demon music, or maybe the enthralled onlookers heard the mellanghar or the mountain pipes in more familiar melody and it was only I who heard the demon music. A fragrant wind stirred the treetops and wafted into the audience, ruffling hair and gowns, stealing the breath of the astonished Derzhi.

Five Khelid stood to each side of the display. One of them walked into the crowd, took a young woman's hand, and drew her into the vision. When she stepped past the granite columns, her formal attire grew blurry and was replaced by country apparel, and instead of a silk fan, she carried a basket of flowers. Soon she was dancing with the rest, and the Khelid stepped out again and took the hand of a young man. There was wild applause and laughter from the audience.

I passed my hand before my eyes and shifted my senses. I expected to find enchantment. The vision was too elaborate; it could only be spell-wrought. And though I prayed not, I expected the Khelid magicians' eyes to be cold and dreadful like those of Korelyi and Kastavan. The presence of such a powerful demon was dreadfully serious, even if I discounted tales that had likely swollen with so many years of telling. But I came near drowning in horror at the entirety of the truth. The magical forest was no enchantment, but a place that was quite real. Somewhere a poor man or woman was clawing his head in madness, tearing at her own flesh, screaming at the horrors trapped inside. Soon the dancing youths would pull out their swords or the maidens bare their fangs. Perhaps the beasts would extend claws of steel or spew out poison or lick the dancers with tongues of flame. All would be blood and terror, destruction and madness. Perhaps the Derzhi spectators would see it; perhaps it would only play out in the broken mind. The demons might have other purposes in view. But it would happen, and the sad wretch whose soul they violated would never be the same again. I could not allow this to go on. For the forest was a landscape such as I traveled when I was a Warden, when I would step alone through the portal of a human soul and do battle with demons.

Chapter 14

I tried to go back to warn Aleksander. I begged, I groveled, I pulled out every reason, every excuse, offered every bribe or favor I could think of, whether possible or not, to persuade the guards to let me back up the stair. But they had seen the Prince kick me away, so they were in no mind to be persuaded that he would want to see me again. After ten fruitless attempts to sneak, push, and talk my way through, the guards threatened to put me in chains if I bothered them again. One of the guards threatened to tell Durgan I was mad, and in my frenzy of helpless dread, it was very near the truth.

The danger was unimaginable. The Khelid were working enchantments with the most profound sorcery that existed in the world, drawing on the madness of a tormented human soul. Yet I had no idea what they were trying to accomplish with it. Were the Derzhi guests the target, or was Aleksander, or the Emperor himself? Even if I could get to Aleksander, what could I tell him? That every Khelid in the palace might carry a demon within, and that their magic was dangerous, unholy, soul-destroying? That his father, the Emperor of the Derzhi, was likely in the thrall of the Gai Kyallet, the Lord of Demons, the most powerful of their kind, prophesied to lead the demons in a war to end the world? He would never believe me. Nor could I explain to him how he, Aleksander, carried within him the very thing demons hated most, the spark of strength and honor that could enable a man or woman to hold out against them. But only if he used it. Only if he nurtured it and humbled himself to its power.

Impossible. He is an arrogant, murdering Derzhi. His own people had stripped me of the very tools I needed to discover what was happening. I wished myself a thousand leagues away. Better to be dead. Better to be chained to the rocks in the depths of the Derzhi mines than to be faced with a dilemma so monumental in consequence and so wretchedly impossible to solve. Oaths and wishes had no bearing on the matter at all. I could not even get close enough to warn him.

From the ballroom came laughter and applause, and the howling music that covering my ears could not silence. The liveried sentinels who ringed the ballroom were not so obviously armed as the guards on the stair, but their ranks were no more penetrable. I could not see what was going on . . . and, in truth, I did not want to see. Whatever were the purposes of the demons, I could not stop them. Never had bondage been so bitter.

I slunk away from the ballroom, half sick with the aura of demon, and found Sovari, captain of the Prince's personal troop. I delivered Aleksander's orders, and Sovari immediately sent word to handpicked riders to make ready, and to the kitchen to prepare provisions for the group, and to the stable to have the horses saddled and loaded. Then he proceeded to Aleksander's chambers to collect the Prince's preferred weapons and riding clothes and winter cloaks. I snatched the opportunity. When the Derzhi captain walked past the door guards and into the Prince's apartments, I followed close on his heels. I lit candles and sat purposefully at the writing desk as if I had work to do there. Sovari sent the extra clothes to the stables, and piled the riding clothes and weapons on the table. Then he left. Pages of nonsense flowed from my pen as I waited, hoping to get five minutes with the Prince before he set off to chase Dmitri.

But Aleksander did not come. The hour passed, and then a second one.

"Are you sure of your message, slave?" Sovari demanded when he checked the room for the fifth time in half an hour.

"Upon my life, sir. He said to be ready to leave in one

hour. He planned only to make his farewells to the Emperor and the guests in the loge. Five minutes, he told me. Has the entertainment ended?"

"More than an hour since."

"I'm sorry, sir. I know nothing else."

"Maybe the Emperor forbade him to go," he mumbled to another warrior who stood in the doorway, dressed in thick clothing suitable for a midnight ride into the mountains.

"I'd like to think it," said the other. "Chasing into the Jybbar in the middle of the night . . . it's not how I'd choose to spend my dakrah feast."

"I'd surely not do it for my likai," said Sovari, and the two of them laughed as they walked out. I couldn't imagine how anyone could laugh on that night.

I let my pen fall on the sheet of gibberish in front of me, put my head in my hands, and tried to figure out what in the name of the stars I was to do. I had been trained from the age of five to see beyond the evidence of my eyes, to hear nuances unnoticeable to ordinary ears, to taste and feel and smell the slightest variations in the textures of the world so that I could oppose the works of demons. Yet these skills were honed to work with melydda, power I could no longer use.

Another hour passed. One by one the candles winked out. As the night winds howled, blowing rain and sleet against the windows and whining behind the draperies, a servant came in and built up the flagging fire. I stayed quiet in the dark, and she never saw me. Periodically Sovari would open the door, peer into the room at the untouched pile of riding clothes, and mutter a curse before slamming the door shut again. The world might have ended beyond the gilded panels of Aleksander's door.

I needed to leave. At some time soon, the Chamberlain's men were going to start looking for me, and the consequences of being "out of control" for so long would be severe. I was numb with dread, and I craved the safety of darkness and solitude and ignorance. One more hour. Then I would go.

I must have fallen asleep, for when I heard the door close softly, the fire was no more than glowing coals and my hand lay numb under the weight of my head. I held still and silent in the dark. Listening.

From the floor between the blue couch and the pulsing red coals of the hearth came a low growling. A mournful, animal sound. Aleksander had a pack of hunting dogs—sleek Kuzeh hounds that could outrace the fleetest fell-deer—but he didn't like them in his apartments. Perhaps someone had let one of them up from the kennels.

But on second hearing the quiet moan of anguish was very human. I crept across the room, my bare feet silent on the carpet, and peered down at the source of the noise. Curled up on the floor just next to the hearth was the Prince. Water pooled on the hearth tiles beneath his sodden black finery, and he was shivering violently.

I dropped to my knees at his side. "Your Highness, are you injured?"

He recoiled at my touch. "Who's there?" His voice was hoarse and wrenchingly tight.

"Seyonne, my lord. I was waiting to speak with you. Should I send for Giezek?"

"No . . . gods, no."

I grabbed blankets from his bed to throw over him, then stirred the coals and fed the fire to bring it back to life. Next I found brandy and a cup, and helped Aleksander sit up to drink it. There were dark smears on his face and on the shaking hands that gripped the wine cup. While he sipped and huddled close to the fire, I warmed a basin of water and found a clean towel.

"May I help you clean yourself, Your Highness?"

He was puzzled until I gestured toward his hands. The wine cup clattered to the hearth, and the dark liquid pooled on the tiles, then crept gleefully along the mortared crevices, hissing as it dribbled into the coals. "It was only a dream," whispered Aleksander. "A nightmare. I drank no wine or spirits. . . ." When he dipped his hands into the basin, red blood swirled into the clear water, and he jerked them out again as if they were scalded. "Madness."

"Are you injured, my lord? There's more blood on your face."

"It's not possible." He pushed the basin away, then snatched the damp towel and scrubbed wildly at his face before throwing the towel in the fire.

I took the basin away and emptied it. When I returned to the Prince, he was no longer shivering, but only staring at the fire with clenched hands pressed to his mouth. The orange flames left his skin sallow.

"Your Highness, is there anything else I can do for you?"

"No. Go away."

"If I may speak, my lord, there are things I must tell you about the Khelid. I suspect that my news might bear on whatever disturbs you so."

"Nothing has happened to me. I got drunk and walked about outside. That's all. Nothing more. Cut a finger . . . or something. . . ."

He offered no explanation of why no cut was visible or how he'd gotten drunk without drinking anything. I tried again. "What I was trying to tell you earlier was that this Khelid Kastavan also bears a rai-kirah—a very dangerous one. Far more dangerous than Korelyi's demon. My lord, I suspect all the Khelid in the palace are possessed by demons. I've never seen the like . . . so many at once, working together as they are. I cannot imagine the danger . . . and I know a great deal about demons."

"You look in their eyes, and you can see who bears demons and who does not. Is that the way of it?"

"Yes, my lord."

"Then, tell me what you see here." He jabbed a finger at his own eye. "Tell me that I am taken by a rai-kirah, then perhaps things will make sense."

I did as he asked. It was certainly possible, though rare, for a demon to reveal itself voluntarily. But the feadnach still burned within him, which meant no demon ruled there. He was not untouched, however. A veil of enchantment shadowed his bright center—exactly what I should have been able to guard him against.

"So it's true, is it?" He leaned back on the cushions heaped by the hearth and poured himself another cup of brandy from the flask I had left there. "I see it in your face. I'm one of them, too."

"No." Sluggish with fear and despair, it was very hard to make the shift back from the distance of my true seeing, so I had no sense left for caution in choosing words. "No, my lord, there is no demon in you—none you were not born with."

To my astonishment, after only a moment's pause, Aleksander burst into laughter—hearty, healthy, hopeless merriment. "I have never known anyone like you, Seyonne," he said, raising his cup in mock salute. "You mourn the universe while ignoring a knife pointed at your eye. Come, slave, tell me what you really think of me."

His laughter nagged and nipped at my spirits like an annoying pup, and before another moment passed, I was laughing with him. For ten minutes we wallowed in the silken cushions and chortled like drunken drovers. I had not laughed in a century. It cured nothing, reduced the magnitude of the dilemma not a whit, yet I took strength from it.

I rubbed my hand over my short hair trying to return some wit to my head. "We cannot laugh this away, my lord. I wish we could. There is no demon in you, but they have managed to bind you with an enchantment—a very nasty thing. It happened at the performance tonight, I would guess. The magic they worked was very powerful."

He lay back and gazed thoughtfully on the golden wine cup as it gleamed in the firelight. "I should kill all of you. Khelid and Ezzarians. Perhaps I will. All of this is words and mirrors and distractions. Theater props. None of it real." He wasn't going to tell me what had happened to him. He felt stronger, too, and believed he could resist it, whatever it was, just as he had resisted the sleeplessness.

"If you can control whatever they've done to you, you are stronger than any sorcerer."

"Nothing happened."

"Then, you should send me away, my lord. The farther, the better, for I am the one who is mad. But if whatever didn't happen should happen again, I might be of some help." I pressed my forehead to the floor, and started toward the door. "Shall I take a message to Captain Sovari?"

"Sovari!" He sat up straight. "Athos' balls, what time is it?"

"Somewhere in second watch," I said.

"Damn. Tell him to wake me at dawn, and we'll be off. Tell him . . . tell him I decided we needed to ride in daylight."

"As you command, my lord."

I left him poking at the fire, and crept past the attendants sleeping outside his door. After delivering his message to the Derzhi captain, who had been snoring under a horse blanket in the stables, I slipped up the back stair to the attic room and collapsed onto my pallet. Tired as I was, I could not sleep. *The Lord of Demons . . . here, working such magic . . . the war to end the world.* As I lay in the dark stale air, listening to the harrowing moans of slave dreams, my thoughts wandered into the dusty corridors of Ezzarian prophecy. The Scroll of Eddaus foretold a lost battle—a prophecy that many of my countrymen believed had been fulfilled with the Derzhi conquest. That writing was the same that spoke of the Gai Kyallet . . . and foretold a second battle, which, if lost, would leave the world in the thrall of demons. My people had been confidant that, however terrible our first defeat, this second and final battle was far in the future. All we had to do was make sure that some of us survived, to grow strong again. But what if we had been wrong? I threw my arms over my head and added my groans to those of my sleeping brethren. I could not bear to think.

The Prince did not leave at dawn. He was nowhere to be found when Sovari came to wake him, so I heard. I heard a number of the rumors that flitted through the palace that day. After administering five lashes and a solid beating with his

padded truncheon and putting me on half rations for a month
for my evening's disappearance, Boresh set me to scrubbing
floor tiles. I guessed that the expanse of floor in the Summer
Palace could have paved all the kingdom of Manganar. But
even through the haze of hunger and pain and too little
sleep, I heard the talk as I worked.

*The Prince is ill. The Prince regrets his impulse to search
for Lord Dmitri. After all, he detests the old man. Has
threatened to poison him. Has cursed him and tried to keep
him away from Capharna. There's ill luck hanging over this
dakrah: the Marshal Dmitri missing, the bandit raids at
Erum. Beasts have come down from the mountains and been
seen in the city. A tavern keeper was mauled in the last
night.*

Sometime just after midday, I moved my aching knees to
yet another square of cold slate in the gallery that separated
the residential wing from the administrative wing of the
palace. As I gritted my teeth and dipped my raw hand into
the water pail yet again, two men hurried past. One of them
was Aleksander, fastening the high collar on a green tunic as
he walked. ". . . do not need to explain myself to anyone,"
he said. "Now, I'm late. . . ."

Aleksander hurried on, while his companion stopped and
put his hands on his hips in exasperation. It was Sovari.

"May I be of service, Captain?" I said, pausing for a moment to ease my burning shoulders.

In one glance he took in my identity and the bloody tunic
stuck to my back. "We've both felt the brunt of this night's
doings it seems," he said.

"I've had better mornings," I said.

"He changed his mind. We're not to go after the Marshal,
after staying up half the night to be ready. He's sent another
party into the Jybbar. I've been put on report for upsetting
the household. I may have lashes of my own coming."

"I'm sorry, Captain. I only brought the message I was
told."

"We all do as we're told, but some days it doesn't seem
to matter."

* * *

I saw no more of Aleksander that day. I worked until two
hours past midnight before finishing. Neither mind nor body
could function any longer, and I was glad for it. Not even the
growling in my belly would keep me awake. But as I stumbled up the attic stair ready to ease my weary bones and torn
flesh onto the pallet, a hand gripped my arm and a whisper
burst upon my ear. "Come with me, Ezzarian."

"I've done everything required, Master Boresh," I mumbled. "If you have more floors to be cleaned—"

"Quiet." The hand dragged me away from the barracks-
room door and the snoring guard, and down another back
stair. Who was it? Boresh had no need for secrecy. As we
turned at a landing, a sliver of moonlight penetrated a grimy
window and fell on a broad, flat Manganar face encircled by
wiry, gray-streaked hair.

"Master Durgan!"

"I said to close your mouth. Just come."

I no longer resisted, but went willing, curiosity pumping
a bit of life into my legs. We emerged in the brick-paved
kitchen courtyard and wound our way through the snow-
covered barrels, crates, and piles of rusty stovepipes, and
past the stinking refuse heaps and the bins of smoldering
ashes. Durgan led me not into the slave house, but into a
long, open work shed at the far side of it. At one end of the
shed was a storeroom, where spare ropes and chain and pul-
leys and such things were kept. We stopped at the storeroom
door.

"I grew up in the southern lands," said the slave master,
"where strange tales of good and evil were told at our hearth
fires . . . my gran always said we could feel safe, living
close to the sorcerers' land as we did. She said the Ezzarian
sorcerers kept faithful watch and held the darkness away. In
truth, I've not slept easy in all the years since Ezzaria's fall.
There's evil abroad in the land. These past weeks, I've felt it
close, and tonight I know it. Did you hear of the beast that
roamed the city last night?"

"I heard that a bear or a mountain cat of some kind

mauled an innkeeper. Probably waked hungry from winter sleep. . . ."

"I thought the same. I was watching for it, thinking it might show up here near the refuse heaps, and sure enough, tonight I saw it slinking through the courtyard. I gave chase and it ran in here, but when I got my sword and ventured inside, it was no beast I found."

All the dread from the previous night surged through my veins, shoving my weariness aside. I knew what I would find when Durgan opened the door. "Get blankets and hot tea or wine," I said, and I stepped into the storeroom and knelt beside Prince Aleksander.

"My lord, can you hear me?"

He was cowering in the corner, his eyes golden pools of fear with no sense or intelligence in them. The green tunic was torn and stained, and his feet were bare. Just as on the previous night, he was shivering violently, and a low, feral moan rumbled from his chest.

"We'll soon have you warm again," I said. I tried to examine him for injuries, but he snarled and shrank away. I spoke to him calmly, though, and by the time Durgan was back with blankets and a pot of boiling nazrheel, I had determined that his body was unharmed. I scooped a cup of the strong tea from Durgan's pot and held it close to Aleksander's face so the steam might warm him and the familiar scent draw his senses into some sort of focus. Soon I had him sipping from the cup, the clouds slowly clearing from his eyes.

"We need a fire," I said to the slave master. "Somewhere we won't be disturbed."

"The gardener's workroom," he said. "No one will be there this time of year." He pointed the way, then hurried ahead to light a fire.

I gave Aleksander more tea and tried to get him up and moving. He curled into a tight ball, covering his head with his arms and groaning in shaking misery. "Madness," he whispered hoarsely. "I've gone mad."

"No, you've not," I said. "I told you there was a spell on

you. If I'm to help you, I need to know what's happening."
From Durgan's tale I feared the worst. "But come with me,
and we'll get you warm first."

The gardener's shed smelled of cold earth and damp
wood. Overturned pots and empty barrels, withered plants
and rusty tools littered the place that would not come to life
again for two months yet. Gardeners had a short working
season in Capharna. Durgan had a fine fire going in the
smoke-grimed brick hearth, and we got Aleksander settled
by it. I hinted to Durgan that it was important that someone
stand guard in the courtyard until the Prince was recovered,
and, to my satisfaction, he took my suggestion. I didn't want
to be interrupted.

"How does it begin?" I said. "Do you feel it coming?"

"Hot," said the Prince, rubbing his face with a filthy
hand. "So hot I can't breathe. The first time I thought it was
from dancing. They got me dancing in their cursed playact-
ing. When it was over, I needed air, so I stepped outside. . . ."

"And you felt the change begin."

"Gods of night . . . I've never felt anything like. As if my
bones are bending out of shape but won't break, as if my
flesh is ripping apart. The world . . . everything . . . goes
dark, and when I can see again . . ." He looked up, bewildered, anguished. ". . . I can't think. I can't remember.
Everything looks so different . . . the colors all drained
away, the angles and positions peculiar. And the smells . . . I
think I'm going to drown in the stink. That's when I go mad.
I have this dream . . . It must be a dream." He shuddered and
pulled the threadbare blanket tight about his shoulders. "I
wake up like this. What's happening to me?"

"How often has it happened?"

"Three times. Last night when you found me. This morning . . . I woke before dawn thinking the bed was on fire. I
ran outside and came to myself halfway up Mount Nerod in
the middle of the morning. Then this afternoon, we were
doing something . . . swearing . . . the Twenty Hegeds
swearing fealty. I couldn't finish it. Said I was sick and hid

out in the kitchen garden. No one would be there to see. . . . It's impossible. Why do I even speak of it?"

"It is a demon enchantment, my lord. I saw it in you, but I didn't know what it would do."

"So is it like before . . . some trinket . . . some poison? Tell me how to stop it."

I wished I could tell him. "This one is not so simple, my lord. It's not a spell bound to an artifact, but one that's been buried in you by their magic. It is part of you until a Khelid . . . or someone . . . takes it away. We need to find out what they want of you."

"What they want?"

Exhaustion kept creeping in between me and clear thinking, and my torn back was bleeding again where Aleksander had leaned on it as I helped him to the gardener's shed. I rubbed the back of my neck and tried to shake off my dullness. "Have the Khelid . . . this Kastavan . . . has he said anything to you? Have you argued with him . . . defied him . . . angered him? He thinks to gain something from this affliction."

"No. I've told him I think it's stupid to build a new capital, no matter how fine it would be. But my father is going ahead with it anyway, and he's not likely to die any time soon. It doesn't really matter what I think about anything."

"What happens if you can't finish the dakrah? If you can't be anointed?"

"Not finish . . . ? It can't happen. Whatever isn't done one day, can be done the next. I will be anointed, whether on my birthday in front of two thousand people or a week later in my father's bedchamber with a scullery maid to witness it. It makes no difference."

"Unless your father chooses someone else to succeed him."

Even while trembling with pain and cold, Aleksander could shrink one to the size of a gnat with his scorn. "I'm his only legitimate son. Dmitri is his only brother and has no sons. My male cousins are all of the female line. If I were a puling leper, my father would anoint no one else."

"But your father will want to go back to Zhagad to pursue his plans, not stay here to wait for you to recover from some strange 'illness.' That will mean more delay. And if Kastavan has been able to convince the Emperor to abandon Zhagad—the Pearl of Azhakstan—what else will he be able to convince him of? Perhaps your father will find himself unable to sleep or unable to take a woman to his bed."

"Druya's horns." There was a tremor beneath the quiet curse. "Why don't they just kill me and be done with it?"

I shook my head. "What would your father do if you were found dead?"

Even as he said it, Aleksander's eyes widened in understanding. "He would torture and kill every man, woman and child in Azhakstan until he found out who had done it."

"Therefore, they cannot kill you."

"So the dakrah must be completed." He breathed deeply. "I'll have to tell him . . . something. I'll have you explain it."

"No!" My blood curdled at the thought of Ivan, and thus Kastavan, so much as hearing my name. "It would endanger the Emperor. If the demons have no game to play, then they will take what pleasures they can from chaos. We must get you through the dakrah. There are only three more days." And then I would need to think more about demons and prophecy, and knowledge that I had no means to act on.

"But how do I stop this . . . change? You said—"

"We can't stop it. We might be able to control it . . . no, not completely." I had to quench the desperate hope that flared up in his face. "You must have Giezek give you something to make you sleep. Enough that a turret falling on your head will not wake you from the moment you recline until the moment you absolutely must be up. You cannot afford to dream."

"I can see to that. And what of waking hours?"

"That will be more difficult." Impossible, most likely. The nighttime change would be triggered by dreams, but in the day . . . "If you would, my lord, tell me everything that you remember from this afternoon and last night."

I led him through it three times. Each time he swore he
had told me all, but each time I pulled out more details. But
which detail was the important one? Was it that he had been
impatient? No, or else he would have been shape-shifting
before my eyes in the dark gardener's shed. Was it that he
had felt the stirrings of desire at the sight of a woman? If so,
we would never be able to hold it off. "But you were not
angry at the heged lords for taking so long with their
speeches?"

"I said not! Why do you care? This is intolerable."

"We've got to discover the trigger, the thing that sets it
off. It could be an emotion, a smell, a sound, the touch of
flesh, the taste of cheese, anything."

"I remember nothing about it. So what do I do?"

"You must avoid anything that you ate, drank, or touched
on those occasions. If you find yourself growing angry or
distracted or drowsy, fix your mind on a single image—
something you like. Something that encompasses your entire being when you consider it—and something you've not
thought of these past two days. Submerge yourself in it until
the disturbance is past. Perhaps that will get you through
these next days."

"And if not?"

"Send for me. I cannot prevent it, but perhaps I can help
you endure it. Your mind is not gone away with the enchantment."

Aleksander fingered a strand of pearls that dangled from
his torn tunic. "I can't believe any of this. The longer I sit
here, the more convinced I am that nothing happened. It's all
an illusion, like that cursed forest in the ballroom."

It was too late and we were too tired for me to explain
about the forest. But I could have no mercy on him. "A man
in the town had his throat ripped out last night by some kind
of large cat or bear roaming the streets. Durgan saw such a
beast on this night, my lord. He saw it run into the storage
room behind the slave house, and when he followed it, with
a sword in his hand ready to slay the beast, he found you. No

illusion leaves a man bleeding to death in the streets of Capharna."

The color that had returned to Aleksander's face as we talked drained away again. "Gods of night . . ."

"I'm sorry. I wish I could have prevented this."

He took a deep breath. It was not difficult to imagine the whispers of horror and dread crowding together in the place behind his eyes. "What if the Khelid don't stop it? How am I to be rid of it? I am to be Emperor."

Yes. The essential question. I could not yet bring myself to think of the only answer. "We'll have to find someone to help you." I stared down at my dirty, raw, useless hands and began once more to trace their outline.

As if reading the part of my mind I forbade myself, Aleksander said softly, "Could you have done it . . . before you were taken?"

"Yes."

I expected a barrage of questions, of demands or speeches, perhaps threats. But he just said, "Would I could undo what has been done." And it was not only for himself he said it.

Chapter 15

I slept in Aleksander's chambers that night, on the floor in front of his hearth. In the nine years since I had been brought to Capharna I had never slept warm, so I kept waking up from the strangeness of it, then sinking into blissful slumber again.

The first thing on the next morning, after he had drunk enough strong tea to clear his head of Giezek's sleeping draught, Aleksander sent for Fendular. The High Chamberlain arrived to find Aleksander wearing only a loincloth. The Prince was to run in the footrace to the top of Mount Nerod that morning along with three hundred other young Derzhi men. The loincloth was the traditional garb, no matter the fat, wet snowflakes drifting from the gray sky.

"Chamberlain, I have decided that my writing slave is not available for household service until after the dakrah. He is to be held for my exclusive use. Durgan will see to his sleeping and feeding and discipline."

"Of course, Your Highness," said the man, pursing his full lips into a disapproving pucker. "As you please. But may I ask why? We have need of every hand to keep your house fit for the glory of these days."

"Ah, but you see. It's exactly that." The Prince sat on a stool with his arms outstretched while his body slaves oiled his back and chest and arms, and laced sandals on his feet for the procession through the city. The race would be run barefoot, of course. Derzhi warriors were nothing if not respectful of their traditions. "I have decided that the tale of my dakrah must be written down for my sons to hear. I don't trust these singers and lore masters to get the story right. The Ezzarian has the most pleasing hand of all the palace scribes, so he must write it. Then I shall hear it read and judge if it has been recorded correctly."

"But, my lord, should it not be our own Derzhi scribes who write this tale, rather than some sneaking barbarian?"

Fendular's protest was scarcely aired when Aleksander began screaming at him, accusing him of treasonous insolence. The torrent of abuse was a very model of a princely tantrum. The Chamberlain escaped the room before the wineglasses started flying, and Aleksander dissolved into laughter that his nervous servants and gentleman attendants did not understand. I think he was relieved that he had only acted the beast and not turned into one.

We had agreed that it would be unwise for me to attend the dakrah ceremonies. The presence of a slave would be too noticeable. I would remain in the Prince's map room writing, and Durgan would keep watch on the kitchen garden. The slave master would send for me if Aleksander . . . or whatever Aleksander became . . . arrived there. The Prince was certain he could make it so far, if the change came upon him again.

As Aleksander made ready to leave his apartments, one of his bustling gentlemen called to him, "Shall you win today, Lord Prince?"

He answered, "A race encompasses my entire being. I can fix my mind firmly on it and think of nothing else. I will not lose." His eyes met mine, and he grinned.

It was the tenth day of the dakrah.

Aleksander did win the race, whether because of his true prowess or because no one would dare surpass him, I wasn't sure. Though I had no doubts of his strength and speed, I suspected the latter. He had commanded his attendants to bring me hourly reports for the "history" that I was writing, so I learned that he drank only nazrheel at the victor's banquet, and ate only dakhfruit, claiming that during his run with the god, Athos had told him to purify himself before the day of his anointing.

Many hours later he returned to his apartments to be bathed and dressed for the evening. I remained in the map room as would be expected. Before leaving again, he stepped into the room, followed by two attendants frantically trying to put the final touches on his five resplendent layers of green and gold brocade and silk. He looked over my shoulder, where I was diligently transcribing the latest reports of his activities as told me by the scowling under-chamberlain, who sat on a stool beside me. "So the work progresses," said the Prince.

"Indeed, my lord. Besides writing of today's victory, I have also begun the account of the first day's events, from the recollections of your servants. I pray that my work will honor the trust you've given me."

"I will judge your work when the dakrah is finished. As for now, proceed as I've told you."

I bowed my head. "As you command, Your Highness."

Just as he walked out of the map room, he called to another slave. "Make sure my fire is built up. I've been cold all day."

I smiled to myself, which drew a puzzled stare from the irritated under-chamberlain. "Pardon, sir," I said. "I was distracted. You were speaking of the first night's menu . . ."

It was quite late when a clamor of voices, boots, steel, and glassware from the nearby rooms announced the Prince's return. "Just go," he said, his words running over each other, stumbling over a thick tongue. "I need nothing but to get out of these gaud-rags and find my bed. Get out, all of you. Hessio can do what's required."

After a flurry of honorings and farewells, the noise died away. The quiet, fair body slave Hessio, a Basranni youth gelded before he reached manhood, as were all those destined for such intimate service to the royal family, soon followed the others out of the door. The lamp girl had already snuffed out most of the lamps and candles. I had been sitting in the dark for half an hour, and only after I was sure that no one remained in the rest of the Prince's chambers, did I venture out. Aleksander was sprawled across his bed, only half undressed, sleeping the sleep that was the image of death, a blue vial clutched in his hand. I removed the vial and slipped out the door through the candle room. No one was there to see me. Aleksander had dismissed the guard earlier in the day, sending him to march about the walls until dawn as a punishment for being ugly, and had issued no orders for the man to be replaced.

One day gone.

The eleventh day of the dakrah festival saw a watery sun rise over Mount Nerod. If it was an omen, I had no way to interpret it, but the day started out badly. A search party arrived from Avenkhar with no word of Dmitri. The five soldiers sent by the magistrate of Avenkhar had followed the southern route to Capharna in case the Marshal had taken a detour from the dangerous Jybbar road. The party Aleksander had sent into the Jybbar had not yet returned.

I watched the Prince carefully as he listened to the report. If the demon enchantment was triggered by strong emotion, I guessed it might happen with the news of the fruitless search. Anger, exasperation, impatience, guilt—all made their appearance to a watchful eye, but the Prince showed no ill effects.

The day's ceremonies were to be more formal than those of the past ten: a series of rites and blessings leading up to the solemnity of the anointing on the next day. As on the previous day, I retreated to the map room while the slave master kept his watch in the kitchen garden. From the household gentlemen who came to give me their hourly reports, I learned of ceremonial wine cups and burnings of incense, of recitations of Derzhi history so interminable they would bore a doorpost, of kisses exchanged and symbolic wooden sticks broken. At sunset, Aleksander would surrender his sword and his signet ring to his father as a final gesture of submission, then he would drink away the evening with the other young nobles who were still under the age of majority. The Emperor and Empress would host the older guests in a separate dining room.

I was finishing up the transcription of the most recent report, when a guard dragged in Filip, the albino boy from the slave house. "Says he's got a message for the writing slave," said the guard, holding the scrawny child at arm's length. "I didn't trust him to come into the Prince's chambers on his own. Fryth steal whatever's not nailed down."

Hoping that the pounding of my heart would not alert the guard, I nodded.

"You're wanted," said the boy, picking his nose and gaping at the splendor. "By Master Durgan."

"Of course. Right away," I said, pushing the child aside and starting to run, not pausing to stopper the ink or wipe my hands.

I could not get through the interminable passages fast enough. I had to be with Aleksander before the change was complete. "Ezzarian!" A high-pitched voice called out to me as I ran through the door into the cloisters. Boresh. I dodged into a dark doorway and struggled to silence my breathing as he passed. The prune-faced under-chamberlain stood in the columned passage frowning, looking this way and that and fingering the small whip he carried at his belt. "Where have you got off to in such a hurry, slave?" he murmured to himself. It seemed an eternity until he strolled back the way he had come. I streaked through the cavernous washhouse and the billowing heat of the kitchens, across the bustling kitchen courtyard, past storehouses and workshops, and through the iron gate that led to the winter-blighted wasteland of the palace kitchen gardens.

A single, sharply angled beam of sunlight escaped the dome of heavy clouds, casting an eerie, orange light on the bleak landscape, while the first cold spatters of rain fell from overhead. Dirty snow lay in crusted patches in the corners of the herb garden. Mats of dead plants carpeted the wood-squared sections, and overturned barrows and rolls of rotted netting were abandoned alongside the path. The far wall, lined with trellises supporting a year's dead growth, separated the herb garden from the larger main kitchen garden.

Thunder rumbled in the blackening east as I followed muddy boot prints into the walled enclosure.

Ranks of ancient fruit trees, gnarled and barren, divided the garden, and it was from behind the trees that I heard a soul-chilling cry of agony. I ran toward the sound and almost crashed into Durgan, transfixed in horror, holding his sword in one hand and clutching a spreading tree branch with another.

The Prince was on his knees in the mud, his back bent forward, his clenched fists drawn tightly to his face. As if the worsening rain blurred my vision, the outline of his body wavered: the curve of his back stretching, his head swelling, his torso thickening, his long legs bending into impossible shapes. The green and gold of his clothing pulsed and swirled into a uniform golden tan. For an agonizing span of time the two images wavered—the man and the beast—and such a wave of bitter cold swept through that garden that I thought we must be frozen where we stood. Aleksander stretched out his arms and cried out . . . his groan taking on a fearsome, guttural fury as the images shifted again.

By this time I was but an arm span away. I dared not touch him, but I called out as calmly and evenly as I could. "Aleksander, Prince of the Derzhi, hear my words. Though you feel yourself consumed by pain and enchantment, you are not lost." The words flowed from my tongue as though I had practiced them only hours before, instead of lifetimes. "The enchantment controls your body, but you are in control of your mind. Listen to my voice. Take hold of it. Though I cannot come with you into that fearful place, you will not be alone. Our joining will bridge the barriers of this vile spell and prevent the doors closing on the life you know. You will remain in control of your actions and your thoughts, and you will yield no victory to those who have brought you to this pass."

The change was almost complete. As the last beam of the distant sunset was swallowed by the oncoming night, I glimpsed a last flicker of green satin and red hair and heard a last brief cry of anguish . . . and before me lay a shengar, a

rock lion, the vicious wildcat native to the Azhak mountains.
It . . . he . . . leaped to his feet and confronted me, teeth
bared, roaring in pain-racked fury.

"For the love of Athos, Ezzarian, come away." The trembling slave master laid a hand on my shoulder.

"Prince Aleksander will not harm me," I said. "He is in
full control of himself." I hoped.

The beast, its weight twice that of a man and its length
from head to tail half again Aleksander's height, writhed its
head and emitted a long low snarl that grated fearfully on the
nerves. It moved slowly to the right, then to the left again,
never taking its eyes from my own. I remained kneeling, unmoving, gazing into the wild amber eyes that were yet so
much of Aleksander.

"I will stay with you, my lord, and we will talk. I will
talk, I suppose, though I have no idea what I'm going to talk
about. You'll have to forgive me if I rattle a bit, and I'll have
to hope that you'll forget much of what I say when you
change back to yourself. It has been a very long time since I
had much conversation. As you have observed so frequently,
a slave does not speak openly to his Derzhi masters. And
whatever conversation I had with other slaves, in the early
days when I indulged in such foolishness, is perhaps not
suitable for my lord's ears. Not very flattering to the Derzhi
or their Empire."

The beast lowered its head and screamed such fury into
my face that the heat of it warmed my cold fingers. Durgan
raised his sword, but I laid my hand on the blade and pushed
it aside.

"The Prince will not thank you for sticking him, Master
Durgan. You see how he chastises me for my insolence. But
I know who is there beneath this illusion. And I have told
him several times that he does not frighten me."

"Can you read his thoughts?" whispered Durgan over my
shoulder.

"No. I can only guess his thoughts from what I know of
him. Can't you see him here? I say the least word insulting

the reputation of the Derzhi, and he tries to intimidate me. He is a bully . . ."

"The gods silence your tongue, Ezzarian! He'll have your head."

". . . a rogue, and an arrogant beast. But there must be something more to him, something finer buried beneath his skin, else demons would not need to spend this much trouble on him. He has only to seek it out and pay it heed . . . which, in the end, may be much more trouble than this enchantment."

The Aleksander-beast circled us, gliding smoothly on its dinner-plate-sized paws, powerful muscles rippling under the tawny coat. I stayed still and hoped I had not gone too far. If I angered him too much, he might break off his connection with me and become imprisoned in the small mind and passions of the beast. I doubted Durgan or I would survive such a resolution. If it happened too often, neither would Aleksander.

Hot breath steamed on the back of my neck. I did not move. "You are in control, my lord," I said. "You will do only as you please. But you must not ignore wholly what this body demands of you. If you thirst, you must let it drink. If you hunger . . . you must judge . . . and eat what is fit without shame or disgust. If you need to run, you must do it, combining your own caution and skills with those of the beast to avoid danger. Attend to the senses you have been given, for they will protect you, but use your own mind to understand those things the beast cannot . . . like hunters and bowmen and innocents who will fear you and suffer from your strength. Your people, my lord. Those the gods have given into your charge."

He moved away from my back and circled the garden restlessly. If my tunic had not been drenched with the rain, a torrent of sweat would have made it so.

"Do you think he hears you?" asked the slave master.

"I hope," I said, feeling suddenly weak and chilled, shivering in the steady rain. "Did he say anything when he came?"

"Only to send for you, and to get my sword."

"To get your sword?"

"He said, 'Get the Ezzarian . . . the sword.' So I thought I was to get it."

"I don't think he meant for you to kill him, though."

While Aleksander continued to lope about the perimeters of the garden, Durgan asked if we dared move, as he needed to be off for a few minutes.

"Go ahead. I'll stay here." I didn't expect him to return. Shengars were vicious and unpredictable.

The burly Manganar was back in five minutes. I knew he was come when he laid a scratchy wool cloak over my bare shoulders. Blessedly dry. "Thank you," I said.

"It's only right. You've no call to help him."

"I'm not helping either of you," I said, drawing the dry warmth around me and indulging the bitterness that often welled up when I found myself grateful for the pitiful scraps that should be a man's right. "Never think it."

"But you are one of the guardians? You fight the darkness, as my gran told us?"

"In the only way left to me."

"Does the Prince know what you are?"

I watched the great cat roam the vast garden, stretching its long muscles.

"I am only a slave with a bit of knowledge," I said. "And I will never be anything else."

Unwilling or unable to argue the point, Durgan moved back toward the fruit trees and settled himself to watch the garden entrance.

After a time Aleksander came back to me. He growled softly and circled. I gathered that he wanted me to talk again. "Shall I speak gibberish to you?" I said, drowsiness and the proximity of enchantment leaving me fey and careless. "Shall I tell you tales? Or sing? Or shall I speak of women or books or the life of trees? Or tell of the stars in the southern skies . . . if there are still stars somewhere? Too bad. Once I knew something of those things, but no longer. Perhaps I will speak of cleaning tile floors and the places I

have seen cracks in your foundation, or I'll tell you that your
pen maker is cheating you because the reeds he uses are not
the best."

I cared nothing for Aleksander. His few kindnesses had
been only more scraps. *Give the slave a bite of meat without
gristle. Give him two cups of water. Ah, yes, a hand under
his arm when I've kicked him half to death. Only one lash
today, Ezzarian. No matter that we've taken your life and
your soul and crushed them beyond repairing. No matter
that if you were set free this very hour, you could never go
back. Never.* I rolled onto my hands and knees and vomited
up bile.

Aleksander shied away, hissing at the foulness I left on
the ground. "Come back," I called wearily. I tugged the sodden cloak about my shoulders, then, shaking and empty,
turned my face to the sky, letting the rain cool and wash my
face. "I'll not leave you. Kastavan and his evil twin will not
be rid of either of us so easily."

I spoke of the weather and the land, mostly how the
weather in Capharna was so different from what I had grown
up with, though we, too, had a great deal of rain. It was the
only thing I could come up with that was not bitterness or
horror or implacably dull because I had shut off the well-
springs of thought while I existed in the Derzhi world. And
while any memory of Ezzaria was painful, geography was
about as distant as I could get from anything truly important.

For more than three hours I talked and soothed the restless lion prince, until my eyelids were sagging and my
words stumbling. Then the shengar screamed, and it startled
me awake. I was confused and groggy, and fell backward
into the mud, my heart drumming like a smith's hammer.

"Aleksander!" I called, afraid I had let him slip away.

A blast of heat like that of a dry pine bough thrown on a
fire threatened to set my wet hair on fire. A flash of green
and red. A shapeless form—two entwined images—writhed
in the mud battling with itself. A wrenching groan escaped
amid snarls and growls, as if a living man were being devoured by the maddened beast. I scooted backward, slither-

ing through the mud so the battle could not touch me. Fifteen minutes it took for the enchantment to wane and leave
the long, lean figure sprawled facedown in the mud, rain
spattering on the red hair and green satin. No sooner had the
last trace of the shengar disappeared than I heard a hoarse
whisper through chattering teeth, "A bully, am I?"

"Indeed, my lord, you are. And well you know it." I
helped him up and hung the sodden cloak about his broad
shoulders.

"Then, you must confess that you are my guardian spirit,
Seyonne. If I can no longer pretend, then neither shall you."

Our eyes met for a moment. I looked away first. In the
depths of his soul, the feadnach burned.

Chapter 16

We retreated to the gardener's shed again, though Aleksander swore he was done with skulking about in filth. "I can rid my apartments of listeners well enough," he said, "and I won't have to sit about wet." He was in immensely good spirits, considering what he had just been through. "And I'm ravenous. Next time find me a herd of fell-deer. There wasn't even a rabbit in that garden."

Next time. He spoke of it as if it were a dinner party, even while he was yet shivering uncontrollably from the release of the enchantment.

I, on the other hand, was exhausted and afraid. Dealing with demon enchantments when I was powerless was fearful at best, and Aleksander's frivolous approach to melydda was unnerving. "One more day, Your Highness," I said. "When your father's thumb is on your forehead bearing the oil of chesem, then you may feel like we've accomplished something."

"It was the sword," he said, cupping the steaming mug of nazrheel in his still trembling hands and inhaling the foul odor with satisfaction. "And Dmitri. I'm sure of it."

It took me a moment to realize what he meant. "The trigger?"

"I was to surrender my sword to my father—a symbol of my last night of youth. I unsheathed it and laid it on my palms, and as I stood there looking on it, I couldn't help but think of how Dmitri ought to be here with me in these days. Magical foolery is nothing compared to this punishment he has contrived. Stubborn old villain."

"You don't think—"

"There is no bandit party could hinder my uncle. He's taken as many as twenty of them single-handed without breaking a sweat. And the warriors of his traveling cadre are only slightly less skilled. No. Dmitri, ever the likai, is teaching me a lesson."

"And you believe that the thought of him together with the touch of a sword sets off the enchantment?"

"The first night I was dancing in this damned Khelid magic trick, and I had taken off my sword. When we were done, I put it back on . . ."

". . . and you thought of what you had planned to be doing."

"Exactly. The second time was when I was sleeping, of course, but the third, when the heged lords were swearing to support my father's choice of successor, I held their swords. Baron Demiska is Dmitri's old comrade. . . ."

I sighed. "It sounds quite likely. And so tomorrow . . ."

"I will touch no swords, and I'll do my best not to think of the despicable bastard."

"Stay cautious, my lord," I said. "If the Khelid get any hint that you've figured it out, they could alter the spell or attempt another."

"Tomorrow is my dakrah, Seyonne. I will be anointed Emperor-in-waiting. Were they to make me a jackal, do not imagine I would yield." He was supremely confidant.

I was not. There were never any certainties when facing the rai-kirah, and I could not imagine the purposes of a Gai Kyallet. Had the Khelid made some bargain with the Lord of Demons, or had their greed and ambition only made them fodder for its unfathomable purposes? Nothing in all the lore I had studied gave me any answers. While Aleksander finished his nazrheel, I dredged up everything I knew that might give me some clue as to these happenings. And so I found myself thinking again of the Eddaic Prophecy, and its warning of a First and a Second Battle in the war to end the world. Ezzarians had believed that the First Battle, the Derzhi conquest of Ezzaria, had been lost as the prophets foretold, but had taken solace in the prediction that the Second Battle would only take place when those same "conquerors from the north" had become one with the demons. If any of us survived, we would have plenty of time to recover, to prepare before all of the Derzhi could be possessed. But what if the conquerors from the north were not the Derzhi, but the Khelid, a race already one with the demons? I could not dismiss the thought of it. I no longer had faith in gods or prophecies, but the tale nagged at me as I helped the Prince to his feet, and checked outside the garden shed for prying eyes. There were other parts to the prophecy, too: stories of a warrior, a man with two souls who would step forward to take on the Lord of Demons and prevent the doom of the world . . . and there I had to end my useless ramblings. I didn't know anyone with one undamaged soul, much less two.

I returned with Aleksander to his apartments. Though it was well into second watch, lights were blazing, and soldiers and householders were everywhere. When the Prince was recognized beneath the mud and soggy finery, thirty shocked attendants tried to examine, undress, avenge and interrogate him all at once.

"Where have you been, my lord? The Emperor is most . . . most disturbed at your absence." Sovari, being an experienced commander, got the upper hand on the chaos. "He's got search parties scouring the palace and the town. When he heard you didn't show up for the feasting . . ."

"Clear out! All of you, out of here," commanded the Prince, batting away the hands of solicitous servants, and pushing away cups of wine and nazrheel being shoved in his face. "Is it inconceivable that I have an hour to myself? I'm sick of guests and ceremonies and feasting."

"An hour, Your Highness, but it's been six! You ran out of the ceremony, and no one knew where you'd gone." The warrior scanned the Prince's sodden disarray. "We thought you were ill. What's happened to you?"

"Nothing happened to me. I went walking in the rain. I

wanted to clear my head before tomorrow. To be alone for a while. I slipped and fell and got muddy. That's all."

"Walking alone . . . Then, what of him?" Sovari nodded at me, puzzled, with the slightest flavor of suspicion. I, too, was coated with mud. I had tried to slip back through the candle room, but the way was blocked. "One man suited your company, it seems."

"Hardly company." Aleksander snorted. "He is a slave, not a man." He rubbed his hands together, warming them by his hearth. "Gods' teeth, how is it I let you query me this way? If you didn't suit me so well, Sovari—"

"Of course, Your Highness," said the captain hastily. "I was only curious, as this slave seems to be everywhere these days. What message should I take to the Emperor?"

"Tell him it was nothing."

Sovari laughed bleakly. "If you value me as you say, my lord, you would not send me to the Emperor with such a message. I fear for my head."

"Have Gottfried pass the message. He's always been the one to get me out of my scrapes with Father. Been with him since the dawn of time. Should have been a dennissar, he knows how to tell unpleasant news so diplomatically."

"A fine idea." Sovari wrinkled his nose as he helped Aleksander out of Durgan's wet cloak. "Are you sure you're all right, my lord?"

"I need to sleep. The slave will help me with all this. You get my father calmed down. Tell him I'll be ready at first hour of fourth watch as he has commanded me."

"Sleep well, then." When he got to the door, the young warrior turned and bowed deeply. "May this day see the dawning of your glory and assure the future glory of the Derzhi Empire."

Aleksander nodded quite regally, considering his grime-streaked face, his half-unraveled warrior's braid, and his bedraggled clothing. When Sovari was gone, I helped the Prince strip off his wet things, and I brought him warmed water to clean the mud from his face and hands. When he was done, he pulled a blue vial from a drawer in one of the immense wardrobes in his bedchamber and held it up to me in a toast. "To my guardian spirit," he said. "You did me great service tonight."

"I don't want to do it again," I said. "May you have an uneventful birthday."

He grinned and dived onto his bed. I would swear he was snoring before he reached it.

Two days gone.

Athos at last decided to reveal his glory on the day of the dakrah. Aleksander kept the windows of his apartments un-covered, and I was wakened by the brilliance of a cloudless morning. I had taken the liberty of sleeping by his hearth again. By the time I had put out all the lamps, cleaned his boots, and hidden the wet wool cloak so that no one could trace its owner, it hadn't seemed worth the time to trek back to the slave house. Durgan knew where I was. Besides all that, I was nervous. If the rai-kirah were determined to pre-vent Aleksander's anointing, then the enchantment they had laid on him was not enough. They were planning something else, and I had spent several wakeful hours trying to figure out what it was.

The whole matter made no sense. If Aleksander's beliefs were true—and I had no reason to doubt him—then nothing short of death would prevent his anointing. Whims, tantrums, and odd behavior were not unthinkable in royal circles. Even if some of the Derzhi were to see the Prince in the throes of the enchantment, what would they think? Noth-ing. The Derzhi did not believe in melydda. They would consider it illusion, a joke, Aleksander being foolish again, or some perverse sort of pleasure like that of men who took dogs to bed along with their women. It was odd, but nothing that could turn Ivan against his son.

I left the Prince's chambers before anyone else came that morning. Servants were bringing wood to stoke his fire as I slipped down the passage, and three more were carrying heavy, steaming jugs of bathing water. Durgan was waiting for me in the slave house. His other charges were already dispatched to their day's duties. My guess was that those who worked in the kitchens had not slept all night.

"Has he told you where he wants you today? Are we to be in the same places as before?" asked Durgan.

"I suppose so," I said, making an attempt to clean myself at the slave-house cistern. "We never spoke of it." I didn't think it would make any difference. Whatever happened would not be the same as before.

The sun glared in garish celebration when I stepped out of the slave house. From the parapets, banners whipped wildly in the cold wind, the red and green stark against the ice-blue sky. The banners of the Empire and the Denischkar Heged. The lion and the falcon. Empire and family so closely bound. Ivan, Aleksander . . . Dmitri.

In an instant my own clouds were lifted, and I saw the danger as clearly as I could see the snowy pinnacle of Mount Nerod glaring white in the sunlight.

"Master Durgan," I called, running back into the slave house. He was poking wood into his brazier and setting a pot of water on to boil. I crouched down close to him and spoke softly. "Do you trust me? If I was to tell you that I have a dreadful suspicion about this day, would you do as I ask without asking any questions?"

"It is for your fight against the darkness?"

"Yes."

"And it would not endanger the Prince?"

"If I'm right, it might be the only thing to save him."

"I've seen enough to trust you."

"You must have a horse ready, somewhere. . . ." I closed my eyes trying to think quickly.

"Behind the washhouse there's a grove of alders. Thick. A man could hide there . . . or a horse." He was getting the idea.

"Yes," I said. "Supplies . . . food for several days . . . and clothes, something plain . . . for someone tall. . . ." I looked at him questioningly. For a slave to speak of such things, things that screamed escape, was a death sentence. He could strip my bones bare of flesh for saying the words, or throw me into his dungeon and never take me out.

"It will be done as you say, Ezzarian. But if you dare . . ."

"I'll not betray you, Durgan. Maybe I'm wrong. . . ."

I ran for the palace and arrived in the passage outside Aleksander's door just as he emerged. He looked the part of an Emperor. He wore white—a stiff, close-fitting satin tunic and breeches, embroidered with white silk thread and pearls. Gold threads were plaited into his braid, and a thin gold circlet set with a single emerald banded his brow. A long pearl-encrusted cloak fell from his shoulders, and atop it all was the diamond neck piece. It was made of tight-woven gold mesh that banded his long neck and extended the breadth of his shoulders and a handspan down his chest. It was set with diamonds, hundreds of them artfully arranged, an array so brilliant it could have taken the flame of a single candle and lit up the darkest midnight of a thousand cities. The Prince's lean face was solemn and his bearing regal. If his spirit matched his appearance, the Derzhi could want no finer a prince.

It was too late to warn him of my suspicions. Fifty Derzhi warriors walked beside and behind him, and he swept past without ever knowing I was there.

For want of a better plan, I retreated to the map room, but I did not get out my pens and ink. It was impossible to settle, and within ten minutes I abandoned my post and sped down the passageway. I ran past the ghostly servants and slaves who had emerged from the shadows to be about their interminable cleaning and hauling. Down, down the grand staircase, not stopping to answer the staring indignation of those shocked at a slave setting foot in a forbidden place.

The drone of the mellanghar and the blare of trumpets drew me on, but the crowds bulging out of the Hall of the Lion Throne were too thick to allow a view. Even when the wave of genuflection passed by my position, it was impossible to see.

I ran across the dome-ceilinged atrium to the inner end of the Hall, the end where Ivan would be enthroned awaiting his son. Behind the dais, where stood the Lion Throne, was a storage room, in which were kept the tall ladders for changing the candles in the highest sconces. The storage room was an oddity, a tall narrow niche created when a new wing was added to the palace behind the Hall of the Lion Throne. At one time there had been tall windows of stained glass at the end of the Hall above the Emperor's throne, but since no sunlight reached them any longer, they had been replaced by bronze grillwork inlaid with a sunburst of silver.

I placed the ladder and climbed up. Through thick clouds of candle smoke and incense, I could see out over the throngs of jeweled Derzhi and their guests. Lesser nobles stood, crowded under the broad colonnades on either side of the Hall of the Lion Throne, while higher-ranking guests were seated in the vast expanse between the colonnades. Every lamp burned sweet-scented oils; every candle flamed. The music soared and echoed from the dome of gold and blue mosaic above the throne, drawing the spirit upward to float in the pure spaces of the groined arches.

The tall, broad-shouldered Emperor, wearing robes of dark blue and a diamond and emerald-studded crown that would bend a lesser man, sat enthroned between rampant lions of gold three times the height of a man. His white braid was long and bound with bands of rubies, and his face, lean and intelligent and proud, was the image of his son forty years in the future. Aleksander had prostrated himself on the white carpeted dais between the throne and the steps.

Ivan raised his hand to silence the music. "Arise, Aleksander, Prince of the Derzhi." His deep voice carried with such resonance and such magnificence that no person in that vast audience could fail to hear it, and no person who heard it could fail to understand that the speaker was the most powerful man in the world.

With a grace that was an uneasy reminder of a shengar, the Prince moved into position beside his father, and the ceremony began.

I did not watch the elaborate pageantry: the Derzhi men whirling to rhythmic drumbeats, the choruses of children costumed in dangling gold spangles, the whining pipers, or the white-robed priests with shaven heads, whose chanting echoed from the vaulted ceilings. Instead I searched the sea of faces for the others who were not interested in Derzhi ceremony. There, on the left, in the front row of the most privileged guests, were those were allowed to sit in the Emperor's presence. Though I could not see their cold blue gaze from my high perch, I could recognize the two of them by their smooth, white-blond hair. Trumpets blared a fanfare and Aleksander knelt before his father again, his pearl-studded cloak stretched out behind him by fifteen young page boys. A boy in a stiff, gold-encrusted suit approached the Emperor, carrying a small jeweled cup. Foreboding hung as thick as the smoke, though I could not judge from what direction the challenge would come. But come it did.

As the crash of sudden thunder signals the storm is upon you before you're ready, so the voice rang out across the reverent silence in the Hall. "Murderer!"

The Emperor's finger stopped on its way to the jeweled cup. As one, the thousand observers caught their breath in astonishment and twisted their necks to see the madman who dared interrupt the most solemn ritual in Derzhi life. I, too, raked the crowd for the one who cried out, noting that only two of all that number failed to do the same. The two fair heads on the front row did not turn, but stayed fixed, their attention on the Emperor and the Prince. Aleksander leaped to his feet and whipped his head about to see, causing several of the children who held his cloak to stumble and fall.

"Treachery!" The cry, the sound of the word oddly malformed, hung in the air like the incense. "Glorious Majesty, what viper do you name to follow in your footsteps? Into what bloody hand do you place the seal of the Empire? To what craven coward do you entrust your realm?"

As a tightly stretched fabric splits when a tear opens the way, the crowd parted down the middle to reveal a hooded figure in gray. The smoke coiled about Aleksander, dulling the glitter of his diamonds as the robed stranger walked forward and stood in the aisle just below the steps.

"Who dares speak treachery upon this sacred morning?" demanded the Emperor, his long, straight nose flaring in fury. "Show yourself." Red-liveried soldiers ran to the robed man, but stayed their hands at the Emperor's gesture.

The hooded stranger lifted his arm and pointed a finger at Aleksander. "I stand witness to this villain Prince's crimes, and I bring evidence of a deed so heinous that you will denounce him yourself, Majesty."

"Show yourself before you die, fool," said the Emperor.

"As you command, sire." The man dropped his hood, and those nearby gasped, shuddered, and turned away. Murmurs and whisperings rippled outward as do the waves when a whale breaches the surface of the ocean. I shuddered, too, and pressed my hot forehead against the cool bronze of the grillwork. The man had only half a face. What skin remained on the left side was scarred and shrunken, pulling the eye half-closed. The left side of his mouth was gone, exposing his teeth in a death's-head grin. On what remained of his left cheek were the shriveled purple and red marks of a falcon and a lion. Vanye.

Aleksander did not flinch, but leaned toward his father and spoke quietly.

"You are the criminal who destroyed your Prince's property," said the Emperor. "You should properly be dead or in chains, and your children and your wife turned out to starve. Think you to tempt me into pronouncing the judgment my son so mercifully withheld?"

"Indeed not, sire. I came only to accuse him of murder in your presence." Those watching nearly trampled on each other to distance themselves from Vanye.

"I have affirmed the Prince's judgment in this matter. Lord Sierge was executed properly as a traitor and a spy. There is no dispute here. Guards!"

"No, Majesty, it is not my brother-in-law's foul murder I am here to denounce, but that of one you may think more worthy than a son of the House of Mezzrah. The Lord Marshal of the Derzhi, Dmitri zha Denischkar, lies dead, and it is no one but this foul Prince who has done it."

"Liar!" yelled Aleksander, reaching for his sword.

"No!" I whispered. "Aleksander, don't touch it."

He could not have heard my whispered entreaty above the explosion of horror and astonishment that filled the Hall of the Lion Throne, but his hand paused above the hilt and did not move.

"Silence!" roared the Emperor. "The man or woman who speaks without my leave is dead this instant." Only the hissing of torches and the soft whimper of a terrified child intruded on the heavy silence. The tall monarch pointed an accusing finger at Vanye. "Bring me this man . . . this dead man." His words resonated with earth-trembling fury. The guards threw Vanye across the steps at the Emperor's feet. Aleksander stepped forward, but Ivan's left hand flew out to stay him. With his right hand the Emperor drew his sword and held its edge at Vanye's throat. "Now, say it again."

"I've brought evidence, sire, and a witness," said the young man, snarling in defiance and hatred. With his sleeve he wiped the spittle leaking from his gaping scar. "This is not my contrivance. When I happened upon this story, I only begged to be the one to deliver the message. Call for my servants who wait at your door, and you'll see that the son of Mezzrah speaks truth. And call for Lord Dmitri's own captain Fredek, and you'll hear the tale that will expose your son's rotted soul."

"Fredek?" In the moment Ivan spoke the Derzhi warrior's name in surprise and curiosity instead of rage, I knew Aleksander was lost. If I could have reached out and plucked the Prince from that assembly, I would have done it. But instead I had to watch the demon plot play out.

Four soldiers wearing the orange and white of the House of Mezzrah marched forth slowly, carrying a litter draped in white. They set it at the foot of the steps before the Emperor, and withdrew. Ivan signaled to one of his own men who lifted the drapery and revealed the face beneath. Cheeks sunken. Lips black. Beard matted with blood. But unmistakably Dmitri.

The Prince sank into the red velvet chair beside the throne, staring at the exposed body of his uncle. He said, loud enough for all to hear, "Athos have mercy, what have I done?"

I never imagined so great a crowd could hold so profound a silence.

A sturdy, grizzled man wearing warrior's gear had followed the litter up the aisle, slowly and wearily, leaning on a cane. He eased down onto one knee before the Emperor. "Majesty," he said. "Would your righteous sword might pierce my heart before I speak these ill tidings. My master, Lord Dmitri, lies dead at the hand of bandits, fallen in the Jybbar Pass some fifteen days ago."

"How is it that you, my brother's right hand, sworn to live and die with him, can walk and speak while he lies dead?" said Ivan, his words of iron ringing from the stone walls.

Fredek spoke slowly and deliberately, the dread surety of his words hammering the ancient stone like battering rams. "Alas, sire, I suffered a wretched flux in Avenkhar, and the Marshal commanded me to stay behind so as not to slow the party. He was set on returning to Capharna with the Prince's new sword in time for the opening of the dakrah. The Prince had commanded him to come by way of the Jybbar to have it so. Gaspar stayed with me, and some two days after the Marshal's departure, we set out, planning to ride day and night until we caught up with them. But when we reached the Jybbar summit, where a man can see east and west to the horizons of the Empire, we found the Marshal and his four companions dead. Horses, purses, and weapons were all gone . . . cloaks and boots gone. Sire, they had been cut, bound, and left in the snow to bleed or freeze to death or be devoured by wolves, whichever came first."

"Great Druya avenge your mighty servant!" roared Ivan, thrusting his eyes and his clenched hands toward the heavens as if planning to wrest the gods' cooperation in his bloodletting. "Who were these murdering thieves?"

"Unknown men, Majesty, but the villains were still there, lurking in the pass, when we came. They took our horses, else we would have been here days ago with the news. But they spared our lives . . . on condition we deliver a secret message to Prince Aleksander."

"And what message would these murderers send to my son?" said Ivan coldly.

The Prince had not moved, had not removed his eyes from Dmitri. I could not be certain he even heard the man's words. The grizzled veteran looked from the Emperor to the Prince and back again. "He said to tell the Prince that all was done as he wished."

The Hall erupted in frenzy. As molten rocks and lava spew forth from a volcano, so did every hatred, grudge, and grievance against Aleksander fly into the smoky vastness of the Hall of the Lion Throne. He had insulted people, ridiculed them, made mockery of Derzhi honor and traditions. The Prince had dishonored men's wives and daughters and made light of his solemn duties. A thousand other accusations, petty and not. But the only evidence Ivan cared about lay at the foot of the steps. The Emperor silenced the babbling with a wave of his sword and the thunder of his rage.

"This rite of celebration is suspended for three days, so that we may bid fitting honor to the finest warrior ever to ride beneath Athos' fire. For a full year from this day shall every household mourn his loss with banners of red upon their doors, and with song and story shall we recount his mighty deeds so that Athos will know to place him at his right hand. There will he defend the realm of day and night against the beasts of the netherworld."

The Emperor was most efficient in his resolution. With one smooth motion of his sword he removed Vanye's head, then he kicked it down the white-carpeted steps, where it landed at Dmitri's feet, staring up in a last accusing glare at the Prince. In a swirl of blue robes, Ivan swept out of the

Hall, only half of the stunned witnesses remembering to bow.

Aleksander sat unmoving in his chair. No one dared glance his way as they bustled about. When the Emperor's guardsmen picked up the litter and bore Dmitri's shrouded body away, Aleksander's head did not move, as if the dreadful sight yet lingered in the place it had come to light. Fendular snatched the anointing oil from the gold-suited page boy who stood gaping at the grotesque head and the bloody corpse. Another man packed away the ceremonial bowls and implements, while two women puzzled with what to do with the white strip of carpet, so hopelessly stained with blood.

The crowd dispersed quickly. I imagined they were seeking a place where they could speak freely, away from the fear of Ivan's wrath. Only a small cluster of guests remained at one side of the Hall: two men and a red-haired woman in dark blue. The Lady Lydia. She stood watching Aleksander. Her companions tried to maneuver her through the side door, but she wrenched her arm from their grasp, then left the room of her own accord.

The bright banners hung limp. Empty chairs lay overturned. Flowers lay crushed on the floor. Arrows of sunlight found their way around the edges of the draped windows only to be slowed and deflected by the drifting smoke of snuffed candles.

I could not move, either, as if my very limbs were linked to the will of my master. And he had no will. His diamond collar glittered in gaudy mockery of the ruins of the day.

As I knew would happen, a slave walked hesitantly across the dais and knelt before the Prince, putting his head to the bloody carpet just out of arm's reach. Aleksander did not acknowledge the slave, but evidently the message was delivered. The Prince rose and slowly followed the path his father had taken from the Hall.

Chapter 17

Murder. Surely Ivan would not believe it on such flimsy evidence as the word of an unknown bandit and a vengeful traitor. The love between Aleksander and Dmitri was too deep. Yet, how often had the Emperor had a chance to observe the truth of their affection? He had heard Dmitri condemn the Prince for careless stupidity, and he had heard Aleksander rail at his uncle for every attempt at discipline. Perhaps the affection was only clear to me because I, too, had suffered a mentor who drove me wild, back when I was young and headstrong and intoxicated with life.

I hurried through the passages that led from the Great Hall toward the Emperor's chambers. Stunned courtiers flowed aimlessly in the jammed galleries, their eyes searching the crowds for a trustworthy face. When lucky enough to find a friend, they would clump to the side of the passage like clots of cream in a milk jar and whisper and glance over their shoulders to make sure no one would overhear.

I kept my eyes cast down and ignored any command that might be aimed at a slave. I was desperate to find Aleksander, desperate to understand what was happening. I had never believed my own quiet speculation that the Khelid thought to force the Emperor to name a Khelid-chosen heir. There were too many obstacles of heged tradition to overcome. Even with Aleksander out of the way, the Derzhi would go to war before seeing the throne go to someone else, and war was exactly the thing the Khelid could not deal with. We were hurtling down a steep path, and I could not see where it would end.

I could not get close to the Prince, nor even get information on where he was. No one had seen him enter the Emperor's chambers, though everyone assumed he was there. A harried serving woman said the Prince had retired to his apartments, but the rooms were cold and deserted. I returned to the Emperor's wing and drifted from one dark doorway to another, trying to hear the gossip, trying not to be noticed, trying to figure out how in the name of sense I could get anywhere close to where I needed to be or learn what I needed to know. Hopeless. Powerless.

My heart stuttered when an iron hand gripped my shoulder. "I said, you will come with me, slave." It was a balding man in blue satin pantaloons and a brown vest that exposed a chest full of wiry gray hair. I hadn't even heard his approach.

"But, sir, I—"

The man pulled me so close to his face that I could count the wide pores at the end of his egg-shaped nose. "You are required to come. We will not have a scene here in front of all these people. I would prefer not to be seen with a slave— especially you." He let go, brushed some imaginary lint from his bulging vest, and walked primly around the corner. Cursing silently, I followed him into a nearby passage, quiet, elegant, and deserted, the domain of the most-favored guests, so close to the Emperor's rooms.

He led me through an open door into a room that smelled of flowers. A large bouquet of tall, peach-colored stentia and radiantly blooming roses stood on a polished round table. The room was hung with fine stone tablets carved with stylized images of Derzhi desert life, as stark a contrast to the flowers as were the lingering snows in the garden. The man in blue satin closed the door behind me, then said, "Wait here," and disappeared through an inner door. I crossed my hands on my breast and cast down my eyes, trying to force myself into familiar habit. I was a slave, subject to the fancies of any Derzhi. I could not afford to forget it.

Don't wonder. Don't worry. There's nothing to be gained by it. What comes, comes.

But my own words rang hollow, the echo of a peace I no longer owned. The demons had started a war, and I had to play whatever pitiful part I could, even deaf and blind and powerless as I was. Every minute ate away at my composure. Where was Aleksander? I had no time for the whims of Derzhi nobles. I was on the verge of bolting, when the Lady Lydia hurried into the room, her angular cheeks as red as her hair, her green eyes blazing.

"Did he do it?" she demanded, not waiting for me to rise from my hasty bow. "Answer me truthfully."

"No, my lady. He did not."

"You know him well enough to swear it?"

"I would stake my life on it. He is not capable of such a deed."

"You truly believe that. How is that possible?" I could not understand her anger. "Does it not poison your tongue to say it?" She grabbed the iron ring about my wrist and yanked my arm up in front of my face as if I were a puppet at a midsummer fair, then she dragged me toward a looking glass and spun me around where I could glimpse the ruin that was my back. "Look at what he's done to you. What perverse madness makes you love one who treats you so cruelly?"

"Prince Aleksander is my master, my lady. He has the power of life and death over me, and the capability of every vile possibility in between. I'll not pretend feelings that are impossible for a slave." I spoke over my shoulder, refusing to look at the gaunt, scarred stranger she claimed was me. "But I must be honest in my answers. Despite his faults, the Prince is capable of great devotion. The only person I've seen who owned that devotion was the Lord Dmitri."

A small table went flying past my head, collapsing into splinters as it struck the wall beside the looking glass. I ducked and whirled about to see the lady taking up a chair to follow it. Were it anyone else, I would have flattened myself to the floor and covered my head, but somehow I trusted that her aim was true. I merely stepped to the side. She wasn't throwing things at me. In a quarter of an hour, she had created a sizable pile of sticks and velvet and glass beside the gouged wall, and she had regained a semblance of composure.

As I watched her vent her fury, I questioned the cause of it. I recalled our earlier conversation, and a glimmer of suspicion began to grow. She did not argue with Aleksander, pick at his flaws, and scorn his follies because she despised him. Quite the contrary. I wanted to laugh at the revelation. I leaned against the wall and pressed a hand to my face, fighting to banish all trace of my understanding. But she would not allow me to hide.

"Oh, Seyonne, I've not injured you? I'm as bad as the despicable prince." With soft fingers she pulled my hand away and probed with worried green eyes.

"No, my lady. You will just have to tell me if throwing furniture eases your affliction."

"He is impossible."

"Yes, my lady."

"Cruel, thoughtless, stubborn . . ."

"Indeed."

". . . prideful and foolish. Insulting."

"No one would argue with any of those things, my lady."

"So why can I not cast him from my heart?"

"Clearly reason and logic have nothing to do with such matters."

She grabbed my shoulders and shook me. "You love him, as I do."

"That is impossible. I serve him. Nothing more. A sword loves neither the hand that forges it, nor the hand that wields it. But there is more to him than we see, my lady. At least you can be assured that you do not care for a man who would kill his own uncle."

She sagged onto a velvet couch, now bereft of cushions. "No. Instead I love a madman."

"He is not mad, my lady, no matter how strange his current behavior."

She wrinkled her wide, smooth brow and shook her head. "In that you are wrong. The Emperor has judged him so, and he would never send Aleksander away unless he was convinced. Ivan zha Denischkar dotes on his son, and he is not a fool."

Judged him mad . . . I knelt at her feet. "My lady, forgive my questioning, but you have spoken freely with me, and I must know what's happened. What do you mean that the Emperor is sending him away?"

"The Emperor would not hear it at first—that Aleksander was mad. He dispatched men to burn villages until these bandits were caught. But Aleksander would not agree to lead them or have anything to do with the hunt. The Emperor called me in to convince Aleksander to explain himself . . . not knowing that my persuasion is exactly opposite whatever cause I plead with the Prince. He tried to make Aleksander say he didn't have anything to do with the murder, but Aleksander continued to insist that it was his fault. That he never meant for Lord Dmitri to die, but that he was to blame. What was the Emperor to think? He asked if Aleksander knew where the bandits were hiding and who they were, but the Prince said it didn't matter who they were. The crime was his. Then came that repulsive Chamberlain—"

"Fendular."

"Yes. And he simpered and groveled and began to tell of Aleksander's strange behavior of late: these dreadful events with poor stupid Vanye and Sierge, odd tales from the Dar Heged, insults to powerful families and the Magicians' Guild, consorting with beggars and . . . low women . . . fits of temper and abuse. He said Aleksander had cursed Lord Dmitri and vowed to make a slave his chamberlain. Sovari confirmed Aleksander's change of orders on the night of the Khelid entertainment, and how the Prince had disappeared that night, only to return muddy and disheveled, refusing to say where he'd been. Then other men stepped forward and confirmed Fendular's lies, and added more tales of their own. . . ."

Only they weren't lies. Every word spoken was true, I had no doubt. Exaggerated perhaps. Taken away from its true meaning. Put together in ways that would point up the truths the instigators wanted. Perfectly crafted. Terrifyingly perfect.

"And Aleksander . . ."

Lydia rose and strode to the table, gripping the edge so hard I thought the marble top might break away in her hands. "It was as if he didn't hear any of it. He sat and stared into nothing. The Emperor commanded him to swear he had not harmed Dmitri. He laid his own sword in front of the Prince and said that all Aleksander had to do was place his hand on the sword and swear. Nothing more would be said about any of it. He would be anointed this night."

The sword. And Dmitri living and dying in his head to trigger his change. The plan was exquisite. "He would not touch it," I said.

"His father begged him, but Aleksander drew away and said he could not wield a sword ever again, because he could never shed his guilt for Lord Dmitri." She lifted the vase of roses, then set it down firmly and began pacing the room again. "The Emperor was beside himself. He demanded that a physician be called, but someone said there was a better solution."

There. Now we had come to it. "Let me guess. It was the Khelid who said it."

The lady halted her steps and frowned at me. "It was indeed. How did you know?"

"Please go on, my lady." I forced my words calm, even as dread gnawed at my gut.

"Lord Kastavan is a kind and wise man, a great confidant of the Emperor. He said that his people were quite skilled at healing disorders of the mind. He offered to take Aleksander into his care and do everything possible to cure this illness."

"Stars of night," I said. "The Emperor didn't agree?"

"But of course he did. What other hope is there? He almost embraced Lord Kastavan in gratitude. The Emperor will proclaim to the Empire that Aleksander is devastated by the death of Lord Dmitri and has vowed that he will not be anointed until he has avenged the murder. The emissary Korelyi leaves for Parnifour with Aleksander at first light. From there they will take him to Khelidar."

As fire exploding in a drought-ravaged forest, so did understanding burst upon me. They had him. Gods of light and darkness, I knew what they planned. And Aleksander would not see it. . . . It was almost impossible to keep my voice even. "And what did the Prince say to this?"

The lady closed her eyes and pressed her fingers to her mouth for a moment. Only when she had mastered herself did she speak again. "At first he didn't hear it. Not until Lord Korelyi tried to lead him away. Then Aleksander pushed him aside and asked what in the name of the gods he was doing. The Emperor told him again how he was going to Khelidar, but that he would only be held there until he was healed of his illness. Aleksander flew into a rage. He tried to kill Korelyi, screaming about enchantments and demons and beasts. He cried out for a sword, but they had already taken his weapons away, so he tried to choke the Khelid with his own hands. It took five men to subdue him. Sovari bound him . . . weeping as he did so, for Aleksander called on him to remember how he had sworn to protect his prince with his life. And then Korelyi forced Aleksander to drink something he said would quiet him, so he would not harm himself. I've never seen the Emperor so shaken. The Empress could not watch it."

"Where have they put him, my lady? We can't let the Khelid take him." I wanted to shake the words out of her, not from any fault of her telling, but from the urgency that consumed me.

"He's mad, Seyonne. You could not doubt it, if you had seen and heard all this. If the Khelid can help him . . ."

I would have given much to keep the lady out of it, but I needed help. Aleksander's peril was far beyond mortal danger. The Khelid were going to force him to host a demon— if I was right, the Gai Kyallet himself, the most powerful of their kind, the one who could draw the others to his will. It would rip the fabric of Aleksander's being . . . destroy not only the feadnach, but every shred of reason, of honor, of decency. He would try to hold out, and that would make it worse. Eventually he would yield and become what they wanted, and if he were anointed Emperor, the worst bits of the Derzhi Empire would be a child's sweet bed story in comparison. I could not afford to protect anyone if I was to save him. "My lady, what do you know of rai-kirah?"

I paced the flower-scented room for an hour. The disapproving man in the blue pantaloons, Lydia's bodyguard Feddyk, brought in meat and bread and fruit and set them on the table for me, as his mistress had commanded him. Though it was luxurious fare for a slave, I could scarcely taste it for my fear. I was not used to waiting behind while women went to scout a battle for me.

"You cannot go," the lady had said to me. "They've heard your name too much already today. I'll discover what we need to know, if I must take the Emperor to bed to learn it."

I had implicit trust in her political and social wisdom, but none of that would prepare her for the intrigues of demons. Lydia was a kind and gracious woman, and I would not see her come to harm. So it was with a great release of guilt that I saw her come back through the outer door at last.

"He is held in the west tower. The Khelid have told the Emperor that they must confine him until their departure, closely guarded lest he attempt his own life."

"And they have no suspicion. . . ."

"It was the Empress who told me. I convinced her attendants that I needed to comfort her . . . as a daughter . . . and receive her mother's comfort in return. Lady Jenya has indulged Aleksander shamefully and is overwrought at his downfall, but she is no simpering court lady. When I suggested that Aleksander's caretakers might not be accustomed to giving a Derzhi prince his rightful comforts, she insisted on seeing him. I was not allowed to go, and I didn't think it wise to press, but she told me enough when she returned. She says that Korelyi accompanied her on her visit, and that the two Khelid magicians guard the stair. Lord Kastavan is with the Emperor, preparing his proclamation."

She told me all this scarcely taking a breath. Her cheeks were flushed, her eyes bright. Her pointed chin was resolute, as it had been since I told her of the Khelid and the demons. Lydia was no simpering court lady, either.

Now it was up to me. I just had to figure out how to get Aleksander out of a well-guarded tower and down to the copse behind the washhouse, where—if Durgan had done as he promised—a horse would be waiting to carry the Prince to safety. "You've done exactly right, my lady. I'll do everything I can for him." I rose to leave her.

"But wait, I've not told you all. The Empress was most distressed at what she saw. They had no pillows and only coarse sheets where the Prince was sleeping. And, though the Emperor's servants had taken his jewels away to keep them safe, Aleksander was still dressed in his dakrah clothes. I offered to carry a message to Aleksander's chambers . . . and get a slave to take traveling clothes and linens for his comfort. The Empress was very grateful."

"Lady," I said, smiling. "I have never met a more accomplished conspirator. You put the legendary Derzhi spymasters to shame." I bowed to her and turned to go.

"I should go with you," she said, hurrying after me until I paused at her door. "You might need an ally, a protectress."

"You've done more than enough. From this moment you must never be seen with me. Never must your name be mentioned in the same breath as mine. Forget that we ever met. If anyone should ask, tell them that you sent a servant to the Prince's chambers, so you don't know which slave was dispatched."

Only reluctantly did she agree. "Go with Athos' blessing, Seyonne. You must send me word of the Prince's safety . . . and your own. I'll not rest until I hear it. If you ever have need of anything—anything at all—send a message to Hazzire at my house in Avenkhar. Say it is 'from the lady's foreign friend,' and he'll get it to me."

"I would like to believe the Prince is worthy of your kindness, Lady."

"Save him, Seyonne, and we'll find out."

Chapter 18

I was loaded with such a pile of pillows and silk sheets, soft towels and royal clothing that no one could see my face, so I felt fortunate not to trip and break my neck on the steep, curving tower stair. I had even picked up a letter that had come for Aleksander, to make sure I had a good enough excuse to see him. My guess was that no noble visitor or gentleman attendant would be allowed inside the room without an escort, but no one fears a slave. Indeed the two Khelid magicians made only a cursory inspection of my load, especially once I tried to give them all of it to take inside the room themselves.

"I've heard the Prince is mad," I said, making sure my voice quavered in terror, a disconcertingly easy deception. "He beats me enough in ordinary times. Won't you take his things to him? There's clothes to dress him in for his journey, pillows for his comfort—"

The Khelid laughed, and the echoes of their twisted music clawed at my soul. I couldn't make myself look at them. "We're not here for slave's work. If you want him to have his comforts, you will have to stir yourself to do it. But I'm sure he can do without for tonight, if you're too squeamish."

"Oh, no, sir. The Empress commanded it, so it must be done. There's someone inside, then? To protect me? The Empress said it."

"You will have to take your chances with the mad Prince all alone. Lord Korelyi has retired for the night."

I had seen the pale-eyed Khelid leave and was relieved to hear he was not expected back.

"You won't lock me in there with a madman?"

"We are commanded to keep the room locked. If we should get distracted, you might have to stay with him until he wakes."

"Oh, no, my lords. The Prince detests me. I dare not be inside when he wakes . . . and to touch his body, when I am not his body slave . . . prepared . . . you know, so as not to be truly a man. It's worth my life to touch him." It was unnervingly easy to put on the person of a craven coward.

The demon-infested pair unlocked the door, then kicked me through it so hard that pillows and towels went flying. "But then your life is not worth a gnawed bone, is it? Perhaps we should give the Prince a knife so he can 'prepare' you to be his body slave himself." They took great good humor from this thought. They would leave me with Aleksander a goodly time, I guessed. I hoped it would be time enough.

The small room was lit only by cold moonlight slipping through a tiny, barred window. No possibility a man could fit through it. One alternative gone. There was nothing within the bare stone walls save a small table with a brass wine pitcher and a cup, and the low, narrow bed. Aleksander, still in his embroidered white satin, was laid out like a royal corpse, hands straight at his sides. His dull eyes were open and fixed, as if no one had done him the courtesy to close them when he died, and I took a moment to make sure there was still the pulse of life in his veins. Only when you took a closer look did you see the leather straps binding him to the bed at wrists and ankles, chest and neck.

I rummaged in the pile of linens and ripped open the pillow where I had hidden the Prince's short sword. I sliced away his leather bindings, then filled the mug with wine and knelt beside the bed.

"Your Highness, can you hear me? It's Seyonne. I've come to get you away."

He did not stir, not even to blink. I brushed his eyelids

closed then shifted my senses to examine the spells that bound him. It was as I thought. The demons were very confident. I shifted back quickly to silence the demon music.

"My lord, they've put only a simple spell on you and given you a sleeping draught to make you drowsy. You feel yourself paralyzed, but you are not. You can convince your body to move, but it will take a great effort of will. You must want to do it." I dribbled a few droplets of wine on his lips. "Taste and feel the wine I just gave you. Focus your mind on it. Think of it washing through you, cleansing away this foul enchantment, diluting the sleeping draught until it can have no influence on you." I coaxed and wheedled, giving him more wine, trying every image I could devise, but ten minutes passed with no sign of movement. I began to change his clothes and slip the silk sheets underneath him, lest someone poke their nose into the room to see how I progressed. My pleading and bargaining came to no avail. I soon believed it was a matter of will—lack of it. I needed a harsher tactic.

"My lord, you did not kill your uncle. Of course you are not blameless. You sent him away and toyed with him. You were careless and foolish, thinking only of your own comfort and pleasure as you have ever done. You will never be able to rid yourself of this burden, nor should you. But it was the demons who wanted him dead. Not you. It was the demons who set bandits on him. They take special pleasure in killing with cold, as they suffer from it so themselves. They left him to die, my lord, to bleed slowly and to freeze, and if you wish to make right this great wrong, you must not let them profit from it. Killing Lord Dmitri was the only way they could convince your father to let them have you." I pulled away his pearl-studded tunic and slipped a plain loose shirt of soft linen over his head and arms. "You can move if you wish. If you do not, they will take you to Khelidar and make a demon out of you. Neither your body nor your soul will be your own any longer—and you will have to huddle in a dark corner of your mind and watch it happen. Perhaps you desire this, thinking it fitting punishment for your sins. But can you not guess what the demons plan for you? You will kill your father, and the demon will rule your Derzhi Empire."

I was out of words. If he couldn't or wouldn't walk, then somehow I was going to have to carry him out. As I tugged the riding breeches over his feet and up to his waist, I was planning how Durgan might be able to obtain one of Giezek's blue vials to put the Khelid guards to sleep. My heart set up a clamor when a cold hand clamped around my arm.

"This is all your fault, you know." His hoarse voice was scarcely above a whisper.

I whirled about to see the heavy-lidded amber eyes open, though bleak and dulled with drugs and enchantment and grief. "I didn't ask you to buy me," I said.

"No. Of course, you didn't." He sat up and pressed his fists to the sides of his head. "Horns of the bull, what is this horror in my head? It's like every musician in the world playing together, all of them out of tune."

"It's the music of demons . . . the signature of their spell workings. It will fade . . . if we get you away from them. There are two of them outside the door."

I offered him his riding boots, and he stuck his feet in them. Once I latched the buckles, he rose from the bed, stretching his long limbs. "Stand aside. I can take on two guards."

I moved quickly to stand between him and the door. "No, my lord. You cannot."

"Your tongue runs away with you." Nothing like a spark of temper to burn away the remains of a sleep spell.

"Think, my lord. They are sorcerers, not illusionists. They have a binding on your mind that can send you instantly into a painful transformation. Do not imagine that they are unprepared for you to walk out of this room."

"Then, how the devil do you expect me to get out? Shrink myself to a bat and fly out of the window?"

I picked up the sword I'd brought, and held it out to him. "I think you should give them a surprise. They can't trigger what's already happened."

"You're not serious!"

"I see no other way. I would gladly yield you these." I pointed to my wrist bands and the scar on my face. "But you could hardly pass for anyone but yourself. I can't smuggle you out in a pillow. It was hard enough to find out where you were, so it's already near the end of fifth watch. We've no time for elaborate plots, and we don't dare involve anyone else. They plan to take you away at dawn."

"My father won't allow it."

"He has decreed it. He declares you mad, because he cannot stomach you as a kin murderer. He won't stop it."

Aleksander walked to the window and ran his fingers over the bars. His face was as rigid as the iron he touched. "Then, I'll wait until they take me out of here. I'll surprise them on the journey. You can come after us and help—"

There was no time to parry words with him. "If I am caught walking out of this palace, I'll be beaten until my head is pulp, and my foot will be taken off with an ax. If you challenge the Khelid, they will make you a shengar and carry you in a cage until you reach Khelidar. You must not underestimate them. Choose, my lord. We have only moments."

"But as I change . . . they'll hear it." Revulsion and dread were deep upon him.

"You will have to be silent. I'll be with you, my lord. You can bear it. You must."

"Athos, save us." It was the closest thing to a prayer I had ever heard from him.

"If he cares about his Empire, he will. If he wishes Lord Dmitri to be properly avenged, he will."

Aleksander reached for the sword. "Someday you will explain why you're helping me. You've never given me a sufficient answer."

"Time enough for all that," I said as he took the sword from my hand and gazed on it as if it was itself a demon. "We need to speak of other things right now. You will have to remember the way through the palace. You are in the west tower. You must get to the kitchen garden and not kill anyone along the way, as it might be someone you would regret killing. Can you do it? The alarm will be up within minutes. Your soldiers will be after you with every weapon they can muster. They'll have the palace gates closed, so you must not panic. The beast will demand that you panic, but you will have to control it. No matter where you run to get away from them, return to the kitchen garden. I'll be there as soon as I can. Or if I can't, Durgan will be watching, ready to help you."

In a single moment, the warmth was sucked out of the room. Aleksander dropped the sword on the pile of pillows, sat heavily on the bed, and bent over his knees, his arms wrapped around his middle. "Daughters of night . . ."

"Can you remember all that?"

"Yes . . . west tower . . . kitchen garden . . . don't panic. . . ." He rolled to his side, smothering a groan in the thin bedding. Sweat burst from every pore of his skin, dripping from his face and neck and instantly soaking his shirt. Even as the tower room grew deathly cold, heat radiated from his body as if he were the sun in his own small universe. "Be there, Seyonne."

"I'll be there, my lord."

As his torso began to stretch and blur, he wrapped his arms around the bedding and fought to keep from screaming.

"You are in control, Prince Aleksander. Your mind is not gone away. . . ."

In fifteen long minutes the shengar stood before me, a low, angry, gravelly rumbling coming from its throat as it stretched its tawny limbs.

"Well-done. And now we go. Do not let the Khelid recover from their surprise, my lord. Make for the kitchen garden. No panic. I am going to scream in just a moment, and you must not be startled by it. You will run through the palace, killing no one, and you will get outside and find a place of safety. Are you ready?"

It was indisputably strange to be talking to a beast that could kill me with one blow. Though, as I thought about it, it was not so different from talking to Aleksander any other time.

With no little trepidation I began beating on the door. "Help! Guards, please help! I beg you." I let out a dead-raising yell.

The Aleksander-beast bawled its fury, sounding like the screams of a dying woman. It was not entirely pretense when I hammered on the thick wood. When the door opened, I jumped aside and the wildcat leaped outward through the doorway. One of the two Khelid had a moment to yell before he was tossed against the curved tower wall. The other one had already been batted senseless by the great paws. A golden blur disappeared down the curving stair.

I snatched the sword and threw it out of the tower window. No surer way for me to get skewered on the way out than to be seen carrying a weapon. Though I was likely to die soon enough. It would not take them long to learn which slave had come to succor Aleksander. Perhaps I should have kept the sword, I thought, as I crept out of the door. It would be quicker and less painful overall.

The Prince had not killed either of the Khelid. That was good. Their resident demons would have been set loose and ended up in someone else. Someone we didn't know.

I slipped quickly down the tower stair. The alarm was raised through the palace, like fire racing along a trail of spilled lamp oil. "Run, Aleksander," I whispered as I scurried like a rat through the labyrinth of back passages across the vast bulk of the Summer Palace. By the time I got to the kitchen courtyard, torches were blazing throughout the palace grounds. Shouts of terror and amazement rang from every quarter.

"What was it?"

"I heard that it came from the west wing."

"How could it have got inside? Was there some entertainment planned with it?"

"There's three guards down. Drak thought he got a shot at it, but it didn't slow down."

"The monster's headed for the north parkland. Careful in those woods."

I crept around the edges of the kitchen courtyard, behind the refuse bins, between stacks of wood and barrels of ashes, ducking into corners and crevices every time I heard a step. Two groups of men-at-arms ran through the courtyard brandishing swords and crossbows, but soon the dark expanse fell silent. By the time I reached the alleyway that led from the courtyard past the carpenter's shop, the stonemason's workroom, and the other palace workshops and storehouses toward the kitchen garden, I was convinced the way was clear. But no sooner did I step out from behind a broken-wheeled cart, than I felt a flesh-ripping whip across my shoulders, the stinging tail tearing a streak in my right cheek. I stumbled on the broken cobbles of the lane and fell heavily to one knee.

"Where are you going in such a hurry, slave?" asked Boresh.

I moved to get up, but the whip cracked on the wet paving, scattering broken chips of rock that pelted my side and flew into my eyes. I stayed on my knees, bent forward.

"Well, well, it is the sneaking Ezzarian who knows not his place." The diminutive under-chamberlain grabbed a fistful of my short hair and yanked my head back. "It's time you learned it. The mad prince will have no say in your future, so you will have to put your ambitions aside . . . starting now." He spit in my face, jammed his whip handle into my stomach, and shoved me forward. "Face down, vermin."

I forced myself to submit. It was not yet time to take the step I could never retract. His boot on the back of my neck ground my face into the cold wet grit of the cobbles, and I braced myself for a beating. *Get it over with.* But I felt a quiet scuffling at my back and heard a muffled expulsion of air, just as the weight was lifted from my neck. Quickly I rolled to the side, just in time to see Durgan pull his knife from Boresh's back. So the step had been taken for me.

"Off with you." He wiped the blade on the under-chamberlain's breeches. "I'll take care of this refuse."

I got to my feet, wiped the muddied nastiness from my face, and bowed. "Thank you, Master Durgan." Then I started down the lane again.

"Ezzarian!"

I paused and looked, just in time to catch a wad of cloth. It was Boresh's cloak. I bowed again, this time deeper, and ran toward the gardens.

The dark kitchen garden was as silent as a burial ground after a plague. I couldn't tell where the hunt had gone. Half the palace was lit up, and there were cries and shouts from far more places than Aleksander could possibly be. It sounded as if he'd got outside, at least.

I couldn't go chase him. If he had kept his wits, he would come. If not, I didn't want to be near him anyway. But it was very hard to wait. Twice I heard running footsteps and shouts close by, and I ducked into the corner of the garden and pulled a pile of rotted netting over me. Another hour fled past. If he didn't come soon and change again, he wouldn't have the cover of night to get away. His "episodes" had lasted between two and four hours each time. Longer would put us right at dawn.

It was another hour until a quiet, ominous snarling from across the garden told me that Aleksander had arrived. I peeked out from my hiding place and saw the dark shape creeping through the starlit garden, pausing every so often to smell the wind. I stepped out and called softly. "My lord."

The amber-eyed cat loped across the dead earth and circled about me, as if to make sure who I was.

"Are you all right?" I said, sitting on the bottom of a splintered wheelbarrow. He slunk toward me and settled on the ground. "You set up quite an uproar." I talked of nonsense, dreading to see the dark midnight start to pale. But it was less than half an hour until he began to change. Even coming from beast to man, he was silent this time, smothering his agonies in his throat so no uneasy sentinel on the palace grounds could have heard him. "Come," I said, wrapping Boresh's cloak about him as soon as the transformation was complete. I helped him to his feet and led him, shaking and miserable as before, toward the copse behind the wash-house. I trusted that Durgan had managed what I'd asked. "It's time for you to leave Capharna for a while."

"I'll not run away," he said, shaking his head and struggling to force words through chattering teeth and the remnants of confusion and enchantment. "I'll go to my father. . . ."

"And what will make him listen to you? You've told him you killed his brother—a lie he believes. You've told him the Khelid are demons and that they changed you into a beast—a truth he discounts. Why would he believe you now?"

"I'll be calm this time. I'll explain about Dmitri. I'll show him. Touch a sword and let him watch."

"And if Lord Kastavan is there, I'll be unable to help you; he would see instantly what I was doing. If you can't control the beast—and with a demon watching, that would be quite likely—you could end up killing your father. Is that what you want?"

I had thought his face could get no paler. "I cannot run away. I'm a Derzhi warrior. I am heir to the Empire."

"They'll not allow you to be anointed until you are theirs. You must rid yourself of this enchantment or you'll be a demon emperor."

He had no answer.

We slipped into the copse—a thick little stand of barren alders that had grown up where the dirty water from the washhouse ran downhill and got caught in a shallow bowl of land. There stood the Prince's own Musa, happily munching on a pile of hay. Three filled saddle packs hung over his back, and a large cloth bag hung from a thick branch. I pulled down the bag and helped the Prince get on the dry clothes: a thick shirt, sturdy breeches, and a good, heavy cloak to replace Boresh's thinner one.

Now it was time. I steeled my heart and wished I believed in a god from whom I could beg forgiveness for the betrayal I was about to commit. "Your Highness, the only return I ask for this night's doings is that you not ill-use what

I'm about to tell you. There are those who can help you . . . but they are those that Derzhi law requires to be held captive. I must have your word that you'll not do so."

"You must have my word? How dare you bargain with me?" Even after all, he rankled at my boldness.

"My lord, I'll say nothing more until I have your word. You may do as you wish with me—as always." I held my arms out straight to the side, and I did not look away.

This time it was Aleksander who dropped his eyes. "Of course you have my word."

"In the central market of Capharna is a bronze statue of a dying warrior who has just slain a mythical beast—a gyr-beast." I closed my eyes and forced away the singsong refrain of Llyr's dying. "Do you know it?"

"I do."

"Go there. Clear your mind of every distraction and touch the gyrbeast. The way will appear in your head, something like a map. Follow the direction it gives you, and you will be met and taken the rest of the way. They won't like you. They won't like it that you—a Derzhi—have learned the way. But you must tell them you are fyddschar—enchanted—and that you come seeking their help. They need to know everything about the demons, about the Khelid. And tell them you've been told you bear the feadnach. They won't refuse you."

"I can't remember all that. You can tell them your magic words yourself."

"I won't be there."

"But of course you will. If not to your own people, where . . . Druya's horns, you don't think to stay here? You've blood on you already—wages of this night's adventure I would wager. You'll be dead an hour after I'm gone. And that's if you're lucky."

Curse the man for his stubborn heart. "I'll put you in greater danger. A missing Ezzarian slave will bring the Magician's Guild into the hunt," I said. "Paltry as their skills are, there are a great number of them, and they are good hunters. Your father and the Khelid can't mount too noisy a search for you. How would they explain it? But for me . . ."

Aleksander soothed the restless Musa with a gentle hand and stared at me until my voice dwindled away. "You are perhaps the worst liar I have ever encountered," he said at last. "You shouldn't even bother. Your eyes won't stay still. Your skin turns yellow as if you've eaten poison. Your eyelids twitch. Now begin again and tell me the truth or I'll not budge a step from this palace, demons be damned. Why will you not take me to your own people?"

I wrapped my hands about my clammy, bare arms and stared at the ground. "I cannot. Or rather I can, but it will do neither of us any good. They will look past me as if I don't exist. They will hear no word I speak, and if my words come through your mouth, they'll not hear you, either. I could strike one of them, and he would not flinch. From the day I was taken captive, I've been dead to them—irredeemably, unspeakably corrupt. I can never go back."

That moment of my speaking was, perhaps, the blackest moment of my life. No matter how often I had voiced them in my mind, I had never said the words aloud. The utterance made them real, in the way a gravestone manifests the hopeless truth that breathless bodies, still wearing the aspect of life, cannot confirm.

"Corrupt? You? Are the bastards blind and deaf or are you all infected with some priggish disease?"

"It is our law. There are good reasons."

Aleksander put his hand under my chin and forced me to look at him. Even in the dark his eyes burned. "Do you have the least bit of an idea of what you've done to me, Seyonne? I can't take a piss without you watching me, forcing me to look through your eyes at what I do, judging my ridiculous temper, daring me to be better than I am. Fifty times I've come an ant's prick from sticking a knife in you, because I could make you neither envy nor fear me, and I couldn't understand it. You were only a slave. And now you're going to let my father slit your belly and hang you up by your entrails

because some imbeciles say you're not good enough to talk
to them?"

"My lord—"

"Corruption cannot make a man travel in ways he's unwilling to go, make him see bits of himself, however minute,
that are worthy of true honor—not this pomp and mouth-
music we attach to honor's name. If you are corruption, then
I am already one of these ill-begotten soul-eaters, and I'd
best stay here and watch you die." He planted one boot in
Musa's stirrup, swung his leg over the saddle, and extended
his hand. "But neither of us is what others claim. If I cannot
be afraid to fight my war, then I'll be a whoreson demon forever before I let you hide from this one of yours."

I had made peace with fate, resigned myself to exist
alone in captivity until nature finished what the Derzhi had
begun. Now Aleksander was asking me to take up the battle
again . . . and the immensity of grief and pain that would
come with it. Chances were we'd never get so far as the gyrbeast, much less the rendezvous. Chances were I'd be dead
and Aleksander packed off to Khelidar long before I saw any
Ezzarian turn away from me. Before I saw her.

I shifted my senses and found the feadnach yet burning
within him; then I sighed, snatched Boresh's cloak from the
ground, and took the Prince's hand.

Chapter 19

"Urgent message for Lord Jubai!" screamed Aleksander, not slowing Musa's gallop by even a heartbeat as we raced across the final courtyard toward the solidly closed palace gates. I hid my eyes in his back, deciding I would rather not know at exactly which moment two men riding a Derzhi warhorse would be flattened against the two-hundred-year-old oaken beams. But the impact did not come, and a smell of burning oil and a glimpse of torchlight past the edge of the Prince's cloak told me we were through. Aleksander laughed and shouted over his shoulder as we thundered down the lane, "No hesitation. Dmitri taught me that."

I didn't answer. I was working to get my balance before discovering the exact measure of the considerable distance to the ground. The prospect· of an arrow in the back or smashing into closed gates did nothing to ease the difficulties of remaining astride the galloping horse. I had been an adequate rider in my youth, but on smaller, less aggressive beasts. I had no place to put my feet, too many qualms about gripping Aleksander as tightly as I would like, and a dreadful problem in that I was most inadequately dressed for riding. Slaves were not given undergarments. I had only a few scratchy folds of Boresh's cloak caught between bare skin and the saddle, and I was already raw after only five minutes going. Unable to keep a firm grip on the horse, I felt like the next jolt would send me flying.

We streaked across the causeway and into the town, dodging deserted wagons and shuttered market stalls, galloping precariously fast through narrow lanes and about sharp corners until we reached the grand marketplace of Capharna. The banners of celebration hung limp in the cold, damp air, and the broad expanse of pavement was littered with the remnants of the townsfolk's dakrah feasting, interrupted before it had really begun. Hastily sewn mourning draperies were nailed over every doorway, while shadowy figures scurried about, looking for scraps of food or cloth, or dragging away the collapsed plank tables and booths to burn for a night's warmth.

Aleksander reined in his mount beside the towering bronze monument to bittersweet victory. The bronze warrior slumped lifeless beside the legendary monster he had slain, his sword forever on the verge of slipping from his graceful hand. The warrior's face was classic Derzhi. Aleksander could have sat for it.

"Shall we?" said the Prince, offering me his hand. I managed to dismount without assistance, though my wobble-kneed landing and subsequent grimaces as I stretched out my nether regions gave him pause. "I'd have thought a slave would develop a thicker skin," he said.

The ground under my feet rumbled ominously, and the night sky glowed from the direction of the palace as if a second moon was waxing in the north. "We've only moments, Your Highness. We must be away from here before anyone sees what we're about."

"Well, go do it then."

"It would be better if you did it, my lord. You know the land hereabouts. The map will make sense to you." I dared not have both of us use the enchantment. I had no way to know what limits or wards had been placed on it. And, of course, if something happened to me, Aleksander had to know where to go. I could not yet convince myself that there was any real possibility that I would ever walk into an Ezzarian settlement, else I could not have continued. "Just clear your mind, touch the beast, and say 'dryn haver.' It means 'show me the way.'"

I could hear the shouts of the searchers and hear the horses now, not just feel them. Aleksander could, too, for he didn't argue. He ran to the sculpture, scrambled up the stone block on which it rested, and laid his hand on the gyrbeast's tail.

"I don't see anything," he called. "Or feel it, or know it, or whatever the devil I'm supposed to do."

It had to be there. Llyr had wanted me to know how to find the Ezzarians. When Ezzarians wanted to keep a location hidden, they would embed the direction in a map enchantment. Chances were that only a handful of their own people actually knew the entire way to their refuge. The path would be masked, hidden under layers of spells, so that those sent out into the world would not be able to lead others back to the rest of them. Llyr had said that the gyrbeast would lead the way. This was the only gyrbeast I knew of outside of manuscripts and stories, though I had seen things in the domain of demons . . .

. . . the soft rain fell like tears of grief, washing away the purple blood of the monster I had slain. Wisps of steam curled from the silver knife I wrested from its leathery neck. I stepped along its back and gazed upward, letting the rain cool my face, washing away the sweat and blood and foul sputum of the beast. Even as I watched, the clouds broke, revealing brilliantly clear stars in no pattern that would ever be visible in the realms of men. I felt the wafting breeze, tasted its shape and strength, and judged it enough. It would carry me to the portal easily. I was tired, but it had come out well, and soon I would be in her arms . . .

Fires of heaven, why could I not keep it buried? Aleksander was poised on the stone, waiting. The boy had been dying. What if I'd misunderstood him? "Clear your mind and speak the words," I said harshly. " 'Dryn haver.' Let the image come. Don't try to control it. They wouldn't have left it simple."

Aleksander leaned over to the beast again and was quiet for a moment. An eternity. Our pursuers were only a street

away. The scavengers had already fled into the dark alley-
ways.

"Druya's horns!" Aleksander's hand flew into the air as if
the bronze beast had stung it. He bellowed in laughter, then
leaped from the stone block right into Musa's saddle. It
made my backside throb to watch it, but not as much as it
did when he hauled me up behind him again and kicked the
obedient stallion back to life.

"Extraordinary!" he shouted as we wheeled and shot out
of the southern gate of the marketplace just as the torchlit
chase entered from the north. I could almost hear the leather
of their armor creaking. We raced madly through the sleeping lanes. I couldn't imagine how Aleksander could see
where we were going, as the buildings melted together in a
blur. Perhaps he didn't. Perhaps it was all the horse. But
every time I thought we must emerge from the city into the
countryside, Aleksander would take another turn, and we'd
find ourselves deeper in the old part of the city. I was sure
we were lost.

I thought my fears confirmed when the Prince halted
Musa in a dark, narrow lane near the river. It stunk of pigs,
dead fish, and rotted cabbage. Sour yellow light spilled into
the lane through the smoke-grimed windows of a tavern.

He'd got it wrong. The map enchantment would not lead
us to the Ezzarians themselves, only to a meeting place
where we would take on a guide. But Ezzarians would never
use such a den of filth, of excess, of impurity. Besides, it was
right in the middle of the city. Much too public. I should
have envisioned the map from the gyrbeast enchantment
myself. "My lord, this couldn't be the place—"

"It's not, but we need to stop here anyway. Come on."

A man staggered out of the door and pissed in the lane,
then collapsed in his own puddle. Aleksander stepped over
him and pushed open the door of the tavern. Exasperated
with the willful Derzhi, I followed, mystified, wondering if
he had decided he couldn't proceed without a drink or a
woman.

The air inside the dark hovel was thick with smoke, and

smelled of burned grease and sour ale. The eight or ten ragged men and slovenly women slouched on stools about the room goggled curiously at us. It was not the sort of place a Derzhi warrior would frequent. The proprietor, distinguished from the others by his possessive hand on the single ale barrel, had only one yellowed tooth in his gaping mouth, and his lip was birth-cleft all the way to his nostrils. He jerked his head to a vacant stool for Aleksander, then curled his lip at my bare feet and the steel bands about my ankles. Slaves did not usually patronize taverns, either.

Aleksander did not sit down, but circled the room, examining each man carefully until he stopped behind a slender, long-legged fellow who had his face buried in a buxom woman's bodice and his hand up her skirt. "This one," he said, then wrapped his left arm about the man's neck and dragged the poor victim out the door. The frowsy woman who had been sitting on the man's knee collapsed to the floor with a florid curse, one breast hanging out of her bodice and her skirt bunched around her waist.

"I don't like his looks," Aleksander shouted to the curious drinkers who crowded up to the door to see what was going on. None dared step outside to get in the middle of it. I pushed my way through them, just as confused as the rest. What could Aleksander be thinking? Hooves and shouts echoed through the nearby streets.

The Prince shoved his besotted victim against a wall. "Remove your clothes. Boots and all." The man gaped in uncomprehending surprise until Aleksander grabbed his ear and pulled the slack-jawed face onto a level with his own. "I said, remove your clothes. Your Prince has need of them. And be quick about it. If you take more than half a minute, I'll pop your left eye from your head like a pit from a cherry." He flexed his thumb and forefinger in front of the man's face. Well short of half a minute, Aleksander tossed me a pile of clothes and boots that smelled like tar and wine and piss, and the man was running naked down the street wailing as if a Derzhi hangman was at his back.

"Well, get them on. I didn't go to all this trouble to have

you gaping at me like these hod-carriers. Unless you've developed a steel ass and leather feet, you'll be glad of them and not care that I was ungentlemanlike while acquiring them. We've no time to visit my tailor."

Refusing to wear the clothes wasn't going to put them back on the man they belonged to. And, in truth, the closing chase did nothing to make me think generously. The Prince would be coddled and escorted back to his demon guardians. I was the one who would lose one of my feet and half of my face . . . if I was lucky.

In the matter of one minute, I was wearing the first boots and breeches I'd put on in sixteen years, and we were flying through the streets again, sparks shooting from Musa's shoes as we headed for the western gates.

A Derzhi prizes a fine horse above every other possession, and my presumption that Aleksander would have none but the best was fully justified. No pursuer came any closer to us that night. We raced out of the city and across the open valley floor toward the heavily forested mountains to the west. Even carrying the two of us together, Musa never faltered. About the time the darkness thinned to the color of watered milk, the road narrowed and entered the trees, and the Prince slowed his steed to a walk. The lolling gait made me drowsy. . . .

. . . they kept coming, wave after wave. A Derzhi warrior leading his four cadre brothers, and behind them a troop of Manganar foot soldiers and mounted Thrid mercenaries, ivory talismans dangling over painted breastplates. A scream from behind me. Verwynn, my father's friend, fell, a Thrid spear in his gut. My leaden arms were covered with blood. Still they came . . . unending waves of blood and death . . . I had to hold until the others got away. I was a Warden, sworn to protect them . . .

"Daughters of night!" Aleksander's exclamation as we jerked to a halt startled me awake. The Prince was bent forward, pressing his head into his hands that clutched at Musa's mane. Clawing shivers crept along my spine, more than could be explained by the icy droplets dribbling down my neck from the thick branches overhead.

"Is it the change, my lord?" I said, ready to scramble from the horse rather than share it with a shengar.

"No." Aleksander straightened up again and spurred the horse to a walk.

As soon as Musa settled, so did I. My head rested heavy against Aleksander's back. I could not seem to keep the dreams at bay . . .

. . . the sunset stained the sky red as if the earth could not hold all the blood. I whirled about, kicked the knife from the hand of a Derzhi youth, and slashed at the grinning Manga-nar, who was sneaking up my blind side, his last thought amazement at how I knew he was there. To my left the brothers Giard and Feyn—Searchers called in from their rounds—struggled with at least eight warriors. To my right all was silence—though as I flung the lifeless youth onto the pile of bodies behind me and rushed to Giard's aid, I strained to hear the sound of reinforcements. Ten or twelve other Ezzarians were similarly engaged, and coming up the narrow valley were more Derzhi . . . another wave . . . how had they found us? We had been sure that no one knew of this route. We were hoping to surprise the main body of their force before they could slaughter our left flank, but before we could get out of the shallow valley, we were trapped. Feyn gasped in astonishment when the arm that had slain fifty warriors dropped from his shoulder, severed by a Manganar ax. When the sword released his entrails from his belly, he toppled slowly onto his arm as if to reclaim it. I roared in madness and raised my sword again . . .

". . . for the moment, but they'll bring in Janque as soon as they can get him sober."

I didn't know where the first part of the conversation had gotten off to. "Janque?" My tongue was thick with sleep.

"The finest tracker in Capharna. As I said, it's why I went west when we're supposed to go north. He'll have a harder time following us through here. I've left him six false trails. He'll eat his hounds for breakfast."

Hounds. Trackers. What was I thinking to lead the Derzhi down on the remnants of my destroyed people? "My lord, we can't—"

He knew exactly what was in my mind. "I know what I'm doing. They'll not be able to follow us. Even Janque. Go back to sleep."

"I wasn't—"

"Are you arguing with me? Just because I gave you boots, you think you can say what you please?"

"No. Of course not." We rode on and I lost track of the day again.

The shadows were angled in a vastly different direction when we stopped and I fell off the horse. Well, I didn't exactly fall. Aleksander pulled me off. But it was the same gut-twisting sensation, and I . . . I had been deep in that other place.

"Ho, Seyonne. All's well." He caught one flailing hand in his steady grip, but I wrenched it away, whirled about, and aimed for his neck with the side of the other hand and for his gut with my knee. It was only his own impeccable reflexes and my lack of practice that kept me from breaking his neck.

"What in Athos' name . . . ?" His eyes were huge, and when the thunder in my blood quieted enough to realize what I'd done—and almost done—I was appalled.

"Forgive me, my lord. I was dreaming . . ." I could scarcely speak for the shadows crowding one upon the other to escape my head before I could capture them and remember the fading vision.

"Dreaming? I've not seen three men who could move so fast and so . . . deadly . . . when they were fully awake." He looked at my hands that were clamped in his own, then released them and moved his gaze to my face.

"Happily one of them was you," I said, drawing my cloak about me against wind that was not half so cold as my soul.

"I've heard people can do amazing things in their sleep that they couldn't possibly—"

Aleksander held up his hand and closed his eyes. "Don't. I told you, I'll hear no more of your pitiful lying. I'd rather you say nothing at all."

"As you wish, my lord." We were stopped in a small clearing away from the road. I climbed up a pile of rocks beside the trail and looked out on a high mountain valley still locked in the embrace of winter. Frost snapped a limb somewhere deep in the trees, and the screech of a hunting falcon split the bitter air.

"What I wish is to know what you are, Seyonne. A slave held sixteen years who moves like a Lidunni fighter. . . . Were you in service to one of them, or someone who studied their ways? You watched them, didn't you? Someone allowed you to see, or you spied on him and learned it."

"No, my lord. No one is responsible for teaching a slave things that are forbidden." The Lidunni Brotherhood was a secretive sect of Derzhi who mixed religion and the art of hand combat.

"You snapped my grip as if I were a five-year-old girl. I will know how you learned it. If you knew this from before . . . how in Athos' name were you taken captive?"

The taste of death was in my mouth. It was all too close. "Please, my lord. Not now. I'll tell you some day if you insist, but not now." I tried to keep the moment's disturbance out of my voice, the inexplicable dread that constricted my throat and made my heart race when I dreamed. That battle was long lost. There was no reason for it to take on new life just because I was going to see Ezzarians. The dead were dead. The living . . . had survived. "Is this the place that was shown to you?"

"Damnation, you're stubborn," said the Prince, cheeks and eyes blazing. "You try my patience, and I've little enough of it in the best of times. If I weren't asleep on my feet, we'd have it out right now. After what I've seen . . ."

"You've seen nothing but the remnant of a dream, my lord. Please tell me if this is the place."

"No, not yet." He propped his hands on Musa's saddle and leaned on it tiredly. "And just as well. I'd not be awake to greet anyone."

"We need a fire," I said, shaking off the lingering shadows. The sun was low over the mountains. It must have been weeks since I'd gotten more than three hours' sleep in a sun's turning. The Prince was still staring at the saddle, and it came to me that there were a number of things he had never had to do for himself. "I can take care of the horse, so you can sleep."

Aleksander snorted in irritation as he stirred himself and began unbuckling the girth straps. "You need have no fear. Dmitri would not allow me to have servants when I was training. I can care for Musa, put on my own boots, and even cook a fair rabbit if there is one in such a frozen desolation as this."

"There should be provision enough in the saddle packs for a few days," I said.

"Good. Can't say I want to go hunting at the moment. In fact, perhaps you had better do this part for me." He nodded to the long leather sheath fastened to his saddle. I removed the sword and the three packs, and Aleksander hefted the saddle to the ground. He took the saddlecloth and rubbed down the handsome bay, talking to it more brotherly than I'd ever heard him address any human.

While he saw to the horse, I gathered wood, piled it behind a sheltering outcrop, and tried to convince my cold fingers to strike the flint. A fire would be welcome. The wind was bitter, and I was guiltily grateful for the wool shirt, thick breeches, and serviceable boots. They fit amazingly well. But for Aleksander's whim, I could be facing frostbite, sepsis, and amputation.

Aleksander flopped down beside my miniscule flame and dug the heels of his hands into his eyes. He was quiet, and I went about my business of nurturing the tantalizing wisps of fire. When next I glanced at him, he was trembling, and I thought his clenched fingers might press his eyes all the way into his skull.

"What is it, Your Highness?"

"Unholy . . . cursed . . . so real I can taste it. Can smell the blood. And when I try to think of something else"—he took a harsh breath—"I think my head is going to crack open and spill out what paltry brains I've got." He shuddered. "Vile."

Setting his jaw, he pushed away the damp hair that had come loose from his braid and plastered itself to his forehead, then started rummaging in the saddle pack, pulling out a tin cup, a packet of dried meat, another of dates, and another that, from his sigh of relief, must be the tannet bark and leaves used to make nazrheel. "Wake me when I can do something with this," he said, tossing me the packet, then rolling up in his cloak and blanket, starting to snore before his last word was out.

"As you command," I said automatically. The words lingered on my tongue, then dropped into my mind like stones into a quiet pond. I gazed on the deserted valley where ice fogs gathered in the low places in the fading light. The stones were sharp-edged gold, every ridge, corner, and crack shaped by the steep-angled beams. The wind stirred my hair with a frosty finger. Rarely had I ever experienced such a moment of perfect clarity.

I could walk away. I had a horse, clothes, and provisions, and the only man who could prevent me was half-mad with demon visions—oh, yes, I could guess the seductive horrors they were using to torment him. And now he was so deep asleep I could slice his throat if I wished. I could be free. The consideration was overwhelming. I already knew I would not leave him—my oath forbade it—but for an hour, as I fed the newborn flames and grew them into something that could thaw my bones and boil a cup of water, I indulged myself, setting my mind loose to imagine what it might be like.

It was a most discouraging exercise. I couldn't think where I might go or what I might do or even what I might tell the first person who asked about the mark on my face. I had forbidden such thoughts for so long, I couldn't summon them. All I knew was how to be a slave. Perhaps I could neither think nor act unbidden anymore.

When the stars had wheeled a quarter of the way through their night's path, I boiled water in the cup and soaked the tannet bark, leaving the cup near the fire to stay warm. After another hour, I added the leaves, boiled the stuff again, and when the green-black mess was stinking in all its proper glory, I woke the Prince. A proper duty for a slave.

"Well-done, Seyonne," he said, sipping slowly, savoring the nasty, bitter drink. "If you want to sleep, I'll watch for a while. I've had enough dreaming for three lifetimes. Bad enough they come when I'm awake. To sleep is to invite more."

"I slept all day," I said. "I'll do another stint." I stepped away from the fire to relieve myself. In my unaccustomed fumbling with layers of clothes, I found the paper stuck in the pocket of the slave's tunic I still wore underneath my shirt. It was the letter I'd taken from Aleksander's chamber on my way to his tower prison. When I returned to the fire, I gave it to the Prince and told him its history.

"It's from Kiril." He twirled it in his fingers. "Do you know why we always use red wax?"

"I'd guess it has something to do with blood," I said.

He laughed. "Good guess. When we were boys, we made a blood oath to be closer than brothers. To slay each other's enemies. We cut our palms and put them together as boys do. When Dmitri sent us to opposite ends of the Empire, we started mixing blood in the wax to remind ourselves of our promise. A few years ago we agreed that red wax was sufficient. Do you think that means anything? That our zeal is less true?" He poked up the fire, motioned me closer, and tossed me the letter. "Read it."

I broke the red wax and began.

> Zander,
> If I judge rightly, you should receive this on the eve of your anointing. I trust you have had a merry party and not found the rites too tedious.

You are to be Emperor. Not soon, if the gods are gracious to your honored father, but you will be the next. We have always talked of it frivolously, but certain events of late have caused me to give it more sober thought, and to hope that amidst the wine and music, women and feasting, you have found time to do the same.

Dmitri has sent me news of your falling out. Zander, you must repair it. You joke about me being his favorite, and in truth, he was never so harsh with me as he was with you. With my own father dead so long and you with a surfeit of fathering—at least in name—perhaps it was his way of balancing our fates. But there was more. Only in these past weeks have I come to understand that his strictness with you was not lack of fondness, rather the opposite. You will be Emperor, Zander, and of all things he wishes you strong enough to survive it and honorable enough to be good at it. I have often said I would not trade parentage with you, and though it means I am a junior dennissar forever, I say it again. There is trouble coming. Dmitri sees it and is afraid that you have not. Even here in my backwater post, I am greatly uneasy.

I told you of my mission to find a residence for Kydon, the Khelid legate here in Parnifour, and of his extraordinary demands for its equipage. I found a place that would suit, got him settled in it, and now as I look on it, I wonder what in Athos' name I've done. The castle is the old frontier fortification in the foothills of the Khyb Rash. This Khelid now lurks on the very border of the Empire.

Since the day Kydon moved in, the Khelid presence in Parnifour has multiplied rapidly. I don't see how it's possible. The legate says they are just his staff, who have been scattered through the town until he got a proper residence. But I cannot believe they have been here all the time. Am I a fool, Zander? I have seen Kydon's hired laborers carting stones and timbers into his new keep. He tells me it is for repair, but when I question the laborers, they say they are carving out new rooms deep under the castle, and that once the rough stonework is done, the Khelid do not allow anyone to go inside them. They say there are more Khelid in the keep even than we see here in the town. And all are heavily armed.

Now Kydon wishes to build a temple to his gods on the holy mount in the center of Parnifour. The Emperor's warrant specifically states that I am to do everything in my power to make Kydon comfortable. I have sent to the Emperor for instructions as to whether this project fits the warrant, but Kydon is already warning the nearby merchants and householders that the Emperor will soon be telling them to move away from the base of the mount so a wall can be built about this temple. It will be a fortress in the middle of the city.

I don't know what to think of this or to do about it save lay my misgivings in your lap. I have gone on too long. Fond greetings to our uncle. And listen to him.

May the blessings of Athos shine down on you, cousin. I am ever your sworn and dutiful servant, as well as your devoted kinsman,
    Kiril

The Prince jumped to his feet. "Damnation! I should have sent Kiril a message the moment I knew. And now he'll hear it from someone else, and that I . . . oh, gods! They'll tell him I killed Dmitri. He'll be out for my blood." He paced around the fire, kicking at his saddle pack, at the firewood, at the rocks, at the spikes of dead grass and anything else his boot could find save me. "I won't fight Kiril. I won't. He was never any good. They won't make me do it. Everlasting curses on these demons. You will show me how to avenge myself on them, Seyonne."

I saw no point in explaining that there was no such thing as revenge on demons. Demons care nothing one way or the other how things come out. They feed on pain and terror, and if the source of their sustenance is removed from them, they go elsewhere . . . unless they are destroyed by sorcery.

The Khelid, on the other hand . . . we were going to have to do some thinking about the Khelid.

I still had no inkling of their relationship with the Gai Kyallet. The Lord of Demons . . . everything known of such a being was obscured by a thousand years of speculation. Could it truly command others of its kind to a common purpose? The thought was terrifying, even after dismissing the elaborations of Ezzarian prophecy. If the Prince fell victim to this enchantment, there would be no single field of battle for any mythical warrior—the Empire itself would go up in flames. It was Aleksander's battle that would determine the fate of the world. But his battle with the Demon Lord's enchantment was only part of it; there was also the battle with his own nature—the hand that had beaten me into insensibility and the hand that had lifted me up. His two parts . . . two . . . two souls . . .

"Stars of night . . ." I jumped up from my watch post and started pacing, not believing the fancy that pawed at the doors of my mind like a hungry pup. I had never considered prophecy as absolute truth, only a way of communicating accumulated wisdom. Prophecies of doom were not assurances. Only possibilities. If one didn't take heed. If one wasn't aware and careful. Prophecies of glory and victory were encouragement to strength and honor and hard work. Prophecies were comfort in times of need, and pricks of discomfort in times of ease. People could always fit circumstances to the prediction. Yet never had a man displayed two souls as had Aleksander of Azhakstan.

As I sank back to my rocky perch, I laughed at the outlandish scene my imaginings had conjured. How could anyone ever tell the Ezzarians that the warrior hero who was to fight the Second Battle of the Eddaic Prophecy might be a Derzhi?

Aleksander tried to go back to sleep, but after the third time I heard him cursing quietly under his breath, I knew he was no easier in his mind than I. We were on the road before sunrise.

* * *

We traveled three days northwest, deep into the mountains, avoiding villages, hiding in the trees when the rare traveler would pass. Aleksander could not say where was our final destination, for the map imprinted on his mind unfolded and changed itself as we traveled. I stood watch in the dark hours that we camped. In the daylight, I clung to the Prince's back and slept. He asked how I could possibly sleep on the back of a horse, and I told him I could sleep anywhere; the trouble was the dreams. On the third day I couldn't shake them, and Aleksander's also seemed to get worse as we went on. Thus it was that we were both awake and unsettled at moonrise on the fourth night from Capharna, when a dark figure stepped out of the shadows and said, "Who are you who have followed the way of the gyrbeast?"

I quickly pulled the hood of my cloak down low over my face. So it had come—more quickly than I expected. Rejoicing and despair and overpowering memory all at once. The first Ezzarian I met, and not only did I know him, but he was bound to me by ties of blood and affection and grief. His name was Hoffyd. My brother-in-law.

My older sister Elen had adored the quiet scholar and lifted him from the depths of failure when she agreed to marry him. He had tried to become a Comforter, one who could touch a demon victim and allow the Aife to work through him even at a great distance, but he had too little melydda and was too shy to be sent into the world. After finding his happiness in Elen, he discovered his calling in his talent for formalizing spells and enchantments, a useful scholarly pursuit.

Hoffyd had fought beside my father and Elen on that last day, attempting to preserve an escape route for our Queen. My brave and lovely older sister had refused to leave with the other women when our last refuge was ready to fall. Elen, a red scarf in her dark hair, had been waving and smiling at me as she whirled a pikestaff . . . a pitiful, primitive pikestaff . . . at an armored Thrid mercenary who took her head without slowing his step. My father had fallen ten seconds later. I had wielded a sword and a knife and every skill

I possessed, thinking that somehow I could turn the tide of blood that was drowning us. I had fought for twenty hours straight that day, not understanding how the Derzhi had found us so quickly, in despair because everyone within my sight was dying, and we had nowhere else to run. . . .

Even as I barricaded the doors to that memory yet again, and calmed the shaking sickness that always accompanied it, I blessed Aleksander for making me come. I had seen my father and my sister die, but if Hoffyd yet lived, perhaps others I loved did also. Even if I was dead to all of them, even if they looked through me as though I were a pane of glass, unworthy of stopping the eye, the possibility that I might see friends alive against all expectation swelled my heart. I experienced such a blossoming of hope as can only be felt by one who has lived a lifetime without.

"My name is Pytor," I said, keeping my head down. "My employer was told the way by a slave who took pity on him. The boy said that those who would meet him in this place could take away a demon enchantment."

"And who is your employer?"

"My name is Zander," said the Prince, stepping into the moonlight. The silver beams illuminated his tall form so that one could imagine the feadnach leaking out of his skin. "I am a Derzhi warrior and thus your enemy, but I've come in peace. I've been told you can remove this deviltry."

Chapter 20

"A Derzhi!" Hoffyd spit at Aleksander's feet. "What makes you think I'll take you one step closer to my people? Did you torture the slave to discover the way?"

I prepared to leap in between them, but Aleksander's clenched fist did not stray from his side. "I was given it freely," said the Prince. "In exchange for my word not to bring the law of the Empire down on your heads."

"The word of a murdering Derzhi."

"I should cut out your tongue for that." Aleksander turned his back to Hoffyd and waved at me. "Saddle our horses."

"Please, my lord, I'm sure the gentleman had no intent to question your honor. The boy swore that these people could help you be rid of this curse."

"Even our enemies know that our word is the water of life to us."

"Please, my lord."

"I will not argue the matter, nor will I beg. Just tell me if my informant was wrong. Do Ezzarians heal demon enchantments or do they not?" The Prince was frosted steel. Though I could well understand Hoffyd's sentiments, I wanted to kick him for his careless speech.

I poked at the fire and it flared up, lighting Hoffyd's round angry face like a second moon. Though he was no more than forty-five, his hair had gone completely gray, and he wore a patch over one eye. That must be a sore trial to him. He had been a voracious reader, managing to get his hands on every book that found its way into Ezzaria within a week of its arrival. His cheeks were flushed, and his chin quivered with indignation. "What demon enchantment could harm a Derzhi?"

They weren't getting anywhere. Aleksander moved toward his horse again, but I grabbed his arm, cringing at my own audacity. "My lord," I said. "Did not the slave tell you another word to say? To convince them of your need?" Under my breath I whispered it as if Aleksander might remember it from my silent mouthings.

"Fead . . . something. I don't remember his gibberish. He said I had it along with the enchantment. It sounded like a disease. He said it would make these people listen."

"Fead . . ." It took Hoffyd a moment to grasp it. I wanted to shake him until the word popped from his tongue. "Not the feadnach? Surely not."

"Yes, that was it, wasn't it, Pytor?"

"Aye, my lord. That was the word. He said you bore this feadnach within you, and that because of it, the Ezzarians could not refuse to help you."

Hoffyd's cheeks sagged. "Someone told you that you—a Derzhi—bore the feadnach? Who was it? What was the name?"

Aleksander glanced at me uncertainly.

"He was a youth captured in Capharna a few weeks ago," I said. "He did not want to say his name."

The Ezzarian closed his eyes for a moment—a silent mourning for Llyr, I guessed—before continuing more quietly. "A Derzhi who bears the feadnach? Impossible." Hoffyd's disbelief echoed my own. "The boy was not skilled enough. Who knows what he imagined? Perhaps he thought it would save him."

My brother-in-law was likely correct—though Llyr had a Warden's mentor, it was almost certain the boy had not yet been skilled enough to see what I had seen. But the suggestion of it should be sufficient. Hoffyd was not skilled enough, either. He was a scholar who saw patterns in enchantment and natural objects. Only those who had been trained to do so could see into the soul. Someone else would have to judge.

He came to his decision faster than I'd hoped. "I'll take you."

"And my servant will accompany us," said Aleksander.

"Is he enchanted, too?"

"No. But I'll not leave him out here to freeze. He has no horse."

"If we find you've deceived us . . ."

"If I did not wish so fervently to be rid of this affliction, I would not ride to so desolate an iceberg to find a whole army of Ezzarians. If you can heal me, I might begin to believe there is some point to your existence." Aleksander at his diplomatic best.

Hoffyd gave his opinion more succinctly. "If you bear the feadnach, I'm a jackal's pup."

"Should I load our things, sir?" I said.

"Best do it quickly. We leave now," said Hoffyd. "Let's get this foolishness over with so we can send you back where you came from."

It was some three strange, long days until we reached the Ezzarian hiding place. Three days of paths that seemed to go nowhere, then doubled back on themselves. Of grades so steep we had to lead the horses, and that left us panting for air though we would have sworn we were going downhill all the time. Of turnings and twistings and tunnels and ridges, all of them obscured by fog and mind-haze, so that at the end of the day we could not remember where we'd been.

The journey ended at mid-morning on the fourth day, just as the sun brightened enough to warm my dark cloak. We were sitting on the crest of a ridge overlooking a broad, forested valley, blanketed with snow. A small river wound through the rolling countryside, frozen, and glittering in the sunlight. Five or six stone houses were clustered in the open beside the riverbank, with a few more scattered along the river course northwards through the valley. Thin trailers of gray smoke against the clear blue of the sky told me that most of the homes were nestled in the trees, just as they had been in the ancient forests of oak and pine where I had been born. This was a beautiful place, ringed by the snow-covered spires of the mountains, but it was not the soft green bounty of Ezzaria. It was as if a frost giant from a child's nursery tale had blown his cruel breath upon my home, leaving it frozen and sterile. There could be no melydda bound in those frosted trees, or that ice-clad earth.

Hoffyd led us down a steep trail and along the winding road that took us to the settlement by the river. As I knew he would, he deposited us at a guest house: a small, neat stone cottage at the end of the settlement farthest from the trees.

We had passed only a few people on our way. A woman carrying a basket of linen into a house. A man wheeling a barrow of small bags of grain or flour down the road toward the forest. And two running children—a boy and a girl—streaked by us toward one of the houses by the river. I was filled with indescribable pleasure at the sight of them. None of the four were known to me, but they were most certainly Ezzarian. Alive and free.

"We ask that you remain here until someone comes for you," said Hoffyd, pushing open the door of the cottage. "You're not permitted to walk about the village or speak to anyone without our leave."

"Not permitted? How dare—"

"When will someone come for us?" I interrupted Aleksander before he exploded. "My lord's enchantment is severe."

"If he is demon-afflicted as you claim, then you'll wish us to take our time and do what's best for it," said Hoffyd. "Haste can make it worse."

The Prince threw off his cloak and surveyed the simple furnishings of the cottage. He kicked at the narrow bed as if testing whether it might collapse with use, and he ran a finger over the smooth bare pine of the table. "Get someone here. I have important matters to attend."

"Someone will be with you within the hour." Hoffyd was gritting his teeth. I knew the feeling very well. He pointed to shelves beside the hearth. "There's provender here. Be free of it. If you have your own, we ask that you leave no scraps or waste, but rather take them with you when you leave. There's a latrine behind the house. Water for washing is in the cistern just outside. Water for drinking is in the cask by the door and will be refreshed every morning. These are our ways. Will you abide by them, Derzhi, or shall I take you back the way we've come?"

Aleksander was about to burst. I doubt he had ever been lectured so bluntly by anyone save his father or Dmitri. Certainly not by a commoner who looked like a slightly disreputable shop clerk. He glared at me, then managed to squeeze "I will" past his tight-pressed lips.

"And your servant?"

"Gladly," I said. "We thank you for your hospitality."

"I'll not bid you welcome. It will be a few years yet before we welcome any Derzhi, master or servant." With no further attempt at politeness, Hoffyd slammed the door.

Aleksander flopped on the bed, seemingly assured of its sturdiness, if not its luxury. "Not exactly a hearty welcome," he grumbled. "Insolent beggar."

I was nervous and apprehensive, in no humor to put up with his willful blindness. "What did you expect? They are a few hundred souls, hiding here in the wilderness. Before the Derzhi decided they need a few more hectares of land, Ezzarians numbered in the thousands and had lived in peace for more than eight hundred years."

"No wonder it took us only three days."

"We were no threat to you! You didn't need our land. You took it only because you could, and you killed thousands of innocents in the taking. Must we love you for it?"

"You forget yourself, slave. I'll not argue history with you. What's done is done."

Indeed. Words would change nothing. Passion, desires, grief—none of them mattered. I had to be satisfied with the small graces I had been granted.

I lit a fire in the hearth, then, unable to hold off any longer, I opened the front door a crack and peeked out. The first cottage beyond the guest house would be the Weaver's home, always outside the forest boundary, always in a place of honor in the open village, standing between the outside world and the rest. Fleeces hung in her window, and battered copper dye pots and wooden drying racks were stacked against the side of the house. A string of metal strips hanging from her eaves made a musical tinkling in the breeze.

The boy and girl had run into the center house of the row nearest the river. It was likely the school. As it was morning, they would be doing lessons there: reading and writing, maps and geography in case they became Searchers, mathematics for discipline and logic, herbary for healing and spellmaking, philosophy for health of mind. The mentoring for those with melydda would take place in forest homes all afternoon and into the evening. For some, that schooling would gradually take more and more time, until by the age of twelve one was immersed in it every minute of every day, practicing, learning, studying, perfecting the skills you would need for whatever role the gods had chosen for you, until you were ready to take your place in the secret war Ezzarians had waged for a thousand years. The demon war.

The third house I could not know, as I saw no one go in or out, but I guessed it was the Record House. There one of the Queen's record keepers would compile the reports of the Search teams, and families could come to learn if there was any word of those sent into the world to seek out souls possessed by demons.

The investigator would come from the forest. Those with melydda always lived in the forest, to draw strength and power from the forces of nature in a place so rich with life. I could not settle, so I turned back to Aleksander, who was examining a weaving on the wall beside the bed. It depicted a ring of white stone columns set in the midst of a forest, pairs of men and women walking into it, while the moon shone from the heavens.

"The woman who comes will ask you about the enchantment," I said. "She will examine you—a bit like I do, but with true power behind it—and she'll see it. Tell her about the Khelid, as completely as you can. Everything they've done. How they trapped you with the illusion. How they affected your sleep. How Kastavan seems to be directing the others. And you must be truthful. She'll know if you lie, but she might not be able to tell what about. You need her trust."

"I didn't think it wise to tell them who I am," said Aleksander defensively. "It complicates everything. I didn't think it would matter."

"It doesn't really matter with regard to the enchantment. The other, about the Khelid and the threat to the Emperor and his heir, is far more serious. It turns around beliefs . . . prophecies . . . seeings that we have relied upon for hundreds of years. They must believe you, so they'll take action."

The Prince stripped off his gloves and threw them to the floor. "This is insufferable. To explain myself as if I'm some thieving clerk trying to get a position at court. I don't see what a few fugitive magicians can do about this anyway."

"Maybe nothing," I said. "I don't have any idea what they're capable of anymore. It depends on who survived." I turned my face back to the cold afternoon air.

"And who was enslaved?"

"That, too."

"Will you show yourself to them?" he asked, coming to stand beside me at the door, pulling it open a little wider so he, too, could look out upon the village.

"Not if I can help it."

He was going to ask me about it, but just then a woman walked out of the trees and down the road toward our house. She was bundled in a thick cloak and brightly woven scarf. I abandoned my watch post and retreated to the corner of the room, thinking my stomach might twist itself in a knot when she walked through the open door. She removed her scarf and shook out long dark hair. I didn't know her. What had I expected? That she would happen to be the single person in the universe I would give my soul to see?

"Greetings of hearth and home to you, Zander of the Derzhi," said the young woman. "And to you Pytor of . . .

Your guide did not know your people, sir," she added, tilting her head to the side, as if trying to see my face beneath my hood. I needed to come up with a good excuse to remain hidden. But I couldn't at that moment, so I just bowed and sank to the floor in the corner, making sure the dark wool was pulled low over my face.

She was small, slender, and scarcely as tall as my shoulders. Her shining dark hair fell to her waist, pulled back from her face by a green ribbon at the back of her neck. Her cheeks were flushed with the cold air, and her small, serious face radiated intelligence. She was perhaps in her mid-twenties, very young to be investigating a report of a demon enchantment and a feadnach, not to mention the oddity of a Derzhi supplicant. Very few Ezzarians must have survived. But I refused to be sad. I was watching an Ezzarian investigator. My people lived, and still carried on their work. I had grieved for the dead long years ago.

"My servant is not concerned in this matter," said Aleksander, drawing her uncomfortable attention away from me. "Can we get on with this? I need to speak to someone who can help me, not someone's daughter who wants to gawk at a Derzhi." I groaned inside.

"Certainly," said the young woman, seating herself in the plain wooden armchair beside the hearth. "I would not think of allowing anyone to gawk at our guest. Will you sit here please? I need to ask you a few questions." She laid her slender hands in her lap, calmly waiting for a disgruntled Aleksander to seat himself in the chair facing her. There were perhaps two paces between them.

"Please tell me why you've come here, sir," she began.

"As I told the man, an enchantment," said Aleksander, his face an unsettling shade of red. "A curse from a demon Khelid."

"And how long have you lived with this curse?"

"An eternity." She sat calmly, waiting. Serious. Serene. "No . . . six . . . seven . . . damn, can it be only seven days?"

"What causes you to believe it is a demon-wrought affliction?"

Aleksander was already out of patience. He jumped from his chair, and I feared he might strike the woman. "Because I am not mad, and I have no other explanation for it. The slave . . . I was told it was a demon thing, and I have nothing else to call it."

"Please sit down, sir. I will hear everything you wish to tell me." Her face was impassive. She was not judging, not condemning or approving. Only weighing and watching as was her duty. She would listen to him carefully, and only then would she look inside to see if he was what he said. "Now, tell me of your affliction."

The Prince flopped back into his chair like a sulking child told to sit in the chimney corner, and he told her, though not very thoroughly. He said he was the son of a wealthy man, not mentioning that the man happened to be the Derzhi Emperor. He kept me out of the tale, and did not explain how he had happened to throw the Khelid's gift into the fire or keep his mind together when he was changed into a beast. The first flicker of surprise from her came when he described his transformation.

"Others have seen you make this change?" she asked, interrupting his narrative.

"Of course others have seen it. I'm not mad. I did not see myself. I only felt it and thought . . . But I was myself after it. My servant here has witnessed it." He continued with the story of his uncle's murder, and how the Khelid had turned his father against him, and how he was imprisoned until I had brought him a sword so he could make the change on his own terms.

"This is an extraordinary story, sir, and a matter of grave concern to us as you have surmised. I must now ask your permission to examine you, to view this enchantment that causes you such pain."

"You can do it? A bit of a girl like you?"

"Quite adequately. Better than most men. And I would guess that I'm several years older than you."

"Hmmph. Doesn't seem likely. And I didn't know you

needed permission." Aleksander grimaced my way. "But go on with it."

"To do so I will need to know your true name."

"The whole thing?"

She nodded, wrinkling her brow at the question.

He sighed. "Zander . . . Aleksander, that is. Aleksander Jenyazar Ivaneschi zha Denischkar."

She did not lose her composure, though she very certainly recognized the name. She only widened her eyes a bit and nodded slightly to herself. "That clarifies a great deal." With no more fuss than this, she passed the back of her hand before her eyes. Her pupils grew so large that I could see them from my corner ten paces away. And I could tell the moment she recognized the feadnach. Hands that rested so serenely on her green skirt stiffened and clasped together, and she leaned forward in her chair. "Who was it told you of the feadnach, sir?" she said with quiet intensity.

"A slave." Aleksander's eyes flicked to me again. "A slave boy captured a few weeks ago."

The young woman lifted her small chin and cocked her head as if listening, then shifted her gaze to me. Quickly I held up my hands between us and cast my eyes down so the hood fell further over my face. "Turn your witch-eye away from me," I said harshly. "I gave you no leave."

"My apologies," she said coolly, turning back to Aleksander and passing her hand before her eyes again. "I was only curious as to your employer's lies about the boy. I believed you shared the lie, and I forgot myself. But it is of little importance." The sad undertone to her explanation told otherwise. She would not ask Llyr's name or whether he yet lived. He was dead to them, whether or not he breathed.

"As for everything else . . . you are indeed grievously cursed, sir, and you are all that you have claimed. This news of demons is astonishing and must be brought before our Queen immediately." The investigator rose from her chair. "I'll speak with her right away, and also with those who might be able to heal you of this evil."

"*Might* be able . . ." Aleksander leaped to his feet. "Are you saying you might not be able to cure it?"

"I can promise nothing. We are much diminished . . . as you, of all men, must certainly understand. The one who sent you here must have warned you."

"So it's because of who I am," said the Prince bitterly. "You think to avenge things done when I was in the nursery by leaving me with this horror." He gripped the back of the chair with bloodless knuckles. "I cannot touch a sword. Do you understand what that means? I might as well be dead."

There was no fear, no hesitation, no apology from her. "We will heal this enchantment if it is possible. We have sworn to do so no matter whether you be prince or beggar, Derzhi or Ezzarian. The guilt you bear for those you have destroyed is yours to deal with as you please."

"I bear no guilt."

"Then, you are indeed cursed, and perhaps the light I have seen in you is false. Good morning, gentlemen. I'll be back with news as soon as I can." She nodded politely to both of us, threw on her cloak and scarf, and hurried out of the house.

"Insufferable, pious wench. She's as bad as you!" Aleksander slammed the door after her.

I pulled off my hood only after burying my grin. "Has a woman ever spoken to you so boldly, my lord?"

"Only the cursed witch of Avenkhar."

"The Lady Lydia?"

"Yes. The dragon duchess herself. They are two of a kind. My sympathy to Ezzarian men if all your women are like those two." Aleksander rummaged around the pots and bundles on the shelves, finally throwing a small tin pot at me. "Get me some water. I'm in need of something to clear my head after all this skull work."

I filled the pot from the small drinking cask outside the front door, carefully replacing the lid so nothing would fall in to foul it. Then I hung the pot over the hearth flame and searched for real tea in the guest house stores to boil for myself. "The Lady Lydia saved your life, you know," I said after a while. "If not for her, you would be on your way to Khelidar with a demon passenger."

"She what?" It was truly a pleasure to astonish Aleksander so completely.

I didn't tell him of the lady's admission of love, only how she had given me the opportunity to help him. It was long after we had boiled and soaked and warmed and stirred his nazrheel that he could bring himself to speak again. "So what is this feadnach? Is it another curse that makes me beholden to slaves and shrews?"

"No, my lord. It is your heart. Difficult as it may be to comprehend, there is a possibility you may have one."

Chapter 21

We staved off the pangs of long-delayed hunger with herb-crusted bread and new butter from the cottage shelf. For me it was a feast, for Aleksander, famine worthy of an hour's grumbling. Shortly after we finished and I had cleaned up our crumbs, the investigator returned. She tapped on the door and stepped in at Aleksander's word.

"I am to take you to the Queen immediately. She has only a brief time to spare you just now, but she agrees that the matter is of sufficient importance to hear your story herself."

Aleksander threw on his cloak, but I remained seated by the fire. "Come, Pytor," he said, glaring at me. "You must stay with me."

"Your servant has judged rightly, sir," said the woman. "The Queen has no need to see him. She will see you, and you alone."

"But I insist!"

"Then, you shall not go to her. This is her domain, sir, not yours. We are beyond the boundaries of your Empire"—she quieted his protest with her hand—"because you've sworn not to use your knowledge of this place to harm us. Is that not true?"

"Word twisting."

The lady motioned him through the door.

"Speak truth, Aleksander," I said after he was gone. "If things have fallen out as I suspect, this Queen will read you like a child's first book." I curled up and hid from my thoughts in sleep.

* * *

It was two hours until the woman brought Aleksander back to the guest house. "I'll fetch you at first light tomorrow. Until then—"

"What are we to do until then?" said Aleksander. "I won't stay cooped up in this hovel like a prisoner. I should at least see to my horse."

"I understand this is difficult," she said. "Perhaps . . ." She hesitated just for a moment. "Perhaps you would consider coming to my home this evening for supper. It's certainly not the accommodation to which you're accustomed, but perhaps it would be more comfortable than our poor guest house. We have very few guests here, and our customs are quite strict, but we have no wish to make a prison."

"You would have me as a table guest—your enemy of whom you disapprove so heartily?"

She colored a bit. "I spoke out of turn this morning. My feelings intruded upon my work, which is unconscionable. Therefore I must make amends. Those who come seeking our help are equal in our sight. We must not and should not judge."

"Fair enough," said the Prince. "Then I presume my servant is also welcome."

She glanced at me uncomfortably. I had pulled up my hood again when she returned. "I had no reason to believe he would wish to come. But if it is his desire, then he is also welcome. Will you come, Pytor?"

I shook my head. "I cannot—"

"Of course he'll come," burst in Aleksander. "He's better company than his shy aspect and his boorish tongue would tell. If we are equals here, then servant and master will both sit as your guests."

"I'll come for you after sunset," she said. "And, by the way, your horse is well cared for. You needn't worry save that some of our lads won't want to let him go."

As soon as she was gone, I protested. "My lord, I cannot."

"I'll not argue it. If I go alone, I'll want to bed the wench; she's fair and pleasing when she controls her tongue. It's likely not a clever notion, and if you're there, you'll shrivel my eyeballs for it, so I'll lose the desire right off."

"Bed her?" I was smitten with horror. "I beg you forget any such idea, my lord. It is not our way to be so free about such matters, and she must live here long after you are gone. It's very unusual for her to ask you to her home unchaperoned. It's a great kindness, so you must be—"

"All right. All right. Ease your mind. I had no serious thought of it. I would at least not take her unwilling." He sprawled on the bed and closed his eyes, smiling to himself in smug satisfaction, as if I couldn't see it. I wanted to throw something at him. He knew I could never let him go alone now. "Let me sleep for a while. Your women are exhausting."

"What of the Queen?" I took my petty vengeance by preventing his sleeping until he satisfied the curiosity gnawing at my gut.

"I've never been probed and examined and poked at so thoroughly. I didn't know there were so many questions in the universe."

"But what did she say?"

"That I had a curse on me, and she'd have to think about it. A lot of bloody nothing for all the questioning. Comes of having a woman do it. Her consort was with her. He was listening right enough. Asked a few questions of his own, but left most of it to her."

"We decided hundreds of years ago that women were better at such things than men. In our particular work, it made the difference between success and failure, and failure with regard to demons is more devastating than most failures."

"So Ezzarians chase demons. However did you get yourselves into that?"

I laughed at his question. Only to be expected that Aleksander would hit upon the single puzzle Ezzarians themselves would like explained. "Actually, we aren't sure. We've lost a great deal of information from the past. But we have the power, the melydda, to do it, and we've developed the skills over the years, and if we didn't . . ." I shrugged my shoulders. It wasn't really possible to explain the devastation of the world that would occur if we failed in our task. The cruelty, the violence, the horror . . . there was so much of it already that sometimes it was hard to feel that we made a difference. You had to view each victory in itself: the wife no longer beaten to the point of death, the child no longer starved, the slave left unmutilated, the man no longer weeping with the horror that his hands created, the woman no longer clawing her eyes to rid herself of unceasing visions. ". . . there is no one else. There are horrors worse than those we live every day."

"And women are in charge of it. That seems a demon-wrought thing itself."

"All have their role," I said. "Equally important. Women have certain talents—sorcery you would call them—that enable them to do certain things. Other tasks require physical skills and sorcerous ones that women are less likely—"

"Fighting. You actually fight them, don't you?"

"It's how we get them out—not battling the possessed person, but the demon itself." In a landscape woven of sorcery and the human soul. There was no simple explanation for the Aife's magic—the portal and the land beyond it. "If the ones who did those things also carried the tasks of governing or examining, it would bind up too much knowledge in the person most at risk."

"Like sending your master strategist into the vanguard?"

I wished he would stop his questions. I didn't want to tell him. I didn't want to think of it. "Exactly that."

"Warriors. Warriors who battle demons. And you were one of them, weren't you? Before. What I saw was no dream."

"Please, my lord . . ."

He was quiet for a moment, though I could feel him looking at me.

". . . tell me . . ." Did I want to know or not? "Please, my lord, tell me of the Queen."

"Exceptionally lovely." He rolled over on the bed and kicked off his boots. "Cold as a stone goddess, but fire in her eye—and in her soul, too. When I got there she was playing some kind of lap harp. Thought my boots might start to smoke. Do they ever marry anyone but Ezzarians?"

"Never. Put it out of your mind." I wished I could put her out of mine. It had been a mistake to ask. Music. That wasn't right. She had never played. If it wasn't her . . . Darkness crept into my being. Dread.

Aleksander was still babbling. "It could be a good thing for Ezzarians to have me in the family, you know. Her consort has eyes like a frog. . . ." He caught my attention again. "Not a bad-looking fellow, but his eyes don't sit nicely down in a hollow, more flat on his face. Built like a Manganar, though. If he can fight, he'd be a day's work to get rid of."

"Oh, he can fight all right." He could twist two Thrid into a knot and still crush a Derzhi neck with the other hand.

"You know him, then?"

"And the Queen, she's tall, lighter-haired than most Ezzarians . . ." Streaks of red-gold sunlight in her dark chestnut curls—so different from the straight black hair the rest of us had. ". . . with a cleft in her chin?"

"I could spend a day exploring that cleft. And another exploring under her skirt, and another—"

"That's enough!" I jumped up from the floor. "Gods, will you leave it?"

Of course, Ysanne was queen. Why had I doubted it for a moment? She had been groomed for it from childhood. Her power, her perception, her skills honed every day. Fate, even in the form of a Derzhi conquest, could not have prevented her.

Aleksander came to me and pulled down my hood, cocking his head to one side. "She's not just an acquaintance, is she? Not just your sovereign? A kinswoman, perhaps? I was told you were a royal bastard. Couldn't be your mother unless Ezzarian magic is more powerful than I can imagine. Or was she your lover? That would be a tale worth hearing. How—"

"She was my wife."

"Athos' balls." Odd how heartfelt sympathy could be expressed so crudely.

We'd not yet been formally wed, but the distinction was too subtle for a Derzhi. Ysanne and I had been paired when we were fifteen and had fought our first battle together at seventeen after I passed my testing and became a Warden. We were the youngest pairing ever to dispossess a demon. We had come to think as one, to mesh our talents so that I could move with ease through her portals from the world where we existed into the reality, the battleground, she created for me. There I would seek out the demon to banish or destroy it. Ysanne had been able to sense my doubts and fears before I knew them myself, and send me her strength and power and care to vanquish them. There had never been a Warden and an Aife so attuned to each other as we had been. We were destined for each other, we said, pledged through a hundred battles and three years of such intimacy as husbands and wives never know. I had known she would marry if she lived. I was dead. She was to be queen.

"And the fish-eyed consort?"

That was the true surprise. "A friend." My dearest friend from the day we could walk. "On the day of Ezzaria's fall . . . when things got desperate, I sent him for reinforcements, spellmakers who could cause a distraction, allow us to regroup, anything to get five minutes to think, to get people out. He said that the only way he would fail was if he was dead. He never came, so I assumed . . . all these years, I thought he was dead."

"And instead he was running off with your wife. Sounds like a Derzhi!"

His words at last prodded me out of my confused musings. "Of course not. Something happened. He couldn't get back. And she was free to marry from the moment I was captured. I'm just surprised they're together, that's all. They argued . . . irritated each other, so I could never be with both of them at once. I wouldn't have thought they'd suit."

Aleksander returned to the bed, his large stockinged feet hanging off the end of it. "Clearly you didn't look. You're naive, Seyonne. I'd guess you were the only one not to see it."

I tried to rid myself of my disturbance. I should be rejoicing that two I had loved so dearly lived and had found love with each other. Enough to draw music from one who never believed she could create beauty, but only lunatic landscapes. Of course I rejoiced. Ezzarians were not Derzhi. Ysanne needed a partner to make use of her skill, and a lover to embrace her fire. Rhys was a good and honorable man. There was no betrayal. Aleksander knew nothing about Ezzarians. Nothing.

Chapter 22

I sat in the cottage doorway all afternoon, leaning against the doorpost, listening to Aleksander groan and mumble in his sleep, and watching the quiet activity of the Ezzarian settlement, quite successful at forcing aside all thoughts of Ysanne and Rhys. As surely as the sun moved along its path toward the western peaks, the man with the now empty barrow trudged out of the forest, past the cottage, only to disappear beyond the next rise in the road. An old woman drove a small flock of sheep across a nearby field with the help of a dancing pup. The only excitement was when two youths careened down the road on horseback and reined in hard in the center of the road, laughing excitedly and splattering sun-melted slush. A woman stepped out of the Records House and scolded them, and they began walking the horses back toward the forest. I smiled when, at the very moment she reentered the building, they whooped and shot off again. Some things never changed.

After an hour of quiet, the children—fifteen or twenty of them—burst from the schoolhouse door and ran in every direction, some toward the river, some toward the forest. Two girls went straight to the Weaver's cottage. Perhaps one of them would be the next Weaver, she who was the heart of an Ezzarian community. My mother had been the Weaver for our settlement before she died of fever when I was twelve. Two more girls and a boy, older children, sat on the rocks outside the school talking earnestly, drawing in the air with their hands, leaving traces of silver glinting in the sunlight. Musings on the universe, I guessed, remembering a hundred such conversations. Trying to understand why, among all the peoples in the world, Ezzarians were charged with keeping demons from ravaging human souls. Believing that some-day they would take on their responsibilities and that those thousands of strangers who lived out in the world, never knowing or understanding what had been done for them, would become worthy of its beauties. I longed for a mo-ment's sharing in their innocence and ignorance.

The woman came just after sunset as she had promised. The road was deserted by that time, and so she was halfway to our cottage before I picked out her green cloak against the background of the darkening trees. It was odd for her to in-vite us to her home. Outsiders. Suppliants. My people were sincere in their welcome to anyone in need of help, and gen-erous beyond the world's understanding in the sacrifices they made to hold the power of demons at bay. But their homes were their private refuges—warm, comfortable havens for those who lived close with horror and madness. A cynical voice in the back of my mind said that the investi-gator was but another young woman captivated by Alek-sander's overabundant virility and breathtaking station in life. But I dismissed the thought quickly and told myself it was more likely exactly what she had said. A kindness. And perhaps a desire to converse with someone new.

My Ezzaria had been isolated from the world. It was nec-essary. We dared not reveal our purposes to anyone, lest the demons be drawn to us, or the rest of humanity interfere with our work. But there had been a great deal of travel be-tween our own settlements in those days, and we'd had a hundred or more Searcher teams out in the world, constantly coming and going with news and information and books. With so few Ezzarians left, and all of them in hiding, there could be only a few teams out and only the most necessary contact with outsiders.

I stood up when she came, bowed, and held open the door.

"Good evening," she said, lowering the hood of her cloak, but very pointedly keeping her eyes averted from me.

"Good evening, madam," I said, biting off the apology that came to my tongue. I could afford neither her interest nor her friendship. I needed to stay apart so she would at least acknowledge me as a living being, however boorish.

Aleksander was sitting at the table, his head bent over a cup of steaming nazrheel. When I'd waked him at sunset, he'd almost broken my arm before shaking off his restless dreams. He complained that he'd slept only an hour, and indeed dark smudges circled his eyes, and the skin of his face was stretched tight. But he recovered his spirits quickly when the woman came. He snatched his cloak from the hook on the wall, swirling it about himself dramatically as he fastened it about his shoulders.

"At last! I've begun to despair of Ezzarian hospitality. Lead me away, gracious lady. Anywhere."

The lady's amusement gleamed softly beneath layers of dignity, serious purpose, and gracious formality—a burden of roles for a quiet, graceful young woman. "We must seem a dreadfully dull village to one from so different a life," she said. "I can offer only a pleasant, though chilly, walk through the woods, a simple meal, and perhaps a little conversation. Not exactly an evening in the courts of Zhagad."

"Madam, it is the company makes the evening." Aleksander offered his arm, and the woman nodded and took it. As they walked out of the door, the Prince looked over his shoulder and grinned fiendishly, calling out, "Come along . . . Pytor. You don't wish me to have all the fun."

I trailed along behind, cursing Derzhi princes and the paths of fortune, as had become my unseemly habit of late.

To Aleksander's astonishment our guide made a light with her hand, silvery beams that mimicked moonlight and showed us the way along the path. Every few steps a smaller path would break away, wandering off into the forest darkness, where you could see homely lantern beams winking through the movement of the trees.

My corruption had weighed heavily on me from the first moment we'd entered the Ezzarian settlement, and as we passed under the eaves of the forest, beyond the barriers of enchantment woven by the woman with fleeces hanging in her window, the burden of my unclean soul became almost unbearable. When I inhaled the pure air, every violation of my body and mind came back to haunt me: every unseemly touch, every night of forced intimacy with women or men I did not know, every drop of impure water, the food that was never clean, but half rotten or taken from unclean beasts or dung-fed fields, my blood exposed to outsiders' touch, my hands immersed in their filth, my body, once dedicated to the service of honor and truth, scarred and maimed and forced to grovel before those who considered themselves gods. I knew none of it was my fault. I had done nothing to deserve what had happened to me, despite what many of my people would assume. Yet reason—all the arguments and philosophizing I had used with Llyr—had no effect on my feeling. As I walked behind Aleksander and the Ezzarian woman, I wished only that I could run from that place and never stop.

"Here," said the woman, leading us to the left along one of the narrow tracks and across a wooden footbridge that spanned a gurgling brook. Cheerful yellow candlelight shone from the windows of a good-sized cottage, speaking of comfort and companionship and familiarity. To be a Warden, one had to be able to separate oneself from others, to rely on no one save your partner who held the portal. One had to embrace solitude and self-sufficiency. These were skills and habits that had preserved my life and my sanity in my years of bondage, but they were not without cost. Never in all my life had I felt so alone.

"Come inside and get warm." She pushed open the door and stepped inside. Aleksander followed her. I went as far as the doorway and stood stupidly gazing upon the past.

The room was quite large, the wooden floor covered with woven rugs of russet and forest green, the chairs and table of smooth dark pine, laid with sewn cushions and cloths of autumn colors. It was pleasantly jumbled with books, papers, and baskets of needlework and pinecones and nuts. One end of the long table was laid for three. On the other end lay a mortar and pestle and a stack of small, sewn bags. It looked as if she had been packaging herbs dried from the previous season, for bundles of herbs hung from the rafters above the table, and a few more lay beside the implements. The room smelled of thyme, and rosemary, and roasting meat from a spit over the hearth fire. The walls were hung with weavings, lovely, rich-hued, some in simple patterns, some with detailed depictions of Ezzarian life.

The lady removed her cloak and hung it on a wooden peg inside the door. "Do come in," she said. "Spring comes late here, and the nights are always cold."

"I cannot," I stammered stupidly. "I'll wait outside . . . or go back. I don't belong here . . . eating . . . with the Prince." Nonsense poured from my lips because I could not bear leaving, yet I could not accept the consequences of stepping inside. How could I keep wearing my cloak and my hood in that room?

"Come inside," said Aleksander gently. "My servant is quite affected by the cold," he said to the woman. "Would it violate your customs if he left his cloak on for a while . . . until he's comfortable?"

"He may do as he wishes," said the woman. "Come to the fire and get warm," she said to me. "It took me three winters here to get accustomed to the cold. Are you from southern climes?"

"Yes," I said numbly, and stepped inside.

She closed the door and took Aleksander's cloak, then excused herself and disappeared through a doorway on the left.

"You have to do it sometime," chided Aleksander quietly. "She is not someone you know, so it might be easier with her. Perhaps they've changed their ways."

"Perhaps the Derzhi have become peacemakers."

"You are a man. Tell them they're wrong about you. You've convinced me of a number of things I had no wish to believe."

"You said it yourself, my lord. I am a slave, not a man. They'll not hear me when I speak."

He didn't answer. The lady returned and began setting food on the table. She put out hot bread, potatoes roasted in the coals of the fire, a bowl of dried fruit, and a plate of meat, sliced thin from the piece on her spit. As she poured three glasses of wine, she invited us to make ready.

Aleksander started for the table, but I caught his arm and nodded to the painted pottery bowl and pitcher sitting on a small table next to the hearth. He was puzzled, but I pulled him with me and showed him how to clean his own hands with the water and the small linen towel laid out beside. The lady was pleased.

"No business while we eat," she said, offering the plate of meat to Aleksander, who shifted uncomfortably in his chair. He was accustomed to reclining at table, and he didn't know what to do with the offered plate.

"May I serve you, my lord?" I said softly, taking the plate from the woman and picking up the fork that lay on it.

"Whatever is done," he said.

I filled his plate and my own. The woman seemed not to notice. That is, she was very skilled at ignoring awkward behavior.

"So tell me, sir," she said to Aleksander after everything was served and we'd begun eating. "What is it you enjoy most about your life?"

It was a simple question, seriously asked. Not frivolous. She truly wanted to know and to weigh it along with everything else she had learned. Aleksander understood the same, and he gave it serious consideration, rather than blurting out something foolish as he might have done in Capharna.

"The horses," he said at last, then laughed heartily at himself. "Amazing, isn't it? I'd never considered it quite so plainly. I have been given everything in life a man could want, but the thing I prize most is that I can ride the finest horses in the world."

"Horses are indeed beautiful creatures," she said, her dark eyes fixed on him in such serious attention as a man might bleed for.

"Intelligent. That's what I like about them. Strong-willed.

You can't tame them, not without making them less than they are. To get their best, you must convince them of your worthiness to be their rider."

She drew him into an hour's web of conversation, astonishing for a sheltered young woman speaking with a very worldly prince. They talked of horses and racing, and that led to the desert and Aleksander's love of the hot, dry lands of his birth. She talked of herbs and their many uses, and of the weather and writing and trees. Several times she tried to include me in her word weaving, but I would give only a brief answer, declining to take up her challenge.

After a while I found that I had forgotten to eat while I watched her. She would flush charmingly when Aleksander would get so wound up in a story that he would blurt out rude words—then strangle on them—or when he would quite obviously skip the part about how he took the fiery Manganar girl, who rode so magnificently, to his bed. She was animated by the exchange like an enchanted flower, budding and blooming all in the matter of an hour.

"You are a fine storyteller, sir," she said. Then she shifted her attention to me again. "But as for you . . . I rarely have so much difficulty setting my guests at ease. You put all my skills to the test. Perhaps you take no pleasure in conversation."

"Sometimes the greatest pleasure is listening to those who are skillful at it," I said.

She was genuinely surprised at my answer.

"He has no trouble conversing when he's telling me all the things I do wrong," grumbled Aleksander to no one in particular.

"Indeed?" she said, widening her eyes in interest. "You must be a favored servant to thus have a prince's ear. More a friend than a servant."

Aleksander flushed quite a vivid red.

I, of course, had no wish to pursue such an interchange. "May I help you clear the table, madam? After such a fine meal, the hostess should not bear the sole burden of the cleaning."

"That would be very kind," she said, rising from her chair. She showed me where to put the dishes, then asked if I would bring water for washing them.

I took her pail and stepped out the door, welcoming the cold. I was fearfully hot in my cloak, for she had kept the fire well stoked for my comfort. I found the cistern beside the house and dipped the pail. Perhaps it was the enchantment of the forest or the need to ease my heartsickness with a touch of long-forgotten grace, but I spoke the water-blessing words as I lifted the pail. *"Sych var de navor, caine anwyr."* Gift of earth and sky, purify our hands. It seemed only right to say it on that night.

When I stood up to return to the house, the woman was standing right behind me. She was staring at my hand that held the pail, her body rigid as if the pail were filled with snakes. I looked down to see what bothered her so. I had pulled up my sleeve to keep it out of the water, leaving the iron band about my wrist exposed.

"You are his slave, not his servant."

"Yes."

"Does he forbid you to show your face?"

I wanted to tell her yes, for that might direct her attention away from me. But she would detect the lie, and there was already too much anger in her voice. Aleksander needed her help.

"No. It is my choice." Too late, I pulled down the sleeve to cover the telltale. "We should go in. You wear no cloak."

"I came out to show you where to get washing water, but clearly you knew where to look."

"Hoffyd told us of your customs and showed us the cistern at the guest house. I assumed it was the same here." I was flustered and stumbled over the words.

She walked slowly up the steps to the house and paused before opening the door. "And did he also tell you his name, and the prayer we say as we draw water?"

She didn't wait for my answer, but went in and confronted Aleksander, her cheeks and eyes blazing with more than the fire. "I brought you here tonight to learn more of one who bears the feadnach. I could not reconcile a prince of the Derzhi marked with the light of destiny. You told us you were sent here by a slave, and you allowed us to believe it was a youth, a lost one of our own, whom we believed incapable of such a discovery. You lied to me, but it seemed only a small thing compared to the truth of what you carry and your demon enchantment. But I was not easy with it." She tightened her lips and shook her head. "So I decided you should speak to someone else, someone wiser than I, who might unravel the lie. But now I've uncovered another lie, and before we go further, I must know how far I've been deceived."

She faced Aleksander first, closed her eyes, pressed a clenched fist to her breast, and said, *"Lys na Catrin."* Then she did the same to me. And then she waited, eyes closed. Listening.

"What does she want?" whispered Aleksander.

I sighed and accepted what had always been inevitable. I spoke without whispering. "She has given you an immense gift, my lord—the gift of her name, and the trust and kinship that such a gift bears among Ezzarians. You are her guest, and if you wish to answer in kind, you must do the same."

"But I already told her my name. There's no more of it."

"Give it again—with your unspoken oath that you will never use her name to betray her. Do it here, in this way, and she'll know that you mean it truthfully. Once done, you will not lie to her."

With his eyes and hands he asked if he should make the same gestures as she had done, and I nodded. So he clenched his fist before his breast, closed his eyes, and said, "My name is Aleksander Jenyazar Ivaneschi zha Denischkar."

Then it was my turn. She had not yet moved. I lowered my hood, closed my eyes, and clenched my fist until I thought blood might drip from it. *"Lys na Seyonne,"* I said. "Forgive me."

There was no need to list the offenses for which I needed forgiveness. I had brought my corruption to her home, eaten her food, touched her things, lied to her. But it made no difference if I laid out my faults. She would not hear. When I opened my eyes, Aleksander was watching curiously. The lady's back was disappearing through the inner door, and my heart was stone.

"I must go before she comes back," I said.

"You were wrong," said the Prince. "She saw you very clearly. And it was not with hatred or disgust or anything you expected."

"It was shock. Surprise. She won't slip again. I only hope I've not hurt your chances for their help. I have to leave."

Aleksander shook his head. "It was not that kind of shock. I think you should stay."

There were steps beyond the doorway, and I was in a frenzy to be gone. "Please, my lord. I cannot stay here."

"And where do you think to go, a boy like you, incompetent, ignorant, imperceptive, and ill-suited to your most considerable . . . ah, Verdonne have mercy . . . your most considerable gifts?"

In the doorway, leaning on Catrin's arm, was an old man. A shock of unruly white hair stuck straight up above a square face that was bounded by the most stubborn jaw anyone ever owned. He wore a dark red dressing gown and the bent posture of age, but his dark eyes snapped with everything of life.

"Master Galadon." I whispered the name, then held up my hands between us, palms spread wide as if I could hide behind their meager shelter. I could not bear for my beloved mentor to see what I had become.

"Is it you, boy? Come here to me." Catrin eased him into the chair by the fire.

"Gaenad zi," I said, averting my eyes.

"You are most certainly disobedient, but I alone will judge whether or not you are unclean. Now, come here."

I looked to the woman for help, but her eyes, glistening with love and tears, were on the old man. Catrin. Galadon's granddaughter, the dark-eyed sprite who had watched every agonizing step of my training, who had brought me water and sweets when I was exhausted, and who had told me I was strong and marvelous when I would go three days without doing a single thing right. She had been only eleven when I was taken. How could this luminous young woman be Catrin?

Galadon pointed to the rug in front of him. "Here would be a good place."

I knelt on the rug in front of him and kept my hands, palms outward, in front of my face. "Master, it is the blessing of my life to see you, but I must go. I don't belong here."

His face was lined with age and sorrow, but his eyes were lifetimes younger and shed such joyful warmth on me as to melt my frozen soul. Gently grieving, he brushed the scar on my face and touched the slave rings on my wrists, then he took my hands in his warm wrinkled ones. *"Tienoch havedd, Seyonne. Vasyd dysyyn."* Greetings of my heart, Seyonne. Welcome home.

Chapter 23

There was very little to be said between Galadon and me. I would not speak to him of the corruption I had lived, and he had no need to tell of sorrows that time and logic had already revealed to me: my father's death and my sister's, the abandonment of Ezzaria and rebuilding here in the wilderness, the fact that my betrothed wife was married to my best friend. I made one tentative query as to Ysanne's well-being, but he refused to speak of her.

In truth, no words could equal the blessing of his greeting. I held it in my ears and in my heart, unwilling to let anything of mine displace it, but afraid the law of silence would yet overtake his lapse of age and grief. "Master," I said softly, pulling my hands away from him. "I must leave you before someone sees. Forgive my coming."

He raised my face to look on his own, allowing me to see tears that no student would ever have believed him capable of shedding. "You have committed no offense, son of my heart, save waiting so long to come back to us."

"The law has not changed," I said, knowing he would not contradict me, even while yearning that he might.

"What law is worth a beetle's ear if it condemns—"

"Please, Master Galadon. If you would do me one service in memory of what has been, then I beg you listen to the Prince's story and warn the others of what it means. Did she tell you—Catrin—did she tell you of the Khelid?"

The old man leaned back in his chair and scowled. "I am to believe this Derzhi's tale? A despicable demon carrier who believes he can own another human being? One who's done these wicked things to you?" He flicked his eyes to Aleksander in disgust, and he could not hide his distress when his glance came back to me.

"I am no matter," I said. "And, yes, you must believe him. We were wrong, Galadon. All these years we believed it was the Derzhi warned of by the Eddaic Prophecy. We thought we had time before they became one with the demons. But I am convinced that the conquerors from the north are the Khelid, not the Derzhi. I have seen the Gai Kyallet and watched it involve other demons in its plotting. And this Prince . . ." In the moment of my speaking, my budding theories blossomed into conviction. ". . . master, he could be the Warrior of Two Souls."

"Impossible!" Age had done nothing to quiet Galadon's bellow.

Catrin had taken Aleksander across the room and was showing him the weavings hung on the walls. The Prince was listening to her attentively, his hands clasped behind his back. Neither of them took note of Galadon's outburst.

"Look inside him, master," I said, keeping my own voice low. "Even with no power I was near blinded by his fead-nach. Even while living in the shadow of what he is, I have seen the promise of what he could be. I know it's difficult to believe, but it's so clear to me. If ever a man had two souls, it is Aleksander."

But Galadon would not be soothed, nor his long-held convictions shaken. "You are the Warrior of the prophecies, Seyonne. I've known it since you were a child climbing trees, breathing melydda before you even understood what it was. The Derzhi came down from the north as the Seers foretold, and the First Battle was lost. I know that the Second Battle comes—when the demons will show themselves in the fullness of evil—and you must be ready. All of us must be ready. We've been preparing, waiting, hoping. . . . It's why I knew you weren't dead as some among us claimed. All these years I've trusted holy Verdonne to bring you back. She would not leave us without the Warrior. It's made me rethink everything: the law, the prophecies, our ideas about power and corruption."

"Master, I've been through the Rites. I have nothing—"

But he heeded me no more than a mountain heeds a gnat. "My plan is ready, the groundwork laid, secrets kept and held close, waiting for you to come back and walk the path laid down for you when the world was young. You believe your power is lost. But I believe that you have been forged anew by your suffering—and you will find that the past was but a shadow of your glory."

"Ah, master . . ." I would have given my eyes to believe him, but I had lived too long with the truth. "Examine the Prince and tell me what you see."

Aleksander laughed just then, and Catrin, her dark eyes sparkling in the lamplight, laughed with him, a harmony of life and beauty in the sound of their youthful voices.

"Verdonne be merciful," said Galadon. "You care for him. How is that possible?"

"Examine him, master."

The old man glared at me as if I'd put a gutted rabbit in his lap. "Catya, bring me the supplicant."

If I had been a student again, the steel edge to Galadon's tone would have had me running for shelter. Aleksander didn't know anything of likais.

"So what were you arguing about? I thought you two were going to set me bawling like a Suzaini granny with your sweet reunion, and then, after the old buzzard turns me inside out and leaves me feeling like a puddle of spit, you start yelling at each other."

"I wasn't yelling."

"Well, he was yelling enough for both of you, and it was you he was aiming at."

Aleksander and I were hurrying down the snowy forest path, back toward the village. Catrin had been planning to escort us, but her grandfather was exhausted and needed her care. Galadon could be not a day less than eighty, and though his stubborn spirit refused to admit it, his body clearly knew. The moon was up and full. We weren't going to get lost.

I was anxious to get back to the guest house, where I could sit in the dark and think. I needed to clear the muddle Galadon had made of my head. It hadn't helped that he'd started setting me to recite things for him as if I were ten years old again: a poem about ships, the words to a song, the spell to ripen fruit, the second prophecy of Meddryn, five hundred other snippets of information. I dredged them all out of my head, stumbling over words and inflections, trying to refuse him nothing, who had tried to give me everything. It went on so long, I couldn't keep all of it straight. He never gave me time to catch a breath . . . or to ask him all the questions I longed to have answered. His plan was set, and he did not deem it necessary to enlighten me as to its details.

"So what was the argument about?"

"It's all bound up in a prophecy," I said, as much to keep the Prince from pestering me with more questions as anything. "For centuries our Seers have predicted that a race of warriors from the north would destroy the world. There were to be two battles. The first would leave the people wailing in terror, and the world reeking of blood and destruction. The Second Battle would be worse, for the warriors from the north would ally themselves with the demons. The only hope would be another warrior—the Warrior of Two Souls—one destined to return his people to greatness. This person would challenge the Gai Kyallet, the Lord of Demons, and in single combat they would determine the fate of the world."

"And you believe this kind of gibberish?"

"We saw the race of warriors come from the north. And there was no denying the blood or the wailing."

The Prince halted in the middle of the moonlit path. "You think your prophets foretold our coming—the coming of the Derzhi?"

"So my people believe," I said wearily, trudging onward, craving the fire and the blankets that awaited us at the guest house. From houses deep in the trees, I glimpsed flickering firelight. Faint voices and laughter wafted by us on the chilly breeze. There were so many of the lights, I had the passing thought that there were more Ezzarians here than Llyr had told me.

The Prince caught up with me and stopped me again, this time holding onto my arm. "But you think something else." How could he be so annoyingly persistent after the past tiring days?

"Don't be offended, my lord, but I think the Derzhi were incidental. Prophecy or no, the Khelid are the real danger. They are the conquerors from the north with no souls. We must face them, and the ranks of the Ezzarians are already decimated." Only three Wardens left, Galadon had said. Only three. Two of them untried students, and the third one Rhys. My friend, who had struggled through his training and come close five times to ending it, had passed his testing at last. I had been one of ten experienced Wardens. How was Rhys able to keep up with the burden? "We thought we had time before the Derzhi became one with the demons. That we would have ample warning. But the Khelid are already merged with them. If there is such a being as the Warrior with Two Souls, we'd best find him."

"Sounds a confusing mess—two souls. I can't seem to deal with one properly, according to you. So what of this Galadon? Can he get rid of my curse? He wouldn't answer when I asked him."

"He told me it would be very difficult." Galadon had told me it was impossible, that the damage already done was too severe. Attempting to excise the enchantment would destroy Aleksander, and it might draw the demons' attention just when we could least afford it. Galadon claimed that his plans—including myself—could not be risked. That had been only one of our disagreements. "But someone will take care of it. You will be healed. It is necessary. Critical. They'll see it."

"Damn. You're not thinking to convince them that I am your Warrior of Two Souls? Is that what this feadnach foolishness is?"

"I don't know what to think. I can't think. I'm not sure I want to think." I pushed his hand away as if it was not a hand that could take my life at any instant. "Galadon has very different ideas than mine." And budging the stubborn old man seemed impossible.

"Well, whatever you're thinking, keep me out of it, Ezzarian. I am not here to prance around, pretending I believe in any barbarian prophecies. I might as likely believe in the warrior on the tapestries the woman just showed me—a warrior with wings fighting a monster with only a knife and a looking glass. I will deal with the Khelid the moment I can hold a sword again."

"It seems foolish, doesn't it?" I tried to put it all out of mind. "Whatever comes, please don't mention any of this to the Queen in the morning. Nothing of Galadon or Catrin. If anyone finds out I'm here and they've spoken to me, their lives will be very hard. It is a violation of their law."

Aleksander shook his head. "And you call the Derzhi cruel! I don't understand this kind of punishment. Invisibility. Wouldn't a good beating or a nice hanging suffice?"

"Trade places with me for a day, my lord, and tell me which beating is a good one and which hanging is nice."

"I stand by my point."

"You must understand. Ezzarians spend their lives battling demons. They have to make sure that there is no possible channel through which a demon may reach them. No evil. No impurity. Our history tells us of horrors that can result when a demon follows a path of corruption back to those who are fighting it. I suppose we took it too far. Perhaps our attempt to protect ourselves has coiled about on its own tail and devours us. I don't know anymore."

We walked in silence until we broke through the edge of the trees. Though the valley lay frosted and still in the moonlight, spring was in the air, a moist earthiness beyond the night's chill that soothed the soul with the promise of warmth and growing. I inhaled deeply.

"Who is this old man, Seyonne? I wouldn't have thought anyone could set you so at odds with yourself."

I laughed. "Haven't you guessed it? He was my likai."

At the very moment I said the word, Aleksander's boot broke through an ice-crusted puddle. He slipped and cracked a knee on a sharp rock. "Damnation!" he said, sitting down hard and pressing a gloved hand over his bleeding knee.

Whether it was the sudden injury, the thought of Dmitri, or the combination of the two, in one stomach-wrenching instant I felt every shred of warmth sucked out of my body.

"Blessed Athos," said Aleksander, clamping his fists to his temples. "Not again." He struggled to his feet and sucked in a harsh breath.

I grabbed his arm and pulled. "Hurry. Come back to the trees." I suppose I held some faint hope that the enchantments woven about the edge of the woods might forestall the demon transformation, but as I helped the limping Aleksander across the barrier, it seemed I only made things worse. His body jerked in tortured spasm, and he cried out. The searing heat that poured off him forced me to drop his arm and fall back. He bent double and sank to his knees, groaning in mortal anguish, his torso stretching into impossible shapes, while his human aspect wavered and faded with agonizing swiftness.

"My lord, you are in control," I said, but the stray beam of moonlight illuminating his terror-filled eyes told me otherwise. No more than three minutes passed, and I stood facing a maddened shengar, jaws gaping wide as it roared its fury and pain. One paw was bloody, and the limping beast began to circle around behind me. Smoothly, slowly, I turned with it. "My lord, take hold of my voice. Keep the door open. Your pain will ease."

The huge cat screamed again in the harsh, bone-chilling cry of a tortured woman, so much more fearful than the throatier roar of larger beasts. I stood absolutely immobile, allowing the restless beast to examine me. I kept talking, but words seemed to make him angrier, so I fell silent, whispering my chant under my breath. "Stay calm, Aleksander. You are stronger than the beast. It is only the pain. The surprise.

The crossing of an unholy enchantment with the weaving of light. I should have known. I'm sorry."

He did not attack. Rather, after a while, he loped off into the dark woodland. I sagged limp against the trunk of a towering fir, praying there were no Ezzarians wandering the forest that night. A shifting wind moved the trees, almost blinding me with the beams of the full moon. Distant laughter floated on the breeze along with wood smoke . . . oh, breath of Verdonne . . . of course there were Ezzarians out. It was the first full moon of spring—the birth of a new season. The night Ezzarian families built fires outside and told stories until dawn. A night of merriment and excitement for children allowed to stay up late. A night of wonder and companionship. Grabbing a thick branch broken from the fir, I took out after Aleksander, wondering if, after sixteen years, my legs remembered how to run.

I heard him crashing through the brush ahead of me. I leaped fallen trees and ducked under limbs and paid no heed to scrub and branches that tore at my clothes. Occasionally I caught sight of the dark blur leaping with ease over obstacles I had to climb. But soon I smelled wood smoke, and I could no longer hear his passing. Perhaps it was only my terror, but I believed I heard the soft snarl of wicked anticipation as he slipped nearer the merry fire just ahead. I circled wide and ran toward the fire. "Wildcat!" I screamed. "Shengar! Take the children and get inside!"

I didn't stop to explain to the five or six yelling adults who leaped from the ground and snatched up whimpering children. I just dipped my branch in their fire, prayed it to catch quickly, and kept my ears focused on the snarl of fury to my left. He was moving. I threw down my still-unlit stick and picked up one the Ezzarians had left poking into the fire to stir the coals. It was too thin and would burn down quickly as I ran, but I couldn't wait. Aleksander was running. As I took after him, I heard a shocked voice from behind me. "Verdonne's mercy. Seyonne?"

The shengar had found a game trail. A clearer path, easier to run. But it meant he was faster. Shengars were not like the kayeets of the desert who were the fastest beasts known in the world, fleeter than the graceful dune-runners and sand-deer who were their prey. But Aleksander was fast enough that I soon had a stitch in my side and heard the echo of Galadon's insults from my youth. "Are you glued to the path? How in Verdonne's name will you ever outrun a demon if you have stone feet?"

I cleared my mind and commanded the blood to service my legs and my side and my lungs, and soon I could see him again . . . and at least three fires in the trees. I bellowed with all the breath I could muster, "Hear me, Ezzarians," as if they all could hear my desire. "Shengar! Take shelter!" I ran to each fire and made sure they heard, then took back to the game trail. Which way? I had to stop and silence my breathing so I could hear, desperately wishing for the increased acuity melydda had once provided me. Fool! I was not helpless. I still had senses that would be of use. Quickly I passed the back of my hand before my eyes and shifted into the realm of my extra senses. All I needed was to see enchantment.

When I looked again, the trees of that forest were woven with silver threads, as if the goddess of the moon had dropped her nets to catch what magical birds might nest there. I had forgotten how beautiful were the weavings, and my damaged sight could catch only the merest hint of them, like looking at a rainbow through a smoked glass. But I had no time to savor it. Ahead of me the roiling purple and green ugliness of the demon enchantment was disappearing over a rise, and I took off through the trees, trying to keep my blazing brand from starting any other fires.

I heard screams and ran faster yet, soon arriving at a rocky grotto where two men and three women had plastered themselves against the stone walls, pressing five or six children behind them. The shengar crouched low, bawling at them across the clearing, shy of the fire that burned innocently to its right. But the fire wasn't big enough, and he was beginning to edge around it to get at the terrified people. "Here!" I said, stepping in between the shengar and the people, holding my pitiful torch so that two fires blocked its path. "You don't want to do this. Listen to my voice. Leave these good people alone." He screamed at me with fangs bared and muscles taut, ready to spring, and the children behind me wailed in shrill terror. "Keep them quiet and still," I said over my shoulder. I waved my burning branch, and the cat shied backward slightly. "Think, Zander. You don't want to do this." One of the men got the idea and stepped to the campfire to grab a stick of his own. Aleksander bawled harshly at the man, and I was afraid he was going to leap the small fire and take the man before he could get his branch burning well enough. "Begone from here," I said, waving the torch at Aleksander again. "Stay in control."

The cat backed away a little more, and I stepped toward it, waving the branch until it slunk into the trees and disappeared. Bending over to ease the cramps in my legs, I caught a glimpse of the man standing over the fire. "Garen," I blurted out. He was the miller's son from my home village, a close friend who perennially won any contest of strength. After a year in the world as a Searcher, he'd come home to take over the mill when his father died . . . about two days before the Derzhi invasion.

He stared squinting across the fire. "Thank—" His eyes widened and glazed out of focus. "Come," he said, waving to the others, "let's get the children inside." I had disappeared from his sight as surely as if my body had become transparent. I turned and ran after the cat with the weight of lead in my gut.

The next group of storytellers had already set a ring of fire about themselves, and the next, and soon I began to find the fires deserted. Perhaps the word had spread. About the time I decided I couldn't run another step, I heard a triumphant scream up a small rise just ahead of me. My feet sped forward on their own, and I had to grab a tree to stop myself running right into a place I didn't want to be. Aleksander had found himself a yearling buck, and he lay in the moonlit glade happily gnawing on its belly. His muzzle and the snow were bright with blood.

I sank down by the tree. My chest was on fire. My legs cramped into knots that made me want to howl. If the shengar decided that a wretched slave was a better meal than the fallen buck, I could not have moved one handspan to prevent him. Galadon's surety that I could regain my strength and stamina with only a few weeks of decent food and physical training seemed only slightly less laughable than his surety that submitting to the five days of Warden's testing would restore my power.

I pulled my torn cloak about me and doused my smoldering branch in the snow. While I watched the shengar sate his hunger, I leaned my head against the tree and tried to map out in my mind the route we had run. It was impossible. How were we ever going to find our way back to the settlement?

Shouts from the way we'd come woke me from a drowse. The shengar was still gnawing on a haunch bone, showing no sign of reverting back to the Prince's true form. Soon, if all went as before. Its ears pricked at the closing sounds. I pulled up my hood and stood up, stretching out my cramps and moving around behind the tree.

"This way! See the tracks!"

The shengar dropped the bone and a low rumble of disturbance came from his chest. It wasn't a good idea to interrupt a shengar at its feeding. I slipped a short way down the hill thinking to intercept the hunters, but I hadn't counted on them being mounted. Three riders galloped past, and the shengar roared.

"There!" shouted one of the riders. A woman. "Take it."

"Get behind, so it can't run," called a man.

"Wait!" I cried, chasing after them. Panic muted my senses so I didn't notice the tremor the voices set up in my skin. "Don't!" I crested the rise just in time to see one of the mounted hunters let fly a spear. It fell short, just in front of the furious, blood-streaked cat. "He's human," I cried hoarsely, terrified they couldn't hear me over the pounding of blood in my ears. I grabbed the stirrup of the nearest rider. "You mustn't hurt him. He's enchanted."

"Human?" It was the woman. "Oh, sweet Valdis, this is the supplicant!"

"I've got him!" cried the hunter from across the glade, as the cat screamed in pain. "Finish him with your sword, Daffyd."

I ran to the shengar, who lay sprawled in a pool of blood with a spear protruding from its side. I couldn't tell which blood was the cat's and which was the buck's.

"My lord, can you hear me?" I pressed fingers to the beast's breast and it snarled feebly, trying to nip them off, telling me what I wanted to know. "We'll take care of you," I said. "No Derzhi warrior was ever taken with a single spear. Is that not true?"

The riders had dismounted and come up behind me.

"Does he live?" asked the woman.

"Yes," I said, "but sorely wounded. Bleeding badly. Is there a healer who could help him?"

"None that know of shengars."

"He will change . . . soon." A blast of hot air rippled through the glade, and the shengar growled . . . then moaned . . . and the image wavered. As the two images battled for supremacy, Aleksander cried out in anguish and the people behind me gasped in horrified astonishment. I had no attention to spare for them.

"Soon, soon, my lord," I said, moving back slightly so I would not touch him during his change. "Hold on to my voice. We'll help you as soon as the change is over."

For a moment I thought him dead, he lay so limp and cold in the bloodstained snow. I ripped off my cloak and my shirt, then, hoping I wasn't going to make things worse, I eased out the spear, pressing my wadded shirt to the gushing wound in Aleksander's belly. I used his leather belt to hold the shirt in place, then wrapped him in my cloak, using the edge of it to wipe the blood from his face. "He needs a healer," I said. "If you could take him on your horses . . ."

But they did not answer, and, in an instant, I realized what I had done. I was wearing only a slave tunic with my breeches, and the crossed circle on my shoulder would be

glaring at them. They would see that I was Ezzarian and
know what I was, and perhaps, like Garen, they would know
my name.

"I ask only that you care for him as Ezzarians have always cared for those who come as supplicants," I said, hoping they would listen to what I said even if they would not
acknowledge hearing it. Then I took the offensive in my
own war and looked up . . . into the faces of my wife, the
Queen of Ezzaria, and her husband, who had once been my
dearest friend.

Chapter 24

The moon was sinking toward the horizon, leaving the forest dark and haunted as I trudged down the hill. Ysanne and Rhys and their companion Daffyd, a man unknown to me, had made a litter for Aleksander and taken him away. I tried to help, to ease Aleksander, to speed their departure, but I might have been only a moon shadow for all the notice they took of me. Even in that first moment of revelation their eyes had betrayed nothing, as if the ground beneath my feet was all they could see. I knew how it was done. Gods have mercy, I had done it in the past, never understanding the horror it was for the one unseen, the utter desolation of the spirit to be told so explicitly that one did not exist, that flesh and blood were not enough, and that there was no remedy for it.

At least I had their tracks to follow. Only once did I depart from the horse-scented path, to light a branch in the smoldering coals of an abandoned moon fire. The small torch helped me see the tracks and droppings, and helped to keep a bit of warmth in my hands and face. The first real clothes I'd had in forever, and I'd already lost half of them. I laughed aloud as I walked. Aleksander would think it a good joke. The humor echoed hollow in the silent trees.

The years had touched Ysanne with magnificence. Even in the torchlight I could see with what artistry time had sculpted her girlish softness into true beauty. I longed to look in her eyes to see whether or not the garden of her spirit still flourished behind her wall of stillness. So few had ever been permitted to see it. Her Serene Majesty . . . the brittle

iron of her girlhood now tempered by time and adversity.
She was born to be queen.

Her family had lived in a village some twenty leagues
from my own. Ysanne had been taken into Queen Tarya's
house to train when she was five and found to have an astonishing level of melydda. Too young to be so far from
home, to live in a huge house with fifty courtiers and a busy
woman older than her grandmother. Queen Tarya was set in
her ways and forced Ysanne to train exactly as she herself
had done fifty years in the past, not allowing the girl's brilliance to move her along faster or skip any step, but rather
making her take every step twice over. Tarya never let her so
much as demonstrate the marvelous variations of her talent
she discovered as she grew. Because her awestruck parents
would not dispute the Queen, Ysanne had no choice. For ten
years she bottled up loneliness and fury, determined not to
yield, sure the old woman was trying to make her quit or
crush her spirit. But on Ysanne's fifteenth birthday, Queen
Tarya smiled and embraced her and told her that she was the
most powerful Aife ever born in Ezzaria, and that the rai-
kirah would not prevail as long as her talent was fed by the
fire within her.

"Then, why did you never allow me to use it?" Ysanne
had asked in mystification. "Why did you bury me in the old
ways all these years?"

The Queen had laughed at her and said that her talent
needed little schooling. But her patience . . . that was a different matter. No Aife could afford to be impatient.

Only after I had known her a very long time did Ysanne
tell me of that day. She wasn't one to admit that anyone ever
found her wanting.

To be an Aife, a portal-maker, was the most difficult of
all Ezzarian callings. To weave one's own being into the
soul of another so completely as to shape a physical reality
was hard enough when the person was healthy and whole of
mind. But to do such a thing to a subject who hosted a
demon—a person perhaps mad, perhaps vicious, perhaps vi-

olent—was intricate and dangerous work. Wardens were more celebrated, as warriors so often are, but no Warden could have taken one step into a battle, much less have had the confidence and freedom to do what was necessary, without absolute, unshakable trust in his Aife. If the portal closed behind him, he would be trapped forever in another person's soul, and without the solidity of the Aife's shaping, he would tumble into an abyss of madness where no rescuer could ever find him.

Mentors like Galadon had a network of colleagues throughout Ezzaria, all of them watching for the right pairing for their students. Warden and Aife, Searcher and Comforter, Scholar and Spellmaker, all of our skills were honed to work in pairings, except for the Weaver, of course, who always worked alone. The Searcher's skill at discovering demons lurking in the heart of madness or cruelty was worth little without a Comforter to envelope the victim in enchantment. And the touch of the Comforter that spun the thread of power back to the Aife had no security without the physical skills of the Searcher to protect him. Though all were working toward the same purpose, our talents needed to balance like the roles in some complex dance figure, where your life and your sanity might depend on the footwork of your partner as it blended with your own. The announcement of a new pairing was in every way equal to a birth or a death or a marriage. This is not to say that every pair married. In fact, it was more common not to marry. But the intimacy of Warden and Aife was extraordinary. It was hard to imagine being married to one woman while walking souls with another.

I was fortunate that Galadon lived in my own village, and I didn't have to leave home as so many Ezzarian students did. Though my preparation was rigorous and consuming, my parents and my sister had sheltered me with warm and loving normalcy. Having lived and trained in one small village, I was intimidated when Galadon told me that he'd found me a pairing with Queen Tarya's protégée. A girl celebrated for her extraordinary skills. A girl rumored to be cold and difficult. A girl destined to be queen. A girl so lovely that my youthful urges, suppressed by unending schooling, burst forth full-blown and came near exploding me into bits the moment I laid eyes on her.

Galadon took care of that problem quickly, of course, by plunging me into a course of training that made everything thus far look like nursery coddling. Somedays I would see her only for a brief moment, when the candlelight of the temple reflected on her face as she concentrated on her portal-making. I would stand stupidly and wonder how the small cleft in the smooth line of her chin would feel were I to run my finger across its tantalizing irregularity or how it would be to brush away the little wrinkle of intensity between her brows, until Galadon would say, "Begin now, imbecile! Demons do not wait upon gaping jackdaws." And I would close my eyes and sigh at the remembrance of her loveliness as if Galadon couldn't see me do it, then I would say the words and shift the reality that would take me into her creation.

It was in the portal that I got to know her. There I could hear the voice of her mind without being distracted by the sight of her body. We argued everlastingly at first. She was very sure of herself, and though I was a shy and gawky fifteen-year-old in the matters of women and life, I had no such reservations about my aptitude in the realms of enchantment and combat. Ten years with Galadon had seen to that. Just as with Tarya, you came to believe in yourself or you gave it up. Galadon claimed that the two years we trained together aged him fifty, but we knew better. He gloried in our perfection and our strength and our triumph. When we returned victorious from our first battle—forcing the demon from a Suzaini woman who was on the verge of murdering her children—Galadon toasted us and said there was no pairing ever made that was our equal. We scarcely heard him, for when we opened our eyes and saw each other in the flesh while our blood still thundered with enchantment and danger and victory, there was room for nothing else in the universe.

By that time I had discovered the fiery core within the alabaster goddess, the tender passion that could breathe life into a dead man, the quiet wit that could sharpen a diamond's edge, the devotion that had been waiting all her life for a loving hand to claim it. Her soul was a fifth season, of richer hue than autumn, bursting with more life than spring, hidden away, ready to transform the world with such glory as it had never seen. She had permitted me to glimpse it . . . and she had promised that I could spend my life exploring it.

I shivered in the predawn blackness as I walked out of the forest and down the path to the village. It had all been so long ago.

There were lights in the windows of the guest cottage and a cluster of people outside the door. I debated whether to walk back into the forest until they were gone, but I decided that it didn't really matter. No reason to stay out in the cold when the worst had already come to pass. I hadn't died from it. I wasn't bleeding. I would survive.

The fifteen or twenty people did not part when I approached, but somehow in their movements—one man leaned toward a friend to speak, one man drew a cloak about himself, a woman gathered two children close against the cold—a way was left for me to pass where I would not touch any of them. When I walked in the door, the healer didn't even turn around to see who came.

Aleksander looked dreadful, his skin almost transparent, his lips colorless, and his cheeks and eyes sunken. The woman had cleaned him and bandaged him, and from the implements on the table—needles, silk thread, packets of herbs, a small brazier, an assortment of small stones and bits of metal—I gathered that she had stitched the wound and used an enchantment for healing such a thing. I ignored the healer, who was washing her hands and packing the implements and the blood-soaked rags into a basket so they could be cleaned and purified, and sat down by the bed.

"Sleep well, my lord. Have no ill dreams tonight." He didn't move, of course. Unlikely he could hear me. "I'll wake up every few hours and give you water and check your bandages." The healer poked up the fire, then took a few things from the bedside table, leaving a packet of herbs and a damp cloth behind. The door closed softly behind her.

I drew a small basin of washing water and carefully cleaned the dried blood from my hands and the slave tunic. Once I had disposed of the cleaning water and hung the tunic in the rafters to dry, I rolled up in a blanket on the floor by the fire, wondering ··aguely what I was going to do for a shirt or a cloak. The Ezzarians certainly weren't going to provide me any. But at some time during the next long day, while I wandered in and out of sleep, the shirt and cloak I had used to wrap Aleksander appeared on the table, clean, dry, and folded. Perhaps they thought they were Aleksander's. I put them on, gave Aleksander some tea made with the herbs left by the healer, and went back to sleep.

The healer came frequently to check on the Prince, who alternated between wild delirium and death-like stillness. I watched what the woman did to ease him and did the same in the hours when she was not there. In the evening I fixed myself something to eat, then went back to sleep. I was still good at sleeping. There didn't seem to be much else to do.

It was sometime deep in that night—the moon was hanging huge and low over the western peaks—when I heard footsteps outside the guest house. I was halfway on my way to sleep again, but postponed it for a bit to see if the healer found any more change in our patient. I thought it odd she would come so late. But the dark figure carried no lamp and lit none, and rather than going to Aleksander, came to stand over me. I was poised to roll out of the way, when the person crouched down and touched my shoulder.

"Seyonne." It was a man's whisper.

"He does not exist," I said.

"Then, how else am I to explain the vision I had in the forest? Was it perhaps a spot too much of winter ale?"

I sat up astonished and smiling. "Have you not yet learned about winter ale, Rhys-na-varain? Or has your head

grown porous with age and ease, and all your hard lessons
leaked out of it?"

He crouched down and found my hands in the dark,
clasping them firmly with his own powerful fists . . . until
his thick fingers met the slave rings. Then he pulled back as
if the rings were still hot from the smith's fire.

"Gaenad zi," I said. My own training would not be de-
nied, however much I wished it. I was required to warn him
that I was unclean.

"Curse the law," he said with quiet ferocity. "I cannot
maintain such madness when you walk into Dael Ezzar
alive. I saw you fall, Seyonne. You were surrounded. Eight
Derzhi or more. I saw the sword go in and the blood on your
shirt. I couldn't risk the few—"

"There was nothing to be done. We lost. I'm glad you
survived it. Truly glad." I hoped he would go on to something else.

"I know I swore to bring help or die . . . and I did come
back. Daffyd could tell you. He was in the party guarding
Queen Tarya, but I made them leave her to come and make
spells like you wanted. To get you. But I saw you fall. . . ."

"It would have done no good for you to die, too."

"I still dream of that day."

"I should teach you how not to dream. I learned it early."

"Ah, curse it all, Seyonne. What were we thinking in
those days—that we could fight an empire alone?"

"We saw no alternative. We couldn't surrender."

"We were fools. There's always a way."

He sat down on the floor beside me. Though I could see
the outline of his familiar bulk, I couldn't make out his face.
But when I reached for the poker to stir the fire, he stayed
my hand. "Let it be." His words were a plea for understanding. To talk in the dark was not the same as seeing me.

"I'm glad you've come," I said. "You'll never know how
glad. Tell me . . . tell me anything. About this place—Dael
Ezzar—'New Ezzaria.' How did you find it? Tell me who
survived, who wards, anything." The craving in me was

monstrous, but I didn't know whether it was hunger to be
satisfied or pain to be blunted with a balm of words.

"First, I've got to tell you. . . ."

"About Ysanne and you. I heard it already. When the
Prince told me of the fish-eyed consort, I knew it could be
no one else. I'm happy for it."

"There were so few left . . . we couldn't let her power go
wasting . . . and we'd known each other so long. . . . Once
we were paired."

"It's all right. I prayed she lived . . . and if she lived, I
knew she would marry. I hoped it would be someone worthy
of her." One who would give her music, as I had not. "Who
better than you? Someone closer than a brother? Don't
speak of her, if it troubles you."

"Oh, demon fire, Seyonne, we believed you were dead.
And it wasn't right away. I finally persuaded Galadon to
pass me through my testing. Did you know the old dragon
still breathes fire?"

"I heard it from the boy Llyr."

He was silent for a moment. "We assumed it was Llyr
who'd told you how to find us. What else did he tell?"

"Nothing else. He was careful—and we had no time."

"A slave to the Derzhi . . . for all these years. How do you
bear it?"

"It was not how I planned to spend my life."

There was so much I wanted to hear from him, but I knew
our time was short. So I swept desire aside and broached the
subject of most importance. "What did Ysanne think of
Aleksander's story?"

"You know there's no one can speak her mind."

"But she sees the danger? How we've misread the
prophecies? These Khelid . . . Rhys, I could see the Gai
Kyallet in this Khelid Kastavan. I have no power—not a
scrap—but I could see it. Never, in a hundred encounters,
did I ever see a demon so powerful. We've always suspected
there was a Demon Lord, and my every instinct tells me that
I have seen such a being. I am convinced that this Kastavan

plans to cast his own body aside and live on in the heir to the Empire."

"Impossible. How could you know? You're saying the demon is directing these Khelid."

I hadn't thought of it in that way. "It's the only answer for what they're doing with the Prince. And I saw his eyes. To let demon-infested warriors take control of the Empire . . . we can't allow it. With all the resources of the Empire, with all the horrors they'll be able to devise, they'll be strong enough that fifty Wardens could never clean them out. You've got to take them on now before they're entrenched. I believe you can use Aleksander's—"

"Wait. It's not . . . you've got . . ." Rhys was stammering and waving his hands in the dark, and I felt him shift away a bit. "Are you sure you have no power, Seyonne? None at all?"

"The Rites are very thorough. Believe me. I tried everything."

"You've got to get away from this Derzhi, Seyonne. He's damaged beyond repairing. Ysanne says the rai-kirah have made themselves a proper nest inside him. You mustn't be close when they take him. We'll give you a horse. You can be off before—"

"Get away?" I was completely taken aback. Of all people, I would have expected Rhys to take action, to see the danger and set out to remedy it in his usual hotheaded way. I thought I would have to convince him to be careful. And for him to think I would . . . or could . . . run away. "Rhys, do you understand what I am? This mark on my shoulder proclaims that I am chattel, and this one on my face declares that it is the Derzhi royal house that owns me as you own your boots. There is not a place in the Empire where these marks would not be recognized. But beyond that small matter . . . why would I have to fear Aleksander being taken by a demon in the midst of an Ezzarian settlement? Even if you can't heal him right away, you can protect him."

"Things aren't like they were, Seyonne. You don't know

what we've been through. With so few of us, we've had to change." He was nervous. Uncertain.

"What do you mean?"

"For one thing . . . we don't go searching anymore."

I was dumbfounded. It was as if he'd just informed me that they had decided to make the sun shine at night and the moon in the day. "You don't go searching? Then how do you find the victims?" Even more, how could the Aife make a portal if there was no Comforter to make physical contact with the victim?

"We don't fight the same way. We can't afford to send out Searchers. They'd end up . . . like you. And we have so few Wardens, what would we do with all the victims we found? How would we choose?"

"So what do you do? Just sit here and let them rot? Do you let a woman go mad and slay her children? Do you let a man crucify his slaves to feed the creature who has taken up residence in his soul? What do you tell old men who weep with the nightmares in their heads? Verdonne's child, Rhys, what do you do instead?"

"We do what we can." He burst out with such vehemence I thought the floor might shake. "We've struck a bargain."

"A bargain. A demon bargain?" I was appalled. It was not uncommon to bargain with demons when victory was close in a battle. The idea was to force them out of their vessel, not to destroy them. Demons were a part of nature, no more evil in themselves than a cyclone or a volcano. It was never our aim to exterminate them, lest we upset some unknown balance in the universe. We only prevented them finding their feeding place in a human soul. So if we could force them into submission, we would offer them continued existence in return for their vessel. They would abandon the soul and retreat back into the frozen wastes of the northland to regenerate. Only if they refused did we fight to the death. But to bargain outside of that circumstance . . . "What did you exchange? And with whom? You've sworn to oppose them in physical combat. How do you uphold your oath?"

"You're right about one demon speaking for all of them

now. And you're right about the Khelid being the danger. Our pairing in the northeastern Empire—Kevyra and Do-rach—kept turning up demon-possessed Khelid, and I was about to go crazy with them. It's too long to explain, but I figured out what was happening, and came up with this idea. We fight one combat every cycle of the moon. Keyra and Dorach make the connection with the victim. If we limit ourselves this way, the demons will take no new souls un-willing and will not hunt or challenge our people. We battle for one soul each meeting. It's ferocious combat . . . only to be expected when they know we're coming. I've killed some of the demons, banished the others, lost a gallon of blood along the way, came near losing my arm in one. But it gives me time to help train new Wardens. So you see, we can't protect this Derzhi . . . he's as good as one of them al-ready."

"And Ysanne agrees with this? One soul every moon's turning."

"Of course, she agrees. None of us like it. We have no choice." He must have felt my shock and dismay. "It's only for a while until we're stronger. Until there are more War-dens than just me. It was the best we could do. It took us two years to make our way here—every day in hiding, split up, no possibility of the work. Everything was chaos. You were taken. Morryn and Havach dead, and all the Wardens from the western groves. We had to rush our training. When we tried to start up again, we lost Dane and Cymneng in the matter of a week. There was no one but me. We had to find some other way. Someday—"

"Some other way . . ." It was impossible. No wonder Galadon had been so determined that I should pursue his fu-tile scheme. Perhaps a powerless Warden was better than what they had. "You let them stay . . . but as you get stronger, they get stronger, too. Do you think that in this 'someday,' you'll ever be able to get them out?"

"I had to warn you, Seyonne. There's nothing to hold you here. This Derzhi villain can't do anything to you right now, so leave him. Be free. I'll cut these off you myself." He lifted my wrists and shook them, anger showing through his insistence like stark canvas behind an artist's paints. It made no sense.

I yanked my hands away. "It's not my slave rings I'd lose were I to run away, Rhys. You would have me abandon the only thing in the world I still possess. I swore an oath, as did you—"

"I've got to go. Think on what I've said. I'll give you a horse, provisions, clothes, whatever you need. Perhaps I could make a spell to cover the marks."

I couldn't think what to say to him. How could he not see what he'd done? "Be careful, Rhys. Be sure. A demon never yields what it's not already lost. And only when it thinks it's found another way to get what it wants."

"He's a dead man, Seyonne. Get away from him." He gripped my shoulder briefly, then left.

I poked at the fire once, then again, then threw the branch onto the coals in exasperation. Sparks whirled and danced their way up the chimney. One lost its way and settled on my blanket, flaring up in bright orange bravery before dying its quick death.

"He betrayed you." I came near shedding my skin when the hoarse whisper came from the darkness across the room. I snatched a candle from the shelf over the hearth and lit it from the coals.

"You shouldn't talk," I said, setting the candle on the table by Aleksander's bed. His eyes were closed, damp red curls matted to his brow and cheek. I took a small clean towel and blotted the sweat from his face. "You've lost enough blood to sate a Derzhi Heged for a month."

"Did you not hear it? He said it himself. Gave it away."

I lifted the Prince's head and gave him a sip of water, and his eyes drifted open. His skin was warm and damp. "There was nothing to give away," I said.

"He knew you lived. He chose not to help you."

"Maybe a Derzhi would do such a thing, but not Rhys. I was surrounded. I was wounded by a Derzhi sword. I fell." Though it was only to my knees as they chained my hands and tied a leather strap around my throat so tightly I could scarcely breathe. . . . I cut off the thought. I was not ready for those memories. "He would have died for nothing."

"When he was talking about the others, he said it. 'Everything was chaos. You were taken.' *Taken*, not dead. Very clear. The guilt was leaking out of him."

"You should rest," I said.

"You should watch your back."

Chapter 25

The break in Aleksander's fever was only temporary. Though I had little doubt that his vigorous health would prevail, the dirty wound was deep in his belly. The healer cared for him throughout the morning after Rhys's midnight visit, so I had little to do but watch and stew and wonder what in Verdonne's name to do about anything. I longed to speak to Galadon again, but I dared not approach him now that others knew I was there.

After endless hours of nothing, I was so restless and agitated, I thought I might start ripping shelves off the walls or throwing things. Though he could not have heard me, I sat on the Prince's bedside and told him I was going out for a while, that I needed to clear my head. "The Ezzarian healer is here with you, my lord. I'll be back before she leaves at sundown. I'll not desert you."

I started out walking, passing several people who did not see me. Even the children had been warned. Not one of them slipped, even when two of them came near trampling me when they came barreling out of the schoolhouse door. I might have been made of sunlight. After four or five such meetings, my hand flew to my face just to make sure it was still there. How often since I'd been a slave had I wished for invisibility? Experiencing it was altogether different from my imagining.

I tried to sort out my thoughts, but somehow since my conversation with Rhys I had been incapable of putting any two of them together in any logical order. Every time I tried to consider Rhys and Ysanne and the meaning of their bargain with the demons, my thoughts would skitter away into something trivial. What did they talk about? Rhys delighted in parties and laughter. Ysanne preferred intimacy and quiet pleasures. What wine had he shared with Ysanne at their wedding? Ysanne loved sweet, dark wines, and Rhys disdained such "putrid child's drinks." He would only drink thin, sour white vintages. Idiocy. Why did I care?

Aggravated at my inability to think, I started trotting, and by the time I entered the trees, I was running, faster and faster, first along the main path and then angling off on the game trail that Aleksander and I had followed the night he was injured. The harder I ran, the better my mind settled into coherence.

It was astounding enough to know that the demons were working together and had been doing so for so many years, that one demon could bargain for all of them. But beyond that change in the working of the world, what in the name of sense had possessed Rhys to strike a bargain with them? He had always been rash. It had continually set back his training, and Galadon had despaired of getting him to think before striking. But surely time had taught him prudence, and paired with Ysanne, a strong, decisive, experienced partner, he could not have entered into such an arrangement without consideration. As my feet pounded on the hard-packed dirt, I began to conjure visions. With nothing of magic, of course, only memory long forbidden. Rhys . . .

I envied Rhys his height. At ten he was taller than me by a head and his shoulders twice as broad as my scrawny frame. If we were both to be Wardens, then any advantage of height or strength would place him ahead of me. It wasn't fair to be bested through no fault of my own. But on the day we decided to explore the caverns carved out from under Caenelon by the springs of Valdis, height and bulk were no advantage. We'd heard of a series of crystal-lined rooms beyond the "gargoyle cavern" that everyone could reach. But to get to them, one had to crawl half a league through a low tunnel, then flatten oneself against a wall and squeeze through a short, narrow crevice. I slipped through the crack easily and raised a light, calling to Rhys to hurry, as I'd never seen such a wonder as the sparkling cave.

"Seyonne, wait!"

"Come on," I said. "There's more beyond. It's like diamonds in here."

"I can't fit. Come back."

I didn't want to go back. I was halfway through the slot into the next cave, gapi:.g at amethyst walls, ceiling, niches, and crevices.

"Seyonne, help me!" The rising panic in my friend's call dragged me back. He was in the dark, so terrified at the prospect of being stuck forever underground, that he'd forgotten the words to make a light—the first enchantment any Ezzarian child was taught. He had stooped over to squeeze his head through, then wedged himself tight, caught with one hand ahead of him, one hand behind, and something snagged on the overhanging rocks behind him. He was panting hard and said the rocks were so tight about his chest he couldn't breathe properly. After ten minutes of close examination, including poking my head back through the crevice underneath him, I concluded that it was his leather rucksack—carrying such necessities as cheese and bread and apples, nuts and ropes and sweets—that had caught him.

"Going to have to cut off your balls to make you fit," I said solemnly, unsheathing my knife.

Rhys's eyes, already bulging in fear, dwarfed the caverns. "Merciful Valdis!" he whimpered.

I slashed the straps on his shoulder, and when the rucksack released, his pent-up fear shot him through the crevice like a stone from a slingshot. He bowled me over, sending my knife flying and scattering our treasured supplies, leaving two apples rolling slowly across the stone floor. "Your balls," I said, and we exploded in laughter. For an hour we lay choking on wild hilarity in the diamond cave, flickering our magical lights on the crystals and marveling at the glories of life. He swore on that day that when we grew up to fight demons, he would never fail me—even if he had to cut off my balls to save me.

I ran faster, propelled by worry, confusion, and sickness of heart. By sixteen years of confinement . . . of pain and loneliness . . . of forbidding myself to remember. Even when my side felt like Daffyd's spear had pierced it, my legs knotted in cramps, and my breath came in burning gasps, I could not stop.

What was I to do about Aleksander? Ysanne saw him as too damaged to save. So did Galadon. But were their judgments clouded by the Prince's identity, as Aleksander assumed? Would they say the same if he were not Derzhi? If so much had changed among my people in sixteen years, was I a fool to believe that their impartial generosity still thrived?

Without realizing it I began to control my breathing and the ferocious beating of my heart, slowing them, commanding my muscles to loosen and stretch, to work smoothly. Always my thoughts came back to Rhys. What had he done?

My eyes flicked open to clouds. Or fog. Or some other indefinable grayness. Moisture condensed on my overheated skin and dribbled down my bare back . . . and chest . . . my bare everything. Where were my clothes? Confused, disoriented, beginning to be nauseated, for I couldn't tell whether I was right side up or upside down. My feet felt nothing underneath, and I began flailing my arms in panic.

Where was I? Where had I been last time I knew where I was?

Training, of course. When did I do anything else?

"Aife?" I dared not speak Ysanne's name. Galadon would set me back a week for such a slip of discipline. A week . . . It was not training, but testing. I'd been taking the last test after five grueling days. I had taken the last step. Through a curtain of fire . . . Sweet Verdonne, was I dead?

"Aife! Master!" I flailed and twisted, and felt soft clutching at my arms. Demons? Spirits of the afterlife? I yanked

*my arms away and still they clutched at me . . . and laughed.
Quietly at first, as if at a long distance, then closer and more
boisterously. "Holy Verdonne," I said defiantly. "Take me to
the light if I'm to live with you."*

"Take him to the light!"

"He wants light!"

"All right. Just remember it was your idea."

"Serves him right!"

*Just in front of me a blinding spark set a torch blazing,
and a hand took shape in the mist—a very solid, thick-
fingered hand holding a pewter goblet brimming with
golden wine. It was quickly followed by a pair of exuber-
antly wiry eyebrows topping two bright eyes something like
those of a fish. "You may want this," said the owner of the
eyes, pushing the goblet into my hand. "Verdonne sent it and
said 'maybe later.' For now you're condemned to stay with
us."*

*And, of course, the mist of merry enchantment dissolved,
and I found myself clad in nothing but wood smoke, standing beside a cheerful bonfire being laughed at by Rhys,
Hoffyd, my sister Elen, Garen . . . and Ysanne, who sat quietly on a rock, frowning in concentration as she examined
me. She took a long pull at her own pewter goblet as I stood
paralyzed with embarrassment. "I'd always imagined a
Warden would be more impressive naked, but Galadon
swears he passed his testing, so I suppose we'll have to
make do with him."*

*As I tried without success to shrink into nothing, Rhys,
Garen, and Elen collapsed into raucous hilarity, and Rhys
tossed me a Warden's cloak of dark blue. "We tried to get it
on you while keeping you modestly hidden in the mist, but I
was afraid you were going to crack our skulls." He lifted his
goblet. "Congratulations, my friend. You are the youngest
ever to pass the Warden's testing. May you know nothing but
victory, and return from every battle unscathed."*

*"Here, here," cried the others, raising their cups.
Ysanne's rare smile unfolded like a butterfly from its
chrysalis. For so many years she had been suffocated by the*

ten courtiers Queen Tarya set to watch over and protect her every hour of every day. She had never attended a village school or gone adventuring with those her own age, so she had only just started to be comfortable around my friends. They had been astonished to discover her wicked sense of humor. I would have laid wagers that this "unveiling" was her idea.

After embarrassment and confusion had yielded to elation and shared joy, Ysanne returned to her studies and the others went off in search of food. Only Rhys and I were left by our midnight fire. We sat in companionable silence for a while, letting the echoes of our friends fade into the sounds of a peaceful night. Then Rhys broke the quiet. "You've left me behind, Seyonne. I can't share your path or your battles now. But I will. As soon as I can, I'll follow you. Leave me a few demons to fight." We joined hands and swore our Warden's oath to each other, and believed we had glimpsed the truest meaning of the universe.

I lengthened my stride and increased my speed. The trees alongside the path blurred.

"What did you say to her? I thought she might bring the cliff down on your head." Rhys flopped onto the grass beside the log seat Ysanne had so recently vacated. I was still smarting from her angry words.

"I just told her I needed to go back to Col'Dyath for a few days to clear my head. That's all."

"How can you bear being in that place all by yourself? Rocks, wind, not a twig or a blade of grass. Gives me the twitters, it does."

"These last few encounters have been vile," I said. "It takes me awhile to get my equilibrium back after battles like that, and I don't like to burden anyone with it."

"But you've got the most beautiful, intelligent, marvelous woman in Ezzaria melting at the sight of you. She's been cooped up so long with Tarya and Galadon, she's going to

*burst . . . and you're going to be the lucky man to catch it.
You're insane to leave her for a second."*

Why didn't anyone understand? *"Sometimes I just need
to be alone. I've fought sixty battles in six months. Sometimes I think I can't get a full breath unless I'm out of the
trees and away from . . . everything. A few days is all I need.
Then I'll be ready to go again."*

Rhys rolled toward me and propped his head on his hand,
while chewing on a long blade of grass. *"And you just told
this immensely desirable woman that you have to be away
from her for a week so you can get a full breath? That you
spend too much time with her? And it's only been three
weeks since the last time you did this? You are absolutely
mad."*

"It's not like that."

*"But that's what you said, and that's what she heard. If
Galadon ever decides that some of us more ordinary talents
can possibly be worthy of being named a Warden, you'll
have me making a portal into your soul to find the demon.
And if not that, then what?"*

*"There's more than that. There's something strange hap-
pening with me. A change. Powerful . . . as if I'm about to
open a door into another place within myself. It's so close,
but I can't quite grasp it, and when I'm with Ysanne . . . I
can't think of anything but her. I drown in her, Rhys. And
while I'm doing it, I am a madman. But whatever this is, I'm
going to go crazy if I can't figure it out. So I have to be
alone."*

"And did you tell her about it?"

"I can't. She'll worry." And it wasn't just that she would
worry . . . she would ask and probe and try to help, and
make me tell her that I had a gnawing, growing, lunatic conviction that I could jump off a cliff and not die from it. I
hadn't told anyone about it . . . or about the burning pain
that had cropped up in my shoulders and had me ready to
scream whenever I lifted a sword. They would think I was
mad or injured, and they would stop me fighting. I couldn't
have that. *"It's something I have to work out alone."*

"*Seems like you'd want to bring your partner in on something like that.*"

"*Of course I do. I want to be with her every minute of every day. I want to touch her . . . body and mind. I want to be her eyes and her ears, because the whole world is more perfect when I share it with her. But when I step through the portal, I have to leave her behind. What if I take too much of her with me and reveal it to the demon? What if I get distracted thinking of her or worrying about her? I have to work alone, so sometimes I just have to be alone. I just don't know how to tell her that without making her angry. I can't seem to get out the right words.*" It had taken so long to get her to open up her heart. I was terrified of losing her, or of losing my admission to her inner self, which was just the same.

Rhys sat up and shook my knee as if to wake me up. "*What if I were to talk to her? I've got to go south for a few days to see Gram. I'll get Ysanne to go with me while you're off in your eyrie. I'll tell her Casydda is showing talent for searching and needs Ysanne to test her.*"

I wanted to say yes. Rhys was so much better with words than I. But that was the coward's way out. "*No. I need to tell her myself. And besides, she still doesn't like you.*"

Rhys popped to his feet, ignoring my weak protest. "*Don't worry. Go get your head mended. I'll take care of her for you. I'll tell her you're an independent bastard who never lets anyone help him do anything, so she might as well get used to it. And I'll be very gracious. She'll learn to like me.*"

When the path angled upward I did not slow, and I leaped smoothly across the streams and fallen trees that tried to block my passage. Clarity. Memory. The pain I had banished, so much deeper and more agonizing than chains or lashes. The entirety of my being was encompassed in my running, and my long maintained barriers crumbled in the tide of understanding.

My arms were on fire. Inside and out. Inside with the burning of muscles too long strained, too tired, functioning only from will and necessity. Outside from fifty lacerations of sword and knife and spear, some deep, leaving bloody rivulets dribbling to my wrists. An arrow point was buried in one thigh, threatening to collapse my right leg under me. Everywhere was the stink of death, where men had released their bowels in pain and fear, where warriors had vomited when seeing the mutilated remains of friends and lovers, brothers and fathers.

If Rhys didn't come in seconds, I would be carrion along with the rest. How long had it been since he'd gone for help?

I whirled and kicked the knife from the hand of a startled flat-faced Derzhi, and he summoned two Thrid who had just hacked off the hands of two of my dead friends. I slashed with my sword at a snarling Manganar and feinted my knife at another, while aiming it for the heart of a second Derzhi who thought I didn't see him. My pivot leg was the one with the arrow in it, and I made the mistake of brushing the broken shaft with my swing leg. I commanded the leg not to buckle, roaring as the steel tip ground against bone. No use to hold back the cry when it might surprise one of the growing crowd of hostile faces around me. Pride had no place when you were desperate for any advantage.

Watch their eyes.

The eyes of the flat-faced Derzhi shifted, telling me that another had come up behind me. I whipped about and swung again, this time making sure to leave room for the arrow shaft when I set my foot again.

The Manganar is worried. Nice, but why? Not because of an overtired Warden fighting with the dregs of his skill and stamina. I whirled again, sweeping the circle, keeping them back long enough to see. There . . . at the top of the rise, silhouettes against the orange smear of the sunset. Even as my eyes flicked back to the curved saber threatening my rib cage, I continued to solidify the image in my mind. Broad square shoulders. And beside them, a cloud of dark hair, touched with gold. Rhys and Ysanne come to rescue me. Five or six others with them. Enough.

With a last surge of hope I took the Derzhi on my left and ducked a neck-severing swing from the saber.

One minute . . . a few seconds for them to set up a spell . . . a quick distraction so I could sneak out between the six . . . now seven warriors.

"On your knees, barbarian." The stabbing fire in the vulnerable spot just under my left ribs stopped me instantly. Blood dripped slowly down my side from the shallow contact, and any movement would drive the blade deeper. And, of course, in the moment of my hesitation, there came a knife to my throat, a scalp-ripping grab of my hair, and a most persuasive spear point to my groin. "Drop your bloody little toys. It would be a shame to slay such a fighter. You'll do very well to wipe our backsides with your clean Ezzarian fingers."

Now! Do it now, Rhys! I cried silently, as the flat-faced Derzhi forced me down with pressure on the sword tip lodged in my side. I dropped my weapons and tried to summon an enchantment of my own. Anything. But twenty hours of battle, three days without sleep, and grief beyond bearing laid their leaden fingers on my mind and my body. I could not conjure a will-o'-the-wisp. My only hope stood at the top of the rise.

There's only these few, I thought. The bulk of the enemy is five minutes away, finishing the slaughter of our left flank.

But as the circling vultures screamed triumph and descended on the dead, and manacles were locked about my wrists, the Derzhi leaned to the side to grab a friend's whip. And then I saw. One moment the square shoulders and gold-streaked hair were visible at the top of the rise, and in the next, as the first lash ripped the flesh of my shoulders, they turned their backs and disappeared from my sight.

Up and up. The trail narrowed into a rocky, ice-slick goat track. By this time I was not thinking, only running. And when I reached the cliff edge at the top and could run no more, I knelt in the cold sunlight at the rim of the frozen world, and I wept.

Chapter 26

So I had come to it at last. A "revelation" that I had known full well for half my life. Aleksander would be satisfied that he had guessed the truth so easily, whereas I had tried to reinvent it, reinterpret it, reenvision the memory of my friend's betrayal . . . and Ysanne's. She had been there with him. She had watched. She had done nothing.

I sat on the edge of the cliff, dangling my legs over the vast emptiness of sunlit valley.

So what was I to do now? I had brought Aleksander to the Ezzarians in hopes we could find the help he needed so sorely. Was I wrong to believe that such betrayal had led to true corruption—and that it had crippled the Ezzarians, as we had always feared?

"Are you ready for this particular test so soon?"

Fortunately I had a good hold on the rocky verge of the abyss, or the startling intrusion might have sent me off the edge.

"Catrin! How did you find me?"

"The Prince told—"

"The Prince?"

"Nevya had him awake and eating broth two hours ago. He's very weak. He said you were out working off a disturbing encounter with an old friend." She cocked her head to one side, and the wind caught her long hair, framing her small face with a dark corona. "You've always gone to high places when you were troubled."

I shook my head and laughed as I looked back at the

noonday brilliance. "Did you do nothing when you were a child but spy on me?"

Catrin peered into the immensity below us, then sat down beside me, keeping well back from the edge. "I've managed one or two other things along the way. And I don't think you always considered it spying. You never refused the almond cakes I brought you nor the words of encouragement as I remember. You were always very solemn and proud in your humiliation, but you never refused to listen to my admiration. Nor ever contradicted me, as I think about it."

"I kept hoping your grandfather had sent you to tell me he was mistaken, that I was not the most incompetent student he had ever had the misfortune to mentor. Failing that . . . I hoped you had inherited his meticulous eye and had seen worth that he had not." I smiled at her. "So have you? I have sore need of both wisdom and encouragement at the moment."

"Have you given more thought to what he proposed?"

"Of course I've thought of it. I wish I could believe I still had melydda, or that five days of exertion could bring it back."

"It would take you several weeks to prepare. You'd need to work at—"

No point in letting her rattle off Galadon's arguments again. She couldn't understand. "Do you know what they do to you in the Rites of Balthar, Catrin?"

"Seyonne—"

"They start by putting you into a stone box—a coffin with just enough air to keep you breathing—and they bury you underground. You lie there in your own filth, made worse by your terror, unable to move. You think they won't leave you there long. They want a slave. They're just trying to frighten you. But after a while . . . hours . . . a day . . . thirst begins to gnaw at you, and you feel the walls pressing in. You use your power to hold off your fear: to make a light, to dull the cramps and the thirst, to prevent breaking your fingers trying to claw your way out. After a while you can't hold it off anymore, and while you lie there in the dark feel-

ing the madness come, they begin to twist your mind with illusions. . . ."

She put a finger over my mouth, quieting the shaking
rage and terror that consumed me with the remembrance.
My betrothed wife and my best friend had put me in that
coffin. I had known it and had used every scrap of melydda
to make myself forget, leaving nothing to hold off the horror
of being buried alive. For three days I had prayed to die, but
my captors would not allow it. Only my heart and my power
had died.

"We know what they do," said Catrin. "They believe—
and you believe—that they starve your melydda until it's
gone. They force you to use it up, and they use horror and
pain to prevent you from touching it until it withers away.
But Grandfather believes it is not your melydda they destroy, but the faith that binds your senses to your power. The
power is still there. Your mind and body and will are still
there. You have only to reconnect them. What better way to
do it than to explore the very path you walked before, when
you opened yourself in faith, risking everything to prove
that you could stand against demons?"

I shook my head. She believed what she said very sincerely, but what could a sheltered young girl know of despair? I hated to disappoint her, in the same way I would
have hated to refuse her gifts of sweets when she was seven,
but there was no choice in the matter. "I have no faith. I
don't know where to find it anymore."

"You can start with my grandfather. He has never failed
you."

"But he doesn't tell all of the truth." Galadon knew what
Rhys and Ysanne had done. He knew Aleksander would be
refused. That was why he was so determined I should try to
reclaim my power. But he hadn't told me any of it.

She paused a moment before answering. "Being worthy
of your trust does not oblige him to reveal everything he
knows. It never has. He acts as he thinks best."

"It makes faith all the more difficult, especially when
things get hard."

"Strangely enough, we believe you have already found something of faith in this Derzhi. In time, you will find it where you most need to find it. But that will be another day."

"You seem very sure I'm going to do this."

"If you're going to make a Derzhi into the Warrior of Two Souls, you'd best not dally."

"Your grandfather believes me?"

"No. But he can't ignore you, either—which annoys him greatly. And time is very short. The Queen will render her verdict as soon as the Prince is awake again. She'll send him away."

"How can I even begin such a thing when I can't summon the melydda to light a candle?" I said, still consumed with the morbid shadows of the past. "It would waste your time and mine. Better I should go right to the end—step off this cliff and see how far my faith would take me."

The color fled from her rigid face, and her dark eyes grew huge and horrified, shifting from me to the vast emptiness behind me. "Sweet Verdonne, no! You can't—"

"No, no. I didn't mean that. I'd never . . . I'm sorry." What was I thinking? She was an innocent, generous young woman . . . not a cynical slave who could find humor only in the macabre. I held her cold hands. "I sit here floundering in self-pity while you offer a gift of everything I desire. I wish so very much that I could believe as you do. But you mustn't think . . . I've a number of things to do before I die. I've got to get someone to listen to me about the Khelid, and I've got to find a way to get this annoying Derzhi off my conscience."

Catrin set her jaw and yanked her hands from mine, and for a moment I caught a disconcerting glimpse of her grandfather in her small face. "Don't you dare treat me like a child. Even after so many years, you still think you know everything. You're still the same cocky boy of seventeen who would pat me on the head and tell me that I couldn't possibly understand his problems until I grew up. Well, I've grown up. Perhaps I can enlighten you to a few things. Tell me, cocky boy, do you remember how my grandfather questioned your memory on the night you were at our house? He had you reciting every spell you ever learned or made."

Her fury dampened my remorse quite effectively. "Age hasn't mellowed his annoying habits any more than experience has changed mine. Is that what you're saying?"

She showed no signs of appreciating my attempt at humor. Her complexion was a quite vivid red. "When you were seven, you carved a ship that you could make sail in the air. Your cloud ship, you called it. Do you remember that, too?"

My skin prickled as if coming to life after sleep. "Of course I remember."

She reached into the pocket of her scarlet cloak and pulled out a crudely fashioned sailing ship about the size of her hand. "It has not flown in all these years, because only you were ever able to make it do so." She tossed it over the cliff edge and it spun downward, scraps of faded red cloth fluttering bravely from its thin wooden spars . . . until a soft gust of wind brushed the mountaintop, and it floated back into view, drifting in a wide circle around our heads.

"Three nights ago he had you say the words. It required no faith, for its enchantment was created in you before you knew of doubt. A child's spell. Awakened by your melydda, Seyonne. Only yours."

I could have answered her ten different ways. Cynical, disbelieving ways. But as I watched the bit of pine dip and roll over the currents of the wind, I chose to keep silent and live for a moment in the wonder of my first magic. After a while I plucked it from the air and ran my fingers over its gouged and battered surface: the masts I'd had to replace fifty times, the scraps of my mother's weaving, the ship's wheel my father had shown me in a book, the awkward letters of my name carved proudly on the hull. I held it on the palm of my hand . . . just beside the scar where one of my masters had nailed my hand to a door for a week for failing to open the door fast enough.

I gave the toy back to Catrin. "As you said. It's a child's spell."

She returned the ship to her pocket and folded her arms. Again, the fleeting resemblance to Galadon in the set of her jaw and the steel of her eyes. "Then, tell me how it was that on the night the shengar roamed our forest, sixty-three families were warned of the danger at exactly the same moment by a man with a scar on his face. A man who wore a gray cloak and carried a burning stick. A man who disappeared as soon as he had told them to take shelter. Explain it to me. Was this a child's spell or is it a skill of Derzhi slaves?"

"I ran from one to the other."

"Not sixty-three."

"The number was exaggerated."

"I spoke to them myself. I am an investigator and have the right. There were five families you warned in person. One group of two additional families that you saved by stepping between them and the beast. Sixty-three were warned by sorcery—and the power to work such an enchantment is only a Warden's skill. There are not five Ezzarians yet living who could do such a thing. And none of them did it. I've spoken to them all."

"It's impossible."

"And what if it's not? What if you're the one who's wrong?"

"I don't know. . . ."

"Exactly. And your oath requires that you know." She rose and drew her green cloak about her. "I'll come for you tonight, right after the Weaver's lamp is lit. I'd recommend that you get some sleep before that time. Grandfather will be waiting." She turned and marched down the hill, leaving me speechless and confounded. The only words that came to mind were, "Yes, Master Galadon."

I didn't stay long after she left. Life was too confusing to think about. I needed to run again, and so I did. And that's when I noticed that it didn't hurt, and that I could breathe, and that my stride was smooth and long, reeling up the path so that I was back at the guest house in the short matter of an hour. I hoped Aleksander was awake. I needed to talk to someone who wouldn't leave me feeling as though I'd been tied into widows' knots by little girls playing with string. I'd come to respect Aleksander's gift of seeing through people. If he would just learn the right thing to do with those insights once he had them, he might turn into a decent human being.

The village was quiet and deserted, so I was completely taken aback to open the guest house door and see the Queen of Ezzaria sitting beside Aleksander's bed. The healer stood by the fire with Rhys, and two Ezzarian men, armed with spears, stood just inside the door. None of them moved when I walked in. I wondered what they would do if I attempted to harm their queen.

I genuflected, but of course, Ysanne did not acknowledge it. It was Aleksander, leaning back on his pillows looking exceedingly ill, who waved me up. It was improper for me to stay. Neither Ezzarian manners nor Derzhi slave discipline would permit it. But I decided that rudeness and impertinence were far outweighed by my need to hear whatever was to be heard. So I sat myself on the floor beside Aleksander's bed and watched Ysanne's face as she spoke. Her dark eyes never strayed from Aleksander, and her clear voice never wavered.

". . . sorry. Because we caused you this grievous injury, you may stay until it is healed. But once Nevya says you are able to travel, we will require that you leave."

"I thought we were going to send him away immediately," said Rhys. His back was to the rest of us, and he was staring at the fire, drumming his fist on the sturdy pine shelf over the hearth. "He could be taken at any time. You said he was so far gone that he would accept a rai-kirah willingly, so every moment he's here is a risk. I know how you hate it, but—"

"We are to blame for this illness. We will offer him healing for his body, but nothing else."

"I understood that Ezzarians did not refuse anyone healing for demon enchantments, even a Derzhi." Aleksander's voice was tight, breaking with quick breaths, as if it pained him to move even so small a part of himself.

"We have no love for Derzhi," Ysanne said, "and I'll not say that I would consent to your healing in any circumstance. But it makes no difference. Your enchantment is beyond our skill. We cannot protect you from its consequences, so we must protect ourselves."

Frost had blighted Ysanne's fire. Her words were not unkind. Her sympathy was sincere. Yet the woman I remembered would never have sent Aleksander away without attempting to save him. He bore the feadnach . . . how could she not try? Then I laughed at myself without mirth. The woman I remembered had never existed. She would never have walked away and left anyone in slavery.

The threads of light in her dark hair were a paler gold than I remembered. Was it strands of silver that dimmed it, like mingled moonlight cooling the fire of the sun? Only a single curl was allowed loose to hang beside her face and fall on the deep blue of her cloak. My body was in a knot as I listened, waiting for the sympathetic harmonies that her melodious voice had always set off in me. We had been like chiming strings on a harp, and no matter the betrayal, I expected that hearing her again would tear me apart. But I felt nothing. She sat straight in her chair beside Aleksander, her eyes fixed on him, and I found myself wanting to reach out and shake her, to make her angry, to curse me, anything to prove I was not dead. I had lived in her mind. She had created worlds for me to walk, using everything she knew of me to make them as familiar as possible . . . to keep me safe. Our pairing—the two of us, the work we did—had been my whole life, and I had believed it was hers also. How could she have betrayed me? How could I feel nothing?

A sudden gasp and a stifled moan from Aleksander startled me out of my private argument and had Ysanne out of her chair. One side of the Prince's body had twisted itself into the shape of the shengar, while the other half stayed in the shape of a man. It was only for a single, agonizing mo-

ment, but it left Aleksander's bloodless face rigid with pain
and the two guards with spear points at his heart.

"Sweet Verdonne, haven't you done enough?" I said,
grabbing the spears and twisting them from the hands of the
guards, unable to contain the rage that had so little to do
with their blind reaction. They weren't sure what to do with
me, which left it very easy. I used the blunt end of their
spears to shove the men away, then reversed the shafts, pin-
ning the two to the wall by their clothing. I dropped to my
knees beside the Prince. "My lord, can you hear me?"

"Stay back," he said, struggling for breath. "Tell them to
stay back."

"They'll stay away," I said. "What's happening?"

Ysanne broke in as if I hadn't spoken. "This is your enchantment? Is this how it begins?" Rhys stood behind her,
his broad hands on her shoulders, staring in horror at Aleksander.

"Different . . . these few days," said the Prince, pressing
the heels of his hands into his eyes. "My mind keeps slipping back and forth . . . changing . . . so I see . . . as the
beast sees. Smells . . . Cravings . . . Parts of me changing.
Then it goes away."

"No trigger?" I said. "Nothing sets it off like before."

"No trigger. No sword . . . no Dmitri. . . ."

"If you wish to be heard, Prince Aleksander, you will address your words to me," said Ysanne coldly. "What is it
you're saying?"

"I can scarcely hold one conversation," said the Prince,
trying in vain to moisten his lips. "Can't do two."

I poured wine from the pitcher that sat on the bedside
table, then raised his head to give him a sip. "Tastes beastly,"
he said, then laughed weakly. "Appropriate, eh?"

"Daffyd, you will stay to protect Nevya," commanded
Ysanne, angrily throwing on her cloak. "Rhys, tell the
Weaver to place a barrier about this house."

"No! Ysanne, you can't! It was worse—" I broke off,
cursing inwardly. She would do nothing from my saying.

"My lord, please tell the Queen how it was when I took you beyond the forest boundary during the change."

He told her in words different enough from mine that she could act on them, and Ysanne rescinded her order. "I'm sorry we can't help you, Prince Aleksander. Once we had those among us who were capable of unraveling such things. But they are all dead now. Dead at the hand of the Derzhi. We must husband our resources carefully. You will be gone from here as soon as you can ride." She swept out of the room on Rhys's arm, followed by one of her red-faced guards who had loosened himself from the wall. I wondered how he was going to explain the rips in his jerkin.

"Not very friendly," said Aleksander into his pillow, a sheen of sweat glistening on his bare arms.

"Our Queen holds the care of the world. She can't do everything she would like," said the healer, adjusting the pillow and blankets to make him more comfortable. "But she's brought you her own remedies to strengthen you and to ease your pain. She has more knowledge of these things than any of us." The woman crushed a packet of herbs with a few drops of oil from a glass bottle and dressed Aleksander's wound with it. I watched closely, wishing I had the power to read what was in the mixture. Yet I still could not believe Ysanne would deliberately hurt anyone. Stupid. How many betrayals would it take? Perhaps it was just that I trusted the healer to recognize anything amiss. Nevya was a gentle, capable woman. The Prince did seem more at ease once the medicine was applied and the healer had wrapped clean bandages around him.

"Seyonne."

"Yes, my lord."

"Tell her how I need something to keep me asleep. So I won't change. Please. If it comes again . . . I won't get back."

"You've told her, my lord. That will have to do. And should it come, you will stay in control and return to yourself as you have before. I'll be with you."

The healer mixed herbs in hot water and slipped a few spoonfuls into Aleksander's mouth.

"This will help you sleep," she said, then she gathered her things and slipped out the door, leaving me alone with the Prince.

"Your people are cruel, Seyonne."

I sat on the floor beside his bed. "No. They're right to be cautious. But sometimes they look in the wrong direction for corruption. They could use your skill to see men's hearts behind their deeds."

Aleksander dragged his sagging eyelids open. "I was right about the consort?"

I nodded and bit my tongue to keep from asking the next question. But he heard it anyway.

"She wears a mask," he said. "If she's guilty, then she's locked it away. It does not control her actions. My father does the same. I've always hoped to learn how he does it. Figured I'd need it."

For an instant, feral madness gleamed in his amber eyes, then a shudder rippled over his long body, and he clutched the pillow with bloodless knuckles. "Help me, Seyonne."

"We'll find a way," I said. "Even if I have to start over from the beginning and do it myself, we will rid you of this affliction. The demon will not win."

"My guardian spirit," Aleksander mumbled sleepily. "I've been lying here thinking, remembering that warrior on the woman's tapestry—the warrior with wings who's battling the monster. Can't get it out of my head. The face was so familiar, but I couldn't place it. Now I know. It's you, isn't it?"

I wasn't sure he was awake to hear my answer. "Aye, my lord. It was."

Chapter 27

The Weaver was the guardian of an Ezzarian settlement. A woman of unequaled skill in creating enchantments, she was responsible for the forest barriers that would keep it safe, that would give warning when intruders, especially unseen demons, entered the trees. The Weaver always lived outside the forest so she could monitor her spells, but that meant she was not sheltered or protected herself; thus she was susceptible to risks that others were not. And so at the corner of her house hung a lamp, lit every evening as soon as she had made her rounds and confirmed that all was secure. Someone from the settlement would come to the forest edge to make sure that the Weaver's lamp was lit, and if it was not, would run to give the alarm.

For the two years my mother had been the Weaver and could not live in our home in the forest, I had been the runner. It was a great honor for her to be named, and I basked in the respect it gained from my friends, but I missed her sorely, feeling a great emptiness in our home. When my father told her of my grief, she took me in her arms and said that she had woven my name into the spell to light her lamp. Whenever I saw it burning, I should know her heart was with me for the night. Since then the Weaver's lamp had always warmed me far beyond the security of the settlement. It had been the coldest of nights when I was twelve and saw no lamp lit, the night we found her dead from a sudden onset of fever.

Aleksander was deep in drugged sleep, and I was sitting in the open doorway of the guest house when the Weaver's lamp bloomed from a single spark to a steady yellow gleam across the dark lane. I could not but think of my mother . . . and so my father, too. I missed them both. My mother had been immensely powerful, my first teacher in the ways of enchantment. She had enlightened my imagination with her stories and taught me to explore fully the worlds of my senses, to be observant and attentive even to the most ordinary things. She made sure I knew how to listen to silence as well as sound and see things absent as well as present. And in a strange inversion she taught me to see and feel the things I heard, and to hear and taste color and texture and shape.

But I believed I had actually learned more from my father, who had no melydda at all. He had been a tall, wiry man who loved books. He could have spent his life joyfully as a scholar or teacher, exploring the realms of the intellect. But he was Ezzarian and had no melydda, so he had not that luxury. His days were spent working the terraced fields beyond the forest, growing food to support those who carried on the demon war. Before I started school, I would make the daily trek with him, riding on his shoulders in the dewy morning, happily digging in the dirt, pulling weeds, or napping in the apple orchard until he carried me home in the evening. Those were precious days. After supper he would sit in his study and open his book, but would fall asleep in his chair instantly, too tired to read. It was many years until I understood the quiet sadness beneath his smile when I was tested and found to have melydda. He understood, as I did not, that it meant that our time together would quickly dwindle and disappear. It was my good fortune that my training did not take me away from home, for I learned everything of honor and duty and sacrifice, not from Searchers or Wardens or mentors, nor from my mother, who left our home to be the Weaver, but from my father, whose gift was to give away everything he valued.

I smiled as I sat watching the Weaver's lamp from the guest house doorway. All these years I believed I had walled up my father with the rest of my memory, but in truth, he had been with me through everything. His was the voice of acceptance and peace that had helped me survive. *What comes, comes.* Though he had no melydda, on the day when the terror came, when the Derzhi legion was sighted off our borders, my father was the first to take up his pikestaff and his bow and ask me, his warrior son, where he should stand.

When the shadow that was Catrin walked out of the trees and up the village lane to fetch me, I was already standing up. "I need to be back before Aleksander wakes," I said. "I've promised to be with him. Other than that, I'm all yours. Just tell me where to stand."

She didn't smile. Didn't speak. Just turned and walked back toward the trees.

It was a correct beginning. No one spoke unnecessarily to the candidate in the days leading up to his testing. He was supposed to be focusing entirely on his preparation: physical skills, mental clarity, sensory perception, purity of heart, and a mind-cracking load of arcane knowledge. I sighed as I followed Catrin's straight back. The only question seemed to be in which area I was least prepared. But I was accustomed to self-discipline, at least, so I kept myself from dwelling on possibilities. I would not consider either faith or failure. *What comes, comes.*

Catrin led me, not to Galadon's house, but deep into the trees to a rocky glade lit by three white lamps hung from pine branches. Trailers of steam rose from a dark pool and wreathed about the white-haired Galadon, who stood on the rocks of the bank opposite Catrin and me. The old man wore the dark blue robes of the Warden he had once been, and he leaned on the staff he used to focus his melydda when he was teaching. I stopped at the edge of the glade and bowed to him as was proper from a student to his mentor. He raised his staff and pointed to the pool. No words were necessary. I knew what he wanted.

I cast a sidelong glance at Catrin as I took off my cloak, hung it over a branch, and sat down to pull off my boots. She was occupied with a bag set under one of the hanging lanterns, her back to me. I hoped she would stay that way or leave the glade altogether. Galadon did not intend for me to pollute the pool with clothing, and even sixteen years with the immodest Derzhi had not prepared me to stand naked in front of an Ezzarian woman I hardly knew. And there were other things . . . steel bands, scars . . . I shut off my head and pulled off my shirt, hanging it beside my cloak. *Think of the words. Feel what you're doing . . . only that. To be clean.* How long had it been? I stripped off the slave tunic and my breeches, shivering as a breeze whispered the trees and teased the vapors from the pool. The water looked to be very hot. I wanted to dip my hand or my foot in the pool to test it, but faith had to begin somewhere. Galadon would not give me more than I could bear.

So I walked gingerly across the patchy snow and the damp rocks at the edge of the water, jumped in . . . and came near drowning. The water was well over my head and scalding. I flailed about in panic, inhaling a barrel of the boiling stuff before struggling to the surface and dragging myself onto the painfully cold rocks. I lay choking and coughing, unable to scream at the touch of frigid air on my raw skin. I could feel every stripe that had ever been laid on my back. The burn scars on my shoulder and my face throbbed at the insult. My eyes poured out a river of tears to cool their injury, and I frantically crawled to the edge of the rocks to plunge my hands into the snow to cool the metal about my wrists. I began to shiver, and between bouts of coughing I tried to form words. "I'm sorry, master . . . so stupid . . . so stupid." When I could move again, I would put on my clothes and go back to Aleksander. What had I been thinking?

"Again."

I feared the scalding water had damaged my hearing. Scarcely able to control my trembling limbs, I got to my knees and looked up at the white-haired man who stood over me. His jaw was hard, his eyes uncompromising, unsympathetic. He raised the staff and pointed at the pool behind me. "Again."

It was as well I couldn't speak. What could I say to a

madman? Or perhaps he thought I was mad. How could he believe I would go back into the water? Boiling my skin away would not heal my scars. With blurry eyes I searched the glade for Catrin. She was sitting across the pool on the rocks from which I'd stepped in. Watching. Waiting. No expression. Certainly no movement to gainsay her grandfather lest he torture his too-old student to death.

They didn't think I would die if I went back in. I pressed the heels of my hands into my eyes, trying to dam the river of tears so I could see. The pool steamed in the night air. *Faith.* Galadon did not want me to die. *Discipline. No doubts.* Doubt, not fear, was the Warden's enemy. Fear made you wary. Doubt made you weak. *Discipline. Clear all these thoughts away.*

I stood up, still shivering, and bowed to Galadon. Then I took a breath, emptied my head, stepped into the pool . . . and believed that I was certainly going to die. I could feel the blood boiling in my veins. At least this time I had been wary and stepped in close to the bank, so that within one agonizing moment I was back on the cold rocks again. I felt like one of the sheets Manganar laundry women boil in copper pots, then beat with stones.

"Master," I gasped. "I can't."

"Again."

I didn't even bother to look up. The word told me everything. The staff would be pointing to the pool. How often in my life had I heard that same word in that same insistent tone? Every instance of it came back to me as I lay on the rocks, freezing and on fire at the same time. The words pelted me like hailstones, battering me into pulp so I could be shaped into something better, stronger. It meant I was forgetting something: a word, a movement, an insight, a step. I was failing to see what I needed to see. "Again." This time do it right. This time, don't forget. When you walk the realms of demon madness, you cannot afford to forget, to slip, to fail.

So what was I forgetting? What had I tried? Breath, distractions, trust . . . I knelt on all fours, limp and laughing in exhausted helplessness. What would Aleksander say to this? A warrior's training . . . not to slit bellies or ride horses, but to bathe. To clean oneself. To restore purity.

Aleksander. With the thought of the Prince, he who had brought me to face this trial and whose need demanded that I finish it, the answer came clear. My problem was not lack of knowledge. The knowledge was in me and would come back with practice. And I had correctly banished distractions, but I'd not replaced them with my purpose. It was impossible to fight any battle without purpose. It was your anchor. Your focus. The place you could fasten everything you had to remember.

I struggled to my feet and bowed again to the figure in blue. This time, instead of clearing my mind, I filled it with light—Aleksander's feadnach, the silvery gleam of possibility, my anchor. Once done, everything else fell into place. This was a simple test. I delved into the bits of knowledge floating in my head and prepared. *Breathe deep to fill the blood with endurance. Control the senses. Mute the throbbing of ragged nerves. Cool the skin. Glaze the eyes with thickened tears to protect them while allowing you to see what must be seen. Slow the heart. Control . . . steady . . . focus . . .* I stepped again into the steaming pool.

Smoothly, slowly I slipped into the hot water, as if time scarcely crept along its way. All the way to the bottom this time, feeling only the soft brush of drifting moss and the soothing warmth penetrating my pores. Far above me the white lantern light floated on the surface, and I swam lazily toward it, feeling the water glide past my skin, soaking away years of filth, of horror, of pain. In a moment I reversed direction and returned to the bottom, grabbing a handful of sand and scrubbing my skin and my hair. Then I shot for the surface and burst through, laughing at myself as I crawled out onto the rocks and lay naked in the cold night, feeling as if I had crushed a Derzhi legion.

It was such a small triumph. My victory had involved no sorcery at all. No melydda. I had scarcely touched what I needed to do. But it was enough. I had begun.

* * *

Every night for seven nights Catrin came for me and delivered me to Galadon. For eight hours or more he would work me through elements of my training. He would drill me for two hours in words and spells, strategies and tactics, then set me to running or practicing the martial disciplines to hone my reflexes and settle my mind. In other hours he would set me problems—puzzles or battle scenarios—and have me work them out in my head, never allowing me to scratch them in the dirt or on a rock. I heard the word "again" so often, it was burned into my being anew, and then I would have to twist my mind into knots to discover what I was forgetting. Never did Galadon speak to me beyond the work, and never did he set me any task that required melydda. I did not allow myself to think of that. In truth, I was always too tired to live beyond the moment.

Catrin was with us the whole time, which I found odd. I kept waiting for her to offer me almond cakes or some bit of encouragement in a humorous connection with our past. But her dark eyes never smiled. They watched and judged, and when I would fail at a simple task, she would turn away in annoyance.

I was returned to the guest house two hours before dawn, stumbling to my bed, though never did I remember actually getting there. I woke in the early morning when Nevya came to see to Aleksander. His wound was healing well. The fever had gone, and only a little tenderness remained in his belly. But much to his disgust, he was still woefully weak, scarcely capable of standing up, much less riding. Ysanne came to check on him every morning, reminding him that he was to go as soon as he could ride. Nevya shook her head and said it would be condemning him to death to send him through the mountains in his weakened state.

"The whole damned world just won't be still," he said one afternoon after commanding me to help him up. He had walked back and forth across the room ten times, then had come near falling on his face. "Between the infernal sleeping potions and my cursed head, I feel like a dezrhila dancer.

Never saw how they could spin for an hour and stay upright. Drove me mad to watch them."

I yawned and helped him from the chair, where he had dropped himself, back to the bed. "Rest today, and then to-morrow I'll take you outside," I said. "Fresh air will do you good. We don't want to rush it. Another week might be worthwhile." After a singularly unsuccessful night with Gal-adon, I thought ten weeks could not possibly suffice. I had not told Aleksander what I was doing, but I'd hinted that a slower recovery could be to his benefit.

I gave him a mug of soup that Nevya had left. His ap-petite was certainly revived. I couldn't keep enough going down him. The Ezzarians might run him off just to keep him from devouring their food reserves.

"So what's your plan?" said Aleksander, nudging me awake with his foot. I sat on the floor leaning against his bed. "You're implacably dull these days, always dozing off, making me carry the whole conversation. Nothing about sorcery or demons or what a madman I am to imagine that you told me you could grow wings. What do you care about Derzhi military maneuvers or how Dmitri taught me to carry a sword? I think it's time you told me a few things. About this Gala—"

"I just want us to be away from here," I said, motioning him to silence. "We'll find some place to hide until you can be rid of this curse." Nevya was not in the guest house, but I had no confidence that we could speak without being over-heard. There were ways. For the past three nights I had ex-perienced a creeping dread, a cold itch running up my spine, a sensation quite familiar from demon battles when some-thing nasty was ready to pop out from a rock behind me. On that afternoon it had been worse than ever.

"Maybe the wretched thing will just go away. It could do that, couldn't it? If the demons lost interest or something? Thought I was well out of the way? I know it's been better the last couple of days." Even as he said it, the color drained from his face. He slammed his eyes shut, but not before I saw the wild panic that told me he was once again viewing the world through the eyes of a beast.

I gave him time for the terrible event to pass, then shook my head. "I can't be sure, my lord. But I doubt it. I wish I could tell you differently."

Whether it was his injury while in the form of the shengar, or my taking him across the Weaver's boundary while he was changing, or some other, unexplainable variance in the demon working, his enchantment had taken an ominous turn. It seemed to require no trigger at all. He kept experiencing random "slippage," where one sense or one limb would transform and the rest of his body would not. I wondered if he was ever truly free of the shengar anymore. I had examined him that morning with my reawakening senses . . . and I had been horrified at the damage. His soul was being eaten away by darkness, as iron is eaten away by the damp, leaving ragged, brittle edges that could disintegrate at a touch. I could not imagine the torment of his condition . . . or what slight change might cause his last defenses to fail. We were running out of time.

I didn't know whether it was fear of Aleksander's disintegration or some other sense that had me in such a state of anxiety that day. I stood up and peered through the open shutters. A group of small children were playing tag in the marshy field beside the river, happily trouncing each other into the mud. Three women were coming out of the Weaver's house, carrying rolls of colored cloth. A boy drove a small flock of sheep over the rise in the road. It had been a beautiful day, warm and windless, birds twittering the message that perhaps spring had come at last to this high meadow. Peaceful.

I could not sit still. I shifted my senses and found no enchantments save the ordinary ones I would expect. To keep the water clean. To prevent vermin from invading a house so little used. To make it tight against the cold.

"What is it, Seyonne? You're as nervous as a squire on the eve of his first battle."

"I wish I knew." I moved to the back door and watched a

hawk dive for a mouse that had finally braved the weather to come out of his winter's hiding.

"It seems strange that no one comes here. The man to deliver the water. The woman that brings food. That's all. The healing woman doesn't even come very often anymore."

"The Queen has told them her decision. They won't do anything to encourage you to stay."

He didn't answer, and when I glanced over my shoulder to see if he'd fallen asleep, I saw instead that his left arm had shifted itself into the limb of the shengar. Aleksander was staring at the grotesque appendage in horror and disgust. "Holy Athos . . ."

"Don't think of it, my lord. Think of something else. Tell me . . . tell me of Zhagad. I've never seen it, though I've heard it is the most beautiful city in the world. And not only Derzhi say it."

Aleksander closed his eyes and shook his head. I wasn't sure if he was in too much pain to speak again or if he was afraid that nothing would come out but the shengar's scream.

"Then, I'd best tell you something to keep you interested." The transformation was not reversing itself quickly, as was the usual case. I wasn't sure I wanted to think about it, either. "I suppose it's only fair to tell you a bit of history about the war against the demons."

I dared not tell him anything of importance. I trusted Aleksander, but I knew how thin was our hope to save him from the demons. Whatever I had said otherwise, whatever Ysanne had told the Prince, there was only one living Ezzarian who had ever had power enough to deal with an enchantment as deep, as virulent, as Aleksander's. And I was not ready. Not yet.

Chapter 28

It had taken two hours for Aleksander's arm to return to normal. He was unable to eat after that. When I offered him a cup of stewed barley and a honey-laden biscuit, he said they smelled rank and disgusting.

"My lord, you must regain your strength," I said.

"I told you, I'll have none of it!" he roared, then smashed the cup from my hand, splattering the hot stuff all over me. I jumped up, and by the time I had wiped the mess from my breeches, the Prince was curled into a knot, his arms thrown over his head. "Make me sleep, Seyonne. Bash my head with a rock if nothing else will do it."

I thought I might have to do that very thing. It took three times the normal sleeping draught to get him quiet. By the time the Weaver's lamp was lit, he lay in the image of death. Only a hand on his chest could detect any movement. I had to convince Galadon to help me do something, or we were going to lose him.

Catrin came at the appointed hour, and I argued with myself over whether to leave the Prince. "He's had a difficult evening," I said, not expecting her to answer, as she had said no unneeded word to me for seven days. "I ought to stay with him. Our time might be better spent on figuring out how to help him."

"If you stay, you will assure his ruin." Her words echoed like the faint thunder rumbling over the mountains to the east. With quiverings of pink and silver the magnificent day was giving birth to a storm.

I stared at the short, slender young woman in dark green.

"Are you a Seer, Catrin?" I had not considered that she might have melydda beyond the minor gifting of perception and mind-seeing needed by an investigator.

"No." She stepped from the doorway onto the road. "If you're going to continue what you've begun, then it must be now."

A brilliant flash of lightning lit up her face, and I read such a range of emotion in that brief glimpse as to make a lie of her cool voice.

"What is it, Catrin? What are you afraid of?"

"Come or stay," she said, and she hurried into the night toward the forest.

I went back into the guest house, made sure Aleksander was still sleeping, and laid another log on the fire against the possibility of a storm. Then I took out after Catrin, catching up to her at the edge of the trees. Before we passed beyond the boundary, I laid a hand on her arm. "Is your grandfather all right?" I had been so absorbed in my own dilemmas, I had given no thought to the toll our activities must be taking on Galadon.

"He's waiting," she said, firmly removing her arm from my grasp. "If you want to help the Prince, you must continue working at it. Come or stay."

I went, vowing to get Galadon to help me decide what might give Aleksander more time. But I had no opportunity to speak to my mentor before we began. He was waiting beside the pool, his white hair lifted by the rising wind and his staff already pointing at the water. We started every evening with the purification. In the daytime hours I tried very hard to keep a portion of my mind focused on my training, to keep that bit of me free of anxiety or curiosity. But inevitably I would lose my concentration as I watched Aleksander struggle with his grotesque enchantment. Galadon seemed to understand that the ritual helped me regain my focus.

That night when I came out, clean clothes were waiting for me on the rocks: tan breeches and perfectly fitting calf-high boots, a sleeveless shirt of white linen, and a cloak of gray wool. As I pulled on the shirt, I noticed that Catrin was nowhere to be seen. It was unusual, and somehow disconcerting. The first spatters of rain fell cold on my face.

Galadon motioned me to follow, and I settled my mind into emptiness as I walked the path behind him. It was a way we'd not traveled before, leading into a denser part of the forest, where the spreading firs were so thick they held off most of the rain. The muddy path wound upward, little patches of old snow gleaming dirty white in the faint light from Galadon's hand. The rain brought out the perfume of the thawing earth and the ancient carpet of pine needles.

There was more disturbance to the night than the approaching storm. The air was ripe with sorcery. Even without shifting I could feel it. My breathing slowed as if an anvil rested on my chest; my skin quivered as if the boundaries of my body were the boundaries of the universe, and whatever lay beyond those boundaries was altogether different than it was before that night. *Don't think. Don't guess. This is all part of your preparation. What comes, comes.*

Firelight flickered through the trees ahead of us, but before I could see what manner of place lay there, Galadon stopped and handed me a strip of linen to bind my eyes. I thought nothing of it. He'd had me do it a number of times over the past days to make sure I could still function without sight. One never knew what might come in a demon battle. I would just pay closer attention to my other senses.

But this time he set me no puzzle, only used his stick to bid me follow him again. I listened to his steps. Slow and careful on the rocks and roots that protruded from the soft ground. His left hip was bothering him. I could hear it in his uneven step and in the slight hitch in his breathing when he would put weight on it. Curve slightly to the right. We were out of the trees. Rain drizzled on my head and shoulders, though not enough to soak the gray wool cloak.

Steps . . . three . . . and a flat stone floor. Galadon's shuffling sandals echoed faintly, and no more rain fell on my head, so there was a roof. Walls, too, but not surrounding us entirely for I could still feel the rain-scented breeze. And the

fire was there . . . pine boughs . . . and a few grains of jasnyr
had been thrown in it, making the smoke sweet so it did not
burn the eyes. We were in a temple! Instantly I could feel the
five pairs of stone columns around me and the simple
domed roof over my head. Somewhere the floor would be
inlaid with mosaics depicting centuries of struggle with the
demons. This one likely had the new chapter added—about
the Derzhi conquest and the flight from Ezzaria.

This was an interesting variation of Galadon's teaching.
He was going to set me another puzzle, of course, and
wanted to immerse me in the vision as if it were a real battle. I would watch the scene play out or perhaps make some
attempt to do the fighting myself, then he would pull me out
and quiz me on what I'd seen: the moves, the mistakes, the
hidden meanings, the riddles that could be wrapped in the
land or the weather or the structures or the inhabitants.
Everything had meaning in the landscape of the human soul.

"Recite Ioreth."

I bowed and settled myself on the floor, palms open and
relaxed on my knees. I spoke the words of Ioreth's Chant,
part of a Warden's preparation before going into battle.

"Again."

I recited it again, this time trying to go beyond rote
words, to ease myself into the rhythm, let them take me into
a state of separation from the world. As if he knew I had
gone as far as I could without melydda, Galadon took my
hand and placed in it . . . another hand . . . slender, soft . . .

The portal opened into blistering heat. The path was
steady beneath my feet, and I stepped through instantly, curious to see what manner of riddle Galadon had set me. I
stood on a rocky precipice under twin red suns, looking
down on a landscape of death. Parched, cracked red earth
stretched as far as I could see. Jagged pinnacles of rock jut-
ted out of the caked land like grotesque game pieces. Orange
clouds stained the horizon, and a screaming vulture dived
through the air after . . . what? I squinted into the hot glare,
but couldn't see the prey. Galadon would rail at me for miss-

ing it. I tried to banish such thoughts and immerse myself in the lesson.

Concentrate. See what lies here in this life-destroying heat. What is the meaning of the landforms, so harsh, so devoid of life, the sparse, tangled scrub that could never bloom in such desolation? What dangers lie hidden in the rocks or the smeared clouds? Is the vulture the enemy or is something else lurking, waiting for the warrior who will come?

The land trembled beneath my feet. Out on the seared plains several of the towering rock stacks toppled, raising clouds of red dust, and wide cracks opened in the land. My spine tightened with foreboding. Galadon was a master at creating practice illusions. I had died a thousand times in his creations, astonished to find myself still breathing when he pulled me out. But this one . . . how was it possible that I could taste the faint traces of sulfur in the hot wind and feel the grit of sand between my teeth?

I needed to see what lay at the bottom of the cliffs on which I stood, but I could not convince myself to walk to the edge and peer downward. I would be too visible outlined against the orange sky. *Foolish. This is an illusion like all the rest. Nothing more. He's just convinced an Aife to help him, to make it more real.* Yet I sank to my knees and crept across the hot rocks.

At the bottom of the cliff was a warren of rocks, sharp, dangerous spires reaching a quarter of the way up the cliff. It was impossible to penetrate the thick shadows between them. The flat light shifted subtly, and in an instant the shadows were gone and I could examine the deep clefts and crannies. Nothing moved. Yet there was something. . . .

My hand slipped on the loose talus, and an edge of rock bit into it, cutting the skin, leaving a thin line of blood seeping from the cut. I stared at the blood. Touched it. Tasted it. In a vision you did not bleed—not blood that you could taste. *What have you done, master?*

Before I could reset my mind to consider that the place I stood was real, the dust haze far to my left parted to reveal a shimmering rectangle—a portal. A tiny figure stepped through, too distant for me to see his face, though I could hear his booming voice clearly. "I am the Warden, sent by the Aife, Scourge of Demons, to challenge you for this vessel. Hyssad! Begone!"

There! One of the stacks of rock in the shadows of the cliff moved, but there was no quaking of the earth to cause it. Did the Warden see it? A piercing glint of light from the warrior's hand . . . the knife. My right hand ached for the silver knife and my left for the smooth, palm-sized oval of the Luthen mirror—the artifact from our ancient past that could paralyze a demon by showing it its own reflection.

The warrior moved forward slowly. Hunting. Examining the landscape as I had done. Would he see the lurking danger? Would he locate the source of the demon music that grated on the soul like steel on glass? Was the warrior real, too, or was he some masterful creation of my mentor?

If he was real, then how was this possible? Two portals in the same soul. It was the Warden's burden . . . to be alone in the domain of evil. And how could I have come to such a place unprepared, without sharing in the Aife's weaving that made the passage possible?

"I reject your challenge, vermin." The voice echoed from the rocks, twisting my stomach with revulsion at the sound of it. "I claim this vessel for my own. Its food is rich and satisfies me beyond any I have tasted."

The landscape shuddered. More vents gaped in the plain, spewing foul-smelling smoke. For an instant the sky darkened. With an explosive clap, a crack ripped through the rock where I lay prostrate. I rolled to the right, and when my gaze settled on the plain once again, the warrior and the monster were already engaged. How had it happened so quickly? Somewhere a tormented victim was screaming in agony at the wrenching horror in his head.

The monster had separated itself from the rocks that disguised it. It was red and lumpy, its shape that of a huge caterpillar, but with legs as thick as trees and huge paws at the end of each appendage. Its eyes were set into bony hollows, its neck ringed with jagged cartilage. The hide would be thick and tough; to find the vulnerable spot would require long and careful testing. Yet the Warden had already transformed the silver knife into a spear. Why a spear? What had he seen that I had missed? A spear, once thrown, is useless. You have to be sure. They had scarcely begun their battle.

The Warden dodged a blow from the monster's bulbous paw. Gracefully, for such a large man. A very large man, I realized, considering the distance between us. Broad-shouldered. Tall. He feinted with the spear. A give and take of moves and parries. Slowly. Precisely. Like a dance where all the steps were known and practiced. After only a few exchanges, the monster rose up on its hind end, waving its six legs and bellowing in ear-shattering defiance. The Warden dodged another blow, then launched the spear. It lodged low in the creature's belly. Green foulness spurted from the wound, slathering the warrior and the red dirt.

The land trembled when the beast toppled and lay still. *Now,* I thought, my tense body urging the man to hurry, to finish the deed before the moment was past, even while my mind wondered at the shape of the battle. *Take it now. It must be now.*

As if at my bidding the warrior raised his left hand high and a glare of brilliant silver shot from it as he spoke. "Hyssad, rai-kirah. Begone or die."

Watch out! I flinched—for some reason thinking the man in danger, when he was clearly in control. With his right hand, the Warden wrenched the spear away, changed the weapon into a broadsword, and slashed the monster's belly from its neck to its hind end, loosing its entrails that dried and shriveled instantly in the heat.

Then came a mind-ripping scream of fury as made a shengar's cry no more than an infant's whimper. Demons loathed the Luthen mirror. They could not resist looking at it, though they knew the consequences. Only in the instant their physical form was dead could you capture them with it, for only then would they see their demon aspect rather than the physical being. Timing was all.

The scream told me that the warrior had succeeded in

taking the demon captive, yet something jarred me about the scene, beyond the unbelievable speed of its resolution. Even as the man changed the sword back to a silver knife, ready to dispatch the demon should it choose death, I tried to recapture what I had seen. What was wrong?

A first-year student could have picked it out. The timing! The warrior had dispatched the monster *after* he had raised the mirror. But the mirror was only effective after the physical beast was dead. I had flinched because the demon beast had moved just before the sword bit into its gut. Too quick. Too easy. The Warden didn't have the demon in his control. I wanted to cry out a warning, but I was drowned out by the bellowing demon. Because it was outside of physical form, it spoke in its own nerve-scraping voice, using the demon language, a tongue so vile you studied it only in daylight, lest your nights be forever filled with words of dread. "Never will I yield to such whining scum as you. Take me if you can."

The knife flashed, the silver Warden's knife that could be changed to whatever weapon was needed, that could slice through the incorporeal body of a demon if you could calculate exactly where that was. The faint mournful wail of a dying demon floated on the cooling breeze. The light began to brighten. The warrior knelt and opened his arms wide to embrace victory and peace.

But I had no peace. There had been no demon captured, so no demon was dead. Since I existed in that place, I would have felt it. Every demon death was a palpable alteration in the aspect of the universe. That was why we were so wary of killing them all. The change would be so monumental, we believed that nature could not tolerate it. Better to keep fighting than to destroy the very thing you were out to protect. But this one . . . This demon was gone, but still alive. Unbound. This scene was all wrong.

"Warden, I challenge this claim of victory. This sham. This craven falsehood." The thundering voice spoke the very thoughts in my head, but its source was a white-haired figure in a blue cloak who had walked onto the battlefield while I wasn't looking. Galadon.

I rubbed my eyes and shifted senses back and forth, but still I saw what was impossible. Incredible enough that I was present, somehow able to observe a battle beyond a true portal, but now another had come there, and two humans faced each other on the battlefield.

The warrior was astonished also. "How in Verdonne's name came you here, wicked old man?"

Blast and curse all treachery. The Warden was Rhys. No one but the three of us—Rhys, Ysanne, and myself—had ever dared call Galadon "wicked old man."

"You think you have explored the depth and breadth of power, Warden, but it is only the depth and breadth of corruption. There are many aspects of melydda beyond those you know."

"I know you have no business in this place . . . and neither do I anymore. This battle is done. There is no sham. Let's get out, then you will explain how it's possible for you to be here."

"You claim your business is done. Yet you have allowed a demon to leave this vessel unbound—yes, I saw it. You claim victory, yet it walks the earth again, free to take another for its pleasure. What mockery have you made of your oath?"

"You're mad, old man. I killed the demon, as I've killed every one of them for ten years. It's why they stay away from us and adhere to our bargain. No wonder you've twisted the ways of the world to follow me here. You're afraid to face me with this accusation on a human plane where all can see how you've grown feeble with age."

"I fear nothing save that your corruption continues unchecked. You will bring our people to ruin, and the rest of the world alongside."

"You don't know what you're talking about. If it weren't for me, we would all be dead." Rhys turned his back and walked off in the direction of the portal.

Galadon called after him. "You've not answered my challenge, boy. I demand satisfaction from you. Here. Now. Before your wickedness goes any further."

Rhys halted and looked back. "You can't mean this. I have no grievance with you . . . save perhaps your everlasting blindness."

"Others will know of this violation unless you silence me this day."

What was Galadon doing?

Rhys hesitated, then strolled back toward our mentor. The old man leaned on his staff, the hot wind fluttering his white hair and blue robe. The two were so far away, yet I could hear them clearly, and through their words envision the stubborn resolve on Galadon's face and the nervous cockiness on Rhys's.

Yet it was not just fury that flowed from Rhys, but long-held pain and bitterness. "Who would believe you? They'll see only the great teacher overtaken by age and grief when faced with the ruin of his favorite. Do you think my old friend can save us by playing at Warden's training? Oh, yes, I've watched your games with him these past few nights. Sixteen years, old man. He cannot light a candle with his melydda. You've been afraid to test him, because you know it's true. You just can't bear to give up the hope. Perhaps it's time you gave a little thought to the rest of us."

"He is the Warrior. He will find what he needs. He will save us all—Ezzarian and Derzhi and Khelid. He was born for it."

"What care have we for the Derzhi or the Khelid or the cursed Empire they desire? Let them exterminate each other. We'll take care of whatever is left. Send your failed pupil back to his slave masters, old man. It is I who's done what's necessary to save us, because you were too busy mourning a dead man." Rhys was only a few paces away from the figure in blue.

Galadon extended his arms to Rhys. "It is not your reason that speaks such cruelty, lad. Even now your jealous heart echoes the desires of rai-kirah, as it did the day you abandoned your dearest friend to slavers and tainted yourself with corruption. As it has since the day you lost your first battle and sold your soul to hide it. Did you think I wouldn't guess what happened all those years ago? Did you think you could make such a bargain and never have to pay the price?"

"You don't know what you're talking about."

"It is not too late. Put it away, my son. See your own gifts and crave not those that were never meant for you. Or tell me how long it will be until you look into your own mirror and see the eyes of a demon."

With a roar Rhys raised his knife and changed it into a sword. Galadon did likewise with his staff. Though a formidable warrior in his youth, he would never have been a match for Rhys. Frantically I looked for a way down from the precipice. As far as I could see to the right or the left was a sheer drop to the razor-edged rocks below. Endless wastes behind me. There was no time. Rhys's sword ripped Galadon's shoulder, and the old man stumbled backward. Grotesque laughter assaulted my ears. From wherever he had gone, the demon watched and fed. Galadon stayed on his feet, but his sword wavered in the orange light. Rhys feinted, causing Galadon to stagger left, but the old man recovered and nicked Rhys with a powerful stroke. In pained rage Rhys beat Galadon back and back and back. . . .

I could not permit it. Such a storm of anger and indignation came over me that I was incapable of reason or doubt. Galadon was going to die at the hand of my friend, and a demon was growing stronger as it happened. I could not stand back and watch it.

I closed my eyes and reached into the depths of my being, ripping away layer upon layer of fear and horror, pain and despair, shutting out grief, cooling anger, focusing my inner eye upon the essence, the core that gave shape to the soul named Seyonne. There I grasped the cold hard knot that lay where melydda had once lived, and I breathed upon it, willing it to take fire.

Without waiting to see what came of my working, I opened my eyes, stepped forward, and dived off the rocky precipice.

Chapter 29

I had no thoughts to spare for panic in that initial gut-wrenching plummet from the cliffs. I was desperately trying to remember what to do next. The words. *Caedwyrrdin mesaffthyla.* The movements. *Hands just above your head, fingertips together, not clasped lest the jolt break your fingers. The legs, straight and spread wide to slow your fall. Your back arched forward slightly to bear the strain.* The senses. *Feel the air. Read it, every nuance like the words on a page. Where are the rising airs? Where are the dangerous downdrafts? Be ready. No doubts. Doubts make you weak, and for this, strength is everything.*

I could not watch the battle on the plains, only cry out a quick promise. "Hold on, master. I'll come for you. I will." And even that was obliterated when the fire began to burn in my shoulders. Oh, gods of earth and sky . . . it came, rippling along my arms and back like the searing touch of lightning. In that fleeting instant I thought of Aleksander and the torment of his transformation. How differently such agony can be perceived. For when my wings unfurled and came near yanking my shoulders from their sockets, and as I bent my bones and strained my muscles to their searing limits to bring them under control, I cried out, not with the pain, but with the heart-bursting ecstasy of such magic.

Extend . . . curve the lower veins to catch more air. Sense each nerve connection as it's made so you can control it instantly—like learning to walk all over again in a tenth of a second with a floor of broken glass beneath your feet. How long had it taken? By the time I had full control and was in more of a soaring dive than a full plummet, I was much too close to the jagged rocks. The thin membranes spread out beside and behind me were not immune to rips. A haze of dust hung over the battlefield as I pulled hard to the right and caught the uprising wind that would carry me toward the two vague shapes. One silver—upright, sword raised. One blue. Bent over. Retreating.

"Hold, Warden!" I cried. "This place is not yours. This life is not forfeit."

The figure in silver gaped upward in astonishment and dismay. With one sweep of a gathered wing, I knocked him to his knees just as my feet touched the ground. The move was one of my favorites, but I was unpracticed, awkward, and it made my landing unsteady. Rhys recovered quicker and jumped to his feet. "So you're not entirely dead?" he said as he backed away, his eyes wide, staring at the extent of my transformation.

"Master, are you badly hurt?" I called over my shoulder while holding Rhys at bay with melydda.

"All is well," came the harsh voice from behind me.

"I never believed you when you told me about the wings," said Rhys. "I thought you were trying to prove you were better than the rest of us." With a blurred motion, he changed his knife into a spear, but I was quicker and swept it aside with the fingers of my power. It dropped to the ground, only a knife again. Rhys stepped back, guarded, watching, ready to call down some enchantment if I moved again.

But I didn't move, only stood my ground between him and Galadon. I needed to understand. "What's happened to you?" I said. "We were friends. Brothers. It never mattered who was stronger or faster, or who had wings and who did not."

"It never mattered to you," he said bitterly. "But when did you ask me or Ysanne? You got so caught up in your glory, and you took Ysanne as if she were your right."

"Is that what this is about? You wanted Ysanne?"

"You never knew her. For three years she spent her days

and nights with you, offered you everything, but you would go off into your everlasting silences, leaving her alone as if she were only some annoyance to your purity. Ask her why you could not be with both of us together—because she could not bear to hurt you. Always it was you. No one could match you. No one could help you. You had to be the strongest and do everything alone. It couldn't go on. Then came the war . . . before she could tell you that it was me she loved."

"If you hated me so much, you should have killed me outright. Was it so hard to tell me the truth that you had to make me a slave? Shall I describe what it was like, how I could not hold off their horrors because I had to bury the memory of what you did? Gods, Rhys. I loved you both. I would have done anything for either of you."

He spit at my feet and shifted his stance, edging closer to his fallen weapon as if I didn't notice. "Didn't you hear what I said? We didn't want you to do anything for us." In a move so swift and smooth I almost missed it, Rhys dropped to the ground, rolled to the right, and launched his silver knife at my heart. But I slowed the knife, holding it off just long enough to soar upward, out of the way. The glittering weapon, changed to a spear, sped past to strike the earth.

"So which did the demons take first, you or Ysanne?" I said angrily, touching my feet to the ground. I snatched his weapon from where it had fallen, as he scrambled backward.

"You don't know anything," he said. "I'll take care of the demons. We'll be stronger because of what I've done. And I'll not allow you to get in the way." He nodded his head to something behind me. "You should see to the old fool. He fares ill." Then he leaped to his feet, turned his back, and walked away.

I glanced over my shoulder. Galadon lay facedown on the red earth. Unmoving. I let Rhys go and hurried to the old man, cursing my delay. "Master, can you hear me?" I said, rolling him onto his back.

The old man was struggling to breathe. A gaping wound

in his chest had robbed him of far too much blood. "I was right," he said fiercely. "Say it."

"You were right. Of course you were. Was there no easier way to convince me?"

"Now show me," he said, his red-rimmed eyes blinking away tears. "I've yearned to see . . . since you told me about it that first time when you were a boy. So young. So young to have such power."

"I need to get you—"

"Show me." All the ferocity of his spirit was expended in the demand. A demon could not have refused him.

I shifted him enough that he could rest against a rock, then I stepped back and held my hands high above my head, whispering a wind spell so that my wings were completely spread and filled with air. The rippling pattern of the gossamer strands fell on Galadon's smiling face. "Son of my heart." He sighed. "Come close now."

I knelt beside him again, and he pulled my ear down to his mouth, scarcely able to form the words. "Don't . . . harden . . . your heart. Don't believe all that you . . ." When he did not continue, I pulled away to look. He had stopped breathing.

I had no time to mourn his passing. The light flickered, and I glanced up. The twin suns wobbled in circles about each other, and the dirt beneath my feet shifted uneasily. The portal . . . Ysanne. Powers of night, they were shutting down the portal. I couldn't believe it. No matter what else they'd done . . . to shut a portal on a living man . . .

I gathered Galadon's too light body in my arms and spoke the wind again. "Now. Here." A mighty gust picked us up, swirling dust into my eyes as I worked it, faltering, remembering, feeling, concentrating. The staggering suns began to dim, and I strained to see the portal through the dust and the fading light. A whirlwind could slam me to the disintegrating land. Rocks crashed to the surface, shattering into brittle shards that were snatched into the air and threatened to shred my wings. I fought to go higher, out of the debris, to see beyond the darkening haze. The portal was flickering. Fading. It was too far.

"Aife! Don't leave me here!" I cried. "Face me. Tell me what I've done. But not this . . ."

The gray rectangle disappeared, swallowed by the midnight darkness rolling in from the horizons. Rocks and tangled shrubs flew wildly through the air. There was no longer any solid place to land. When I tired enough that I could not fly, we would fall—the lifeless Galadon and I—into the abyss. Demon music wailed through the chaos as I struggled to stay oriented. Perhaps the portal was still there, hidden by the darkness . . .

"There's another." The soft words were like a finger poking into my mind. "Hurry. Soar high, love."

Another? Another portal? Of course there was another. The one I had used to enter. Catrin's portal. But where was it? Everything had changed. Panic threatened to disintegrate me as surely as the chaos devoured the landscape. *Reverse course. Don't get caught in a circular wind. The wind is behind you now, so the place will come up faster . . . on the right. . . .* My back and shoulders ached with fatigue. My legs dragged. Galadon, so light when I lifted his body, weighed like one of the red boulders, but I would not leave him in that place. *Veer right. Now look for it. Careful of the updraft.*

"This way," said the voice, so faint it was almost unhearable, yet leading me higher and always to the right. "Hurry."

A glimmer of gray. A straight line in a place where nothing was straight. *You must land perfectly on the edge, lest you fall backward. Hurry.* Wavering, wobbling, at the end of my strength, I dived for the flickering rectangle . . .

. . . and banged my head on a stone platform, briefly knocking the wind out of myself on the very solid ground to which I returned.

"Seyonne! You've got to wake up." A hand shook my shoulder so hard it rattled my teeth.

Wake up? Was it an illusion, then? All the emotions that

sped through my mind: elation ... disappointment ... anger ... grief ... were they nothing but dream stuff? It seemed such a waste. "I don't think I'm asleep."

My next movement told me it had been no dream. The wings were gone, sloughed off like an old shirt as I passed through the portal, but the muscles in my shoulders and back spoke clearly of activities altogether beyond those of slaves. And so, Galadon ...

I flicked open my eyes to see Catrin crouched over me. Her small face was tired and filled with grief and worry; her green gown was stained with blood.

"I'm sorry," I said, the entirety of the night's events filling me to overflowing. "I wasn't fast enough."

"He didn't expect to survive it." She straightened up and moved away.

I was sprawled across the step at the base of a stone platform. Galadon lay beside me, his limbs straight, his wild hair tamed. Catrin must have put him there from wherever I had dropped him.

"Rhys escaped. And the demon."

As I sat up, feeling as if I'd just crawled out from under an avalanche, Catrin returned, bringing a small bowl filled with water. With the strip of linen that had bound my eyes, she dabbed at a nasty cut on my forehead. "Are you going to sit here and recount your failures, or are you going to get up and prepare for the Second Battle? Your enemies believe you're dead. You can't let them know otherwise."

My enemies. I had never thought of myself as having enemies except for the demons. Even the Derzhi had no personal antipathy for me, no interest in my identity. One barbarian slave was the same as another. But I had just been singled out for murder of the most horrific kind. And only by the grace of ... I moved Catrin's hand aside so I could see her. "You held the second portal. Somehow you merged your weaving with Ysanne's to let us in. And I wasn't prepared, not able to do my part. How in the name of sense did you manage such a thing?" I searched her face for some hint of the voice that had called me back, but she was intent on business.

She pushed my chin around again so she could finish wiping the blood from my head. At the same moment I felt the prickle of enchantment and a stinging tightening of the skin that meant she had closed the wound to stop the bleeding. It was a quick, but not particularly good method for healing, and it would leave a scar, but I suppose she thought one more wasn't going to bother me. Only then did she answer. "I told you I've not been idle. I can do more than bake almond cakes. Now you must—"

"Does anyone else know you've done this? Or that you're capable? Rhys and Ysanne will be looking for the one who did it. They've already killed." It was unbearable to think of it. Ysanne had been fostered so young that she had known little of her parents. She had always called Galadon her only true father. How could she have left him to die in an infested soul?

"Only Grandfather knew what I can do. But it's vital that you remain dead for a while. You must come with me and do exactly as I say." She dragged me up by my arm, and either the discomfort of the dragging or the discomfort of my thoughts fueled rebellion. Catrin did not seem to bring out the best in me. I must have mistaken her words in the chaos beyond the portal.

I yanked my arm from her grasp, which hurt me more than it did her, and I pointed an accusing finger at the still smiling Galadon. "I think I've had enough mysteries and surprises for one day. I'll not go one step farther until you tell me the whole scheme this nefarious old buzzard has left us to play out."

She didn't want to hear it. "We need to go. Now. When we have time, I'll tell you everything you need to know."

But Galadon's blood still stained my hands, and I could not rejoice in the gift he had given me until I knew why he had to die to give it. I sat on the platform beside my old mentor and refused to budge. "I will not believe your grandfather died just to persuade me that he was right and I was wrong about power and faith. I have to know, Catrin."

"Idiot boy." She set her jaw and fumed and rolled her eyes, but eventually she sank to the other stone platform, her knees almost touching mine. "This is the last time I will allow you to question my judgment, Seyonne. My grandfather has entrusted your training to me. No, don't interrupt. Most of what you have done so far has been of my devising, and you have most assuredly progressed. But you're not yet ready for what we believe must come."

The rain splashed on the roof and the steps, and the treetops beyond our little sanctuary whipped in the storm winds. The jasnyr-scented smoke danced around us as Catrin told me something of the past and something of the future. Not all of either one, for she was an Aife, who shared only what it was necessary for the Warden to know. But enough.

"Grandfather suspected for many years that things were not right with Rhys. In his third battle after passing his testing, he lost his partner. It was a difficult case, and he barely made it out alive. Vedwyn held the portal too long . . . to give him time to get out . . . and she never recovered from it. Her mind was dead, and it was only a few weeks until her body gave up and died, too."

I remembered Vedwyn—a shy, modest girl of great talent, who made everyone uncomfortable with her quiet insistence on correctness. She had adored Rhys, but he spent half his youth avoiding her. An ill-fated pairing it would have been.

"Rhys refused to fight again after that, but we lost our last four Wardens that year one after the other. It was devastating. We had only students left. Children. So Grandfather worked with Rhys. Rhys insisted on going through his testing again, and he did much better than the first time. His concentration was ferocious. The Queen . . ."

Catrin darted her eyes at me uncertainly, but I motioned her to go on. "She tried to kill me tonight," I said. "You're not going to say anything that will make it worse."

She hesitated for a moment longer, then shook her head.

"The Queen and Rhys had been living together for several years, and as the most skilled and experienced Aife, she took him as her partner. It gave us heart to see it, especially when he came back with one victory after another. But ten years ago we began to lose Searchers and Comforters at a terrible rate, and the Queen at last recalled all but one pairing, saying it was too dangerous to have them out. Every new Warden trained fell within months. When Grandfather found out about the demon bargain, he feared that Rhys had been compromised and blamed himself for not recognizing it from the beginning. And of course it signaled exactly what you have discovered—that the demons have been brought to some common purpose by their hosts. But he dared not confront Rhys until . . ."

". . . until I came."

"He had to have a Warden left to continue if something happened to him. His students were either dead or not yet ready, and his belief that you would come back was unshakable. And so he spent his time devising the method to use the second portal. Once you were here and progressing well, he thought to use it for your testing, to see if you could discover Rhys's game. That was all. Until tonight he didn't plan to do what he did."

"So why did he?"

"Because we have no time left." Catrin knotted her fingers together in her lap and fixed her eyes on them. "The demons have demanded that we yield all Khelid souls. This morning, at a meeting of the Queen and the Mentor's Council, Rhys told of it. He said he refused. That he told the rai-kirah that we could do no such thing, for we were pledged to yield no soul without combat. The demons claim that the Khelid are willing hosts, but as a concession to our custom, they have proposed a new bargain."

"And what's that?"

"We will fight one battle—single combat—for the entire Khelid race."

I leaped to my feet. "Madness! Ysanne will never do it. She couldn't possibly. . . ." I could scarcely speak my dismay. Betraying me was one thing—protecting Rhys, desire, anger, whatever it was. But to betray everything . . . centuries of struggle and sacrifice and heroism . . . an entire race. "She can't do it."

"It is already done. She says the demons will hunt us down and destroy us if we don't agree."

I returned to the place where Galadon lay, as if the tether that bound us still held and I might find some comfort or resolution in his stillness. But the voice that had shaped my life was silent. Catrin fixed her gaze on me, watching to see if I understood.

Bleakly, crushingly, I understood. "The demons plan for Rhys to fight. And Rhys, the blind, stupid fool, thinking he can stick his hand in fire and not get burned . . . believes he can win. But he won't. They've been allowing him to win. To pretend. But not this time."

"Grandfather didn't know what had precipitated the demons' threat. He guessed that Rhys was so afraid of you that he revealed something . . . made the demons wary. . . ."

"It's Aleksander. They feel him failing, so the time is coming for their grand play. They want us out of the Khelid so we won't find out what they're doing. Rhys's time is up . . . and Ysanne has to know it." She was going to betray another husband. Was she able to convince herself that this was for the good of the Ezzarians . . . or was she truly bound to the demons by her own corruption? Either way the result would be the same. Surrender.

Catrin pushed at me again. "We have to make sure this battle is won."

The full weight of the night came down upon me then. "Then, I can't leave here. Nor you. If you can make a second portal like you did tonight. Get me in . . ."

Catrin got up and walked to the steps, arms folded, and she looked out on the rain. "The battle will not be fought here. The Queen claims that she must be closer to the one possessed, that she can't rely on Searchers and Comforters in such an important conflict, and she refuses to have a demon-chosen victim brought into our midst. So she will go to the victim instead and take her champion with her. And she says she must take the Prince, too, as once we've freed the Khelid of their demons, she might learn what's necessary to heal him. A good story is it not?"

"Parnifour," I said, all the bits and pieces of mystery falling together.

Catrin whirled about. "How did you know?"

"She's going to bring down the Empire."

"At least it gives us a little more time."

I could hardly feel grateful for that. Not with what I knew. "And have the demons said who is the one possessed?"

"A Khelid. His name is Kastavan."

We rode eastward from Dael Ezzar toward the shrunken moon that was just rising. Catrin had laid an enchantment on her grandfather, to hold him unchanging until we had time to bid him a proper farewell. Then she led me to two horses hidden in the woods beyond the temple, and we were off in the matter of ten minutes. Before very long we were winding down a steep track—not one I would have attempted in the dark and the rain, but Catrin said the horses knew the way and no one else. Galadon had hidden it with spells for many years. Hoffyd was to meet us along the way, bringing Aleksander.

A flash of lightning illuminated the path and the dark crags around us. The moon had been quickly swallowed by the unsettled night. Catrin sat straight in the saddle. Unyielding. There was a great deal more to her than I had ever imagined. It had finally come into my thick head that she was no longer the child I had known, but a lovely, talented young woman, one whose inner strength was unguessable. I wanted to learn more of her, but it wasn't possible to talk while we rode on the narrow way.

So instead I practiced focus and discipline, and spent the hours reviewing strategies and tactics and battle variations, every move I knew, every experience I'd had, every enchantment I had woven. It was astonishing how precisely I could remember, as if they were childhood treasures laid away in a wooden chest for sixteen years, brought out untouched by time. I was going to need them, everything I could muster, and a great deal of luck besides.

After perhaps three very wet hours, we turned into a narrow cleft in the rocks, scarcely wide enough for a horse. Catrin provided a light until we rode into a dry, firelit cave. A man stood in front of the fire, sword unsheathed, but as soon as Catrin was full in the light, he dropped the weapon and called a greeting. "Catrin! It's fine to see you. How did it turn out?" It was Hoffyd.

"Just as Grandfather predicted."

"Ah, sweet Verdonne . . . Though I can imagine what pleasure he took in being right. . . ."

"We have more rejoicing than mourning to do," said Catrin. "And more work than either."

I dismounted, hanging back in the shadows while Catrin exchanged a silent, lingering handclasp with Hoffyd. As he took her wet cloak and urged her nearer the fire, she looked around for me. "Well, come on," she said. "No need to stand back there dripping."

I stepped into the light, heading for the fire, keeping my eyes fixed on the flames and cursing myself for a sniveling coward to be so shy of being ignored after all that had happened. So I wasn't ready for the firm hand on my shoulder or the wry smile beneath the eye patch. "'Pytor,' eh? Could you have no trust in your own brother-in-law?" He wrapped me in his long arms and squeezed away any possibility of reply. "Couldn't you guess that Elen's spirit would come back to give me everlasting torment if I were to cause her little brother one moment's pain?" He squeezed me again, rubbed my hair, babbled unendingly for the quiet man he was, and shed not a few tears from his one eye before whispering in my ear, "I'm damned glad you're here. Is it possible to please this cursed Derzhi?"

"Rarely," I said, grinning at him and not whispering. "Though to be sure his disposition has improved a good deal since I first encountered him. He is only a shengar now."

"My ears are not dead." The slurred mumble came from a long roll of blankets on the other side of the fire. Red hair spilled out of one end of the roll.

"I'm glad to hear it, my lord," I said. "And he has most remarkable hearing. Never believe it if he seems asleep." Then I pulled Hoffyd toward the cave mouth and asked more seriously how Aleksander fared.

"He knew nothing of the journey. He's only waked in the last hour, demanding to know of you. When I could tell him nothing, he tried to fight me. He couldn't even stand up because of the sleeping draught—a matter of great relief to me—but he cursed both himself and me with such a volume of invective as I've not read anywhere. And when cursing did not change anything, he began to threaten various forms of murder and mayhem if any hair of your head was harmed. About that time he experienced an . . . episode . . . dreadful . . . and he begged for more of the sleeping draught. I didn't know what else to do, so I gave it to him."

"There's little to do to ease it. Just talk to him. Distract him. Keep his mind working in human channels. And have your sword ready to protect yourself."

"We've no time for getting reacquainted just now," said Catrin, returning from the back of the cave where she had put the horses. "We all need sleep. We've a long journey ahead."

As I rolled up in a blanket a few steps from Aleksander, I wondered if the journey ahead could be half so long as the way I had just come.

Chapter 30

We traveled hard for the next ten days, though a messenger bird could have covered the same distance in three. We wound through the mountains by way of bandit trails and herdsmen's tracks. With three sorcerers and a Derzhi warrior in our party, we had little fear of bandits. It was more important to avoid Capharna and the trade routes that spun out of it like a spider's web. There would be Derzhi spies and Khelid lurkers on those roads, as well as slave hunters from the Magician's Guild seeking an Ezzarian runaway.

It was the mysterious, primitive wilds of northern Azhakstan we traveled. In one village the inhabitants wore only animal fur; in another they painted their faces with mud. In one settlement they fermented such strong spirits from local berries, that we thought never to leave the place . . . or care whether we did or not. Happily for us—or unhappily—Catrin never drank spirits. She shoved and insulted and yelled at us until we were on our horses, then led the three of us down the road until several hours of driving rain brought us back to our painful senses.

One night we accepted the meager hospitality of a small village where no man, woman, or child had a tooth left in their heads. After two years of devastatingly poor hunting, they had decided that their gods—of whom they suspected we might be representatives—did not wish them to eat meat anymore. So they had pulled all their teeth as a way to prevent sin should a stray rabbit or fox show up in their little valley. They were dreadfully malnourished, and Hoffyd spent the evening trying to teach them what local plants were good to eat. Finally, in desperation, he suggested that they had hunted their little valley bare. Perhaps their gods would allow them to move. Aleksander told them of a valley just north of Capharna where he had taken five deer in an hour. The next morning when we woke, the entire population had disappeared. Hoffyd flushed a brilliant red when we teased him about his "holy teachings," and Aleksander swore to build him a temple in Capharna.

Mostly we spent days and nights in endless rain, walking, riding, climbing, and descending toward Parnifour and the Second Battle of the Eddaic Prophecy.

Aleksander was physically healthy again, and the lingering weakness that had plagued him in Dael Ezzar had vanished. Being astride a horse seemed to restore him far better than any healer's remedies, rain or no. But his enchantment continued to get worse. Scarcely an hour passed that he was not subject to a physical or sensory change or one of the horrific visions that accompanied demon spells. I worried that we might damage him by giving him too much of Nevya's sleeping draught. It took him a long time to come completely awake in the morning, which made that the most dangerous time for him to undergo a change. It was very difficult for him to maintain control when he was so groggy.

Only once in those days did he undergo a complete transformation. It happened in a particularly wild section of the mountains, which was fortunate, as there was no one for him to harm. But it took us eight hours to find him, collapsed in a snowbank beside the bloody remains of an elk. We wrapped him in blankets and built up a towering bonfire, but he sat there dull-eyed and unspeaking until we put him to sleep for the night.

Though he regained his own form after that incident and was capable of speech, he did not regain his spirits. He rode in brooding silence, winding his fingers in Musa's mane or stroking the horse's neck. When we stopped for the night, he would take the sleeping draught before eating and fall asleep in mid bite. The most ominous part of the matter was that we could find no trigger. Just as with the lesser incidents, there was no defining activity or thought that precipitated it.

"Are you sure there's nothing?" I said one day after an hour's halt to allow his arm to return to human proportion.

Aleksander shook his head and mounted Musa. "I dream shengar dreams. Sometimes I think there is more of it than me anymore."

I was afraid he was right. From the beginning of our journey he had eaten only meat, refusing cheese and bread and even the dried dates and figs that Derzhi considered the foundation of any diet. As the days passed after the transformation, he could no longer stomach anything cooked, but cut his portion from our day's kill before we put it on the fire, and ate it without looking at any of us. He kept his hood drawn over his face in the daylight, saying the sun pained his eyes, and he began to leave Musa's care to Hoffyd, as he could no longer settle the beast with his touch, only put it in a nervous frenzy. I think that distressed Aleksander beyond anything, but he would not say it. He said very little at all.

"You must not yield, my lord. We will find a way."

I was not yet capable of healing him. Though I had taken the largest step to regain my power—I still had unsettling dreams of my dive from the precipice—I needed time and practice to build it back to what it had been. Every day as we rode, Catrin drilled me on more and more complex enchantments and the patterns of thought required to create or destroy them, as well as the other skills I needed to fight again as a Warden. Every evening after we had eaten and helped Aleksander to sleep, she had me running and climbing, jumping, stretching, and practicing with sword and knife. She was very determined . . . and very good at the business.

I quickly dismissed any idea that she would somehow be easier or kinder or more understanding than her grandfather. Rather she was stern and demanding, and invited no intimacy of any kind. In our first days on the trail, Aleksander swore that she and Hoffyd were lovers. I told him that she could stand likai for an entire Derzhi legion, and was no more likely to be anyone's lover than such a one. I had come to believe that the care I'd felt from her beyond the portal was only old friendship and her concern for our success in the coming battle. She certainly did her best to make sure I had no time to consider anything beyond our work.

On one afternoon we camped earlier than usual. Another league would take us into the rolling grasslands that skirted the mountains, stretching all the way from Avenkhar to Parnifour, but we preferred to sleep one more night in the safer hiding of the foothills. Hoffyd took his usual uninventive turn at cooking, while a silent Aleksander huddled in his cloak by the fire. It was a fine afternoon and would be a lovely evening, with the light lingering noticeably later than just a few days earlier—perhaps because it had finally stopped raining. The hills were sculpted by the afternoon shadows, the velvety new green touched with gold. The tangy air was cool and washed clean, leaving every rock and tree and blade of grass sharp-edged all the way to the horizon.

Catrin was in no mood to take note of the pleasant weather, and she had no intention of letting me waste the extra hours. Ten days had passed since Rhys's last battle, and we still had more than two weeks to Parnifour. Without waiting for Aleksander to sleep, she commanded me to run ten times up and down a short, steep hill, carrying two of our saddle packs with fully extended arms. When I came down the tenth time, proud of myself because I was not out of breath and my arms were not quite at the point of breaking off, Aleksander stared at me, puzzled enough to break his day's silence. "What are you doing? Have you gone mad while I wasn't looking?"

I had told Aleksander nothing of my experience beyond the portal. All he knew was that Galadon was dead, Ysanne and Rhys determined to be rid of us, and that we were seeking a remedy for his enchantment in Parnifour. "We don't know what we'll run into up ahead. I deemed it best to be fit, at least," I said.

"If demons run footraces with goatherds, you'll do fine." He hunched his blanket up around his shoulders.

"Have you ever run a race where the other runners did not let you win?" I said, more irritably than I should have.

"Indeed! Your tongue is very bold tonight." It was the first sign of spirit I'd seen for five days.

"I've run up this thing ten times already while you've reclined quite royally here by the fire. Do you think you can take me? Ah, no." I threw up my hands in mock denial. "You're likely still weak from your wound."

"Damn your insolence!" The Prince threw off his blanket and his cloak, pulled off his boots and stockings, and stripped off his shirt. "I'll be back here in my boots before you reach the top."

If it had been a higher hill or a smoother path he might have done it. His stride was long and graceful, and with every step he gained a half step on me. But rocks and roots on the upper half disrupted his rhythm, while I sprang easily from one to the other. He was two strides ahead by the top, but I beat him down by four. And he was winded.

"Wretched . . . bloody . . ." He leaned over with his hands on his knees, breathing hard. "All that wallowing in bed . . . disgrace . . . goatherd." Just then the enchantment came over him again, fully half his body wavering between man and beast. He clenched his fists and cried out in pain and fury, "No, I will not!" For the moment his determination won out. The illusion faded, and he downed his sleeping draught with shaking hands. "I will not," he mumbled as he dropped off into death-like sleep.

From that evening on he went through every physical exercise with me. I even taught him the kyanar, the slow, repetitive martial disciplines to which Galadon had introduced me in my youth. They were designed to draw one's being together in the center of the body, to create a harmony such that the mind and body could work as a seamless whole. Only when I brought out a knife or a sword would the Prince sit back and watch. Though my training was different from his own, he was able to see the flaws and rough spots in my technique. He quite enjoyed pointing them out.

Whether it was the physical activity or the fact that we

were soon on the flatlands and could easily cover ten
leagues in a day instead of two, the Prince became more
cheerful and more alert. The incidents of transformation
continued unabated, however. We no longer dared wake him
with a touch. Catrin already wore a long scrape on one arm
from a raking claw. And we kept close watch on him at
night. The sleeping draught had less and less effect, leaving
him at the mercy of demon-wrought dreams. His moans
were terrible to hear, and we began to consider whether we
should bind him at night to prevent him harming himself or
us.

But I watched the Prince bring all his stubborn strength to
bear on his deterioration, refusing to shrink into terror or silence or low spirits as he had early in the journey. If it had
been possible to reverse the curse by will alone, he could
have done it. At least he felt like he was fighting again. He
was more like himself, and began to pester me about our
plans. It might have been safer to keep him in ignorance.
Hoffyd and Catrin were of that mind. But I still had the conviction that the Prince had an important part to play in the
Second Battle—I just didn't know what it was. His feadnach
yet burned, as unlikely in the rotting devastation of his soul
as an unbroken crystal wineglass in a war-ravaged village.

The matter came up on the star-filled evening that we
camped in a treeless hollow two leagues from Avenkhar. We
had run almost to the city gates and back, and sat devouring
a pair of rabbits that Catrin had snared while we ran.

"So you've found your wings again, eh?" he said.

I looked up, startled. "What do you mean by that?" I'd
never been sure whether he believed what he had said about
the tapestry . . . or what I had answered.

He laughed. "You still don't say what you're thinking,
but you show it very clearly these days. You're worried, but
you carry a confidence backed up by more than a stout heart.
It has not escaped my notice that you could be quite a formidable warrior . . . even without the possibility of such
mobility or the sorcery it implies. So are you ever going to
show me?"

"I can't . . . I mean . . ." This wasn't how I was planning to tell him . . . flustered with ridiculous embarrassment. ". . . it only happens in the place where I work. . . ."

I told him all of it. About portals and demon battles. About the night when I was eighteen and in the most desperate battle of my experience, the night when I discovered that I could transform myself into a *caer gwillyn,* a winged defender, a legend so old it was only a sketch on a crumbling scroll. I told him of Galadon's claims that my melydda still lived even after the Rites of Balthar, and of our long nights of work while he—Aleksander—slept. And I told him of my final lesson, where I learned the full measure of Rhys's and Ysanne's treachery. Catrin was near apoplectic with my telling. She kept interrupting, commanding me to silence, and calling me a fool. But once I was started, I could not stop.

Aleksander summed it up nicely. "So your treacherous lover will create this . . . battlefield . . . in Kastavan's head, and your treacherous friend will meet this Demon Lord, probably the most powerful one they've got. The demons will win and do as they please with the Khelid, meaning they can use foul enchantments like this that crazes me to do as they please with my Empire. And you are going to try to sneak in some back door, grow wings, avoid getting slaughtered, and prevent the whole thing."

"Sounds fairly unlikely, I suppose." I sipped the dregs from our last wineskin and wished I had a full one. Perhaps draining another might make our plan sound more reasonable.

"Unlikely is not the word I would choose." He was reclining on the grass, leaning on his elbow. "But even if, by some chance, you were to win, the Khelid would not die. And from what you've told me, they were no models of virtue to get themselves so entangled with demons. Am I right?"

"Yes."

"So we will have Khelid warriors in every major city of

the Empire, believing they have to fight to get what they planned to obtain through guile."

I had not considered what would happen beyond the battle. Always in the past, defeating the demon had been enough.

"I need to warn . . ." Aleksander could not go on. He shuddered and rolled over onto all fours as his shoulders and arms and head blurred and shifted into grotesque combinations of man and beast. The surrounding air was drained of warmth, while searing heat poured from his body. But after five minutes' struggle and a roar, not of bestial fury, but of defiance and determination, all traces of the shengar vanished, and he was himself again. He had stopped it. He sat back on his knees, sweat dripping from his face, and he rubbed his eyes tiredly, taking up the conversation right where he had left it. "I've got to warn them, but damned if I know how. No one will listen to me now Dmitri's gone. Veldar was his friend. Zarrakat had him stand likai to his son. The Mezzrahn generals bear a bit of a grudge. None of the northern marshals will give me hearing."

I swallowed my astonishment at his act of will and tried to follow his thought. "Is there no one to speak for you? No one with influence who might put concern for the realm above their grievances with you?"

"Kiril would do what he could . . . if I could convince him to listen before sticking a knife in me to avenge Dmitri. But he's got no influence beyond the Parnifour garrison. I fought beside two or three of the southern marshals in Vygaard and eastern Fryth, but they're a long way from here."

"We're on the doorstep of Avenkhar. The Lady Lydia could convey a message if you could think of someone to send it to."

"Lydia." Aleksander pulled his hand from his haggard face. "Her father is the most respected tactician in the Twenty. He's got influence everywhere. In Zhagad. With Father. And one could say he has a great deal at stake in me, since he's planned to marry Lydia to me since she was born." He narrowed his eyes. "Would she do it? There's no love lost between us, as you saw."

"I would say you could leave your case in no surer hands."

I needed writing materials. Hoffyd carried a journal in which he recorded his observations of the natural world: the birds and beasts, their habits, the weather, the landforms, the patterns of the stars. From his studies he extracted a deep understanding of the mechanisms of the world that those with melydda used to build enchantments.

I begged a few blank pages from his journal and the use of his pen and ink, and I had Aleksander dictate his urgent instructions to certain Derzhi commanders on how to quietly prepare for a war starting some twelve days hence. I said I would go into Avenkhar and deliver it to the Lady.

Catrin and Hoffyd protested furiously as I sat beside the fire and cut off my hair. "Let him take his own messages," said Catrin, eyeing Aleksander who was sitting under a tree twenty paces away, his head buried in his arms. "Your work is far more important."

"He can't go. He could transform at any moment, and be killed or lost. He's right about the Khelid. Our war is with the demons, but there are other evils in the world and they are just as much our responsibility."

"Then Hoffyd or I will go. We can't risk losing you."

I exchanged my shirt for the slave tunic I still carried, and pulled off my boots and my breeches. Though the night was the warmest of the season, I felt cold and exposed. "Neither of you has any experience of cities or the Derzhi. Neither of you could recognize a member of the Magician's Guild. If you're seen, you could be taken. I'll be in and out in a few hours."

"Then, at least wear something to cover—"

"I have to go as a slave. I am recognizably Ezzarian. If anyone decides to check, they'll find the marks and the rings. If I'm disguised . . . I'm done for."

"I don't know why you've not had me get those despicable things off you," said Hoffyd quietly, trying to keep from staring at the steel bands about my wrists and ankles.

I had wondered about it myself. Aleksander could not prevent me, and I wasn't sure he would try. But on that night, as the first stars popped out of the deep turquoise of the sky, I finally understood my hesitation. Something extraordinary had come about between Aleksander and me. Something beyond oaths, beyond duty, beyond necessity and desperation. If the Prince unlocked my chains, I would not walk away. But until Aleksander believed it, I had no name for him but master, and no name for myself but slave. "I'll take them off when he tells me," I said, then I set off running for Avenkhar. The gates would be closed at the beginning of sixth watch. I had three hours.

Chapter 31

It had been less than four weeks since our escape from Capharna. Not long enough for me to forget the unending fear of a slave's life. From the moment I slipped into the throng of drovers, wagons, slaves, and laborers of a fur trader's caravan just outside the gates of Avenkhar, I felt the walls of Balthar's coffin closing in on me again.

Eyes down. Weariness in your step. A hand on the mule's harness to make them think you belong. The drover can't see you in the darkness and confusion. Stay to the left of the beast to hide the mark on your face.

The voice in my head was calm and focused. The hand that held the mule's harness was steady. But my gut was in such a knot, the Weaver herself could not have untied it.

Through the gates. I ignored the sounds of painful lashing behind me in the caravan. No slave would look. Rather I waited until we turned into a narrow lane in the warehouse district near the Vodyna River, the broad sluggish water-course that gave Avenkhar its prosperity, then slipped away into a dark alley that stunk of tanneries and fish markets and slaughterhouses. I tried not to consider the ankle-deep filth in which I waded with bare feet, but rather concentrate on Aleksander's instructions on how to find the town house of the First Lord of Marag, where lived his daughter, the Lady Lydia.

The house was on the southwestern edge of the city, where the airs were sweet off the mountains and the river still flowed clean before it flushed out the bowels of the city. I hurried head down through busy streets of prosperous shops and taverns. No one paid any attention to me in the crowds. It was only after I got into the wider streets of elegant houses with stone porticoes and carriage yards that I was stopped and questioned.

"Delivering a sword to Demyon the swordsmith for my lord, your worship," I said to the mounted watchman who had slammed the shaft of his spear across my throat to bring me to a halt.

"And who is your lord, slave?"

"My Lord Rodya of the Fontezhi, sir, who has come from Capharna to stop with his cousin Lord Polyet." Aleksander had come up with the names to use. "Lord Polyet told my master that Demyon was the finest sword smith in the Empire, and that my lord could get his sword balanced properly and have a new guard put on it that would—"

"All right. Enough of your blathering. Get back to your master. We don't like slaves loose in the streets."

"Of course, your worship."

He gave me a boot in the back as he rode past. I commanded my heart to slow down, and in a quarter of an hour I stood at the kitchen door of the House of Marag.

"I was told to ask for Hazzire," I said to the rosy-cheeked serving girl.

"Hazzire?"

"It's most urgent that I speak with him."

"Most urgent?" She sounded like the echoes in Galadon's grotto.

"Most urgent," I said, trying to hold patience. "I must deliver this message and be back to my master before he takes offense at my delay. Please try to understand."

"Oh. I suppose it's all right, then." She scratched her head. "I'll bring him. Don't want such as you in the house." She sniffed and glanced at my feet before closing the door in my face. No hope that she would be quick.

I sat in the doorway and began to review the twenty-six steps a Searcher used to verify demon possession and the history, reasoning, and tests for each. *Antipathy for water . . . Blood in the bodily fluids . . . Craving for salt . . .*

Enlargement of the pupils . . . I was on the twenty-first when a slender man with a dark, curling beard opened the door and almost stepped on me.

"Oh!" He stepped back and allowed me to get up and bow. "I am Hazzire. Who asks for me?"

"I bring an urgent message from one known as 'the lady's foreign friend.' I was told you would accept it."

The man's dark, intelligent eyes drilled into me. "Indeed. I can see such a message to its destination."

I gave him the letter. "The one who sends me cannot stress enough the importance and the secret nature of this message, sir."

"You need have no concern. Is there anything I may do for you? I was instructed that if ever such a messenger came . . ."

"Thank you, but no. My only need is a safe exit from the city before the gates are closed for the night."

"Alas, I cannot help you there," he said. "It is well-known that the House of Marag owns no slaves. For me to provide safe passage for you would attract more attention than you want, I think."

I had expected as much. "Then, I'll be on my way."

"So the letter is all?"

"Tell the recipient 'he ages well.' "

He smiled kindly. "I will deliver the report. May the hand of Athos defend you, good messenger."

I bowed and hurried away, back the way I'd come, staying in the shadows while not appearing to hide, holding the path to the gates in my head. I had a close call when a brawl spilled out of a backstreet tavern just as I passed. Five large hairy fellows, stinking of sour ale, burst through a broken door and fell on top of me and two other passersby. There were too many flailing fists and flying knife blades for my comfort, and a crowd of onlookers was gathering like ants to spilled wine. I hoped the brawlers were too drunk to notice that the hand that disarmed three of them and broke quite a number of their fingers belonged to a slave. I poked fingers in two bloodshot eyes, squeezed out from under the noisy pile, and ducked into an alley.

I thought I'd got out of it very well as I retraced my steps through the warehouse district and slipped around behind the stables into the shadows of the gate towers. But then I had to wait. No one was going out of the gates, only in. Six guards arrived to take the next watch. They would close the gates at the change of the guard.

A large party of Chastouain came crowding through the arched gateway at the last minute. Chastouain were wandering tribal herdsmen who bought and sold the desert beasts— from whom they claimed direct descent—to caravan owners. Everywhere they went, Chastouain dragged their wives (three or four apiece) and children, their grandparents and cousins, their tents and wagons, and of course, their herds. They considered solid roofs as profane, and thus pitched their tents in city marketplaces when they came for a fair or a sale.

The confusion of their arrival looked to be the best chance I was going to get. I darted from my hiding place right into the middle of the milling crowd of bleating chastou, whip-toting herdsmen, and uncountable women and children carrying heavy baskets of their household belongings on their backs. Chastouain considered it unworthy to burden their beasts with their possessions—after all, they were relatives. They only sold the animals to other men who were perhaps not relatives and would do as they wished with the beasts. I pushed against the flow, doing my best to avoid being noticed, trampled, or carried back into the city by the sheer force of their movement.

I was under the massive granite arch of the gates, ready to take an easy breath, when my good fortune came to an end. A loop of rope was dropped over my head and yanked tight enough to pull me backward through the crowd. I fought to keep my balance and loosen the rope, even while bumping into cursing, hard-faced women and spitting chastou, and bruising my shoulder on the corner of a cart. But I soon lost my footing and was dragged, choking, between the feet of the chastou herd and the wheels of the Chastouain wagons. I threw my arms over my head and drew up into a ball.

The noose only came loose when I bumped to a stop on the edge of the crowd in the yellow, hissing light of a torch. "I do believe I've found me a runaway," said a weedy voice from above my head. "Watched him sneaking through the alleys for an hour, waiting for his chance. There's new rewards out for runaway slaves."

I gasped for breath. There was no time to weigh the consequences of resistance. I could not be taken. Absolutely could not. As the first boot landed in my side, knocking the newly regained breath out again, I whispered a spell of breaking for the rope about my neck. A second boot landed in the small of my back. I wiped a handful of sticky muck on the right side of my face to cover the royal mark. By the time the boot intended to roll me onto my back landed in my ribs, the rope snapped apart, stinging my neck. I leaped to my feet, taking the boot with me and upending its owner.

There were three guardsmen still standing, and a grinning, unshaven man, who was not a soldier, looking on. All were heavily armed. Two I could take easily. Three most likely. The fourth would be harder, and if the fifth got up again . . . I swung my foot and disarmed the unshaven man, who was crouched low and waving a knife at me. From the sound of it I broke his hand. I was glad, for he was the one who had caught me with the rope.

It was wrong to be thinking. I needed to move, to use my instincts that were so much faster than thought. So I did. While dodging swords and daggers, and inflicting what damage I could with hands and feet, I tried to call up spells. The only ones that came without thought were the simplest ones I had recited for Catrin, but I managed to set one man to vomiting and had another convinced that a snake was sharing his breeches. If three more soldiers had not come running to aid their fellows or if I'd been able to get my hands on one of the weapons that kept flying inconveniently out of reach, things would have turned out differently. But inevitably I ended up facedown in the muck with chains fastened to my wrist and ankle bands, and the angry feet and fists of twelve guardsmen convincing me that a demon was far more pleasant than a soldier who has just been made to look a fool in front of his comrades.

There was always a jail built next to the city gates. Smugglers, thieves who preyed on travelers, escaping felons, or wealthy foreigners who appeared to be ripe to supply hefty bribes could be locked away until the proper authorities could be summoned. Runaway slaves were so rare that the guardsmen weren't sure of what to do with me, but they knew it wasn't to be anything pleasant. So they hooked chains to my wristbands and hung me from the roof beams of their little stone hut, so that my toes just barely touched the floor, and they spent the rest of the night venting their displeasure at my audacity in fighting them. I tried to retreat into sleep, but the calling of the hours by the gate watch seemed to remind them that I was there. They took great glee in speculating as to which of my feet was to be cut off when the magistrate came in the morning, and they made sure to set the dark-stained wooden block and the broad ax where I could see them—as well as I could see anything through the blood and mud caking my battered face.

Once, early on in the evening when the guards were all out, I curled up my feet and tried to kick a hole in the roof, but the old oak boards were thick and hard. After the soldiers had come back and reminded me of their unhappiness with the broken bones I'd left them, I was incapable of such an effort again. I needed to be gone from there. I could not melt chains, not without expending so much power that I would have nothing left with which to fight my way out of the city. Melydda was an extension of the laws of nature, not a replacement for them. I could change the way a fire burned, grow it or quench it, but I could not easily make fire where there was none, especially not for something like iron, which has no nature to burn. And any noticeable sorcery would bring out the Magician's Guild, and then I would be truly done for. Even losing a foot would be better than losing my mind in Balthar's coffin. It was an endless night.

By the end of second watch, thick, soupy grayness came in the jail door with my guards. The magistrate would arrive within the hour. I would have perhaps half a minute from the time they unhooked my hands until they had me pinned to the table, where he would exact the mandatory punishment for slaves who ran. Half a minute was time enough to surprise them. But when the heavy-jowled magistrate, annoyed at being roused so early, pronounced my sentence, a ham-handed guardsman with bruises on his face laid such a blow to my gut that I never knew when it was they unhooked my hands and bound me to the table.

"You'll not run again, slave," said the burly guardsman, smiling and scraping the ax blade against the soles of my feet. "Nor use these to insult your betters. Which one shall it be?"

"Get on with it," said the magistrate. "I've not had my breakfast."

My feeble struggles to get loose got me nothing but another fist. I could not summon the wit to break the ropes, to make an illusion, to create a distraction, to do anything but lie there like a pig at the slaughterhouse. I was only vaguely aware of the ax being raised . . . and vaguely aware of it being lowered . . . but without the terrible consequences some remote center of my mind kept trying to warn me of. People were yelling, but I couldn't move my head to see, or work up the passion to care.

"Where is the vermin? No one punishes my slaves but me."

Somewhere in my throbbing head I held tight to the arrogant voice.

"Druya's horns, if you've ruined my property, I'll have your balls for it. I'll take his foot . . . both feet . . . and his tongue for the lies he told that got him this far. But I'll do it at my own pleasure."

What was so reassuring about the cursing fury of the

newcomer who burst through the jail doorway like sunlight through a storm cloud?

"Get him up on his feet while he still has them. I want him leashed to my horse within five minutes, or I'll have you all strung out behind him."

"What was your name again, my lord?" asked the magistrate. "I need it for my report."

"Vanye of the House of Mezzrah. And you can write it that I take it most ill when mindless bureaucrats presume to interfere in my affairs."

"Our most sincere apologies, my lord. Most sincere."

Vanye. That wasn't right. As I was yanked off the table, shoved out the door, and a rope stretched from my bound wrists to the saddle of a very large horse . . . somewhere in the painful glare of the morning sun, I caught a glimpse of red hair. Wouldn't do to smile where anyone could see. I wasn't sure I could do it anyway. Drool kept rolling out of my mouth.

"Out of my way." Several of the guards stumbled aside, jostled into me by the tall man mounting the horse.

"Where is it you're taking him, Lord . . . Vanye, is it?" The magistrate and the unshaven hunter had come up just beside me, and though the blood was pounding very much too loud in my ears, I was able to hear something new in his voice.

"Go, go, go," I mumbled under my breath.

"None of your business. Just get your minions out of my way."

I let out a groan when the magistrate grabbed what he could of my shorn hair and twisted my neck, scraping with a fingernail at the mud and blood crusted on my cheek. "What mark is this on his face, my lord? Your mark? We've had reports of an escaped slave . . ."

No, no. This was not going to do at all. We could not afford delays. The magistrate let go of my head, and I worked hard to clear it. A rumbling ahead of me told me that the man on the horse was getting very upset.

"What's going on here, Livan?" A woman's voice broke

through my muddled panic. "Why is this man tied to a horse?"

"My lady! You should not be in a wicked place such as this. This is nothing but a runaway slave."

A horse walked up beside us bearing a woman in dark green, riding astride as some bold Derzhi women did. I looked up, and somewhere in the blurry field of my vision swam the face of the Lady Lydia. Her glance was like the bracing freshness of a winter morning after being too long huddled by a smoky fire. For a moment I could think again.

"We were going to punish him according to the law, but Lord Vanye has come to claim him as his property and says he will exact his own punishment. But now I see this mark on the slave, and we've had reports—"

"Vanye?!" The lady was astounded.

"You remember me, Lady," said Aleksander—of course it was he—bowing from his horse. "We met in Zhagad, I believe."

Lydia stared at Aleksander, and the sun hung suspended in its course until she spoke. "Of course, I remember you, Lord Vanye. I should have known I would find someone like you involved in these despicable activities. I heard that a slave was taken last night, and I thought perhaps to buy him before he was harmed."

"But you own no slaves, Lady."

"Exactly," she said.

"Well, this one will be of more use to me than to you, then, so I will bid you good day and be on my way."

Lydia nudged her mount past me, until it stood shoulder to shoulder with Aleksander's Musa. With a sudden move that left everyone in the courtyard silent, she raised her hand and slapped Aleksander. "Indeed, my lord. We all have duties of importance to undertake this morning. I must be about mine. Do not bring your vile practices into Avenkhar again."

"My lady. I look . . . forward to our next meeting. Perhaps under happier circumstances."

Lydia pulled her horse around and came back to the magistrate. "I want them out of here immediately," she said. "My father despises Lord Vanye and will not tolerate him in our city."

"Of course, my lady. As you say."

Aleksander touched Musa's side and rode through the gates and down the road. I stumbled after him, wishing he would either go a little slower or speed up so I could just give it up and be dragged along. Passing travelers laughed or spit or threw things at me—sometimes very nasty things. A few turned away in shame or disgust. Unfortunately, there were no trees for half a league along the flat road, and no turnings or hills that would take us out of sight of the city walls. When Musa at last came to a halt beside a spring in a grove of willows, I walked into his backside and promptly crumpled into a heap.

"Seyonne, come get up." I was wishing very much that I could crawl away from the horse's hooves and its hind end, so it was a considerable relief when I felt the chains and ropes detached from my wrist bands and a strong arm lift me to my feet. "Come on. There's water over here."

He helped me lie down, and I came near draining the little pool. It was sad when I promptly lost half of it again. At least I managed to crawl away so I didn't foul the spring.

"You drank it too fast. You need to take smaller sips." He pulled off the shredded bloody remnant of my slave tunic, dipped water from the spring with his hand, and wet it down. A proper Ezzarian way to treat the spring. Then he dabbed at the blood and filth on my face. "They did as good a job on you as I did."

"Twelve," I murmured drowsily. "Twelve of them."

"Well, that's good. I wouldn't want to be outdone in the matter of random beatings by any mere six or eight." He yanked at my lolling chin. "No. You will not be allowed to go to sleep just yet. We want to make sure your head's still serviceable after all this." He brought my clothes and a cup from his saddle pack, and proceeded to give me sips of water while checking my injuries and getting some clothes on me.

"You were a fool to go," he said, dabbing at my bruised belly so ferociously I almost lost the rest of the water I'd drunk. "I was a fool to let you. When you didn't come back, I knew . . . I knew . . . exactly what had happened and what they were going to do to you. Gods, what a wretched world."

He stopped for a moment and turned away, his breathing tight and painful. I could not see how his curse was manifesting itself. After a few minutes, he turned back again, his cold, shaking fingers tugging awkwardly at my breeches, trying to get them on over my feet. "Wouldn't want to scandalize your fine Ezzarian lady or her gentleman friend." The thought of young ladies kept his mind away from me for a minute, for which my bruises were grateful. "Am I right that you got the message to Lydia? Was that what she was saying to me?"

I nodded. "Did."

"She was magnificent, was she not?"

I nodded again.

"Never thought of her playing intrigue. I think it suits her. Her face was so . . . Damn, what spirit! You must have made a great impression on her for her to do all this." I grinned at him, which he took to mean I was in pain, so he became uncomfortably solicitous again.

"Thank you, my lord. I'll be all right." I managed to get the words out without slurring them, so maybe he would leave me be. "And what of you?"

"The beast still keeps its share of me," he said, leaning back against a tree and sipping from a wine flask. "I try—with occasional success—but it will have me in the end. My likai never taught me how to fight such a thing."

"We'll take care—"

"No. No more of that. Catrin told me how unlikely it is that you can do anything for me, and that if you allow yourself to get distracted and try some magic working, you might not be ready to face this demon."

"She had no right to say that to you."

"She had every right. And I had every right to hear it."

"My lord—"

"Listen to me, Seyonne, and don't interrupt." He leaned forward and wore such passion in his demeanor as would force any man to heed him. "I want your word . . . your word as an Ezzarian Warden . . . that you will not allow me to destroy the Empire. For everything wretched in it, there is good, too. You've not been allowed to see it, I know, but there are thousands who live in peace because of what we've built. Thousands more who would starve in one bad season did we not make it safe to trade and travel. It encompasses honor and traditions that are good and worthy and could be a great deal more. If Dmitri lived, he could tell you, as he tried to tell me for fifteen years. I cannot, will not, destroy it. If I am taken by these demons or if the day comes when I cannot control the beast, I want you to kill me. And when you've fought your battles and run the demons from my realm, I want you to tell my father the story of it."

"My lord—"

"Swear it, Seyonne. Swear that I will die by a warrior's hand and not trapped inside a beast . . . or become one." Even as he said it, I watched him fight off the savage shengar yet again. I could not imagine the strength it took to do such a thing.

"As you wish, my lord."

Perhaps it was a holy spring where we drank. Perhaps it was some blow to my head that jarred the words into place. Perhaps it was that Aleksander and I had each lifted the other from the abyss of pain and despair, and I could see clearly what I had known for a long time. For once I spoke what was in my mind. "If we could but combine your strength and my power, there is no demon could stand against us." I slowly slumped down into the long grass as my hurts were eased, and the long night weighed on my eyelids and made my tongue thick. "Unfortunately, the only way for you to be there is for Kastavan's demon to take up residence in you instead of him."

A wave of blissful sleep carried me far away from the quiet morning. But at some time as I drifted in dreamless oblivion, Aleksander laid his cloak over me and spoke softly in my ear. "I would be honored to fight at your side, Seyonne." A day later when I woke, four broken steel bands lay beside me in the grass.

Chapter 32

"How could you let him go?" I yelled at Catrin and Hoffyd when I came out of the healing stupor. "Do you understand what he's planning to do? The stupid, arrogant fool is going to give himself to the Khelid." I was beside myself with fury and helplessness and grief.

"He was right. You were in no condition to ride," said Catrin, with no hint of the defensiveness I believed she should be displaying. She had put me to sleep for a day, deciding I needed the time for my injuries to heal. "And if we had let you ride after him, you would be in no condition to fight. Your life is more important than his. I won't argue about it."

"Aleksander is worth more than all of us put together," I said. "He will change the world. Am I the only one who can see it?"

Aleksander had met Catrin and Hoffyd at the crossroads where they had waited while he'd gone after me. He returned alone, but told them that I was living, though injured, and where to find me at the spring. Then he'd asked Hoffyd to take the slave rings off of me.

"He said it was long past time," Hoffyd told me, once my initial rage was spent and I stood leaning my head on my horse, trying to settle my mind. "He said it was his damnable pride got in the way of it. But he wanted you to know you were free to do what was best, and he didn't want anything to come between you and the oath you swore to him." Hoffyd wrinkled his brow and knitted his hands together uncomfortably. "And one more thing he wanted me to tell you.

He said that Vanye—I think that was the name—used to take his slaves out to a place in the desert, where he and his friends would hunt them for sport." Hoffyd laid a hand on my shoulder. "He wasn't threatening you was he? He wouldn't do that?"

"No. It wasn't a threat." It was a gift.

Aleksander had such a head start on us that there was no possibility we could catch him. Musa was the finest horse in the Empire. Yet once we were on the road, I could not hold back. I rode like a madman, stopping only long enough to rest the horses. Aleksander's surrender could change everything. And there was the dreadful truth that the Prince did not understand, that once the demon took him, he would not be able to fight alongside me. His soul would be my battleground, and all his strength and determination and obstinate perversity would be wedded to the demon's magic to create my opponent. The demon would know everything I had told Aleksander, including my name.

I cursed my foolish tongue that had picked that one moment of weakness to flap so loosely, telling Aleksander just enough that he believed some grand, heroic gesture was going to make the difference. I was very much afraid he was going to kill us both . . . and the thousands of others who would die when the Khelid and the demons took what they desired.

Parnifour. It was an unlikely place for the fate of the world to be decided. It lay on the fringes of empire, grown up in layers from the ebb and flow of tribes and conquerors over a thousand years. Next to a street of windowless Veshtar mud dwellings would be a street of tall, narrow wooden houses and shops with carved lintels and painted shutters as the Kuvai preferred. Upon stonework ruins left by builders so ancient we didn't know their names, the Derzhi had constructed palaces with open-air courtyards and interconnecting archways designed to funnel the light airs of the desert to cool the stone. The people were just as intermixed. A statuesque, dark-skinned Thrid woman might have

the round blue eyes and curly hair of a Manganar, or a fair
child of Basran heritage might be wearing the colored beads
and striped robes of the Suzaini. It was a medium-sized city,
heavily fortified. Underneath it the land was riddled with
springs and caves, making it a lush green spot between the
boundless seas of golden grass to the south and the harsh
black granite cliffs of the Khyb Rash—the Mountains of the
Teeth—to the north.

I crouched behind the remains of a stone bulwark half
buried in the crown of a small hill within sight of Parnifour's
outer gates. We were waiting the few hours until sunset, not
daring to walk in openly during the day. There could be
watchers . . . waiting for us. Kastavan could know everything by now. *Damn, damn, damn you, Aleksander. Why
couldn't you trust me? I would have found a cure for you. I
promised it.*

It was the twenty-second day.

The afternoon sun baked the hilltop. Catrin and Hoffyd
were sleeping in a meager strip of shade. I sat leaning
against the stone wall, unable to do the same, though we had
ridden all through the previous night feeling the nearness of
the city pulling us on. Vultures circled lazily above some
deadness in the distance; a kite dived screaming into the
grass soaring upward soon after, carrying an unlucky mouse.
A cool wind stirred the long grass, easing the unshielded
blaze of the afternoon.

I wished I could sleep. Instead I stared at my hands and
my bare scarred wrists. I was free, my melydda lived, and all
of it was ashes in my mouth. Of the four people I cared for
most in the world, one lay dead and, if Catrin and I were
successful, the other three could be destroyed by these very
hands. Long years of pain and rage boiled from my soul in
that moment, bursting from my lips in a cry that made the
birds on the nearby hills rise in dark nervous clouds. My two
companions stirred and asked sleepily if anything was
wrong. "Only a nightmare," I said.

I was soon distracted by a dark shape moving toward me
from behind the next hill. A horse. Dark, shapely, fast. A fine

horse . . . riderless. I rose and moved slowly down the hill. The horse stopped. I clicked my tongue in the way Aleksander did, and the nervous beast edged closer. "Where is your master?" I said softly, reaching for his dragging reins. Musa shied, but I kept talking and threw a calming enchantment into the air so that when I gathered in the quivering bay, he did not pull away. "Now show me where you've left him." I could not believe Aleksander would abandon his prize voluntarily.

I worked what small spells I knew that were effective with horses, got myself into the saddle, and let the horse take me where he would. Some two leagues west through the waving grass we came upon the mauled remains of a rudah—a huge, vicious wild pig native to the grasslands. So Aleksander had transformed again on his way in. And not too long past. The vultures and the flies were still cleaning the bones, scarcely anything left of a beast that weighed almost as much as a cow. A short distance away, I found wads of grass torn from the soil and stained with blood and bits of dried flesh. Aleksander had waked here and tried to clean himself . . . and Musa would have been nowhere close to a shengar and a rudah. The Prince would have had to walk the rest of the way to Parnifour. Maybe . . . just maybe . . .

I dug my heels into Musa's side and held on as the horse shot eastward. Catrin and Hoffyd were already awake, draining the last of our water supply. "I've got to go now," I said. "He's not far ahead of us. I'll meet you just inside the north gate at the change to fifth watch. There may be time to save him."

"But where are you going to look?" said Hoffyd.

"I'm going to make inquiries with the junior dennissar of the Derzhi."

"Seyonne! You don't know what—" Catrin called after me, but I ignored her and rode away.

Of course he would go to Kiril first. Only the matter of Dmitri would delay his bullheaded plan. Catrin had found me a long red scarf in one of the villages where we stopped to buy food. I wrapped it around my head in the Manganar style to cover my short hair, and I raked it to the side to cover the scar on my cheek.

"Transporting a horse for the Derzhi dennissar," I said at the gate. "He's bought it from Drafa, and I'm to deliver it before the summer racing season." The guards admired the beast, recognizing that it was indeed too fine for a man who looked as if his face had been used to plow a field.

"Run into trouble along the way, did you?" asked one of them, staring at my fading bruises. "Or is it that the beast is high-strung?"

"Bandits," I said. "I wasn't to ride this fellow. But they got my old nag and my gear. Tied me to a thornbush, but then they drank a few too many toasts to their cleverness. When they passed out, I got away. Figured I'd have the best chance to stay ahead of 'em if I took this one and rode hard."

"And now you're going to deliver him to his owner?" The second guard was skeptical.

"I've served Lord Kiril's family long enough to know they value their horses above their wives," I said. "It don't do to cross that kind of master. I'll take my payment and be glad of it."

The guards laughed and sent me on, telling me where to find the junior dennissar's house. It was a modest, walled town house near the center of Parnifour. It had probably stretched the funds of a junior dennissar who, though an off-shoot of the royal house, was descended from the female line and whose own father was dead.

The gate was open, and I prevailed upon the old man in the gatehouse to take a message to Lord Kiril that a man had brought him a horse suitable for a wager-race from Zhagad to Drafa. The sharp-eyed old man pointed me around to the back courtyard to await an answer. The tree-shaded court-yard had a stable at one end, a workman's shed beside it, and a small garden area near a well house. The enclosed space made me nervous. I was ready to bolt when a man burst out of the back door of the house. He was a short, square-faced young Derzhi with a blond braid. A dusting of freckles across his long straight nose made him look much younger than I could remember ever being.

"Zander, you've—" He bit off his quiet greeting when he saw me, then whipped his light-colored eyes about the courtyard. When his gaze rested on me again, he examined me so closely I worried that he might see things I would as soon stay hidden. The young Derzhi bit his lip and started to speak, then Musa tossed his head, and the young man laid a hand to quiet him. With an almost undetectable shake of his head, the young man stepped backward and lifted one hand. Five well-armed soldiers ran out of the stables and the corners of the courtyard.

I spread my arms and held still, resisting the urge to break the arm of the soldier who was holding a spear point to my gut. I thought better of resistance when I noticed that three of the five had pale hair and pale skin and hooded eyes. Khelid.

The young man rubbed the horse's neck and crooned to it for a moment as Aleksander did, and only then did he return his gaze to me. His momentary uncertainty was no longer in evidence. "Where did you come by this horse?" His voice was a chilly reminiscence of a winter morning in Capharna.

"My lord, I was given this beast this morning by a man on the Avenkhar road. He said to bring it to you and give you the message, and you would pay me for it. Please, sir, I meant no harm."

"And what was the man like?"

"He was a slave, sir." Let the Khelid be unsettled. Chances were that Aleksander would tell them I was living. And if not, let them wonder.

"A slave . . . Did you see the master, the owner of the horse?"

"No, sir. The slave said his master had no more need of the horse. I didn't ask more. Didn't want to know. Mayhap he murdered his master. I need the money, so I didn't ask. I would have brought the slave, too, to sell him or take the reward for a runaway, but I had no weapons, no chains . . . no way to manage him. Forgive me, sir, if the master was your friend. . . ."

"Not my friend. A heartless, vicious bastard I once called kin. He murdered my only father, and I'll have his head for it. To hear he has no use for a horse soothes me, yet rumor is not enough. If he yet draws breath, I will have him. No one but me. So I am pleased and angry at once."

"I understand, sir." But I was curious. Why then had he come out looking so eagerly for "Zander"? "May I leave, sir? I know nothing else."

Kiril gave Musa's reins to a groom. "I would see his body before I'm easy, so I think you'll stay here tonight. Tomorrow you'll show me where you met this slave, and we'll look for evidence of the master." He jerked his head to one of the Khelid guards. "Tell Lords Korelyi and Kydon that I will be unable to attend their celebration tomorrow. I'm still in search of my bloodthirsty cousin. This could all be a ruse to put me off my guard. Aleksander is not stupid." The pale-eyed soldier nodded and left, while Kiril spoke to the others. "Bind our visitor and lock him in the shed. I'll see to him in the morning."

"Please, sir, I have urgent business in the city. My wife is ill. . . ."

Kiril caught the front of my shirt in his fist and spoke through clenched teeth. "She will survive a brief time without you. Once you've done what I want, you'll be free to go. This is necessary. Do you understand me?"

I believed I did. I hoped I did. Though as they trussed me like a goose and locked the hasp of the dirt-floored shed crammed with crates and ash bins, broken furniture, dented pots, and rolls of mouse-chewed canvas, I fully imagined what Catrin could say about stupid men who couldn't be trusted to think straight about strategy. Like a naive child, I had been so sure that Aleksander would go to Kiril and convince him of his innocence.

Fifteen minutes later, about the time I had worked out a few enchantments, including the one I would need to break the hasp on the shed, the door opened and a man slipped

from the waning daylight into the dark shed. When the door
was closed again, he uncovered a lantern and showed proper
shock to see me quite unbound, leaning against a pile of rotted carpet.

"Shall I tell you why your cousin always sends your letters sealed with red wax?" I said, since he seemed to be at a
loss for how to begin.

He yanked the red scarf from my head and stared at the
scar, then gestured at my hands. I pulled up my sleeves and
showed him the marks of slave rings. "So you are the one he
told me of," he said at last. "I thought it was but another aspect of his madness . . . to think a slave would come looking
for him."

"I am a free man, my lord. And I must find your cousin.
He is in such peril I cannot begin to explain it."

"I wanted to kill him."

"But you didn't."

"No. What satisfaction comes from killing a man who
hides in the shadows, unwilling to show his face in his own
city? He could scarcely speak, and he had blood on his
hands and face, though he said he was not injured. If he'd
not reminded me of things only the two of us would know, I
would not have believed it to be Aleksander. He tried to tell
me that he didn't kill our uncle, while in the same breath
speaking of demon plots, and slaves who are sorcerers, and
mustering troops to protect the city. Then these Khelid come
looking for him, saying the Emperor has declared him mad.
They claim they are here to protect me, as my cousin has
sworn to kill me as he did my uncle. Everything I saw con-
firms their charges. What am I to believe?"

"Believe everything your cousin told you, my lord. He
did not kill the Lord Dmitri, only felt the guilt of his own
folly. The Khelid did the deed. It is your warning, your misgivings and those of Lord Dmitri about these Khelid, that
helped convince him of what was happening. The threat is
real. The danger beyond your imagining. And Prince Aleksander will likely not survive it if he's taken by the Khelid.
The Khelid are joined with demons, and they plan to make

him one of them. If they succeed and your cousin is made Emperor, there will come such a rule of terror over this land that there has been no equal of it in all the past ills of the world."

"I don't believe any of this."

I tried to hold patience. We might need Kiril. "Please, my lord. Do you know where he's gone? We must go to him now. It may already be too late."

"He said he had business with Lord Kastavan. I told him that Kastavan wasn't in the city, but that he'd be here by tonight. They're building a temple on the Watch Mount. Kydon and Korelyi and their priests are going to dedicate the foundation stone tonight at moonrise, and Kastavan is to attend."

"I must go, then," I said, trying to rein in my excitement. The moon was rising early, just after sunset, but that meant there was still an hour. "And you must do as he asked you. I don't know how much he told you, but the Khelid may try to take the city by force. If it happens, it will likely be six days from this. There will be no warning, so you must be ready for it."

"And if they don't?"

"Then, I would take anyone I cared for, run as deep into the mountains as I could, and never come out again."

"Bloody Athos."

"Now can you tell me how to find this temple?"

Aleksander's cousin was an unassuming young man, his manner as unlike the Prince as was possible, considering they had been raised in the same house by many of the same people. He was not comfortable taking advice from a "barbarian slave," and I watched him wrestle with the demands of breeding and duty, faithfulness and doubt. But he either had to accept that Aleksander was mad or do as his prince had bid him. Because he loved Aleksander, he grasped at the explanation that held him innocent, and from his first moment of acceptance, he never questioned my authority.

"I'll take you there," Kiril said firmly. "As you've seen, there are a great many eyes watching my house. In case anyone asks, I'm taking you to visit your sick wife, but I have no intention of letting you go until tomorrow."

I nodded, allowed him to bind my hands loosely with rope, then he steered me firmly out of the shed, across the courtyard, and into the street. We'd gone no more than fifty paces down the lane when I leaned my head close. "There's a man following us who's got teeth like a badger. Is he one of yours?"

"No."

The light was failing. A few of the public houses already had torches lit outside them, and laughter and music of skirling pipes and scraping strings came from inside. Fifty plans raced through my mind, but when I saw a hunchbacked woman stumble out of an alley just ahead of us, I nodded toward the dark lane and said, "Shall we take him aside and see what he wants?"

"Are you planning to work some sorcery?"

"No need."

But no sooner did we dodge into the alley and turn to grab the badger-faced man than he was joined by the hunchbacked woman, who confronted us, poised to throw a very long knife. "Give him over," she said to Kiril, "or this knife will find a home right in your throat. I'm quite accurate." Somehow the voice didn't fit with the slack, lumpish face.

Kiril pushed me behind him. "I am the Emperor's dennissar. Who are you and what do you want with my prisoner?"

The badger-faced man used a short sword to motion Kiril to his knees and made as if to cut his throat. In the time it takes for a hummingbird to flit beyond reach, I slipped my hands from the rope, shoved the young Derzhi to the ground, and twisted the sword from our assailant's grasp. Then I lunged, kicked at the woman's hand, and raised my hand, on course to break the man's neck and the woman's arm, when they yelled together, "Seyonne! Wait!" I aborted the move at the last instant, stumbling into the wall and shaking my head as I watched the two faces slide into more familiar lines. Catrin and Hoffyd.

Kiril gaped, and I sagged against the wall. "You should give me a little more warning," I said.

"We saw him bring you out with your hands bound," said Catrin. "We thought . . ."

Well, it was clear what they thought. I explained quickly, and introduced them to Kiril, who merely looked from one of us to the other repeatedly, squinting and widening his eyes. Catrin's illusion had been amazingly good. A transformation of appearance was extraordinarily difficult to sustain for more than five minutes. And for two of them . . . It was no wonder she looked tired when we took off again.

The temple site was on a rocky height in the center of the city. Watchtowers, built by the same ancient stoneworkers who had crafted the foundation of the city, had stood on the heights for as long as anyone could remember. These builders had left their work scattered, not just in Parnifour, but throughout all the lands that had become the Empire. There were those among my people who claimed we were somehow related to these ancients, for their ruins were strong with melydda. Our ancestors had certainly modeled our own temples on their works.

The Khelid had taken possession of the land and torn down the old towers, so Kiril said, and it was there they planned to build the temple, to introduce their gods to the people of the Derzhi Empire. A single narrow track zigzagged to the top of the rocks.

It was impossible to go up by way of the road. Khelid guards were posted, preventing anyone from passing without being identified. As Kiril had written Aleksander, there were hundreds of Khelid in Parnifour. I was almost sick with the aura of demon. "We've got to find another way up," I said as we mingled with the townspeople who stood on the fringes of the Khelid crowd watching the goings-on.

"Come this way," said Kiril, leading us through crowded lanes around to a deserted saddle-maker's shop on the far side of the bluffs. "There's another path up, but it's wickedly steep. I've been trying to keep an eye on the Khelid for a while, and Jynnar, the man who owns this shop, showed me this way."

"I'll wait down here," said Hoffyd when we reached the deserted shop. "I don't do well with heights in the dark since I lost the eye."

"I'll wait here, too," said the Derzhi. "It would be well to guard your rear. There's no other way down save through the middle of the Khelid, and if you were to bring Aleksander . . ."

"I've got to go," I said, chafing at the delay. The sun was sagging toward the horizon, and the hints of demon music that hung in the still, warm air had my nerves quivering.

"I'll go with Seyonne," said Catrin. "Someone has to keep him from going off and doing something stupid."

"Watch yourself," said Kiril. "The path is tricky."

So Catrin and I started up the crumbling goat track. Pebbles and rocks rolled out from under our boots and crashed down the hillside. In some places the track was only wide enough for one foot, and in others it was missing altogether and we had to stretch over a sheer drop to reach another foothold. We grasped at twigs and stunted trees that grew out of the rocks, and more than once I ended up flattened against the rock with a mouthful of dirt, clinging for my life with fingertips and boots. It was too slow. I wanted to scream at the delay. What was Aleksander doing?

It took us over an hour to get up the path. The moon was up by the time we crawled over the edge onto a knob of rock overlooking the flat top of the bluff. We lay flat and scooted to the edge to peer down. There must have been five hundred Khelid on the rocky promontory, standing in a ring about a flat gray stone set into the ground. I could scarcely breathe from the weight of demon enchantment in the still air. Every heartbeat was a struggle; every moment passed slowly and with effort, as if you were running in chest-high water. Catrin pressed her hands to her ears, but I knew how futile was the attempt to block out the grinding noise. The horror pulsed in the veins until it seemed as if the only way to be rid of it was to cut the vein and let it bleed away.

We were too late. Aleksander stood in the center of the ring, the livid crescent moon hanging low in the east behind him. A man knelt before him, laughing uproariously—a strange gurgling laugh mixed with strident breathing. But it was not to do the Prince honor that the man knelt. Rather it was only a transient pose before he toppled onto the gray stone, his face purple and distorted, and a knife hilt protruding from his chest. Kastavan. Aleksander had guessed the surest way to get the result he wanted.

If there had been a word I could say that might change what was to come, I would have said it. If it would have made any difference, I would have leaped from my rock for Aleksander as I had leaped from the precipice for Galadon, wings or no. But the Khelid host was dead, and therefore his demon was savoring his last unholy terrors, licking his lips and belching in a surfeit of hatred and lust, as it began the search for a new home. It would not have to look far. For there stood before him a vessel: waiting, prepared, nurtured by the demon enchantment.

Hear me, Aleksander, I said, willing my thoughts to penetrate the grotesque din. *Hold onto yourself. You are not alone. You will not be abandoned when you fall into the abyss. I'll come for you. Never doubt it. Never.*

I would have sworn the Prince looked up at me and smiled in that moment, just before he went rigid and fell to his knees, his fists pressed to his temples. Then there came from him such a cry as would shrivel the stoutest heart. It was the essence of pain and uttermost desolation, distilled from the fullness of the world's nightmares. Every childhood fright, every midnight disturbance, every mother's pain as she watches her child in torment, every father's despair as he buries his last son, a young wife barren, a young husband impotent, a scholar blind, a musician deaf, a gardener condemned to everlasting desert . . . such was the agony that welled from Aleksander's bright center as he was drowned in darkness.

Hold, my prince. I will come for you.

This time when he gazed to the top of the rocks where I

lay, two beams of frigid blue gleamed from the eyes that should be bright amber. *What voice is this? Come . . . and we will see who has him in the end.*

My skin grew clammy and my throat constricted. My heart tried to claw its way from my body to escape the hissing voice that crept into my thoughts, hungering to know who I was. Every mark of hatred on my body screamed with fire. And as the demon music soared in hellish symphony, Aleksander yanked his knife from the dead Khelid and began to cut out his victim's heart.

"Come away." Catrin's voice stung like ice on burned flesh. "You can do him no good here. It is the battle will set him free or not, and it is time to prepare."

Chapter 33

When we rejoined Kiril and Hoffyd at the saddle maker's shop, three men lay on the dirt floor, immobilized by Kiril's sword and Hoffyd's magic. They were townsmen, known informants who were in the habit of watching Kiril's house. They had seen the incident in the alley and were following us, hoping to profit from such a strange occurrence. Kiril shipped them out of Parnifour that night in a wagon he designated as tax revenues bound for Zhagad. By the time they woke up, the three spies would be abandoned in the heart of the Azhaki grasslands fifty leagues from anywhere.

It would be too dangerous for us to stay with Kiril, so we took shelter with one of his friends in a stable just outside the city walls to the north. It was a large, well-kept place, centered in rocky pastureland that rose gently toward the mountains. But all the stable lads had been taken away to work on the Khelid temple or the old Derzhi fortress, where Kydon the legate had taken residence, so most of the horses had been sent back to their owners. The stable owner came out for a few hours each day to care for the remaining horses. He would bring us food and supplies and ask no questions.

I watched as the spies were taken away, listened as the arrangements were made, walked out of the gates, down the rutted road, and up the wooden stairs to the dormitory above the deserted stables, carrying whatever was put in my hand. I made my bed where I was told and lay on it unsleeping. But all I could hear in those hours was Aleksander's cry, and all I could see was his face in the instant the demon took him, the moment he realized what he had done and what was to come. However terrible my dreams were going to be when I slept again, they would be no match for his.

"I'm sorry we were late," said Catrin, handing me a cup of hot wine and sitting on the straw pallet beside me, picking at the dirty canvas ticking.

"I was supposed to protect him. He thought this was what I wanted."

"Grandfather was right, wasn't he? This is not just about your oath anymore, not about saving the world from demon chaos. This is about Aleksander."

"I would give my life for him—a stubborn, arrogant, murderous Derzhi. I think I've lost my mind."

"You sound just as he did, cursing you for an insolent barbarian . . . just before he went dashing off to Avenkhar to find you. It took me a while to understand how you could care so much for one so absolutely opposite yourself in background, feelings, and beliefs. I thought him handsome and charming, but little more. Only in those last days did I begin to see it."

"There's so little time."

"So how long will it take you to put this behind you and go on?"

I looked up at her small face, so unlikely a façade for an iron will. "If I could step through the portal right now, I would do it," I said.

She nodded. "And you would lose. You must put him away before you go. Clear your mind. You know how dangerous it can be if you think too much of the victim or care too much." She yanked a dangling thread from the worn cloth of the bedcover. "You've never fought in the soul of someone you know."

"No."

"Grandfather did. It was not the only battle he lost, but it was his last. He never forgave himself, because he knew he should have let someone else fight it."

I raised up on my elbow to listen. I'd never known what

made Galadon stop fighting. It was not something he would discuss with his students. "Who was it?"

"It was my mother."

"Ah, Catrin . . ."

"She was an Aife, a brilliant one. My father was her Warden. His talent was weak, and he struggled with his tasks, but she would not withdraw from the pairing. Eventually, inevitably, he lost a battle . . . and the demon took him captive. It was a villainous soul where he battled, and she would not leave him there."

"So she tried to get him out." It was hard enough for an Aife to leave a dead Warden behind. But it was infinitely more difficult to have to abandon a living Warden when he had been taken captive. If she kept the portal open too long in hopes her partner would escape, trying to shift the weaving to give him a chance to get free, she left herself vulnerable, for the demon would make the captive speak her name. And if she fell, the demon could find its way back into the Comforter and the Searcher, and eventually into Ezzaria, endangering everyone. Yet to close the portal upon one you loved, to leave him there trapped with the demon in the abyss . . . Aifes were the strongest of all who fought the demon war.

Catrin folded her small hands and leaned her chin on them. "My mother finally closed the portal before the demon could come through, but she herself was taken. When Grandfather went in, he was not able to save her. It came near killing him, Seyonne, because he could not keep his focus, could not stop thinking about her. He tried to see his beloved daughter in the landscape his Aife created for him, and so he did not look for the demon. He stayed his hand when he should have struck, because he could not separate the monster he faced from her. You must not make the same mistakes."

"So tell me what to do."

She did. For the next five days we worked at every mental discipline. Everything I had learned while a slave—of focus and barriers, of single-minded purpose—I put to use.

She would create visions—horrific, terrible, beautiful, distracting—and force me to solve problems as I lived in them. She painted such accurate portraits of Aleksander in the midst of her weavings that I was sure he was standing before me, laughing, arguing, swearing at me. And after a while it wasn't only Aleksander in the visions, it was Rhys . . . and then it was Ysanne . . . plucked out of my living memory and set before me as friend and lover, as monster, as demon-infested opponent. I killed all of them fifty times over, saved all of them fifty more. We worked from dawn until Catrin could not conjure another scenario, and I could not lift my hand.

Only one thing nagged at me in all our preparation. Catrin and I never worked a test together. When a Warden and an Aife trained together, a third person would summon the vision, and the Aife would create a portal into it, weaving her own magic so that she and the Warden could become accustomed to each other. Hoffyd was strong enough to create the vision, if Catrin would tell him the problem she wanted.

"We don't need to practice like that," she said as I lay sprawled on the floor, panting from the exertions of a just finished session on our last afternoon. "Making and using a second portal is not the same as a true pairing. The Queen will be the actual Aife, as you know. All I do is let you in."

"But I may need your guidance. There are a thousand things, just like—"

"I cannot speak to you in the way of an Aife. I cannot hear you or know what's happening. That's the way it is. I'm sorry. There's no need for us to practice together." She averted her eyes as she spoke, and I wondered if she was embarrassed to think of the words she had spoken beyond the portal. Or perhaps she really didn't understand that I had heard her. It was strange that she wouldn't try to practice with me when she was adamant about my own training.

That night when I called a halt, fearing I would have nothing left for the real battle if I were to attempt one more practice, I asked Catrin if she would walk with me outdoors for a while.

"I should get some sleep," she said, glancing over at Hoffyd, who had dropped off over his journal as we worked late.

"As you wish. I just wanted to get a breath of fresh air." And to look at the stars and the moon and the peacefully sleeping world that I might never see again after the next day. And to feel the warmth of someone walking alongside. The burden weighed heavy on me that night.

She hesitated, then picked up her cloak. "You're right. We've been bottled up inside too long."

The night was pleasantly cool on my face. We strolled across the pasture toward a stretch of spring-fed trees in a gully beyond the fence. The yellow moon hung low in the west. Four horses nudged our arms and nosed our pockets looking for treats. Catrin laughed and shooed them away.

There was nothing to say. Our preparations were made. I was as ready as I could be in six short weeks. She could give me no more reminders, no more tests, no more words that would move me one step beyond the level I had reached. Unfortunately, she could not remedy the lingering doubt that we both knew would be my greatest danger.

At some point her hand found its way into mine, a sweet human comfort that had nothing to do with desire or love or anything but companionship. It was enough. We wandered through the wooded gully, the broad ash leaves making dappled moonlight on the path, a nearby spring whispering its way along beside us. When we came to the edge of the trees, we stood for a moment gazing up at the looming blackness of the Khelid fortress high above us on the rocks. Then we turned back, and in far too short a time we were back at the stables.

"Thank you," I said as we paused at the door before stepping back into the roles we had chosen. "For everything. You've given me back my life."

"It was never lost. Only mislaid."

"You are your grandfather's worthy heir. Your students

will call you a nefarious old buzzard and twist their brains into knots and their bodies into mush to earn a single word of praise from you."

She laughed and stretched up on her toes to kiss me on the cheek. "And you, my dearest Warden, my first and most prized pupil, will never, ever tell them that I once made you almond cakes."

We stepped inside the stable and slept soundly until dawn.

Catrin had not yet told me how she was going to know where and how to open a door on Ysanne's enchantment. As far as I knew there was no temple in Parnifour, no place where Ezzarian enchantments were drawn together like the center of a great spiderweb. It was why we had to come ourselves when Ysanne agreed to meet face-to-face with her partner in treachery. But it was not for me to know how an Aife planned her business. Catrin had given me all that she could.

Kiril came that morning. Hoffyd had cleaned out one of the large rooms above the stable, swept and swabbed and wiped until the place was bare wood with a small, clean window open to the sky. It was there we had practiced for five days, and it was there that I was working through the exercises I needed to stay loose and to put myself in the proper state of mind. Catrin tried to keep the Derzhi away, but I heard the disturbance on the stair and peered down.

"He's busy," she was saying, her small hand set firmly on Kiril's broad chest. "He needs to be alone."

"It's all right," I called from the top of the stair. "One minute more or less isn't going to turn the tide, and if I can't put aside one more distraction when the time comes, then we've wasted a great deal of time this week. Besides, I need to eat."

"You said this was the day," said Kiril a few minutes later, downing a cup of wine, while I drank strong tea and devoured such a pile of bread and cold chicken as might satisfy a shengar.

"It is."

"So what's going to happen? And when?"

"I have no idea when. But at some time Catrin is going to tell me it's time and where we need to go . . . and then, we'll see."

"That's when you fight this demon."

"Yes."

"Damn. It's all too strange. Well, you can be easy about my part. The garrison is ready to move at my word."

"Good."

He hesitated a moment, then pulled something from his pocket. "I've received a message from Aleksander."

I shook my head. "Don't tell me. I mustn't think about him. I'll do the best I can, and that will have to be good enough."

"But I think you need to see." He gave me a folded paper. "It was sent yesterday."

Kiril,

I've just arrived in Parnifour to learn more of the Khelid and to inspect our fortifications here on the border. I've heard reports that you think to avenge Dmitri by cutting my throat or taking my heart or drinking my blood or some other nasty business. It will not happen. I am well protected, and even your skill cannot touch me. If you wish to avoid charges of treason, you will put aside such idiotic notions and come to greet me by week's end with proper respect and humility, proclaiming an end to all grievances against me. If you do so, I may consider allowing you to retain your post as well as your life, for you have done good service these past months in accommodating my Khelid friends. We will put your past behavior up to grieving. But if you refuse and continue to mouth these scurrilous charges, I will see you hanged—kinsman or no. You cannot imagine that my father would countenance such behavior.

Aleksander

The broken wax seal was red.

"He is not theirs," I said softly.

"That was my thought. When he left me six days ago, he knew I wouldn't kill him. I'd had the chance and couldn't do it. And as for my 'skill' . . . I've never bested him in a fight. Not since we were in the nursery."

"You mustn't trust him, though," I said, returning the letter to him. "This could be only one small secret that he's kept his own. And it could change at any time. You understand that? This demon lives inside him, and for every moment he resists its will, he must pay a terrible price."

Kiril smiled. "I've known Aleksander a great deal longer than you have, Seyonne. Even from your hard experience, you can have no idea of his stubbornness."

Catrin was hovering around the door like a moth trying to get into the light. "You should go now," I said. "Catrin will explode if I don't get back to work. Thank you for coming."

"Athos be at your right hand, my friend," he said.

"With us all."

Once he had gone, I spent one minute savoring Aleksander's tiny victory. Every moment he could hold gave me a moment to strike. If he could avoid revealing my name, the demon could not worm its way into my head as easily. If he could refuse to allow his knowledge of me to be put to use, it gave me the advantage of skill and surprise. I wished I could believe that stubborn resolve could protect him against the creature devouring his soul, but after only the moment's indulgence, I put it out of my mind. I could not afford that kind of faith. I had to fight this battle alone.

In only half an hour more, Catrin came in and said, "We need to go. There will be a private place for your preparation."

I nodded and followed her down the stairs into a cloudy morning. Hoffyd was nowhere to be seen, but the horses were saddled and waiting. Catrin's hair was bound in a heavy braid, wound about her head. As we rode through a wooden gate and onto a narrow path across the meadowlands, the freshening wind picked at her braid, luring dark strands from their confinement to brush her flushed cheeks. She wore her usual attire, a brown riding skirt and a dark green tunic, tinted light and dark by the changing patterns of sunlight and racing clouds. A formidable warrior, riding into battle. We didn't say anything. It wasn't forbidden, just unnecessary.

Our path led us a short way into the foothills of the Khyb Rash east of Parnifour and through a wide slot between two sizable rock formations. I was surprised to see that our narrow bridle path followed what had once been a paved road as wide as the rift. Broken fragments of stone too smooth and too uniform to be of nature's making were nestled in stirrup-high weeds, and every so often we passed a stele not quite ruined by centuries of weather and falling rock. After no more than two thousand paces the narrow gorge opened into a lush little valley of knee-high flowers and thick-boled ash and hemlock, centered by the ruins of a long, open building. Half the ruin was roofless, huge slabs of granite fallen amid the crumbling giants of its toppled columns. The farthest portion of the building still held intact. It was an ancient place. Hoffyd's horse stood at one end.

I should have known we would come to one of the builders' ruins. Comforters often took possessed victims to the fallen temples and houses and colonnades. The melydda found in those places made it easier to set up the enchantments that would link the victim to the Aife who waited back in Ezzaria.

As we dismounted and tethered our horses beside Hoffyd's mare, fat raindrops plopped heavily on the dark green leaves. Hoffyd came out to meet us, clasping Catrin's hands and sweeping her face with a lingering gaze that left no room for anyone else in the world. When she brushed his cheek with her hand, a number of things became very clear. I smiled to myself and thought that Elen would approve, ignoring the faint twinge of regret that flitted through the remote corners of my mind. And Aleksander would be pleased. He had been right again.

"This way," said Hoffyd quietly, as if reluctant to disturb

whatever ghosts might be drifting about the place with the wisps of fog. He took us up a broad flight of steps onto the main floor of the building—a bathhouse as it seemed. There were a series of five rectangular pools, each one smaller than the last, as we progressed into the less-ruined section of the place. The larger pools all had sides cracked and caved in, and the only water in them was the scummy, sludge-laden remains of winter snows and spring rain. Around them, on the columns and fallen walls, were carvings of men and women occupied with activities impossible to guess from the faint traces. A few bits of red and blue gave hints that once the place might have been bright with color other than the somber grays of the Khyb Rash stone.

We walked up another set of steps into the less damaged part of the ruin, the patter of rain echoing on the old stone. In one hall most of two walls still stood outside the rows of fluted columns. In a corner of its small pool, water seeped from a spout shaped like a bird, its head long broken away. Beyond that pool was one more, the smallest, perhaps only twenty-five paces around. It was lined with dark blue tiles inlaid with sworls of red. Steaming water welled up from the bottom, filling it until the water ran out into a broken con-duit that should have carried it to the next pool, but now spilled into a crack in the floor. The little pool was a wonder, the water clear, and the beauty of the tiles not dulled by mosses or deposited stone.

Wide stone benches had once surrounded the pool. Only one bench remained intact. The surrounding debris had been cleared away, and cushions not at all ancient had been laid on and beside it. Candles had been placed at five points around the bench, and a small brazier gave off the faint sweet scent of jasnyr. It was the traditional setting for a demon battle where the victim was to be present. So this was the place where Ysanne and Rhys and Aleksander would be. I could not guess where Catrin and I were to be or how we were to insinuate ourselves into the enchantment.

Instead I followed Hoffyd down a long, wide passage to the doorway of a room that remained fully enclosed. It had most likely been a dressing room, or perhaps a dining room for bathers who brought servants and supper with them on their pleasurable outing. The room had a series of long narrow windows along the outside wall that let in enough of the gray light to see, and someone had cleaned it quite recently, for there was no dirt, no grass or weeds showing through the cracked stone, and no sign of animal habitation. On the floor beside the windows sat a brass basin filled with water from the pool, still steaming in the damp air, a red pitcher, which would also contain water, most likely from our rain barrel at the stable, a white towel, a folded blue cloak, and a slim wooden box, polished to a high luster.

At the threshold of the room, I turned to Hoffyd and embraced him, then to Catrin and smiled down into her solemn face, where her dark eyes expressed everything she could not voice. "At moonrise tomorrow we will drink a toast to your grandfather," I said, and I kissed her forehead. "I'll be ready for you in an hour and a half." Then I closed the door of age-darkened oak and left my life behind.

For an hour I worked at the exercises of the kyanar, smoothing the last ruffles that the sights and sounds of the short journey had awakened. Then I stripped and used the water from the jar to wash myself, speaking the words of purification that I had not needed to practice because they were as much a part of me as my heart or my hands. I had no clean clothes, but I smoothed the ones I had been wearing and put them back on. From the wooden box I lifted the silver knife and a small pouch that held a smooth, cold oval of clouded glass, replacing my knife with the silver one and tying the pouch to my belt. After drinking my fill of the clean water from the red pitcher, I fastened the blue Warden's cloak about my shoulders, pulled the deep hood over my head, and sat down cross-legged in the center of the room.

My hands lay open and relaxed on my knees, and in my mind I began to repeat the chant of Ioreth, the first Warden. *Nevyed zi. Guerroch zi. Selyffae zi. I am whole. I am life. I defend the light . . .* Carefully, clearly I fashioned the words, drawing myself together, reeling in the threads of melydda that extended from my soul into the trees and grasses, into the city and its unsuspecting residents, into the sun and moon and stars and whatever lay beyond, until my body thrummed with power, and I sat relaxed, unthinking, waiting.

There was no sense of time passing. I could sit that way for days, if necessary, suspended in time, like an arrow nocked and ready, awaiting only the release of the bow. But it was not days. Only a few hours perhaps until a hooded figure dressed in a white robe opened the door and motioned for me to follow. I could not wonder, could not worry at how close we might be to those who would do us harm. I was already half removed from the plane of ordinary existence.

Yet my inner senses stirred at the direction we walked. The light that danced on the stone floor was torchlight disrupted by moving shadows. Where I had expected silence, because Catrin would not speak to me until we were ready to begin, there were voices.

"Shall we not be introduced to this extraordinary physician?" The cold voice cut into my ease like a knife blade across the palm of my hand, but instantly I shoved it away to a distance so immensely remote it could not affect my composure.

The woman shook her hooded head and motioned toward the stone table. Her white robe shifted softly in the faint breeze, sculpting her form, and the ripple passed through the warp and weft of the world into my being. Strange.

"Bring him in," the man said.

There was the sound of struggling, a low moan of desperation, a snarl of hatred. The victim. Questions flitted across my mind like the feathery detritus of mingallow trees in spring bloom. How was it that we were to be with the victim? Had Catrin managed to take Ysanne's place? I kept my eyes down and held my concentration, not allowing the words to settle. Only when I knelt on the cold stone beside the little pool and saw the ravaged face—the flicker of ice-blue hatred in a visage so racked with pain and dread, I could not bear to look on it—only then did I come near breaking. He was strapped to the stone slab and his wrists already bled from his struggles to be free. His mouth worked as if he wanted to speak, but no intelligible word emerged, only foaming spittle. When the woman with the white robe held a cup to his lips, forcing him to drink the potion that would keep him quiet and still as we did our work, he spit it out, staining her white robe.

I will come for you. As I said it in the stillness of my waiting, the mad blue eyes darted toward me, but I averted my head so he could not see, and I banished him from my thoughts.

"You don't mean for us to leave him with these two, Lord Korelyi? With Lord Kastavan already dead. . . ." The voice from behind me was filled with doubt.

"We'll be close by."

"But you can't trust them?"

"We have every reason to trust them. We have made a bargain and will see it fulfilled. No need to worry, Zyat. Our new friend will be very well looked after. Lord Kastavan's legacy lives on in this prince. As soon as he is healed of this lingering madness, all will be well." Their steps rang on the stone paving and faded.

There was a long pause. The air about me grew thick with sorcery. I waited.

At last it came. "It is time, Warden," said the woman who knelt opposite me across the tormented body. "Come with me if you choose again this path of danger, of healing, of hope."

My skin tingled with her speaking . . . not with the ancient words that had been scribed in my soul with fire when I was seventeen, but with the soft voice, so close I could hear its music and feel its shape. Not Catrin's voice. Nor were the pale slender hands that reached out across my friend's body Catrin's short, capable fingers.

And into my mind came the words. *Step onto the path I have built for you and know that I will hold it steadfast, unyielding, until you return. And in this distant world you venture, my dearest love, you will never be alone.*

As I touched the hands and the world disappeared, I caught one glimpse of dark hair streaked with gold, and deep violet eyes so ravishing a poet could find no words to describe them. Ysanne.

Chapter 34

The portal stood open, a shimmering gray rectangle in the nothingness in which I existed. Before me lay the doom of the world. Behind me, wavering like a painted image on a square of sheerest silk, lay the overgrown ruins of the ancient bathhouse and a life that was suddenly so precious that every second I clung to it was a piercing sweetness.

The path was steady beneath my feet. Ysanne's path. So much had become clear with that moment's glimpse of her violet eyes. Catrin had never made a second portal. It was Ysanne who had drawn me into her weaving in Dael Ezzar, able to take me across the boundaries of reality unprepared because she knew me as well as I knew myself. She had shut the first portal after Rhys so he would think me abandoned . . . dead . . . and she had held the second long enough for me to get out. She had ventured so far from home, into danger that no Queen of Ezzaria had ever before faced, so that I would have time to be ready. "Soar high, my love." No wonder I could not attach those words to Catrin or to feel the bond of the spirit that should have come with such intimacy. Ysanne . . .

Later, my beloved. When the day is won. The finger of her care brushed my lips before I could speak her name aloud and break the enchantment we had woven together. Later. I would not fail. Not with such a promise. I centered my thoughts on my purpose, and stepped to the threshold.

The world that lay before me was very near its ending. A leaden sky hung low over a vast gray ocean, the only remnant of life the threads of white foam where the sluggish tide broke upon a desolate strip of shingle. No bird flew in that mournful sky; neither bone nor scrap of weed lay on the dismal shore to give evidence that life had ever existed there. The shingle might have been the last fragments left as the relentless pressure of the sea crumbled the world. A thick damp wind stirred my cloak as I stepped through the doorway.

I stood on the rocky shore between the advancing ranks of the waves and a line of low cliffs some fifty paces from the water. The insistent whisper of the waves was almost indistinguishable from the soft buffeting of the wind. It was very difficult to see, the only light coming from the livid iridescence of the breakers. I shifted my vision and crouched low, pivoting quickly to scan the vicinity for signs of demon. Nothing moved save the water. Slowly I moved down the rugged shore, peering into the deepest pockets of rocky darkness, tasting the salty wind, straining to hear the first traces of demon music. Somewhere the Gai Kyallet—the Lord of Demons—lay waiting.

"I am the Warden, sent by the Aife, the scourge of demons, to challenge you for this vessel. Hyssad! Begone! It is not yours." The words fell dead. Feeble in the vast emptiness. Yet they should force the demon to take shape and answer.

Mirthless laughter greeted my declaration. "It's a bit late for such pompous speeches, is it not? This is exactly my place, and there is no human vermin can budge me. Certainly not my own hireling, come to perform the last service I require. Do you forget your piteous groveling, when you begged for your life and bartered power for your soul?"

It was the voice of evil that whispered through the unholy quiet, a muted sigh that clung to the soul like a foul odor, that fell upon the ear like whispered wailing, that lingered on the tongue like ash. Yet I smiled as I heard it. The demon did not know who I was. Aleksander had not broken.

I would not parry speech with the demon. With every word it would learn more of me and spoil my small advantage. Instead I picked apart the darkness, hunting for any glimmer of demon fire, listening for any sound that was not wind or wave. Never had I seen such an expanse of nothing. Was this all that was left of Aleksander? A pale smear of light drew my eyes to the right, even as Catrin's warning flickered through my mind. I could not afford to look for Aleksander. The light was swallowed by the murk before I could see what it was.

The strip of shingle narrowed, and soon there was nowhere to go but into the sea. I had no intention of stepping into the water—a notorious lurking place for wicked surprises—so I removed my cloak and my shirt, stuffed them under a rock in case I needed them later, and triggered the enchantment that would cause me to transform. As my back and shoulders began to burn, I walked back the way I had come, pausing in the lee of a massive boulder just long enough to bring my wings under control as they materialized. The final moment of transformation was a dangerously vulnerable time. But soon I was able to read the wind and shape it to lift me from the rocky beach and take me a short distance out over the water so I could get a better view. Where was the demon?

"Come, servant. Where have you gone?" hissed my adversary from within my head as well as outside. "I feel you hunting. Is that needful? Your posturing has come to an end, as you knew it would, and you must pay the price. Aid me in this conquest and kneel before me, and perhaps you will survive to share in the changing of the world."

I had faced a hundred demons in my life, many of them bound so intimately with their evil hosts that they had taken on their names and personalities. But this one . . . it had absorbed the corruption of a thousand hosts throughout its existence. Every vileness a human could devise was given form in its words. It had taken on a life of its own—perverse, corrupt, unclean—that came cascading out of its mouth in a vile vomit of hatred. At last I recognized the missing piece of the Khelid mystery. I had wondered how Kastavan could cast away his life so easily and allow the demon to move on to Aleksander. But it had not been Kastavan's choice at all. The Khelid had not bent the demons to their service; it was the other way around. The Khelid had been nothing but a succulent opportunity for a demon who had grown into its own purpose and was determined to take its place in the world.

I glided over the water's edge looking back toward shore to seek out the demon, and there ahead of me, across the rolling deadness of the sea at the end of the shingle, loomed a monstrous blackness. The smell that wafted from it told me that it was what I sought.

On the day I crawled out of Balthar's coffin, drowned in filth and shame and hopeless terror, I had been forced to strip the bodies of Ezzarians who had lain dead in the summer heat for the three days I was buried. I had believed that nothing could ever cleanse that stench from my nostrils. Time had done the impossible, but now as I flew toward the shapeless darkness, the same stink floated on the wind.

I circled once to get a lungful of the clearer air over the water, changed the silver knife into a longsword, then I stretched my wings straight behind and plummeted toward the monster. It seemed the size of the Derzhi Summer Palace, but was probably no larger than one of the towers. I could make no assessment of its vulnerability in the darkness, but I could certainly not count on any sunrise to give me a better view, so I relied on surprise and strength, plunging the sword into the beast with all the force of my dive. Quickly I wrenched out the weapon, streaked upward, then came down on another side. The beast was made of flesh, not armor or scales, a thin, tough outer hide stretching over rippling bulges of gelatinous tissue. When I pulled out the sword, large globs of the stinking mess came off in my hands, while the outer hide grew over the wound instantly, like cooling grease on a pot of stew.

The beast shuddered when I yanked out the sword the first time, and when I stabbed it again, a low growl rumbled at the edge of hearing, so dreadful in its timbre that sweat beaded on my forehead and between my shoulder blades. The sultry air held the stink close.

Stab. Withdraw. Fly upward. Circle and stab again. And again.

A ferocious roar exploded from beside me as I struck, shattering one of my ears. It felt like a knife had been driven into my head, and hot fluid flowed down my left cheek.

Again. Stab. Withdraw. This time when I flew upward, a thick arm of darkness reached after me, shredding my breeches above my boots and raking my thigh with acid tendrils. No question I had hurt it. I struck again.

"Who comes here? I will know you!" It didn't matter that one of my ears was useless. The words vibrated in my bones, and the world itself began to writhe in pain. The darkness folded in upon itself. The sky swelled like boiling syrup. The restless ocean behind me exploded in inky waterspouts that clawed at the burgeoning clouds. And behind the tumult I perceived a soundless cry of such hopeless torment that I almost dropped my sword and fell from the sky.

Aleksander. His agony threatened to rip the weaving of the world. Such violent madness made it almost impossible for an Aife to maintain her enchantment. She had to hold all of it in her mind. From every expression of Aleksander's being, she drew a thread that she wove into the unpatterned weft of the world's essence, giving it shape and substance. I walked upon the threads of her creation, breathed the air she shaped from them. The water of this ocean could drown me; the stones crush or support me. And if her threads snapped too quickly, we would both be lost . . . and Aleksander would go mad.

To my right a pale light flickered, but I could pay it no heed. A thick tendril had wrapped itself about my ankle and was pulling me toward a gaping maw awash in luminescent green drool. I slashed at the writhing arm, cursing myself for the distraction.

Forget Ysanne. Forget Aleksander. Concentrate or you'll be dead.

"The slave! It is my own slave who comes sneaking in here claiming to be a warrior."

The timbre of the voice had changed. Sneering contempt.

Bone-chilling softness. Agonizing familiarity. I refused to listen to the sound or what it signified. I circled the thrashing monster and landed on the rocks. Standing amid the gross remnants of the beast flesh, I struck upward at the stinking bulk. But before my blade could reach it, it vanished.

"Shall we play a game, slave?" The voice slithered past my useless ear. "Let's make this a merry hunt. Come find me. Show me your warrior's skills." A laugh from behind me had me spinning in my tracks. A man stood a hundred paces away, hands on his hips. His face was only a blur in the darkness, but I could not mistake the tall, lean shape. He retreated, running and laughing, and I gathered the wind and took after him. I traversed the length of the shore, but I could not find him, so I caught an updraft and soared above the cliffs.

The face of the land was as I had already seen, a broken and scarred wasteland. Great slabs of rock were tilted crazily one upon the other. Cracks and fissures scarred the wide barrens, so deep they glowed red in the darkness as if the land were bleeding from a violent lashing. The heat rose from the molten deeps, buffeting me as I flew. Where would he go? Why lead me on this chase?

The land broke upward into mountainous ridges. I settled to the top of a narrow shoulder of rock that allowed me to see back across the wastes to the cliffs and the sea, and forward into the mountains. I needed to think.

A cold wind blew off the mountains, pelting me with grit from the ridge top as I tried to come up with a plan. I could explore for days and never find him if he chose to stay hidden. An Aife could hold for a day; Ysanne for a few hours more than most. But there was no precedent for a demon that would not reveal itself when challenged.

"Hear me . . ." The whisper was almost indistinguishable from the wind. The pale smear of light I'd seen earlier glimmered a few paces ahead of me. ". . . danger . . . the fortresses . . . Parnifour. . . ." I stared at a wavering image of Aleksander taking form in front of me, and I strained to

make sense of the words with my damaged hearing . . .
when I sensed a movement of air behind me. I whirled
about, just in time to avoid having one wing sliced from my
back. The sword left only a long tear in the wing, but a deep,
fiery gash in my left side.

The figure behind me gave voice to my doubts. "Can you
fly with only one of those grotesque appendages?" Aleksander—a fully fleshed image instead of the wraithlike
glimmer. His blood-streaked sword was pressed tight
against my own. "A slave with aspirations of glory. Can't
permit that." He whipped his blade around and lunged. I
parried, and we fought up and down that ridge, moving so
quickly a human eye could have seen nothing but a blur.

I did not let his face deceive me. He was no more Aleksander than was the gelatinous creature on the shore. Unfortunately, he was also no less. He had Aleksander's skills and
reflexes joined with the demon's speed and tirelessness. And
he knew my moves. Aleksander had watched me train, cri-
tiqued my form for two weeks. I could not make a move he
failed to counter. We battled for an hour or more on that narrow strip of rock. I left a bloody streak on his arm, but he
had me to my knees. Though I got out of it, I took another
wound on the right thigh and another painful rent in my left
wing. I was considering a leap from the edge of the cliff to
give myself a moment to breathe, but the demon was relentless, and I wasn't sure the damaged wing would hold. A
shard of rock broke off under my foot, and I slipped backward, my left leg dangling over the edge. I was afraid that in
the moment's vulnerability, I was going to lose a limb or an
eye or my life. But in the same instant, the demon Aleksander stepped back, laughing, and stretched his arms to the
sides in invitation. "Find me, slave. You know me well . . .
as I know you. You don't say what you're thinking, but now
I am joined with this being of power, I can read it for myself.
You can hide from me no longer. I know your name, and I
will use it to bind you in heavier chains than you had before.
You will fear me at last, and there will be no end to it. But
not yet. I want to enjoy this little duel a while longer. It gives

me pleasure to watch you pursue your own doom. For the present you must use everything you know of me to seek me out. Your oath commands it." He laughed uproariously. "You see? You have always been a slave and will never be anything else." Then he vanished.

I crawled back onto the ridge top and lay gulping for air, the sharp rocks cutting into my face and chest. The wind whined off the mountains, making me shiver as my sweat dried. I had to force myself to keep breathing in spite of the wound in my side, which burned with the slightest movement. The cut in my thigh was less painful, but was bleeding heavily, so I tore a strip from my shredded breeches to bind it.

I didn't understand the demon's game. He could have had me. But I dared not sit still, lest he change his mind. So I summoned the wind and gingerly flexed my damaged wing. The same sensitivity that enabled me to feel the slightest variation in the air ensured that there was no such thing as a "mild" tear. But I let the wind do most of the work, and made sure I was no more than an arm span from the ground until I was sure it would hold. My course was wobbly, with an alarming tendency to curve to the left and downward as I favored my left side. But after a time I learned to compensate and put aside any thought of it. There were more important concerns.

Where would the demon hide? It was no use wondering why. I had to find him. Ysanne could not hold indefinitely. My injuries weren't going to get any better. I hunted up and down the valleys, using every trick of discernment I possessed. Several times I caught sight of the ghostly shimmer, but I ignored it. I could not allow myself to conjure such imaginings of Aleksander. It had almost gotten me killed, and I couldn't help him if I was dead. Yet the apparition was persistent. As I entered a valley that looked eerily like Capharna, I heard the whispering again. ". . . danger . . . the border castles . . . portal . . . warn . . ." Words designed to catch my attention. To make me vulnerable. I was vulnerable enough.

Where would Aleksander hide? Sleet bit at my skin, and frost coated my eyelashes as I flew deeper into the mountains, where, buried in a snow-clad valley, I found the corpse of Capharna. Charred timbers had fallen against the stones of broken towers, all rimed with frost to make it an eerie white in the black midnight. Carefully I explored the ruins of the Summer Palace, the kitchens where iron stoves lay rusting, the graceful galleries now collapsed, their treasures scattered, tapestries ripped and rotting under a blanket of filthy snow. I leaped from one pile of rubble to another, until I reached the great throne hall where Aleksander's life had crumbled. The wall at the inner end where I had hidden behind the brass grillwork still stood, but the domed roof had fallen in, its brilliantly colored mosaics shattered and scattered like colored sleet amid the destruction. The Lion Throne lay crushed beneath a fallen column, the virile beast itself staring upward, helpless under the mass of stone. Fitting.

". . . must listen . . . their plan . . . open to Khelidar . . . beg you listen . . ." Haunting desperation from the wraith that shimmered in the gloom. But every lesson of my life demanded that I stay apart, especially in that place where the specter of my captivity walked with the other ghosts. The vision was so real that I could feel iron bands about my wrists and gnawing helplessness in my belly.

I shook it off. It was a ruse to distract me. To make me weak.

". . . for the love of the gods, hear me . . . danger under the mountains. Parnifour, Karn'Hegeth, all of them . . ."

Despising myself, I turned my back on the apparition.

"Where are you?" I screamed. "Come out and be done with this foolery!"

I clambered over the stones, snow swirling into my face.

"Have you come back to your proper place, slave?" Searing fire ripped across my shoulders, a brutal lash knocking me to my knees.

But this time I would not stay down. I gathered all of my strength and infused it with my anger, then I brought my gathered right wing around with the force of a whirlwind. The demon Aleksander looked astonished as he slammed into the standing wall. I transformed the silver knife into a spear and launched it at the slumped figure, but in the instant before it struck, he disappeared.

"Face me, coward," I screamed. "Who is it has forgotten his place? You are no prince, but a nightmare lingered too long into day. Hyssad! His soul is not yours. His body is not yours. His life is not yours. I will not allow it." I yanked the spear from the dirt and summoned the wind.

"Your prating rings hollow unless you find me." No laughter this time. "If you don't do it soon, your Aife will never wake from her enchantment, and you will live here with me for eternity. Your past servitude will be as honey to the gall of my lash. Find me, slave." The world shuddered once more with the silent horror of Aleksander's torment.

I spiraled upward from the ruined city, trying to decide where to hunt next. The demon was correct in every point. My victory in one skirmish was of no significance whatsoever. The wind tore at my ragged left wing, and every effort to straighten my course pumped blood from the wound in my side. The blow I'd struck had ripped the gash wide open. The cut in my thigh throbbed, and the acid burns on my thighs and knees had blistered so badly I had to cut off the tatters of my breeches to keep them from flapping against them.

Where would Aleksander hide? Where would he feel safe? Desert. The dune seas where he was born . . . where he would race his horses, the sands in a cloud behind him . . . where he could see his enemies for leagues around . . . where the stark beauties of sun and sand in a thousand subtle shadings fed his soul. But I could find no desert in the dark realm Ysanne had woven. No sun. Parched, lifeless ground, but not the serene openness of Aleksander's home. For endless hours I made long sweeps across the landscape, feeling my strength and the precious time leaking away with my blood. At last I stood on the cliff tops overlooking the boundary of the desolate sea, where I had stepped through the portal.

Ah, fool. See what is before you. The sky was not lifeless, any more than Aleksander's desert was lifeless. Winging its way through the low clouds was a bird, a solitary patch of white against the looming darkness. I smiled and launched myself from the cliff, ignoring the sticky warmth on the arm I had kept pressed to my side as I rested, ignoring the fresh trickling wetness below my ribs. Across the uneasy waves I followed the bird, sure that I would find what I sought in the midst of the watery desert. "Thank you, my love," I whispered, and a soft breath of wind caressed my cheek.

It was an island fortress, poking up from the gray water like a fist. I circled, hunting for some weakness, and I believed I'd found it on the battlements, where a small wooden door led into one of the towers. I landed on a stone parapet and changed the silver knife into an ax.

"Come out," I said. "There's nowhere else to hide." I raised the ax. The wraith appeared before me, holding out its hands as if to stay my blows. I paid it no mind, but struck the door. Twice. Three times. The wood began to splinter. My anger, my impatience, everything pent up for sixteen years was mustered into the blows of that ax. I could have destroyed the stone battlement itself with my fury.

But the wraith took on more solid form . . . Aleksander's form. It did not speak, but brandished a quite lethal sword, threatening me away from the door.

"So you've come out," I said. "I thank you for not forcing me to dismantle your refuge. Shall we get this done?"

The wraith did not speak and did not attack, just held its ground. So I changed my ax for a sword and went after it. I had no time for games. A blizzard of feints and blows. Ordinarily the wings gave me more in power, flexibility, and mobility than they hampered in weight, but not that day. The shredded one had little strength and could not furl tightly when I needed it to. Yet even so, I did not fall, for never did the apparition attack. When I stepped back, it did also. I could not understand it. What was it defending, when it had summoned me there?

"Can you not find me?" The voice came, not from the Aleksander I had been fighting, but from a second apparition that materialized just behind me. Hoping I would not have to fight both at once, I gave him no time to taunt. I spun, ducked a wicked slash, and grazed his shoulder with an upward cut. He growled and came after me. Advantage. Disadvantage. Forward. Backward. Battle unending . . . unrelenting . . . unthinking . . . no difference between the blade and the arm that wielded it. I became a whirlwind, a hurricane of edged steel and anger . . . and every time I gained an advantage, he would disappear and shift position. I knew how to manage such a fight. Each time he began anew, I watched and learned how the manifestation was to be different, and I adjusted my technique. Eventually we would finish it. Eventually he would make a mistake. I would not falter. I would not.

Across the battlements, up onto the merlons, teetering on the edge of the vast drop to the rocks and the sea with my left wing weak and dragging, my lungs on fire, half of my body slathered in blood that I feared was mostly my own. The demon laughed and dropped back to the battlement. I leaped from my merlon across to another, closer, ready to sweep down on him . . . when he vanished.

In mindless, exhausted rage I switched the sword to the ax again and attacked the door. It was almost off its hinges. "Come out. Come out and fight. No more play. Finish it."

"Breach these walls, and you will have the battle you desire." The voice echoed in my head.

I swung again, but the silent wraith stepped forward and insisted on preventing me. Why were there two of them? How was it possible? Maybe this one wasn't there at all. The blood flowed unchecked from my side and my leg. I was getting dizzy, seeing two or three of everything. I couldn't trust my seeing. Laughter and voices came from every side. ". . . help me . . . slave . . . get out and warn them . . . pitiful, groveling vermin . . ." I whipped my head from one side to another, trying to use my single working ear to judge where the demon might appear next.

Galadon's testing, Catrin's warnings drummed with my exhausted heartbeats. "Your senses are your last defense. Know when they are compromised. If you've lost, get out. Dying just to prove you cannot win profits nothing. Honor, pride, and foolhardy death are luxuries a Warden cannot afford." My knees were like straw. My sword arm quivered with the strain, scarcely able to lift the blade tip from the ground. I could not get a full breath without risk of passing out from the fire in my side.

It wasn't going to work. Even if I got the door open and found the demon, I had nothing left with which to fight. I stepped back, bent double with the pain in my side, heaving for breath and hoping I could hold myself together long enough to limp back to the portal. Another day. If I could survive . . . if Aleksander could hold . . . I could try again.

The silent apparition held back, protecting the door, his face pale and rigid, very like the face on a stone table so far away. Unyielding.

"I will free him," I said, defeat bitter on my tongue.

The specter nodded and reached for my sword, placing the tip in the center of its breast. I stared, uncomprehending.

Breach these walls . . . the service I require of you . . . aid me in this conquest. . . . Like a trumpet fanfare the echoes of the demon's taunting blared through my muddled head. I gaped at my blood-smeared sword and at the image of the Prince that stood before me. Aleksander. Not a mockery, not some monstrous concoction of demon shape-shifting, but the true image that bore his need and his desperation, that still fought to give me his message, though the demon had tormented him into silence.

And this place? Merciful Valdis, what was I doing? He had trusted me to understand. He had sent Kiril the note so that I would know he would be with me. Ready. But I'd failed to heed him. Instead, I'd led the demon right to his hiding place and done half the work to destroy it.

"Oh, my lord, I'm so sorry. Forgive me."

And now it was too late. Aleksander was calling on me to redeem my promise to kill him rather than leave him to become a monster, and I could not even do that. My sword slipped from my hand that could no longer grip, and clattered onto the stone. I tried to shape the wind, but a wave of dizziness overwhelmed me, and I sank to my knees. The chill of death crept into my body and my soul, while demon music began to twine itself about my limbs, and insinuate itself into my being, a sick, cold emptiness, a promise of unending misery and everlasting despair. As my life bled away, I called up spells to hold back the demon music. I croaked out words of protection and pressed my arm to my side to hold in the blood.

But I couldn't do it. I was not enough.

The wraith stood watching . . . waiting . . . his hand outstretched as if I still had something left to give him.

You are not alone. The whisper came from inside me and around me, a faint accompaniment to the clamor of the demon.

I wanted to laugh, but it came out a grotesque moan. Of course I was alone. I knew no other way. If I were the Warrior of Two Souls, perhaps I'd have another soul to give him. I shook my head. "I'm sorry."

But he did not withdraw his hand. Each one of us had pulled the other from the depths of pain and despair . . . in Capharna, in Avenkhar, in the mud of his kitchen yard, in the tower of the Summer Palace. Perhaps it had come around again. Perhaps it was that he had something left to give me. Aleksander had come to this place because I told him that if we combined my power and his strength, no one could stand against us. But I had not listened to myself. I had tried to do as I always had done . . . fight the battle alone. What if the Warrior of Two Souls was exactly that? Two . . . together.

With my last shred of will, I reached out.

A strong and gentle hand reached under my elbow, lifted me up, and guided me through the door into the fortress.

*   *   *

Time has little meaning within the human soul. We are as we have been since birth and as we will be until death and beyond, the changing landscape only the face of an unchanging spirit. I was not long in that luminous place that was Aleksander's refuge, the bit of himself he had managed to keep whole. The wraith disappeared as soon as I was inside. No words were exchanged, and I saw no further manifestation of Aleksander's body. It was only a few moments' rest and peace alone in the light. There was a fountain of cool, sweet water, and I gulped it down with the wry observation that I might see the stuff spouting out of all the holes in me. An observer might think I was part of the fountain. I bathed my face and washed the blood from my side and my leg. I believed it was Aleksander that had me laughing as I bound up my wounds with the shreds of my clothes. "Can't you keep yourself covered?" I imagined him saying. "I give you clothes and what do you do but lose them again? I thought Ezzarians were a modest people."

The storm of the demon's wrath was breaking on the walls as my weakness was washed away. "He will not breach them," I said as I stood up again, refreshed in body and spirit, trusting that the Prince would hear me. "Together we will have him out of here." And indeed when I stepped out upon the battlements and picked up my sword, Aleksander was with me, for my body and my wings shone with his silvery luminescence, casting light upon the dark ruins of his soul.

The Demon Lord came after me then, shifting forms as rapidly as the desert sand moves with the wind. His power was incredible, but no match for the combined power of Aleksander and me. A man with four eyes and six arms. We tangled him in a lightning bolt. A fire-tongued dragon. We confused it with torrents of rain and drove a spear into its throat. A raging shengar. I, we, laughed at that and took its head in one stroke. A beast of living stone. Images of Aleksander, of Ysanne, of Rhys, of Dmitri, of my father. But all were flawed. Now there was light to see with, the imperfections were clear. The demon did not know them any more than it knew me, any more than it knew the Warrior we had become. Aleksander had not revealed my name.

In the end it was the green heart of a three-headed serpent that I stabbed with the silver knife, while choking its meaty neck with a leg hold and blocking its six fangs with my damaged wing. I felt the heart stop beating under my fist, yet the body did not dissolve into a new and more ferocious monster as had happened every time thus far. My left hand clamped about the cool oval in the pouch that hung from my sword belt. With every breath of melydda I had left, I focused my sight and discerned the shape of the demon that was crawling from the serpent's body. *"Delyrae engaor. Hyssad!"* Look upon your nothingness and begone. The horrific wail as the demon looked upon itself in the Luthen mirror came near ruining my undamaged ear. The creeping shape grew still, paralyzed by seeing its own image. "Now is the time I present your choice," I said, my voice hoarse after the long hours of battle. "You have made a bargain with the Aife for all vessels known as the Khelid, based on this single combat. Your bargain is now forfeit. Do you yield and command your cohorts to yield?"

The grating horror that was demon speech hissed in my head. "You will pay for this, slave. Do not think our battle is over. There is another yet to come." But its words were empty. With much writhing and protest, the command was given.

When I was sure it was done, I continued. "For you, Gai Kyallet, there is no further choice. You are no longer an elemental spirit, a storm that returns its water to the sea when spent. You have taken on the mortal aspect of your victims, and you have violated the laws of humankind. Therefore in the name of the Queen of Ezzaria and the Emperor of the Derzhi, I declare your existence ended." And with my knife of silver, I killed it.

"It is done, my prince," I whispered, kneeling on the serpent's carcass. And as the dawn broke over the distant horizon, I summoned the wind to carry me back to the portal and Ysanne.

Chapter 35

I knew something wasn't right when I heard the bees forming words out of their incessant buzzing. I knew it was bees, because somewhere beyond my eyelids was a flickering pattern of light and shadow, and the delightful warmth on my face could be nothing but the morning sun. A perfectly reasonable place for bees. A stirring of air tickled my nose, its damp green scent speaking of the last coolness of morning before a hot day. I knew I ought to move before I got stung, but the warmth held me down as if the sunbeams carried the weight of lead. I decided to risk the bees just for the pleasure of staying where I was. And it was certainly intriguing to hear their speech.

". . . to leave . . . stubborn . . ."

". . . weeks, if ever . . . just don't know . . ."

I ought to listen more closely. My friend Hoffyd would want to know of bees that could speak. But someone must have stuffed my left ear with silk, for it didn't seem to work at all, and in order to free up the other one to listen more carefully, I would have to roll over. I was reluctant to try that, for my body sent a warning from one spot just below my left rib cage that I wasn't going to like moving. So I mumbled, "Speak up," hoping the bees might hear.

Instantly the words stopped, and I felt sorry for startling the creatures and missing the chance to find out what they said when they thought no one was listening.

"Seyonne?" A woman's voice, far away and very worried. That was worth opening an eye for.

The sunlight was exceedingly bright, and the patterns of

shadow were caused, not by bees, but by the fluttering leaves of an ash tree outside a tall window beside me. Somewhere in between me and the open window was a lovely face, smooth, red-gold skin. The woman had long black hair, and I could not bring her name to my tongue, but seeing her caused such a monstrous anxiety to rise up in me, that I thought my heart might wrench itself from my chest.

The dark-haired woman laid a finger on my lips. "She is well. She's gone back to Dael Ezzar for her safety and ours."

My fear soothed, I closed my eyes again and envisioned violet eyes and gold-brown hair that smelled of rainwashed grass, and I immersed myself in the image that had never left me in all the years I refused to speak her name. Ysanne. And, of course, on the heels of her name flowed the tide of waking memory . . . of the battle . . . and the demon. . . .

"I got back," I said, once the flood had subsided a bit and I opened my eyes to the present.

"You did. And a fine mess you were." And of course Catrin heard the real question, for she moved aside and let me see the room beyond her. A large, airy, pleasant room. Tall ceilings. A whole wall of windows like the one beside the luxurious bed on which I lay. From a deep chair nearby protruded a pair of knee-high leather boots. Their owner, whose head was propped on a long arm and whose snores I had mistaken for bees, sported a long red braid. When I glimpsed a sword dangling beside the long legs, I smiled.

"He has been with you every moment possible," said Catrin, lifting a cup of water to my lips. "If any man could will another back from the dead, I would believe him capable."

"Never doubt it," I croaked. "He has done exactly that."

"Is it impossible for an Ezzarian to let a man sleep?" The body in the chair shifted. "Some of us have had other things to do besides wallow in bed for a week and constantly threaten to die and thereby frighten two of the finest-looking women I've encountered since I knew what to do with my parts besides piss."

"A week . . ." I looked up at Catrin, and she nodded, her brows raised in sympathetic humor.

"You lost a great deal of blood," she said. "Do you have any idea of how long you were inside?"

"Long. A full day I'd guess." Though I spoke with Catrin, my eyes did not stray from the lean, smiling face that appeared over her shoulder.

"Three."

Three days beyond a portal. It was unthinkable. No wonder I couldn't move. And Ysanne . . . All the worries that had been eased cropped up again. "The Queen . . ."

"The Queen was very tired, but she suffered no ill effects. Now that I can trust you for a moment not to die"—Catrin bent over and kissed me on the forehead, then nodded to Aleksander—"I have things to do."

Three days. I worked at sitting up, a ridiculously difficult maneuver, as I was wrapped in a cocoon of bandages about my middle, my shoulder, and most of one leg. Every movement set off a barrage of fireworks inside my left ear and a pain in my side that felt as though one of the Demon Lord's monstrous manifestations had left its claw there.

Aleksander put his arm around my shoulders, and without my having to ask it, helped me out of bed, as if he knew I couldn't think straight wallowing in pillows. Once he'd got me into a chair, he went to stand by the hearth, propping one elbow on the mantelpiece. When his smile faded, the residue of pain and horror were etched clearly in his face.

Three days. "I'm sorry," I said. "I'm sorry I made it last so long."

He shook his head. "You owe me no apology. Quite the contrary." He stretched out his hands toward me, staring at them in wonder. "These are my own again. Such a gift . . ." He transferred his gaze to me. "I must believe that you understand the grace you have given me."

I tried to answer him, but he waved me off and continued. "I am called a priest of Athos, yet before seven days ago I could not tell anyone of a single moment of my life that was changed by the hand of a god. But on that day I saw a god's hand . . . you, with your wings spread, sword in hand, lighting the darkness inside me like the moon and the sun together. Athos, Druya, your Verdonne or Valdis—whatever the name, male or female—one of them sent you to save me. Never had I understood the truth of good and evil, of light and darkness, of the shapes they take in the world, of the depths of horror . . . or the glory that exists in beings that walk and breathe as I do. Daughters of night, Seyonne, why didn't I know? Why don't any of us know?"

It was very like the question Ezzarian children asked when they at last understood how different their life was to be from that of anyone else in the world. I gave the Prince the answer that had been given me. "Because someone must do the living—the eating and drinking, planting and birthing, the dancing and arguing and forgiving, all those things that are the proper business of life. They make the world strong enough, safe enough, joyous enough to be the bulwark against darkness. There are enough terrors in the world for demons to feed on without adding more. And if you remember . . . the light was yours."

A grin poked its way through his somber mood. "We did well, did we not?"

I raised the cup of water Catrin had left me. "Exceedingly well."

He poured wine and matched my toast, but as our eyes met over our cups, the smiles fell away. We had been one soul for those terrible hours, an intimacy so profound that the finest words wrought by poet or scholar to describe the event would seem but trivial prattling beside it. I had heard the screams of his uttermost pain and madness, and drunk from the fountain of his joy. He had witnessed the terrors of my loneliness and defeat, and shared with me the ecstasy of my transformation. Our eyes fell away quickly. We knew. There was nothing more to be said.

The Prince settled himself to the thick woven carpet and leaned against a chair, heaving a sigh and trying to begin a more mundane review of events. "Someday you will explain to me exactly what went on in these past days. I remember

going to the temple site, walking up the track and seeing Korelyi and Kastavan waiting for me. They asked if I was
ready to be healed of my affliction. I told them I was . . . and
from that time I saw things, thought things, felt things . . .
but I was never sure what was actually happening and what
was only . . . imagination or dreams or visions. They played
such havoc with my head, I couldn't tell what was real."
There was a slight tremor of remembered horror at the edge
of his words.

"Someday," I said. "If you wish. Let a little time pass,
and it will likely sort itself out on its own. For now you must
tell me how you fare and what's happened since. Where are
the Khelid? And Rhys . . . I never knew what became of
him."

Aleksander laughed, dismissing his own hurts with his
most reliable weapon. "I assumed you would have heard
everything we said while you slept."

"I can do a number of things that could surprise you, but
I can't read minds or see through walls or eyelids, whether
I'm sensible or insensible. And my hearing is about as acute
as that of a tree stump at present."

"Your friend Hoffyd—quite a ferocious fellow, I've discovered—took care of Rhys. Put something in his water
pitcher, he said, that knocked the villain over before they
began. The Queen arranged everything and brought you to
me instead of him . . . as Mistress Catrin says they planned
all along. Were you as surprised as I was?"

I nodded. "You have no idea."

"Hmm." He waited for me to say more, but there was
nothing to say. Not until I had a chance to speak to Ysanne.
When Aleksander saw that I wasn't going to elaborate, he
went on. "It took so long to get the business over with, the
treacherous bastard came to himself and disappeared. No
one knows where he's gone, though, one of Kiril's men reported that he was seen riding south with Korelyi, who also
managed to escape our sweep. The first I knew of anything
was when I woke up in that ruin with you on the floor carved
up like a roast pig, and your queen collapsed beside you.

Mistress Catrin was fussing over the two of you, while her one-eyed lover was asking me if I was mad or not and deciding whether he dared untie me. I had the bloodiest awful headache any man has ever endured, and he kept trying to make me be quiet. If I hadn't felt like I'd just had my entrails drawn through a sieve, I would have throttled him. But he finally got through to me that there were Khelid about, and that if you had won your battle, which he sincerely hoped, then they were going to be mightily angry and upset. I said I would take care of it."

"And did you?"

"I did. I commanded them to guard the temple site or I'd have their hearts out of their bodies." He grimaced. "I knew what words to use with them. I've used such threats often enough through the years. They were afraid and unsure, and they couldn't see that I wasn't . . . as I had been. So Hoffyd and Catrin and I got the two of you and brought you here— Kiril's house—and then I went and found my cousin exactly where I'd told him. He said you had told him that if he didn't hear within a day, he should leave, but being the stubborn Derzhi that he is, he waited and watched. Then we set out to root the Khelid out of their nest. . . ."

He told me what he had learned from the Demon Lord, the information he had tried so hard to impart to me, hoping that I could get out and use it even if he could not. The demon-Khelid had entrenched themselves in twenty cities around the borders of the Empire, and in each one had created a magical gateway to Khelidar. Through these gateways they could pour troops, as soon as Kastavan—or Aleksander—gave the word. The portals were still a risk, as the Khelid were determined to take the Empire, and the other nineteen garrisons would have time to recover from the shock of losing their demon cohorts. But Aleksander had also learned what was necessary to seal the portals—a simple enchantment that Hoffyd had been able to work once the Derzhi routed the Khelid from the border fortress. The Khelid were not exceptionally talented sorcerers.

". . . and now I have to get word of this to Lydia's fa-

ther . . . and mine . . . else the Khelid will continue to bring
troops through the other gateways. Hoffyd says that Derzhi
magicians can work these closing spells if they're taught."
The Prince lost his animation and gave me a weak smile.
"So I'm on my way to stick my head in the old lion's mouth.
I'm glad you chose to rouse yourself today. Kiril is ready to
go."

"Your cousin?" My head was still muddled, for I couldn't
see where he was leading.

"He's taking me to my father. There's an imperial 'summons' out for me, and orders to arrest anyone who hinders
me from answering it—which means anyone who helps me.
So to ensure Kiril's safety . . . and to make sure he is listened to even if I am not . . . I've asked him to escort me to
Zhagad under guard."

"But if your father still thinks you mad . . ."

"He'll lock me away for the rest of my life, take a new
young wife, and make sure he has another heir. My mother
will be ill-humored, don't you think? And if he agrees that I
am not mad, but still believes I killed Dmitri, he will take
my head and do the same. So I must convince him that I'm
not mad and that I didn't kill Dmitri." He did not look confident. "I'll keep the Ezzarians out of it. I've a number of
witnesses among Kiril's men as to what was found in the
fortress here. My father knows the Khelid can do magic beyond our own practice of it, so perhaps he'll believe they
could control me in some way. About Dmitri . . . I'll just
have to tell him what in the name of the gods I thought I was
doing." He shook his head. "Was ever a man so stupid as I
have been?"

"I can think of a number of instances," I said, and proceeded to demonstrate the point. "Are there perhaps some
clothes around here?" I was clad in nothing but a thin sin-
glet.

Aleksander frowned. "What are you thinking?"

"I'm thinking I've never seen Zhagad, and it would be
well to visit it before the season gets too far toward summer.

And I'm in no condition to fight bandits along the way, so I'd best go with the surest protection I can find."

"Absolutely not. I forbid it." He was on his feet, and I thought he might pick me up and throw me back in the bed. "Have you forgotten?" He clamped his fingers on my left arm and pulled my shoulder forward slightly. "What will you say when someone sees this mark and puts you back in chains? I can't protect you. Not until my own business is done . . . and you know as well as I how unlikely that is to come out well. And Kiril has too little influence to help you. He's risking everything to take me in." He let go of my arm and strode to the door. "You've done enough. You are free. Go home and make love to your wife."

But I had not done enough, not until the demon's plot was completely unraveled. "If I am a free man, my lord, then you cannot prevent my going. And in case you've forgotten, my home remains under the yoke of the Derzhi. And I have no wife . . . not as long as Rhys is alive."

"Then, go chase the bastard and cut his throat. Leave me to sort out my own mess. It's time I learned how." With no further farewell, he left.

But in two hours more when Aleksander rode out of the gates of Parnifour, escorted by his cousin and twelve Derzhi warriors, I rode along, tucked in a wagon alongside piles of confiscated weapons and the other evidence of the Khelid conspiracy that Kiril had collected in the raid on the border fortress. Aleksander did not know I was there until we were too far down the road to send me back. Kiril, less concerned for my safety than Aleksander's, had been willing to risk his cousin's wrath to enlist my help.

Catrin had been slightly more difficult to persuade. "We need you in Dael Ezzar, Seyonne," she had said when she found me struggling to get on my boots. "All these demons you've just dispossessed . . . what do you think is going to happen? A year for them to regenerate, and we will see such an onslaught of demon madness as the world has never experienced. If they've all grown into this human evil . . ."

"Then, go back and get your students trained. A few

weeks and I'll be there to help. I promise. But if Aleksander's father executes him, we will have lost after all. The
world is going to change, Catrin. I know it. We've got to ensure it changes for the better."

She probed deep with her dark eyes. "And what of the
Queen? You've had no chance to speak with her."

"When I come back, I will serve her in whatever way she
commands."

"Serve her?" I thought Catrin's indignation might set my
hair ablaze. "Are you blind? She never betrayed you, Seyonne. Never. Will you not give her hearing? How can you—"

I laid my hand on her flushed cheeks. "I walked her portal, Catrin, so I understand more than you think. But she
knows, and you know, that nothing can be done. We were
not wed when I was taken. She was free to marry, and she
did. Her husband lives. Such an oath as marriage cannot be
voided because one party is not worthy. Therefore I can be
nothing to her, not without risking the very ill that Rhys
brought upon himself. Beyond that . . . she knows my
heart."

Three weeks later I stood with the Prince on a rocky
height and looked across a sea of red-gold sand at Zhagad.
The pink spires and golden domes of the capital city rose
from the desert as if sculpted by whimsical fingers, while on
the western horizon the red sun lingered, as if reluctant to
yield its mastery of the world when such a fair sight lay before it.

"Ah, gods of day and night, it is beautiful, is it not?" said
the Prince, ruffling Musa's mane. "There is no city in the
world so marvelous. Wait until you see the flowers. You'll
think your own sorcerers must live there to make it bloom
so."

I stood beside him, reveling in the pleasure of feeling
more like myself and invigorated by the cooling evening
after the sapping heat of the afternoon. For two long weeks
of the three-week journey I had ridden in the wagon. In the
first I woke from uncomfortable sleep only long enough to

eat and drink and have one of Kiril's men help me change my bandages. The second week I spent shoving aside the piles of confiscated swords and spears and lances that kept crowding me into the corner of the wagon bed, while I read the evidence that rode in the wagon with me. There were map rolls of the entire Empire, sketches of fortifications, reports of Derzhi troop positions from every posting in the Empire, and letters from Kastavan detailing everything from guard schedules in the imperial residence to the ways the water supply of Zhagad might be compromised. I studied every scrap of paper as we traveled, and I was sorely afraid the evidence was not enough. In none of the correspondence, notes, or reports was there any mention of either Dmitri or Aleksander. Perhaps the Prince could convince his father that his mind was intact and the Khelid were traitors, but there was nothing to prove him innocent of murder.

One long, leather traveling case was sealed with an enchantment. Kiril's men said it had belonged to Lord Kastavan, but the locks scorched their fingers when they tried to open it. After half a day of false starts, I managed to get past the spell, but found only the Khelid's clothing and a casket crammed with gems and jewelry: necklaces, pendants, bracelets, and rings of every variety. I threw it all back into the case and slammed the lid in disgust. Aleksander was going to die if he couldn't come up with something beyond his own guilty conscience to explain why he had confessed to the murder. A guilty conscience was something Ivan was unlikely to understand.

By the third week of the journey, I was willing to do anything to get out of the wagon, even to riding double with a soldier who had likely not bathed since the ritual washing at his birth. The discomfort was made doubly bad by the fact that we were entering the heart of the Azhaki desert. We were continually starting and stopping—the Derzhi method of preserving their horses' stamina on long desert treks; therefore it was impossible for me to sleep. After a few days Kiril had mercy and let me ride one of his packhorses.

Aleksander was subdued. He rode alone or with Kiril,

scarcely speaking. Every day he would ask after my health and comfort, but he did not speak to me privately at any time. Kiril's men were curious as to my position, a foreigner neither slave, nor servant, nor companion, but they were well disciplined and treated me respectfully, as their commander required.

But on that last evening the Prince had motioned me to ride with him up the rocky ridge, while the rest of the party waited behind. To my surprise Aleksander removed Musa's saddle once we had dismounted. Then he walked to the edge of the rocks, and as we looked across the desert to the Pearl of Azhakstan, he folded his arms in front of him and took a deep breath, half laughing as he did so. "Stupid that I should be more afraid of this than giving myself to a demon."

"You never believed in demons," I said.

"It's not the dying that bothers me so much. I'd not have him withhold justice for the sake of blood ties. But I hate him thinking that I could take Dmitri's life for my own petty grievances."

I had no words of comfort. "I'll be close by," I said. "Whatever you need of me, you have only to ask."

Aleksander laid a hand on my shoulder. "I'll have to fight this one alone, my guardian. And no use delaying. Stay close to Kiril."

As the sun sagged low on the horizon, he threw himself on Musa's bare back and pulled his scarf around his mouth and nose. With a long lingering whoop and a touch of his heel, he and the horse flew down the path and across the rippling waves of sand. Never had I seen such joy in a physical being as I saw in Aleksander on that evening, as he raced across the desert raising a storm of purple and gold behind him.

Chapter 36

The rest of us followed Aleksander across the desert more slowly, Kiril holding his men back firmly when they tried to release their own exuberance. Only when we came to the first of the monumental stone lions that guarded the approaches to Zhagad did we catch up to the Prince. He stood waiting beside Musa, stroking the horse's graceful neck. A grim Kiril dismounted and removed something from his saddle pack before walking to where his cousin waited. I nudged my mount close enough to hear.

"Ah, Zander, are you sure of this?"

Aleksander did not speak. He opened his arms, and the two embraced fiercely until the Prince pushed his cousin away and drew his sword. Kiril's men stiffened in their saddles, but Aleksander reversed the weapon and presented it, hilt first, to his cousin.

"Until you reclaim it," said Kiril, attaching the weapon to his own belt.

Aleksander nodded and held out his hands. Without meeting his cousin's steady gaze, Kiril bound Aleksander's wrists together with silken cord. The two Derzhi mounted up again, and Kiril gave his men a curt command. One of them took Musa's reins, and the rest fell in close about Aleksander. There was no deeper humiliation for a Derzhi than to be forced to yield the reins of his mount.

Night had dropped over the desert, and the soldiers lit torches to lead us on our way down the Emperor's Road. On either side of us loomed the paired stone lions designed to strike the heart with awe and terror of the Derzhi and their

Empire. It was a road Aleksander should have ridden in triumph, as the anointed Emperor-in-waiting. He should have heard the cheers of his subjects instead of the silence of the desert. He should have worn gold and diamonds, not a prisoner's bonds—even ones of silk. He should have ridden in the shining glory of his god, but he passed in the night, and the torchlight flickered from light to shadow on the empty eyes of the massive lions, as if the beasts were closing their eyes in shame.

Aleksander displayed no shame. He held his back straight and his head high. His demeanor was haughty and cold, even when we passed through the towering gates that marked the outer ring of the city, and the people began to gather to see their disgraced prince come home. His name rippled through the city like the night wind, stirring the people from the lamplit courtyards, where they sat sipping tiny cups of steaming nazrheel. His name fluttered through the graceful houses and from stone benches around the flower-bordered public wells, where people sat gossiping with friends in the cooling evening.

Though I wore the desert robes, and it was unlikely anyone could see the mark on my face, I could not help but be uneasy as the crowd gathered. I felt their eyes on my back, probing, curious, and found myself searching the sea of faces for eyes that knew more of seeing than ordinary senses. So many Derzhi. A few of the ever-present Manganar, who seemed to enjoy the hard work of empire that other warrior races disdained. Suzaini merchants. Slender Kuvai who gathered around the foundries and art studios of the great cities. Few Thrid, for the dark-skinned mercenaries were not comfortable in commercial centers and tended to stay in their own lands.

Foreboding hung over us like arrows aimed at our backs. I shifted my senses, looking for vengeful Khelid, but it was not a Khelid that brought me up short. What in the name . . . ? For one brief moment, I caught sight of a pair of dark slanted eyes, something like those of a fish, set on the surface of a broad face. Rhys! He was glaring straight at me as if he could see through the scarf that was wound about my face. Why would Rhys come to Zhagad? He was lost instantly in the mass of bodies as we rode through the second ring of stone into the heart of the city.

Only Derzhi were allowed to live within the inner walls of Zhagad. And the closer we got to the Imperial Palace, the bolder was the crowd. They pressed against Kiril's soldiers. "Murderer . . . his kinsman . . . for shame . . . madman . . . Athos, spare us a monster . . . kin-murderer . . . madman."

Kiril and his men held the surging crowd away from Aleksander, and once, when the people blocked the way entirely, the young dennissar shouted angrily. "He submits himself to the Emperor. The Emperor will judge. Not you."

Without moving his head or shifting his eyes from their position straight ahead of him, Aleksander whispered a quiet word to Kiril. The young Derzhi said no more, just forged a way through the churning mob to the Palace steps. Once there, we dismounted, and Kiril marshaled his men about Aleksander, motioning me to stay close beside him. I was swept up the broad steps and through the vast atrium of the Imperial Palace with the rest. There was no time to stare at the grandeur; I got only a fleeting impression of the soaring height of the ceilings, the brilliant colors of the murals, and the graceful arches that led whispered breezes through the cool stone. I blessed the trailing white scarf I had been given to wrap about my face to keep out blowing sand and prying eyes.

Kiril conferred with a half-naked man of awesome physical perfection, who wore three earrings in one ear and a braid that reached below his waist. He must be the padish, the Emperor's Lidunni bodyguard. I had heard that the Lidunni could snap a man's spine without taking a second breath. On seeing him, I believed it. With a nod the padish led us across a circular atrium, ringed with columns, and he opened a pair of wooden doors five times a man's height.

Ivan sat on a raised dais at one end of a spare, undecorated room, a council room as it appeared, for it had several long tables rowed up around the sides with dark cushions piled up behind. No one reclined on the cushions at present. The padish took up a position to the left of the stone-faced monarch. At the Emperor's right hand stood Korelyi.

My stomach constricted. Though he could not have failed to see the danger, Aleksander did not hesitate, but walked into the room and knelt, touching his head to the white stone. He stayed in the submissive posture, awaiting his father's command to rise. Kiril stood beside him and bowed as was proper for a soldier on guard duty. Before a word had been spoken, a flick of the imperial finger had the door closed in front of the rest of us.

Kiril's adjutant, a man named Fedor, formed up the troop of soldiers just outside the doors. He wasn't sure what to do with me, so I indicated that I would wait in a small alcove between a row of fluted columns and the wall. It was a position from which I could watch the doors without being seen myself.

I had told Aleksander truly. I could not hear through walls no matter how hard I tried it. So I had to wait with everyone else until Kiril burst through the door. It had been less than half an hour.

"Fedor!" The young man's voice was tight and urgent.

"Aye, my lord?"

"Have the rest of the evidence from the wagon taken to . . . gods, where?" Kiril pressed a clenched fist to his forehead for a moment. "There's an old priests' room behind Druya's shrine out beyond the west wing. Do it quickly, and don't let anyone see what you're about."

I stepped out from my alcove, ready to accost the square-faced young Derzhi before he could go back, but he motioned for me to stay where I was. He strode across the atrium and spoke to one of the courtiers who spent their lives hovering outside the Emperor's door, waiting for the chance to perform some service. When he came back to my niche a few moments later, Kiril was trembling with suppressed rage.

"He will die at dawn, and until then is allowed to see no

one. Not his mother, not his cousin, not a servant, not a friend."

"Gods' fires!" I said, unprepared for such finality so quickly. "Did he get no hearing?"

"Before allowing either of us to speak, the Emperor demanded proof that Zander did not murder Dmitri. Zander tried to explain about his foolishness and the Khelid, but my uncle wouldn't hear it. 'First the proof,' was all he said. Zander admitted that he had only his word. But the Emperor claimed that Zander had already given his word that he had done the deed, and that if he had no other life to exchange for that of the Emperor's brother, then it must be his own." Kiril leaned his head back against the column and spoke through clenched teeth. "At least it seemed to grieve my uncle to pronounce the sentence. I thought he might bend the arms of the chair. As you would expect, Zander refused to argue it, but only asked permission to speak of treachery within the realm."

"And what of that?"

"It was not permitted. The Emperor would not hear 'slander created to hide a weak man's crime.' Gods of night . . . a weak man." Kiril clenched his fists and pressed them against the stone behind his head. "I was required to come out and send notice to the headsman . . . Athos have mercy. Then he commanded me to turn over everything seized from the Khelid fortress to the damned, smirking Korelyi. But that I will not do. They'll have to cut off my hands before I'll give it to him. I'll take the letters to every noble in the realm and make them listen. Zander will have that at least. I'll set this Empire on its—"

"Quietly, my lord." I was afraid he was going to blurt out the treason that was on the edge of his tongue. "Where have they taken him?"

"It won't work this time. You'll not get him out of this one. They've sent him to the deepest dungeon in this pile of rock, and that is very deep indeed. Unless your magic can melt steel and stone, you'll never touch him."

"I won't let him die."

"Listen to me, Seyonne." Kiril clutched my arm and pulled me deeper into the shadows. "I do know this. He'll not welcome your dying alongside him. You have your own work to do. And don't think you've gone unnoticed. Three times, Korelyi asked about 'the Ezzarian slave' and what role he had in my cousin's escape from Capharna. Zander said only that you had done as he commanded, and he'd set you free when he had no more use for you. He said he didn't know or care where you'd gone, but I don't think the Khelid believed him."

"We've got to help him, my lord."

Kiril rubbed his face tiredly, all his anger spent. "I've got a few people to talk to. I sent some messages before leaving Parnifour. Perhaps I've had a reply. And I'll find out for certain where they've put Zander. For now, you should go with Fedor. You need to stay out of sight."

I nodded and hurried after Kiril's men, leaving the young dennissar slumped against the column.

I spent the next two hours in a small stone room, its walls lined with peeling frescoes depicting the ferocious Derzhi bull god. We stowed the letters and parchment rolls in cracked stone chests that had once been used for vestments and ritual implements. All the valuable items had been taken away when the earthy Druya had been shoved out of favor by the showier Athos, leaving the priests' room stained with ancient animal blood, and littered with rotting shreds of cloth, burned-down candle stubs, and a large supply of spiders and dead flies.

While Kiril's men carried in the hundreds of weapons from the wagon, I pored over the letters and notes again under the light of a dented brass lantern. I was looking for anything, any hint of the plot that had brought Aleksander to his knees. It wouldn't have to be much. Ivan doted on Aleksander, and only his stubborn Derzhi head was forcing him to impose this terrible judgment. But as before, I found nothing.

Resigned to a fight, I began poking around in the

weaponry for a blade. I needed something fairly new, something that had little legacy of blood and hatred that would make it more difficult to bind with my own enchantments. There was every kind of blade, curved and straight, double-ended gerraws designed to be held in the middle, rapiers, longswords, daggers, short swords, dirks. Many of them had demon spells attached. I had warned Kiril's men not to nick themselves on any of the weapons. Halfway through the pile I came on a long cloth-wrapped bundle tied with cord. Curious, I cut the cord and unwrapped a magnificent new-forged blade, still coated with oil from its making. Its edge could sliver a moth's wing. I wiped it with the cloth so I could see the engraving. The guard was fashioned in the shape of a falcon's wing, smooth, simple, graceful to curve about the hand, and the hilt—my hand trembled as I moved the lamp closer and examined it. Amid the fine and elegant graving of vine leaves were set the devices of a lion rampant and a falcon. Aleksander's dakrah sword. Carried by Dmitri as he hurried into the mountains, venturing the bandit-ridden Jybbar Pass to bring his beloved nephew a sword worthy of an emperor. If Aleksander's sword was there, then what of Dmitri's own?

So it was that Kiril came in at the calling of the first hour of Aleksander's execution day to find me examining one sword at a time, then throwing it onto a grim heap in the opposite corner.

"What in Athos' name are you doing?" he said, standing in the doorway with hands on his waist.

"Come here," I said quietly, determined that no word of my discovery should find its way to Korelyi. I showed him the sword, and he took the meaning immediately. He set to work, giving me a description of Dmitri's sword that made our search go faster. After a few minutes he paused. "If they have his sword, they might also have his signet. The damnable murdering thieves took that as well."

Immediately I thought of the jewel casket in Kastavan's traveling case, and I rummaged through it while Kiril kept searching for the sword. At almost the same moment, we cried out, "Here!" and turned to each other, Kiril with a well-used broadsword, I with a falcon-crested signet ring.

"We've got him!" said Kiril fiercely. "I'll go to the Emperor at once."

"No. Wait." I hated to hold him back. We both felt the dawn creeping up our backs. "We've got to think. Korelyi will say we've had them all along. That we placed them among the Khelid blades."

Kiril looked stricken. "I'll swear it on my father's grave. On my mother's honor."

"No. We've got to be sure." I sat staring at the ring, racking my brain for some way to convince Ivan of the truth. And, of course, my conclusion was that we couldn't. Korelyi had to do it. And if we were to force him to it, we were going to have to risk everything. The question was whether Korelyi knew that Dmitri's things were in Kiril's hoard.

"I'm sure of it," said the young Derzhi. "He's had the Emperor's messengers hounding me all night. He's frantic to get this stuff. I thought it was to prevent the letters getting out, but this makes more sense."

The Khelid wanted Aleksander dead. They had no demons to put in him, and he had shown himself too strong to succumb to their more ordinary magic. He would be a dangerous opponent. I took the two swords and the ring and put them all in Kastavan's case, resealing the Khelid spell and making sure that no trace of my own working remained on the case.

"What are you doing?"

"We're going to give everything back as Korelyi wants," I said.

"Indeed we will not." Kiril blocked the doorway as if I were planning to haul out his hoard in my pockets.

"If you wish Aleksander to see another sunrise, you will do exactly as I say."

At one hour before dawn the Derzhi junior dennissar, smelling strongly of spirits, stood in the central courtyard of the royal residential wing of the Imperial Palace pelting certain second-floor windows with stones. He was cursing and weeping at the top of his lungs. "Come out, Khelid pig. Come take your damnable belongings and with them the sum of Derzhi honor. What care have I for our beloved Empire, if the most noble of princes is dead? Take your foul treasury and choke on it. Do you need weapons to stab at the heart? You can take your pick here in this fine display, though no weapon will be needed when the puking miserable sun takes up its watch this cursed morning." After another handful of rocks, heads were poking out of the unshuttered windows that overlooked the courtyard. "Come out, villain, and claim your blood price!"

Spread out on the carved paving stones, on top of the flower gardens, and in the trickling fountains were every packet of letters, every sword, every book, and every jewel that had been taken from the Khelid fortress . . . with the exception of Kastavan's traveling case and the additional two swords it carried. I knew this because I was sitting on the palace roof behind a carved stone cherub that was strangling a snake in its fist. Kastavan's leather case was in my lap.

Three guards ran into the courtyard, but Kiril held them off with his own sword and dagger. "No, I will certainly not leave here. Not until Lord Korelyi comes to claim his belongings and swears to my Emperor that every piece is here. I'll not have my honor questioned by accusations of thievery. Is it not enough that he claims our prince a murderer?"

No one in the palace was likely to be sleeping, not with a royal execution less than an hour in the offing. And from Aleksander's comments over the months, I knew that Kiril was well loved by all, including Ivan and Jenya. So I was not surprised to see the Emperor himself come out to see to his distraught nephew.

"Come, boy. This profits nothing."

"Ah, honored sire," said Kiril, dropping a knee even while keeping his sword and dagger positioned to fend off the guards—a most difficult feat for a man so drunk as he seemed. "Will you not weep with me? Will you not save my honor so that something of good will come from this black day?"

"There is nothing of honor here, Kiril," said the Emperor harshly. "I have commanded you to return the Khelid possessions that were taken illegally from their residence. You are doing as you must. As every Derzhi warrior must do, no matter how painful."

"Then, have him come examine these things and say I have not withheld anything. Please, my liege, my uncle. Save one life this day, for I swear I will not see the ending of it if I am named thief on the same day as my cousin is named dead."

As I had hoped, the purple-cloaked Korelyi swept out of a vine-draped gallery below me. "So your nephew has decided that obedience must be drowned in wine, Majesty? Not a good lesson for one in the diplomatic service of his Emperor."

"I have no time for foolery, Korelyi," growled Ivan. "Collect your belongings and be done with it."

I did not stay to hear the rest of it, how Kiril would insist that Korelyi inventory everything before taking it, how Ivan would bluster, yet would surely take every moment's reprieve he could from his dreadful duties of the morning. As I scrambled back through the attic window and down the narrow steps that led to the upper corridor and the Khelid's apartments, I could not allow myself to think of anything but what I was doing. I had given enough thought to Aleksander in his cell, his fine clothing replaced with a coarse gray prisoner's tunic, his hair unbraided, waiting for the black-hooded man who would lead him to the prisoner's courtyard and the bloodstained block waiting there.

There! Two Khelid stood outside the next door. Summoning the enchantment I had created over the past hours, I conjured an apparition that, in the dim light, would look very much like Korelyi. The apparition beckoned the two guards and disappeared down the stairs. The guards ran after, and I hurried to the door. Quickly, before my head cracked with the strain of two simultaneous workings, I dis-

cerned the lock spell and countered it. I set the case incon-
spicuously beside Korelyi's own wardrobe. Then I stepped
out of the door, reset the seal, and retreated to my position
on the roof.

Korelyi was screaming at Kiril. ". . . also be separated
from your head this day, for aiding a treacherous murderer.
Your cousin took my Lord Kastavan's life unprovoked, un-
manly, and now you have stolen his belongings, those things
which are his children's legacy, jewels that have been in his
family for generations. This sobbing clamor is nothing but a
screen for your knavery."

"Enough," said Ivan. "Is there no respect in either of
you? What mockery do you make of this most wretched
day? You may both hang for all I care." Ivan turned to leave
the garden.

No. No. No. That was not the way it was supposed to go.

Kiril, still brandishing his weapons, glanced up and
caught my signal. He pressed his back against a stone
obelisk and sheathed his sword, using his hands and his suddenly sober voice to stay the guards. "Your most gracious
Majesty, I seek only to defend the honor of our name—your
name. Grant me this hearing for the love of my Lord Dmitri.
He was my only father, sire, and I will not have his memory
sullied by this foreigner's lies. You must judge why this man
feels it necessary to drag our family's honor through the
mire."

Ivan paused . . . and so did my heartbeat.

Kiril pressed his moment's advantage. "My lord, this Korelyi claims that I have withheld a case belonging to Lord
Kastavan, but why would I desire anything from those I believe have slain my likai. I would rather rot in slave rings before possessing one jewel, one trinket, one gold coin that
crossed the palm of Lord Dmitri's murderer. I'll wager my
life that these 'treasures' are in my Lord Korelyi's possession already. I think he seeks to have all males of the House
of Denischkar disgraced or dead."

The dawn light slipped from gray to red as the sun sent its
first warning, and every eye in that courtyard turned up-

ward. Korelyi laughed. "Does this boy, this murderer's hireling, think to thwart his Emperor's judgment by such a pitiful show? If these weak accusations are the best intrigue he can deliver, I fear for the future of the Derzhi." It was perhaps not a good time for the Khelid to laugh.

"We will settle this now," said the Emperor. "Take me to the Khelid's apartments." Ivan strode into the palace by way of the door beneath my perch.

Remember, Kiril. Remind the Emperor that your men burned their fingers on the case. No one but a sorcerer could open it. Remember to guide, not lead. Let the guilt unfold. Let Korelyi's cockiness ruin him. Keep things moving, so the Khelid doesn't have time to speculate on how this has happened.

I waited in breathless silence, then from the room beneath me came such a roar of anguish that it shivered the red tiles on which I sat. Ivan. Was it only the sight of his dead brother's belongings drew such agonizing grief from him? Or was it the revelation of the dreadful mistake he was about to commit? Or had he . . . oh, gods . . . had he given the final execution order before he came out, lest in some moment of weakness at Kiril's sorrow he might relent?

A beam of red light glanced off a metal facing on a chimney across the courtyard. Without caution I leaped up and ran across the sloping tile roof, faster, up and down, leaping from one roof edge to the next. Slip, grasp for a fingerhold. On my feet again. Summon the wind. I had no wings, but I needed anything to speed my feet, to bear me up. I had memorized the way across the roof from the residential courtyard to the prisoners' court. Why had I waited? Because I had never expected Ivan would fail to witness his son's execution. I had thought him irredeemably hard, but he was only a father trying to live through terrible necessity.

I leaped from the east wing roof, across the gulf to the barracks, up the steep rise and down to the wall of the prisoners' courtyard. "Stop! In the name of the Emperor!" I cried.

The burly, black-hooded man blocked my view of Alek-

sander. All I could see were his hands bound behind his back
and the long bare legs sticking out from the gray tunic as he
knelt, bent forward, on the steps. Was he dead or living?
Would the gray-clad figure slump and fall? The broad ax
rose slowly into the air. Unbloodied.

"Stop!" I cried again, this time in Ivan's voice. "Your
Emperor commands it!"

The executioner paused and looked around, wondering
where his sovereign stood that he could hear him so clearly.

"Do not let this ax fall, headsman," I said, "or you will be
the next under its blade. This prisoner has my reprieve. He
will not die this day."

Chapter 37

The rumor got about the Empire that Ivan zha Denischkar once touched the hand of Athos, and that was why he kept to himself so much in the last years of his reign—to contemplate it. It was said that on the day he saved his son from the Khelid conspiracy, he was able to transmit his voice throughout the Imperial Palace, and because it was at the moment of dawn, it must have been Athos that gave him the power.

I was well content with such rumors. As Aleksander had learned, Ezzarians are, of necessity, shy of fame, and need no reports of miracles to complicate their lives.

I sat on the roof and watched as Ivan ran into the prisoners' courtyard and found his bewildered son still kneeling at the headsman's block, and his son's executioner gaping about in search of the body that went with his liege's voice. A few moments later, as the Emperor held the Prince in a fierce embrace, I took pleasure in the brilliant grin that blossomed when the searching eyes of amber came to rest on a particular gargoyle beside the guard barracks waterspout. Kiril was the one who had the sense to cut the bindings from Aleksander's hands, and after a cousinly embrace, he also turned a smiling face to the roof . . . or the sky, as rumor would have it.

Had it been anywhere but Azhakstan in early summer, I might have stayed on the roof, content to find a shady spot out of anyone's line of vision and sleep away the daylight. But I had no wish to be broiled, so I crept back across the red-tiled vastness, then dodged running slaves, excited servants, and a platoon of guards to make my way back to the old priests' room behind Druya's deserted shrine. There I drained a water jar left from our long night of preparation, curled up in the cool darkness, and slept.

Inevitably someone came to wake me up before I was ready. "Seyonne, come on. Time to go."

It was Kiril, cleaned, trimmed, and polished like a new sword. Candlelight illuminated the eager young face and the gold chain work that hung over his dark red tunic. "He told me you'd be holed up somewhere sleeping." Though I'd have sworn I'd been asleep less than an hour, it seemed to be after dark already.

I sat up, dry enough to spit dust balls. "Didn't see much else to do." I wasn't about to set out through the Derzhi stronghold during the scorching daylight after a night with no sleep. I still wore marks that could get me in serious trouble.

"Well, you must come with me now. Here, put this on." It was a long, flowing white robe such as some of the more traditional heged lords wore. "We've got to get going. I'm expected elsewhere." I threw on the robe over my clothes and allowed him to drag me through courtyard after courtyard, through lamplit galleries and breezy cloisters.

"Is all well?" I managed to hold him still while we waited in a doorway for a wide stair to be clear of people.

"Very well. Lord Marag arrived an hour after dawn. I'd sent for him to witness to what he'd seen in Karn'Hegeth. Almost an hour too late, but he did what was needed, and he brought reports from other garrisons. Zander and the Emperor have been in war councils all day."

I grabbed Kiril's arm before he could take off again. "And what of Korelyi?"

"Ah, well, we've not managed to nab him yet. The Emperor was so worried about Zander . . . and the guards didn't understand what was going on. They saw the Khelid going three different directions at once . . . but we've searchers out, and the gates are closed. He'll not escape us. We've taken care of all the other Khelid in Zhagad. Now, come on. I've no time to talk."

He led me up the flight of winding stairs to a wide gallery, past two stone-faced guards who might have been blind for all the notice they took of us. On one side of the gallery wide-open windows welcomed the flower-scented night, and on the other, curtains woven of gold thread hung in five or six arched doorways. Kiril pushed me through one of the curtains into a dimly lit room. "You'll be safe here. Just stay until I come for you. And enjoy yourself. You'll want to take a look out the back curtain after a bit."

There was food inside the small, luxuriously furnished sitting room, and the smells had my stomach growling louder than a shengar. The repast—cold fowl, fruit, pastries, bread, salted fish, slices of savory pork and mutton, rolls of green leaves containing delicate shellfish and shredded vegetables, spicy sauces with nuts and tart berries, and innumerable other delicacies—was the finest I had ever sat down to. And in the midst of it all was a voluminous pitcher of cool water and another of red wine. I almost drowned in the pleasure of it.

About the time I filled my plate for the third time, I heard a trumpet fanfare followed by pipe music beyond the heavy curtain of brilliant colors on the far wall. The pipe music was haunting and lovely, echoing through the ancient stone of the Palace, beckoning me to pay attention, but I ignored it for a long while, preferring the food as entertainment. Only when I sat back and wondered why Kiril had brought me to such an odd place, did the young Derzhi's obscure remark at last penetrate my gluttonous madness. I jumped up and peeked out the curtain, afraid that I had missed something very important.

Far below me, in a vast cavern of a room illuminated by a thousand candles, Aleksander knelt before the Emperor. Ivan's thumb was on the Prince's forehead, and the words of the anointing were just fading into the music.

"Arise, Aleksander, our successor, our son. Heed him, all

of you, and fear him, for he is the voice of his Emperor and the living surety that our glory will never end."

Aleksander was in dark green. No diamond collar this time, but his lean face wore a quiet and solemn dignity that became him better. He stood up and kissed the man who, only a few short hours before, had sentenced him to death. Then he turned to acknowledge the genuflection of the small crowd—some six or seven hundred onlookers. The beaming Emperor motioned to his attendants and swept from the dais. When Aleksander rose from his genuflection at his father's passing and followed him down the steps, Kiril stepped forward and whispered in his ear. Aleksander turned in the direction of my observation post and bowed from the waist, setting off a turning of heads and general murmuring that would no doubt feed rumors for years ahead. The curiosity would be enhanced by the fact that he immediately greeted the Lady Lydia—breathtakingly beautiful in dark blue and silver—in such a manner as to preclude any question of other dalliance.

I wasn't worried about being discovered. The Emperor-to-be and his cousin were no doubt capable of keeping me private in the heart of the Palace. Once they had passed from the hall, I went back to eating. The journey back to Dael Ezzar would be a long one.

For the first time in almost seventeen years, I allowed myself to think of the future. Five years. Our law said that if one spouse went missing, the other would be free to marry again after five years. Five years was not so long a time. Ysanne . . . When someone stepped in the door, I whirled about and said, "I need to be off, Lord Kiril. I'd be most grateful—"

"Do not imagine that you will go anywhere of your own accord this night, Ezzarian, or ever again for that matter." From behind the gold curtain stepped a pale-haired man with blue eyes, not the ice-blue horror of demon's eyes, but the natural blue of a human, boiling with anger and hate and lust for vengeance.

I tried to raise my hand or my foot, anything to defend

myself, but Korelyi held a small, oval medallion that gleamed ruddy gold in the candlelight and screamed with the dissonance of demon music. "A little trinket left from my former companion," said the Khelid. "We had prepared it for the Emperor himself, but I think I would rather use it for my true enemy." He walked around me slowly, and I could not so much as turn my head to follow. "The catalyst. The slave. Always at the periphery of events. Who would have believed it was the pitiful Ezzarian sorcerers who were the nemesis of the rai-kirah—the *pandye-gyash,* they call them, 'the hidden warriors'? Won't they be pleased when I tell them how to find the rest of you? The rai-kirah are much more attuned to the way of things in the human world now. I'll make sure to be there to watch when they come."

He stepped closer. I could smell the aura of murderous vengeance on him. "But you . . . you will have to imagine it." The brass medallion was suspended from a steel chain, which he placed about my neck. It might have been a mountain, it hung so heavy on my chest. It was a fight to breathe, and speech was out of the question. I desperately hoped that Kiril would show up soon . . . with a Derzhi legion behind him.

"Come with me. Now I've found you, it is time to walk out of this place."

Against my will my feet began to move. Korelyi pulled up the white scarf to hide my face and took my arm companionably—not quite breaking my elbow doing it. Down the corridor and the stairs. Through the galleries and court-yards and passageways. The Palace was a hive of activity and excitement, but even with so many, no one challenged the Khelid. Many nodded and greeted him respectfully. I didn't understand it.

"A glorious night, Lord Kiril," said a young Derzhi as we passed.

"Indeed. A touch of swordplay on the borders will make it perfect."

Kiril . . . It took me a moment to realize that they were addressing Korelyi as Kiril. I couldn't turn my head, but he reached to open a gate, and I glimpsed his aspect. He had worked an illusion, giving himself a mask that resembled Kiril. Though imperfect and lacking the earnest innocence of the young Derzhi, it was enough for eyes that expected only truth in their seeing.

I delved into myself, trying to come up with some bit of sorcery that might throw off the demon working, but his surprise had been complete. All I could do was name myself a fool and five thousand worse names. How could I have let down my guard so completely?

Out of the palace gates, through the inner-ring wall, through the outer walls into the teeming tent cities of those too poor, too diseased, or too unsavory to be permitted into Zhagad. Korelyi pushed me through dark lanes lit by spitting yellow torches, through the crowds of hawkers and thieves, prostitutes and lepers, goats and pigs, to a dark, stinking corner of the tent city. Compared to the clamor of the lanes, it was eerily quiet. A moan from the shadows was followed instantly by the sound of a lash.

I was shoved into a filthy wooden stockade, and Korelyi kicked a diseased-looking youth who lay snoring on a pile of hides in one corner. "Strip this one and bind him to the post so your master can see what a fine prospect I've brought him. But on your life, do not remove this." He tapped the brass medallion and leaned into the boy's face. "He turns into a monster if you take it off him. He eats carrion like you."

The lad did as he'd been told, tying my hands to a tall post and gloating over my decent clothes as he removed them. Korelyi walked across the pen to speak with a cadaverous man wearing striped pantaloons and a necklace of bones—a Veshtar slave keeper. My blood turned to ice. Veshtar kept their slaves constantly in chains or cages; they starved them and mutilated them, allowing no speech, no thought, no movement that was not hellish misery. The Veshtar claimed that their gods commanded them to treat barbarians so, to work them to death in the desert to purify them. Purify. If I could have made a sound, I would have laughed at the irony of it. Even the worst of the Derzhi refused to deal with the Veshtar, considering them too cruel.

A third man joined Korelyi and the Veshtar, and soon the three of them came over to me. Bad enough to have the gloating Khelid examining my scars. Bad enough to have the Veshtar sucking his broken brown teeth and running his dirty fingers over my arms and back as if to decide where to leave his own marks. But the third man . . . it was the third man that made my heart go dead. The third man was Rhys.

Oh, my friend, how can you hate enough to do this? In unspoken pleading, I begged Rhys to hear me, to wait, to save himself from an act of murder that was far more deliberate than killing Galadon. But he could not hear me, so I battled the demon enchantment with everything I could muster, bringing my memories, my love, my too-late understanding of my friend into the working. It felt as if my face might crack with the effort or my heart burst. And what words do you say when they might be your last forever? Croaking, rasping, my tongue burning with the Khelid spell, my mind unable to make any rational choice save that I must speak, my soul spilled out the few words entirely on its own. "Once . . . long ago . . . you swore to cut off my balls. Has the time come?"

Rhys did not change his expression. He did not move when Korelyi snarled and touched his finger to the medallion, and I screamed from the fiery waves of pain consuming my mind and body. I might not have existed as I hung limp and quivering from the post. He watched, his broad face impassive, as the Khelid and the Veshtar haggled over my price. Arms folded he listened when the Veshtar swore to have me away from the city within the hour and to take me so deep into the desert that I could never be found. He said nothing as the Khelid showed the slave keeper how to embed the little medallion in the Veshtari slave collar without removing it from me, so that I would never be able to move unbidden, never be able to summon power. Never in his watching or listening did Rhys meet my gaze, and my soul sank into the midnight of despair.

"We shall each have our desire, shall we not?" said the Khelid, nudging my old friend as the Veshtar went to fetch his gold. "I have made the arrangements as we agreed. A fine pillow upon which to lay our heads this night. And you have no need to wreak this crude vengeance of your swearing. The Veshtar know how to manage such things far better than Ezzarians, I think."

Rhys ran his fingers idly over the knife hilt at his waist. "You said nothing about a Veshtar," he said at last, softly, evenly. My skin itched with more than the rapid cooling of the desert night.

"You wanted him in bondage, not dead. I wanted him in everlasting torment. This seemed a proper solution. And we shall both have a pocketful of coins to ease our distress."

Rhys walked away from the Khelid, toward me, as if to inspect me closer. Only then did he meet my gaze full on . . . and his cold dark eyes were filled with resignation. With death. "The gold would be very nice," he said. "But all in all, I mislike this bargain." And with a movement swifter than a bee sting, he drew his knife in one hand and his sword in the other. With the knife tip and a word of binding, he lifted the medallion from my neck and flipped it into the fire, and with a furious spin he slashed the ropes that bound my hands.

I ducked, for Korelyi was also quick, and his saber came near taking off my hair shorter than Durgan had ever done. With his foot and a bone-cracking double blow of elbow and wrist, Rhys disarmed the slave keeper. The Veshtar's blade spun through the air and landed, hilt-first, in my hand.

It did not take us long. These were mortals, not demons. The Khelid lay dead at my feet, along with the Veshtar slave keeper. And five other Veshtar, including the youth who had bound my hands, were piled in front of Rhys. My old friend was bent over them as if to make sure they were dead. "And so you've won," he said. Slowly he stood up and faced me. Blood was trickling from the corner of his mouth, and even in the sallow light of the slave-pen torch, his face had no color. The color was all on the front of his shirt, and it was all the wrong color. I caught him before he fell to the ground.

"*We* have won," I said, pulling his great shoulders into my embrace. "You've saved my life as you promised."

He shook his head. "This was not for you. You need nothing from me. Never have. You would have survived the Veshtar. But there are things even I cannot stomach."

"The past is done with. I've learned—"

He wouldn't let me speak, but gripped my arm with his huge hand. "Do not lay all this on Ysanne. She never betrayed you. I told her"—a spasm wrenched his giant frame—"I told her that you commanded us to leave you. Because you were dying. Unclean. I never meant . . . my oath. . . . I thought I could still fight."

"I know. It's all right. The paths of fortune have led me where I never thought to go, Rhys. You were right. You tried to tell me. I always believed I could do everything alone. But I've learned better. Even this, tonight, you've shown me again. We have changed the world as we always said we would."

"Just not as I wanted it." He turned his face away, and his hand loosed its grip and fell to the dirt.

For an hour after he died, I sat with him, rocking him gently with the waves of grief that welled up inside me. *"Nevaro wydd, Rhys-na-varain."* Sleep in peace.

I used the Veshtar's gold to hire men to carry Rhys and Korelyi back to the Palace and to induce some of the locals to free the terrified victims who were locked in the Veshtar cages. Kiril had alerted the guards to watch out for me, and when I showed up with two dead bodies, they were content to shuffle me and my burdens through the gate without too many questions. It was only a few minutes' wait in a stable yard until Kiril came running. Once he had sent Korelyi's body to the holding place for the Khelid to be identified and burned, and given orders to wrap Rhys's body in clean cloth as I asked, he dismissed the staring guards. "Are you all right? Where in Athos' name did you get off to?"

"I relaxed a bit too much."

"I'm glad to see you well." He screwed his square face into a puzzled frown, as if by setting it just right, he might understand all the things I had no wish to speak of. "The Prince will be relieved. I thought I might experience a most unpleasant ending to a fine evening."

"I need to go," I said. "The moon is up, and I've a long way to travel. I just wanted the Prince to know he didn't have to waste his time worrying about this particular Khelid. Remember to do as I told you. Burn everything the Khelid touched, all the weapons, the gems, everything. Even Lord Dmitri's things and Prince Aleksander's sword. After an hour in the fire, they'll be safe."

"He would keep you with him, you know. Not as a slave, nor even a servant. But as his companion and valued adviser."

"He knows I can't stay."

Kiril acknowledged it. "But you will at least allow him to give you transport and protection for your way?"

"I'd rather—"

"He will insist. Please don't make my life miserable by fighting over it." He grinned at me. "Can't I persuade you to pity me as everyone else does and do as I ask?"

I returned his good humor. "An Ezzarian feeling sorry for a Derzhi? Unlikely. I need no protection, but I would appreciate a horse. Nothing too fine. I'm not a good enough rider to manage one of your firebrands. And two pack animals. One for supplies and one to carry my friend."

"Across the desert?" Kiril wrinkled his nose in horror.

"We have ways. I need to take him home."

"It will be done. Give me an hour. Wait in the fountain court behind Druya's shrine. I'll have everything brought to you there."

"Thank you, my lord." I bowed to him . . . as a man bows, not as a slave.

Kiril extended his hand. "You have done the Empire— the world—such service as there are no words to express.

Even if we fully understood it." We shook hands, then he hurried away, sending the guards back to their posts.

Music—wild desert pipes against the droning mellang-har—drifted from the brilliantly lit Palace. They would be drinking toasts and watching the whirling dezrhila dancers spin out the legends of Derzhi history. I sat in the little garden outside the priests' room and thought of Rhys, stories from the past, when we were young and invincible, and would emerge from danger excited and glowing, as Kiril was, instead of tired, and lonely, and homesick.

I was suddenly overwhelmed with such a longing to be home among my own people that it was a physical effort to remain in the little garden. It would not be easy to go back. Ysanne could not revoke my undeath on her own whim. Though I believed she would fight for me—and Catrin could be no mean ally—there would be a great number of my people who would strongly resist violating our oldest traditions, even to regain the services of the only living Warden. And that would not be the last change they had to face. The world . . . the demons and our war . . . were going to change. We had to be ready.

As for Ysanne . . . I knew she was waiting for me. Her love had followed me into horror and held strong and unyielding until I returned. Her music had always been for me. Yet we would need to find our way back to each other, Ysanne and I. So many stones had fallen into the stream of youthful passion, it would take some doing to discover how the water ran. *Soon, my love. Soon.*

If not for a remaining sliver of reason, I would have set out right then and run across the desert without stopping until I had the high valley of Dael Ezzar in sight. Yet I would make the journey sooner and safer if I had transport, and I would not leave Rhys behind. It was the only thing I could give him. Ysanne and I would always carry a burden of guilt about Rhys: Ysanne for her childish flirtation with my friend, I for the pride and self-absorption that had blinded me to his need. I had been so sure of him. So sure of myself. So sure of Ysanne. She had rebelled and dallied with Rhys, never thinking he would believe her or link his feeling for her to his other problems with me. Neither of us had listened to him, and so together we had woven a landscape where his weakness could flourish. Our regret would not change what had happened, only make our grief for the big laughing youth more bitter.

So much to consider. So much to remember. The weeks of traveling that lay before me would not be idle.

It was more like two hours until my mounts arrived. I kept my guard up this time, so I heard the steps on the path and stood ready long before the young steward came through the garden gate leading two horses and a chastou. The desert beast was laden with water casks and leather food bags, and one horse was burdened with a long wrapped bundle, tied securely and respectfully to its back and draped with a white velvet cloth. Across the saddle of the other horse was laid a white desert robe and scarf. "Speak Lord Kiril's name to the gate guards," said the boy. "Tell them you're the one he told of, and you'll be passed through."

I thanked him, checked the bindings, and prepared to mount up. But when the lad was gone, there was still breathing from the shadowed corner of the garden.

"Did you think to leave without seeing me?"

I smiled and turned, discovering the lanky form sitting on a broken fountain, his arms around his knees, almost invisible in the darkness. "You have a great deal to keep you occupied," I said.

"A great deal more than my prospects of the morning warranted." He unfolded his legs, but stayed where he was. "We're off to finish the Khelid tomorrow. I go east, Kiril north, Marag south, my father west. I'm even in the good graces of the Magician's Guild again."

"Be careful with them, my lord. They have only a smattering of melydda, but no concept of how to use it carefully." I clamped my mouth shut. "I'm sorry . . . always one more lesson."

"Never apologize for telling me what I need to hear. I am

not as I was before I knew you. I have fallen as low as a man can go, and you have raised me up again. I won't forget it."

"Whatever I found in you was there all along."

He growled in mock ferocity. "Of course, you've caused me a lot of trouble. I've had to find a new scribe."

I laughed and adjusted the stirrups on the horse. "And I've no time to give him lessons . . . or warn him about your habits."

"Lydia loaned him. I think he'll do well. He doesn't say what he's thinking, either, but then, I don't believe he's thinking all that much. You'll find some of his work in the small pack on your mount. Review it when you have time and let me know what you think."

"I will," I said, mounting up. "If you ever have need of me . . ."

"Be safe, my guardian."

"Be wise, my prince."

He was laughing as I rode away, through the streets of his city and into the desert.

It was on the next morning when I stopped at a small rocky outcrop to wait out the worst heat of the day that I unwrapped a rolled leather bundle to find the two well-written papers. The first was a writ sealed by the newly anointed heir. It stated that, despite physical marking that might indicate otherwise, the Ezzarian who bore the letter was a free man, not to be detained, made captive, abused, or mishandled in any way under penalty of banishment from the Empire or death. A precious writing indeed. Even an illiterate warrior could not ignore Aleksander's seal.

But it was the second paper that caught my breath.

A Continuation of the History of the Glorious Dakrah of Aleksander, Crown Prince of the Derzhi Empire, as begun at Capharna and continued this fifth day of the Month of the Bull by the hand of Illeos of Avenkhar.

After this most holy anointing in the manner prescribed by the overlord Tyros when his son Athos came

to his majority in the Courts of the Sky, the Emperor Ivan
zha Denischkar did proclaim Aleksander to the people as
his beloved son and heir, as their Emperor's Voice and
Hand. And after they had retired from the place of the
anointing, the Emperor did ask Prince Aleksander what
gift he desired to remember the day: horses or lands,
gems or gold, slaves or wine, women or titles, or perhaps
songs to be made of his trials and his victory over the unholy Khelid treachers.

The Prince contemplated the riches offered him, but
without hesitation spoke his mind. "One thing, honored
father, I would ask of you. Far to the south lies a warm,
green land once known as Ezzaria. Some of your nobles
have occupied it these past years, but I am looking for a
suitable site to build myself a palace, a sanctuary where I
can take my bride on the day my marriage is blessed by
your hand. I would ask that you grant me all titles to Ezzaria, compensating those displaced with twice the lands
in Khelidar or other territories that are under my rule. I
will take possession of this land at the summer solstice
and travel the houses there to see if any are to my liking.
I desire it to be a private territory, no trade routes through
it, no use of its timber or game unless I say it, and this to
be written into the law of the Empire so that it will extend
beyond my death for as long as the Derzhi rule."

The Emperor expressed his astonishment with the
modest request of the Prince and his pleasure at my lord's
care for those noble families displaced by his desire.
With his hand and his seal the Emperor has commanded
that all be done as the Prince has spoken.

At the bottom of this finely written page were a few
words, drawn in crude, childlike letters.

It is yours.
A.

ABOUT THE AUTHOR

Though **Carol Berg** calls Colorado her home, her roots are in Texas in a family of teachers, musicians, and railroad men. She has a degree in mathematics from Rice University and one in computer science from the University of Colorado, but managed to squeeze in minors in English and art history along the way. She has combined a career as a software engineer with her writing, while also raising three sons. She lives with her husband at the foot of the Colorado mountains.

Read more in the Rai-Kirah saga from *CAROL BERG*

REVELATION

Seyonne, the slave-turned-hero from Berg's highly acclaimed *Transformation*, returns to discover the nature of evil—in a "spellbinding" (*Romantic Times*) epic saga.

RESTORATION

A sorcerer who fears he will destroy the world. A prince who fears he has destroyed his people. Amid the chaos of a disintegrating empire, two men confront prophecy and destiny in the last battle of the demon war...

"Carol Berg lights up the sky."
—*Midwest Book Review*